Endorsements

*"**The Fearless Moral Inventory of Elsie Finch** is a highly recommended work not just for religious collections, but for readers of literary suspense stories. The tale revolves around the carefully arranged legacy of parents who inject chaos into the next generation.*

"Some families leave legacies of positivity and gifts. Others leave behind angst and confusion.

"Lynn Byk writes with a lyrical hand that captures passion and emotion with equal aplomb: 'She didn't shed a tear into this river. Instead, she began to breathe. It was time to figure out what had happened, and when. To finally begin to live her own life without guilt or compunction, she needed the timing of things. Timing was the only way to get a feel for each family member's motives and to answer this: how had her warm, vibrant father died a broken stick of a man washed to the riverbank by the runoff? Her aim was to learn how to get past these wretched years since she first fled the nest and later, when she tumbled headlong into the rushing waters.'

"From her childhood's evolution and her early passion for reading books, to guideposts of faith and touchstones of building a connection with her higher power, Elsie's journey and coming of age details her psychological family dynamics and community influences."

— D. Donovan, Senior Reviewer, **Midwest Book Review**

BookLife Prize: "Alluring and convincing, this multi-generational work has an unusual premise and there's a grandness to the scope. The novel offers an intimate exploration of relationship dynamics and emotional conflicts... An epic accomplishment."

"We are pleased to announce that our judges of the 2022 PenCraft Book Awards for literary excellence voted your book "_THE FEARLESS MORAL INVENTORY OF ELSIE FINCH_," published by Capture Books, as our _Christian - Fiction 2nd Place Winner_.

i

"We want our PenCraft Book Awards to represent books of distinction, and your book certainly met that criteria. Books that win our competition are not just examples of literary excellence but also have demonstrated a notable popularity with readers.

"To select our winners, the many PenCraft Book Award submissions are culled down by using a judging criterion that incorporates a recommendation from the initial AuthorsReader's reviewer or PenCraft Book Award reviewer and then finalized by further evaluation by our judges. Their final evaluation considers not only how well the book was written and crafted but also things such as the book's marketplace popularity and how professional the book cover looks."

– David Hearne, Editor In Chief, **PenCraft Book Awards**

"ELSIE FINCH is brave and startlingly candid; her character is lodged in my heart of hearts. She gives us all permission to delve into our own complex family dynamics!

"Elsie Finch managed somehow, to explore the darker side of human foibles – while at the same time weaving in a bright thread of hope."

– Kathy Hoffner, Editor

AuthorsReading: "The Fearless Moral Inventory of Elsie Finch is an illuminating memoir that reveals life secrets with vibrant narrative prose. Every page of this nuanced account of the multigenerational family comes alive with the force of history, the wonder of place, friends, and strangers that shaped the author's sensibilities.

"The author captures family life's oddities and pain with frankness, sharpness, and a sly-witted style. Each of the sisters portrayed is distinct, with a background and personality that sets one apart from the others. The distinctiveness contributes to her way of thinking, her reaction to family trials, and her interpretation of her place in the family. The palpable tension doesn't let up in this character-driven story. As old wounds and heartaches bubble to the surface, each character involved tells their story from their unique point of view. Rarely do both sides of the story match.

"Distinct Christian undertones throughout the story add layers of complexity without being preachy. Spiritual dilemmas are brought to the surface, allowing readers to wrestle with spiritual conflicts in their own lives."

ELSIE & FINCH

Donovan's Literary Services: "Byk builds her story with the passionate search for God's will and mounting tensions in the story of evolving personality disorders that ripple across the landscape of America.

"As grief, redemption, and human follies weave through the life of this faith-rooted protagonist, readers will appreciate the persona and challenges Elsie navigates as she tries to change her family's catastrophic legacy.

"Christian fiction collectors looking for literary novels will find Elsie Finch replete with thought-provoking moments. But it's the book club that will find *The Fearless Moral Inventory of Elsie Finch* of special interest, certain to spark a variety of soul-searching conversations about faith, family, and the evolution of both."

– D. Donovan, Editor

"A Heart-Wrenching, Grace-Soothed Epic. Author Lynn Byk tells a remarkable tale of Elsie Finch's quest to understand her family— and to refuse its dysfunctional generational patterns. As she untangles lifetimes of tender, rough, and heart-wrenching stories, only her developing faith serves as a reliable guide through destructive lies, confusion, and self-centered, misguided decisions.

"It's a long healing for Elsie, as most of ours are. But in this courageous, unblinking portrayal of the human condition, Elsie gradually discovers truth, forgiveness, and hope practical and relevant to Christians and non-Christians alike. It's unconventional, this book—a hybrid of memoir, diary, and fiction—but it worked for me, and the characters are still giving me pause."

– Cheryl Bostrom, Author of SUGAR BIRDS

"I absolutely love a long family saga. Finishing the whole book yesterday, I realized how brave and difficult story this story is to tell. Writing it must have been both emotional as well as cathartic. The characters evoked all sorts of emotions.

"ELSIE FINCH helps us remember that every family member has a unique point of view. I am able to relate to each of them and believe in what turned them as they are, one way or the other."

– Sandy Fisher, S.A. Writers Coach

"The Fearless Moral Inventory of Elsie Finch by Lynn Byk is a bold, brutally honest multigenerational family saga that explores the limitations imposed by family relationships and the legacies parents leave. After the death of her father, Elsie researches her family's history, hoping to finally understand her family members' motivations and move forward from the past. The brokenness in Gail and Rich's marriage is laid bare. The couple's moments of pain, disillusionment, and disappointment in each other are examined.

"There are some uplifting moments within the story including moments of growth, forgiveness, and reconciliation.

"The Fearless Moral Inventory of Elsie Finch blends multiple genres, offering an absorbing story full of heart, suspense, and practical lessons. I loved the authenticity of the characters and the in-depth exploration of their motives and actions. The account also offers opportunities for introspection on matters regarding family relationships and how our actions influence and impact others around us. I found the characters' courage and resilience inspiring.

"The story offers important discussions about how dysfunction, trauma, and personality disorders affect a family. Readers will benefit from its many essential life lessons including its deft coverage of the effects of parental favoritism and sibling rivalry.

"Lynn Byk's compelling novel is a remarkable work with lessons for all readers. It is cleverly written with intriguing characters."

Five Stars, All Categories – **Edith Wairimu, Readers' Favorite**

"The work of a peacemaker is not easy, and Elsie knew that. I was obsessed with this story right after finishing the preface and was ready to explore the three generations of history that shaped Elsie and her siblings, from discovering family secrets to understanding why her parents' marriage failed and where everything went wrong. I found bits and pieces of myself in Elsie. I wanted Elsie to figure things out and form lasting relationships with her sisters. The relationship between Elsie and Gail was sweet and filled with adoration, and Lynn Byk capitalized on that. The narrative was soothing, the timeline was perfect, and the pace was remarkable.

"The Fearless Moral Inventory of Elsie Finch was riveting and fascinating. I loved how resilient Elsie was and how hard she worked! I highly recommend this novel! Five Stars, All Categories"

– **Rabia Tanveer for Readers' Favorite**

The Fearless Moral Inventory of ELSIE FINCH
LYNN BYK

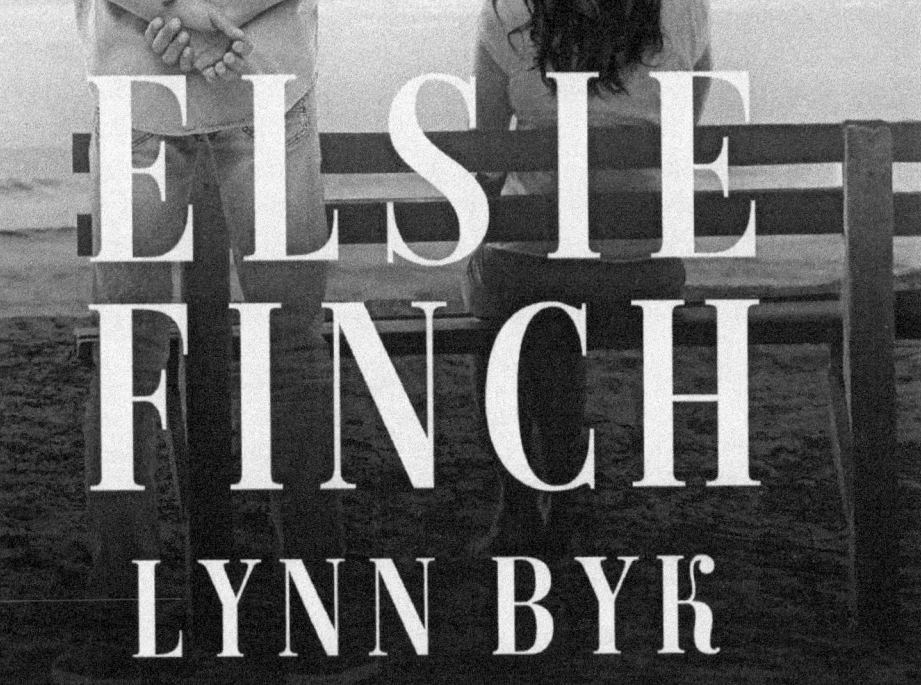

CAPTURE BOOKS   LITTLETON COLORADO

ELSIE & FINCH

Publisher's Cataloging-in-Publication (Provided by Cassidy Cataloguing Services, Inc.).

Names: Byk, A. Lynn, author.
Title: The fearless moral inventory of Elsie Finch / Lynn Byk.
Description: Littleton, Colorado : Capture Books, [2023] | Includes bibliographical references.
Identifiers: ISBN: 978-1-951084-47-9 (hardcover) | 978-1-951084-49-3 (paperback) | 978-1-951084-48-6 (Kindle)
Subjects: LCSH: Mothers and daughters--Fiction. | Sibling rivalry--Fiction. | Dysfunctional families--Fiction. | Family secrets--Fiction. | Heirs--Fiction. | Faith--Fiction. | Psychological abuse--Fiction. | Loyalty--Fiction. | LCGFT: Christian fiction. | Historical fiction. | BISAC: FICTION /Family Life / Siblings. | FAMILY & RELATIONSHIPS / Life Stages / Later Years. | FICTION /Christian / Contemporary.
Classification: LCC: PS3602.Y44 F43 2023 | DDC: 813/.6--dc23

This book is a work of narrative fiction. Though some passages may resemble real life occurrences, nothing in this story may be considered as fact. All rights reserved. No part of this publication may be reproduced in any form, or by any means, electronic or mechanical, including photocopying, recording, or any information browsing, storage, or retrieval system, without permission in writing from the publisher.

Copyright © 2022 by Capture Books
Lynn Byk
Published in the United States by Capture Books
lb.capturebooks@aol.com
Editors: Kathy Hoffner speakwonder@coffeewithkathy.cafe
Crystal Schwartzkopf crystalschwartzkopf1@gmail.com
Brieanne Smart brieanne.smart1@gmail.com
Sue Carter sl.carter@comcast.net
5856 S. Lowell Blvd. Ste. 32-202
Littleton, CO 80123
978-1-951084-47-9 hardcover
978-1-951084-49-3 paperback
9781951084554 paperback 6 x 9 large print
978-1-951084-48-6 digital online

ELSIE & FINCH

For the "normies"
and
for John Kleinig,
also
for Colin Richards, Jason Weckel, Peter Cassel,
and
LORD & Richards:
fluidity takes a team of professionals.

"If there is a soul, it is a mistake to believe that it is given to us fully created. It is created here, throughout a whole life. And living is nothing else but that long and painful bringing forth."

– Albert Camus

ELSIE & FINCH

AUTHOR'S NOTE:

Some fathers leave a legacy of sweet, silly humor. My own father embodied a no smoking, fiery humor, not a wisp of wandering beyond borders like myself, curling hooks for laughs. No, he suffered greatly and was rescued by Mercy more than once. He had been given extraordinary giftedness perhaps because his own father gave him a stone and his stepmother, a snake. The compensation was that he was a musical, romantic man, sensitive, with a beautiful smile. A man devoted to me.

For all this, in many years, I adored him.

My broadest scope of emotions and my love of creativity I owe to my father's influences. Because of him, I also learned how precarious it is to order life by sentimentality.

As I lie here tonight, turning over my mysterious relationships, the characters of people I do not understand dog my sleep.

I lift my arms into the night, hooking my hands into a cloud of comfort. From there, I can swing out over the landscape of my years. Tomorrow, I may step into the boots of a whistleblower, becoming the most disloyal of daughters, the black sheep. But I have lived my life in search of an answer, the point of which is now burnished along the edge of a reflective knife by my father's passing. I will grasp it and use it to flay open the corpse.

Comes a verse like a telescope pointing toward another kingdom. "I heard a loud shout from the throne, saying, 'Look, God's home is now among his people! He will live with them, and they will be his people. God himself will be with them. He will wipe every tear from their eyes, and there will be no more death or sorrow or crying or pain. All these things are gone forever.'" Amen.

 - Revelation 21:3–4 (NLT)

TABLE OF CONTENTS

LONE TREE, 2022	11
WESTERN GROVE, 1927 FROM THE START, A WRITER DESCRIBES THEM ALL	15
OAKLAND, 1945 IN DIRE STRAITS, WE HEAD STRAIGHT TO THE OCEAN	47
PHOENIX, 1957 WHY SO PUNISHING, MY DARLING?	78
SAN LUIS OBISPO, 1960 A CAREFUL GUNNER CANNOT BE DISARMED	97
PHILADELPHIA, 1965 TO THE COUPLE WHO GOT TIDE DOWN, SEAS THE DAY	122
COLORADO, 1968 A FAMILY DISASTER IS A DISORDERED EASTER	140
SOUTHERN SUBURBS, 1985 IN A DOG-EAT-DOG WORLD, HER DOG WORKS PRO-BONE-O	198
SIDES OF A SQUARE WORLD, 1986 YOU HIDE A HORSE IN THE DESERT WITH CAMELFLAGE	219
OKLAHOMA, 1994 WELCOME TO THE FINCH NEST, A SHADY NEW HOME WITH BEAKS, CLAWS AND WINGS TO FLY	278
LONE TREE, 2018 PETER PAN ALWAYS FLIES BECAUSE HE NEVERLANDS	337
EPILOGUE	391
ENDNOTES	393
GLOSSARY	394
AUTHOR ACKNOWLEDGMENTS	396
BOOK CLUB QUESTIONS	398

LONE TREE, 2022

BEING A LITTLE FOREWORD, A STORYTELLER BEGINS WITH A PROLOGUE

Only a day after Richard's memorial service, Elsie's dry mouth began watering again.

Her accounts of the Finch family landmarks began writing themselves into consecutive dramas. The accounts became melting snows, an avalanche, ice patches shifting as tectonic plates do. The elements of Elsie's life heaved together in a channeled torrent to meet the grinding stones of the riverbed. They busted in sprays over boulders, they curled in deep-rolling combustible events—where there should have been eddies—in the coursing river path down, down the mountain to the sea.

She didn't shed a tear into this river.

Instead, she began to breathe.

It was time to figure out what had happened, and when.

To finally begin to live her own life without guilt or compunction, she needed the timing of things. Timing was the only way to get a feel for each family member's motives and to answer this, how had her warm, vibrant father died a broken stick of a man washed to the riverbank by the runoff? Her aim was to learn how to get past these wretched years since she first fled the nest and later, when she tumbled headlong into the rushing waters.

To this end, the thumb drive her father had sent of his life's memoirs would be helpful. He was always noting things. Surely his notes would provide sequencing. She figured she'd read that now since she had not given him the satisfaction of reading or commenting on it while he was alive. He also kept all his little pocket diaries in the top drawer of his filing cabinet. For now, the things she'd heard from her mother were hearsay. Was there anything to corroborate what had happened to Elsie's baby brother?

"Carlene, can you send those diaries to me, please?" she asked her older sister. "I'd like to put the pieces together from Dad's perspective."

Her sister did not respond, typical as of late.

Opening the thumb drive, she read her father's first ten pages. Emotionless little ditties, practical jokes of a teen braggart, lists of gas prices, song lists, and notes on the work he'd done at people's homes. How could these strange idioms of her father's life represent all his values and emotions, all the shared stories of their lives? Elsie felt she was reading an understated argument for what he believed to be the meaning of his life.

When Elsie explained to Gail what she wanted to do by collecting all the memories, her heart's desire to rake through all the leaves of her life and her family history, eighty-five-year-old Gail opened the volumes of data stored in her memory banks. She pulled out stacks of pictures from four generations past to shake the archives out of hiding. She began to help her daughter with names and dates, not only from her grandparents, the Fowlers and Sanders in Western Grove, and her mother Beryl's life, but also memories of her own early childhood and later marriage.

She offered the facts and clarified timelines Elsie had missed. "Now, these memories are to the best of my ability, honey. They may not be exactly the way things were, but they are the way I remember them." These facts changed the face of the family decoupage. The images grew up and adult truths were glued between a child's scrawl and memory sticks.

Elsie varnished whole sections of mirages and mosaics together one at a time, improving the portrait, offering perspectives. A picture emerged of loss, beauty, and wisdom. Personalities permeated the beauty, making sense of irrational acts, faulty memories, and, finally, a sort of reckoning. Whether it would support her indictment of the family slide show was yet to be seen. Elsie wanted these consecutive pictures to be the story she could lie down on, the one she'd take to her grave.

Gail and Elsie's relationship had been growing. "You're my girl. You're more than a daughter to me, you're my best friend," Gail told Elsie when Elsie enlarged her mother's computer font and changed her ink cartridges. It was a best friend trade arrangement she supposed when she changed Gail's oxygen tubing, took her to get her nails clipped, or drove her to a hair appointment, because Gail offered to treat her to a meal for her services.

Elderly people don't just need a doctor's appointment, or a jaunt to the bank. They don't only need their loved ones to pack a walker into the backseat to go out a couple of times a year. In their waning years, they need something sustaining from their children. They need an authentic devotion, a true heart with no agenda. These things can be taken to the grave as treasures. These sentiments alerted Elsie to now, more than ever, restrain herself from handing over her drafts to her mother. If she managed to read it by doubling up her glasses and magnifying lens, it would give her a heart attack.

Why sabotage the very thing she'd longed for all these years?

Feeling uneasy with Gail's comments, and unable to trust her mother's sentiments as being anything more than affirmation and approval for her duties towards Gail, Elsie repeatedly let them slide off her back. She continued to meet her mother's needs, while encouraging her identification of memories and family photographs all the while delaying the inevitable. "It's coming along, Mom. I'll let you see the manuscript soon."

Like Beryl had been an open book after Dorjan's death, Gail too remembered page after page of her own memoir, and Elsie's fingers flew across the keyboard claiming her mother's memories as best she could.

Seagulls swarming, Elsie kept her nagging guilt at bay. She tried to remain as peaceable and honest as the diving birds allowed. There were thrashing, painful episodes unexpected as a phone call from one of her sisters. There were days of calm correction of childhood beliefs as her mom's perspective adjusted the memories she'd collected.

While pieces of family history continued to be gathered and decoupaged like a child's art project inside Elsie's computer, Elsie wasn't sure she should wave the outline for the birds of the air to claim. "Still working on it, Mom," she said.

Why was she reticent?

Elsie met with a counselor, naming her troubled skies as having some animosity to rid herself of. Then it became, "I'm seeking the truth of what happened to my parents, my siblings and myself. I'm starting to write down everything I remember. My mother is helping me by relaying her side of the story. Since I've never known whether to believe her renditions due to natural instincts of self-preservation—the recitals of things she's done being so different to what others say—and because she doesn't apologize for her choices unless they no longer serve her ends, I feel skeptical.

"Honestly? I'm still dealing with my mother's everlasting betrayal. I want to value what we have and what is healing between us, but every time a good memory comes to mind, a banner of her betrayal snaps in the wind over it warning that my mother is a billowing cumulus cloud building up moisture for a pelting. I've been wondering, after a tree is blown one way for years at a time, is it possible to right itself?

"I need wisdom about whose story to write."

The counselor said, "Everyone writes their own story. To make sense of their lives, you know, everyone needs to live at peace with themselves. Elsie, write what you know."

"I'm still learning what I know. If I write her side of the story as what I now believe, will it become a shrine, a bed of comfortable lies?"

"You'll put the pieces together and delete what doesn't fit the picture. You'll know what you need to know eventually."

Elsie went home and kept writing. "Mom, it's the details in your stories that convey credibility to me. I'm glad you're getting the last word."

"Me, getting the last word? I don't think so. You're the one writing this story."

So she understood the risk.

WESTERN GROVE, 1927

FROM THE START, A WRITER *DESCRIBES* THEM ALL

It's the little things. What do they say? It's a small deed that changes the outlook of a young heart. It's the lack of meat on a dinner table day after day. It's the muttering, cursing, and the first cigarette. It's one night of drinking. The first time stealing from the gaping mouth of your children. It's also one little vision and one bit of opportunity that people latch on to.

Beryl saw her opportunity and she took it. Mrs. Deaton handed the young woman a hat in lieu of her wage. What could she do? Mrs. Deaton explained that since her husband had not yet returned from New Orleans, the hat was all she could offer her employee this week. She promised to make it up to her next Friday. The fancy hat inspired all five-foot-three inches of Beryl to stand up like a lady. She'd admired it on Mrs. Deaton many times. Now, Mrs. Deaton set it firmly over Beryl's petite dark braid, and tenderly pushed back the fine wisps of escaped hair from her quiet, disappointed face.

"I have to feed my childr'n, ma'am."

"You look mighty fine, dear."

"Yes, but—"

"No buts, dear. I'll throw in some eggs if you can carry them."

"Yes, ma'am."

Looking on the bright side, a hat like this could give her grim, skeletal appearance the boost it needed to find properly paying office work in a proper business.

On her Saturday walk to town, Beryl, who had bathed most carefully in the family's tin tub, placed that woolen hat on a tilt and donned her best Sunday skirt and blouse. She'd placed some lamb's wool in the soles of her strappy boots making them almost as comfy as piled velvet. She tried out her smile in a hallway mirror and sent up a whisper, "Do you see this, Jesus? I'm here. I'm right here, and I need that secretary job. You know what you have for me and the childr'n, so I'm marching in there, and the rest You'll have to manage."

Her husband's family home, inherited from his dead parents who'd inherited it from their immigrant parents, was built by some of the rare wealthy Welsh. Their deaths served to prove an inheritance had its limits; nevertheless, living in the Hudson home provided her with a feeling of substance that she had never felt in her childhood home. White siding and a wraparound porch decorated her husband's two-story homestead. A large living room offered the occupants a feeling of opulence. *"Though they may starve to death inside it,"* she thought.

Age eighteen, Dorjan Otis Hudson was a fine looker, but he talked funny—funny like an estate auctioneer full of tongue twisters and jokes. He had made her laugh with his muttering performances and strange Welsh accent. Beryl noticed on her walks with Dorjan that his younger brother, Dennis, followed her suitor about like a pet dog. He seemed to worship him. "Pay no mind to Dennis, Beryl. He'll find his way soon enough."

She watched the boys stop to rescue a turtle out from an oncoming horse cart filled with walnuts. She decided right then that the ruff-n-tumble fast-talking Dorjan mightn't be all that bad. Certainly not as bad as her daddy.

Ten mostly older brothers and sisters came loosely packaged with the boy. His loss of a mama and pappy from the flu epidemic of 1918 twisted her feral heart so that the cords of compassion entwined the wild youngsters to her. It was true, Dorjan said he loved fishing, and he could catch 'em. He loved walking through the tall oak woods with his brothers bragging about what he could build with all that wood. And he loved working with his hands.

If'n he could fish, she'd not starve. If he liked making things with sawed up wood, she believed he'd be able to provide. So, when Dorjan tossed her body into the air with a working man's grunt and laughter, taking her breath away, she brought him home to meet Mrs. Sanders. "Be respectful," she warned, pointing her finger. "No practical joking. My mama's been through it and don't need no more."

"What's your pappy do?"

"He's a barber. He's a rascal as well. Make sure your hair is combed."

"A rascal with fringe benefits, darlin'?"

"If so, I bet he'd make 'em hair raising benefits for you, mister."

Dorjan laughed. "You'll do just fine, Beryl. Just fine."

Nothing was easy, but Mama and Beryl served cornbread with boiled pinto beans and onions, and gave all thirteen children, plus Dorjan and Dennis, a half mug of milk a'piece. Dorjan sat on the floor with the little ones, two who belonged to Beryl's older sister, Hattie, who worked across the state line in Oklahoma City, and one who belonged to her other sister, Harriet, working just as far off in Ponca City. Mrs. Sanders sighed with relief to see a young man taking interest in the young'ns' entertainment. She and Beryl washed up the kitchen while the daughter plied her mother's heart for acceptance of the boy who might become her newest son-in-law.

Retiring to the front porch through sunset, Beryl pointed out her daddy's pile of whittlin' sticks lying next to the big rocking chair. Dorjan picked one up asking, "Does he carve anything real, like for decoration or tools, maybe?"

Beryl and her mother looked at each other and shook their heads. "Never seen anything pretty or practical come of Jim's whittlin'," said Mrs. Sanders. "It's jes a nervous twitch, I guess."

"I'll be. I know a little woody joke. Did you gals hear what happened when Geppetto's saw slipped on Pinocchio's nose? They both saw dust."

The women stared at Dorjan dancing around, jumpin' on one foot and then the next in the dusk, laughing.

"Guess'n he'll be all right."

Beryl smirked. "Clever, you are then."

When the bugs began biting, Beryl took Dorjan's hand, "Best come in and maybe start a fire till Daddy gets home."

Hope rising with the fire in the hearth, Beryl and Dorjan quickly stood to attention when Papa Sanders strolled through the doorway smelling of whiskey.

The drunkard took one look at them and waved them away. He stumbled to the marital bedroom with a draft of cigar tobacco and whisky trailing. Everyone heard the metallic springs crunching as he tumbled onto the bed.

"Your pappy's a barber?"

A MAN'S HOME IS HIS CASTLE, IN A *MANOR* OF SPEAKING

Despite the awkward introduction, Mr. Jim and Mrs. Lugilla Sanders managed to provide a proper wedding on March 11, 1927 with a traveling preacher in the only real church in town for Beryl and Dorjan Hudson.

At the front of those standing on the groom's side were Dennis, and Dorjan's elder sisters, Mildred and Maxine with their families. On the bride's side stood Beryl's sisters, Harriet, Bertie, Bertie's husband, Helen, and her husband Homer and their children. The handsome groom, Dorjan, with his thick swarthy curls and easy laughter, had been taken to by the whole Sanders household. Some of the Sanders girls who'd sought work in neighboring cities and states managed to come to the wedding to gossip that their plain little sis had managed to land in the arms of a real man. Beryl noticed all the raised eyebrows and giggling at her expense.

Her petite sixteen-year-old frame attempted to fill out the recycled bridal garment, but it hung off her shoulders just enough that Mama Sanders sewed a stay at the back of the bodice and padded the shoulders to hold it onto her daughter's body. Mama said, "Room to grow—" with a wink.

Lugilla was prematurely achy in her backside. Never mind that, Beryl was to get her rightfully due wedding. Lugilla bossed everyone with the duties she assigned to them.

The sisters and Lugilla's friends served two plucked turkeys with collard greens, scalloped potatoes, and a hard-earned black walnut cake from Mrs. Sanders' mama, Granny Fowler. Beryl's sister and best friend, Bertie, also brought her a plum cake with meringue topping as a wedding gift.

Times had always been hard in Arkansas. Dorjan's feet took him wherever rumors and newspapers dictated construction or highway workers might find a dollar. Leastways, Dorjan's family home was paid for by his mysteriously wealthy parents. God rest their souls. The bank couldn't claim it back no matter what happened. Both Lugilla and Beryl took refuge in this small mercy while they scoured the surrounding fields for fallen apples, mushrooms, sassafras, asparagus, peaches, corn, wheat, and greens to cook, boil, and can. They put these into the ready-made shelves lining the root cellar for winter.

There was no toilet in the house, no running water, and no electricity. The well was full of good water in the side yard, and none of Dorjan's brothers or sisters laid claim to their inheritance, seeing as nothing much was ever going on in Western Grove. With the closest real town being Harrison and average people still needing wagons or trains to transport themselves and their goods, Dorjan's older brothers and sisters had fled to better holdings in cities after the death of their parents. Some went north to Chicago, and others went west to Oklahoma. Only Dennis hung around, unwilling to leave his brother.

YOU'RE STUCK WITH YOUR DEBT IF YOU CAN'T *BUDGE IT*

Beryl shook off the string of wedding memories as she approached town. She knew that in the nearby town of Harrison, Work Project Administration (WPA) workers were still trying to serve hot lunches to school children, while the schools in Western Grove were barely able to stay open as there were so few children. She had to find a way through for her children's sake.

The bell to the surveyor's entrance jangled as she entered, waking Beryl from her reverie of the past. "Hello." She held out a gloved hand. "My name is Beryl Hudson and I'm here to see about the posted position."

"Of course. You a bookkeeper?"

"Yes. I currently work part-time keeping the books of a construction company." She would keep her answers succinct and to the point. On one side of the office, an oak stairway led to an upstairs workroom, where large papers, as wide as a formal dining room table, draped from the hands of a young engineer.

"Are you willing to sit for a simple business test?"

"Of course. That's why I'm here." Beryl felt her breath shorten and her face redden. Could they tell how difficult this was for her? Would they ask her to come back another time for the test? She thrust out the calling card for the construction business where her husband worked. On the back, Dorjan had signed his name as if he was somebody to recommend her. Beryl's plain face, pasty from lack of food, held its color in her cheekbones. Her grim, thin lips made her application appear without frivolity for a job that was all more business than she'd ever tried for.

"Did you graduate?"

"Only eighth grade, sir, but I made good marks. I learn quickly."

He looked her in the face.

"My great uncle was Senator Joseph Fowler of Tennessee. My mama says I came naturally by the brains in the family."

"Pfft." The young man shook his head, but then looked young Beryl over again.

"We might as well have a go. You ain't no coon's ass." This comment shocked her, but she found herself sitting in short order for the mathematical test and then the business test. While the youthful engineer looked over her answers, she interviewed with the gentleman up the stairs. To be fair, her tests reflected her education accurately, but the men were almost as desperate as Beryl, and she appeared eager to learn.

By the time she left the building, she had secured her first corporate employment. She leaned against the building for a moment, faint from the fright of the possibilities, or perhaps consequences, and hope for her children. "Thank you, thank you!" she prayed.

Beryl stopped by her sister Bertie's house along the way home, taking the path through the black oak woods. Since they each had children, visits had been narrowed to the Sundays when they could both find each other in church. Personal quiet visits with just the two of them were practically non-existent.

"My, my! Don't you look spangled!" Bertie took her sister in her arms and welcomed her. "What a fine hat you have! Let me get some buttermilk."

The notion of buttermilk quickened Beryl's spirit. "I've got news! I don't know the first thing about it, but I landed the job at the new surveying business in town!" she exclaimed.

"Of course, you did. Drink this."

"I thought you'd disapprove."

"Me? Ladies, and wives 'specially, gotta do what we can, and you're a clever woman."

"They must'a been desperate for a new hire, Bertie!" Quiet Beryl, undone by her moment of moxie, took the glass of buttermilk and suckled it down. "I'm grateful, Bertie. I needed a refresh. My nerves are like nails. What if I can't manage the accounts? I've only had to deal with my husband's business."

"Strike an Ebenezer into the ground this day, my dear. God has brought you this far, and apparently, He intends to take you onward. Congratulations! Lord knows you needed this job."

"Where'd you get that talk about an Ebenezer, Bertie?"

"Oh, that's the revival meetin' going on this week, Beryl. You should come!"

"What I really need is something to feed Laila and Coalbert tonight. Could I borrow some beans and buttermilk?"

"Of course. You can have a little sack of lima beans here, and can you carry the buttermilk?"

"I can and I will. But I want you to have my hat as a thank you. I only needed it for the interview."

"Oh, no you don't. In fact, Auntie May Fowler left me a little hat pin that I think would suit that hat of yours extremely well." Bertie hurried to her bedroom and returned with a long showy hatpin. At the end was a peacock made of green and purple gems.

"It's so fancy! Oh, no, I couldn't. No." Beryl shook her head.

"Yes, you will. You need to look the part of a professional girl at a place like that. Impression is everything, you know."

"She obviously wanted you to have it, Bertie."

"Here, let me tuck it in. Oh, there. It is fanciful and quite splendid!" Bertie ran again to her room and picked up a mirror for her sister.

"About that revival tonight. Mama would be proud of you taking the childr'n to the revival. If you could manage it, I mean."

"Well, maybe I will manage it. The good Lord musta' known I needed to feed my childr'n, so maybe He's watching over me as Mama says."

Beryl left with a full heart, a jug of buttermilk for her two young'uns, and a satchel of beans. It was enough for a day or two, with the last of her nut flour to make poor man's bread, and the dandelion greens would fill the gaps until she got paid. If only Dorjan would come home!

Beryl determined to keep her new job as quiet as possible. It just wasn't natural for a young mother to leave her babies and run to an outside workplace. Her brothers and other sisters wouldn't understand. She would have to tell her mother.

Dorjan worked with his crew far and wide, sometimes catching a wagon to the worksite, sometimes taking a train. He was faithful to bring home his salary, unlike her own father had been. Yet, he seemed to have no idea how close his family came to starvation between paychecks. He would be proud that his wife had landed a job as they planned, but now came the problem of caring for Coalbert and Laila.

When Beryl told Dorjan about her job, his elbow ribbed her as he joked, "My little ewe's been chasing 'round the yew tree. I know we got ta' get a she-goat, darlin', but you jes' talked yourself inta' buying it yourself."

Lugilla Sanders came through with her typical good humor and laughter as she always did. She was standing at the stove, with her dress hiked up, warming her backside and making faces at the children watching her, when Beryl walked in the door.

Beryl didn't know where her mother found the energy to do what she did. Lugilla was not only the childcare provider for all three of her daughters, but she also washed and dressed the dead bodies in the area and became the local midwife whenever she was called. With no church nearby, she did what she could, no matter how difficult, to earn a living because, as everyone knew, her husband was not keeping the family in clothes or giving them a roof over their heads. "The Lord will provide," she often comforted herself, but Beryl saw that what the Lord provided was health and energy for her mama to keep up with the needs around her.

"Beryl, where'd you get that fancy hat?"

"It was a trade for payment by Mrs. Deaton, who didn't tell me until I was done with my chores that she lacked funds."

Lugilla pursed her lips. "She'll get her come-uppance."

"That hatpin is something from Auntie May. Bertie gave it to me an hour ago. She said it'd give people the right impression because, because...Mama, I'm needin' to go to town for awhile to work. We're starvin' here, and I got the bookkeeper's position at the surveyor's."

Lugilla's mouth hung open for a moment. She cleared her throat and wandered to the window.

"You know, I remember May's hatpin. It was a prize for somethin' or 'nother. Can't remember what. It certainly is news—"

"Mama, Bertie told me about the revival going on. I'm thinkin' I might go along there this evening with Coalbert and Laila, if you don't mind. Get us all caught up on some religion."

Mrs. Sanders studied her most serious young daughter. "Go along to it, then. Just be careful of the snake biting and holy rollers. Stick to what the Bible says, Beryl, and get some good music back into that soul of yours. And you'll be needin' someone to sit with these childr'n of your'n, so that'll fall to me, and I'd be happy to help as I'm able."

"Thank you, Mama."

Beryl dressed Coalbert up in his dark pants and white blouse. Laila squirmed and kept saying she didn't want to go, but when her face and hands were washed and her curly hair was all braided flat, she smiled and took her mama's hand willingly.

The other children still slept in one bed together, or on the floor beside the bed when they weren't with their parents. Someone had to raise them, and Grandma Sanders seemed to be the soft and broad shoulder to carry the souls of many. Two of them were working school problems under the lamp while Grandma rocked in her chair and read her Bible softly when Beryl marched out the door.

As the threesome skipped closer to the revival, Beryl's heart began beating with the hymns pouring from the tent. The children leaped over the wheel ruts in the road to keep pace with her.

As the meeting progressed, neighbors stood and gave testimonies of how God had come through for them. One told of Jesus healing their son. One man claimed he'd never go back to distilling liquor; he was law-abiding. Then, another hymn was sung, it was the theme song for the revival, the leader said. Everyone stood and clapped in rhythm,

"Come Thou fount of every blessing, tune my heart to sing Thy praise. Streams of mercy, never ceasing, call for songs of loudest praise!"

A middle-aged preacher shouted out his stories of the Israelites wandering through the land of the Philistines, being at their wit's end without water, until God told Moses to strike the rock. Being at the Lake of Bitterness, Moses threw in an ax head, and it sweetened the waters. Beryl's heart twisted.

She had been living in the land of drought with her mama and with her children. She had been standing at the edge of that lake of bitterness herself. She glanced at Coalbert. His handsome little face craned forward listening to the stories, his sister's ears were wide open. She smiled at them. Funny how the Bible was as good for the children as it was for her.

When the preacher called for the altar to be brought forward and for those who hoped for salvation to come and touch it and repent of their sins, Beryl found herself standing and walking forward with others. She touched the altar and went straight down to her knees. Sweetly singing, "I've got a mansion, just over the hilltop" accompanied her prayer of confession and confusion.

The second night Beryl was able to get away, the subject of the revival service described how the Philistine army stole the Ark of the Covenant from God's children. Coalbert made fighting noises from his seat. They heard how the prophet Samuel's two sons, Hophi and Phinhas, ordered the Israelites to carry the ark into battle promising that God would go before them. All the men chanted loudly to cause the Philistine army to retreat, but their leaders rallied them. "Do you want to be enslaved to the Israelites as they were once enslaved to you? Rise up against your enemies or be subject to them!" So, the Philistines ran into battle, subdued the Israelites and slaughtered 30,000 foot soldiers that day, killing Samuel's two sons with them.

The groans and gasps from the pew sitters rose with Coalbert's shouts and his little fist against the storyteller. But the hands of the preacher hushed them. "I'm telling y'all this Bible story because ya need to know that one revival in Western Grove is not a lucky charm to save ya from all your enemies or the ills of this world. Ya need to consult the Word of God personally for every decision. If y'all set out on your own thinkin' ya know best, the good Lord may humble y'all severely."

Again, Beryl went forward with Bertie and a host of farmers, young people, old cripples, and just about the whole town.

As Beryl knelt, she felt a rough hand clamp down on her shoulder pulling her back. Dorjan's muscular physique stood over her. "Get on your feet, baby," he growled. "I'm not having my wife become a holy roller. You have them childr'n!"

She stumbled to her feet, a victim of her husband's grip down the aisle. Laila was in her seat, but Coalbert was gone!

"Coalbert!" she shouted. Just then, she saw the boy had followed her to the altar. Dorjan marched back to the altar and grabbed his only son's arm. Beryl linked hands with Laila and made it to the tent flaps as Dorjan and Coalbert caught up to them. As they marched home, Dorjan raged against such preaching, false religions, and pfaffy thinkin'.

About this time, Grandpa Sanders found himself succeeding as a partner in an uptown business cutting hair in Saint Joe. One of his buddies, having bought himself a barbershop with all the bells and whistles, needed, "a partner to keep the customers satisfied one after'n-other," he said. The only requirement was that Jim Sanders had to stop drinking.

Maybe it was ruminating long enough over his failures, or facing ill health, or the bright carroted future of the barbershop gossip with friends, but Jim pulled up his suspenders and acted out his new barber identity with the gumption of a phoenix. Soon, he managed to buy a Chevy sedan with a jump seat and storage. Soon after that, he sweet-talked Lugilla into the idea of moving her household to Saint Joe.

"It's a far cry from the wagons we rode in on!" Lugilla sang boisterous songs and hummed as she packed up. How could Beryl say a word to steal anything from her mama's big hopes?

The Sanders took their hopes and their new motor car and moved away from Western Grove, landing in a newer, smaller house appropriate for middle-agers so that they, "didn't have to worry with raising the grandchildr'n as well as their own," Jim Sanders stated, looking each of his daughters emphatically in the eye.

WHAT HAPPENS IN THE *MEAN* TIME ISN'T A GOOD TIME

At the sight of their best support leavin' town, Beryl plopped down to Laila's height, blocking the sad view of her grandparents leaving. She shook her daughter's shoulders playfully. "You are going to have to take the part of your grandma, now, my little helper. You are going to have to keep an eye on Coalbert. Can you do it?"

"He's big enough to take care of hisself." Laila turned out of her mama's grasp.

"Well then, you watch out for each other." Beryl rose up, wondering at her daughter's strong will.

"I'm gonna lay down my burdens, down by the riverside," she sang to herself. Maybe she should consider putting New Orleans into that husband's head of hers instead of California. Leastways, there was music coming from down there.

"I can help watch your childr'n, Beryl," offered Bertie, "if'n they're ill."

"I'm the one with pain in breathin', sister. I just can't take a full breath."

"Then you best get yourself into the doctor."

Beryl dragged herself to the doctor who diagnosed her with pleurisy. Kindly, he called her a cab home and gave her some Acetanilide to reduce her fever and cure her pain. He wrote her a note to be excused from work. Nevertheless, Beryl still had to pull up the water from the well and carry it into the house in her condition. Little Coalbert ran to grab the bucket when he saw his mama clutching her chest. He also slopped their hog.

When the pleurisy continued as a dull ache, Beryl returned to the doctor. This time, he inserted a tube between her ribs in her back to drain the fluid. She felt so much better!

It had been years since any of the Sanders or the Hudson children had visited the dentist, but Beryl's teeth had been hurting her, in addition to her lungs. She'd been losing weight from the sickness, but also because her teeth ached.

Beryl's dentist examined her twenty-two-year-old aching mouth. Then, he told her at her ripe old age, she should have all her teeth extracted because they were rotting, and they were the cause of her pleurisy. At first, the young woman chuckled. Perhaps this dentist knew her daddy and was pulling one over on her because she could take it, but in a moment, the grim, unchanging expression of her dentist told her otherwise. "If'n you don't lemme take action, you won't be able to hold down that job you like so well, young lady."

He informed Beryl he'd take impressions of her upper and lower teeth and make her a new set just like them. When they came in, as shiny as porcelain china, he'd send her a postcard, so she'd know when to get fitted and come get her natural teeth extracted. He was a regular salesman. Beryl fell into shock. Losing one's teeth can be the most humbling and humiliating experience a young woman can think to endure.

When she explained to Dorjan what the problem was, he looked her in the eye and began to laugh.

"I'm not kidding."

"You ain't? We'll have to see if you're worth it, then, won't we?"

Her husband's sinister reaction to her plight drove her bravery through her leather soles and right into the bedroom floor. He set about trying to prove to himself that his wife was worth the billion-dollar teeth he'd have to pay for. That night, Beryl felt only like wicked flesh to her husband, and though she cried, he kept at her until the fire was wrought out of him.

With no heart to eat much, due to the pains in her teeth and chest, and with her husband and herself working away from home during sunshine hours, Beryl's miserable garden just didn't get the attention it deserved. Though, her children were the best scavengers in the county.

Summer and fall were the usual seasons of feasting for the Hudson's and Bertie's family. They made the cousins compete to see how full their baskets and pockets could be when they came back home. With bringing her fish and crawdad strings, they also competed. Bertie taught the children to bake her favorite plum cake, potato cakes, and braised chicken, fish, and pork. They'd be fine.

She prayed on it a week, trying to maintain her daily chores before and after work. Then, Beryl rang the dentist and made a date for the surgery.

MAKE ALL THE *POUR* DESCISIONS YOU WANT

Sometimes, Grandma Sanders still arrived on the doorstep of Dorjan and Beryl's large white, shiplap sided home to stay safely away from the grasp of Jim Sanders. Lugilla learned to drive out of necessity. She convinced her husband that when a baby was on its way, there was no time for making other arrangements. She was a careful and determined woman, a character aspect she'd passed along to Beryl, so when she proved to Jim that her own hand was a safer bet than the hands of a barber otherwise engaged who was driving in a rush and a hurry, he allowed her to use the car. "Who don't like being chauffeured?" he asked. "Well, it's nice, but it is also nice to have m' thoughts to m'self, and if'n I'm out the Western Grove way, I'd like to stop and visit with the childr'n."

She sped the motor car all the way out to Western Grove as often as she dared. She enjoyed spreading out her dresses, her perfume, and her purses in the larger rooms of the Hudson abode, and the Hudson family relished the laughter Grandma's visits brought along with her fresh biscuits and delicious chicken or pork chop dinners when she arrived.

Beryl had no gripe with her mama's short vacations of that sort. Her mama watched Coalbert and Laila safely, and in return, Beryl could offer her mother a comfortable couch and larger kitchen table for rational conversations and discussions of a more family nature. She couldn't help herself from singing "We're Going to Hang out the Washing" when washing day came round. Beryl and Lugilla made a pair of happy doves. When the young'uns helped wash the laundry, carry the wet baskets, and fold the fresh dried garments from the line, they were especially glad.

Dorjan and Jim Sanders, each other's allies, often voted together in town meetings, siding with the Cherokee if ever there was an Indian issue on account of Jim's mama. Sitting in the yard, in their cotton A-shirts smoking cigars, Jim's commentary on the price of tobacco and Dorjan's talk on costs of labor and immigration laws boosted each man's feel of worldly politics and family economy. Jim pointedly assured Lugilla his drinking was the exception rather than a habit now-a-day. He was on the wagon.

Beryl heard Lugilla spilling her merriment from the screened door that Friday before Beryl's extraction procedure. The Chevrolet was parked in the yard as she arrived home praying about her teeth. Leastways, she knew Mama was here like she said she'd be.

Inside, her children were jumping wildly on their beds, metal springs screeching, headboard clattering against the wall, and the kettle was boiling in the kitchen. Beryl poured two cups of tea and called her mama from the bedroom into the living room. "Well, what brings you home to visit, Mama?" she asked, handing her a teacup and a cloth hankie.

"Oh darlin'! We could be in deep trouble, an' I just couldn't face it!" Mama was giggling. Something didn't sit right.

"What is it? What's happened, Mama?" Beryl set her cup on the table between them and grasped her mother's hand.

"Well, the sheriff in Saint Joe collected Mr. Sanders and put him in jail to sober up."

"That won't hurt him too much, Mama."

"You don't understand, dear. His chums packed some dynamite at the base of the wall at the back of the jail and they blew the new jail wide open an' he came home to me, dear Jesus! Well, after he told me all about it, just about then, the sheriff decided to knock on our door."

"Of course, he did."

"Well, I told the gentleman sheriff that it was news to me. He barged in and started looking around. I had 'ta say I hain't seen him. Anyway, where was the sheriff gonna put your daddy if he arrested him again? So, he got on his horse and left!"

The strait-laced funny bone on Beryl was tickled. Seeing as no one was hurt, the ladies snorted and giggled.

"I didn't do nothin' but a little white lie for my husband cuz everything he told me about those boys' dynamite was just hearsay." She huffed and puffed a bit more. "And I wasn't goin'ta sit around that house 'ta find out what was 'ta happen next, so I high-tailed it out here!"

"Well, you're welcome any ol' time, of course, Mama." The ladies picked up their cooled tea and sipped it straight down the hatch. "Now, tell me, have you got any news about Harriet and Helen?"

"Nothin' so excitin' as your daddy. My, my, life can get excitin'. Lemme tell you what exactly was the reason he was in that jail."

"Aw, Mama, you are sounding like the gossip train now that you have nothin' to keep you busy."

"I can't help it if my husband is the sole source of my entertainment these days, darlin'."

"Okay, what was the reason?"

"Mr. Sanders was barbering the head of a touring sharecropper about this time last week, see. The sharecropper was telling him that he burns the fields of the tenants who have finished harvesting, and he was goin' on an' on about the works of burnin' fields and saying what a nice day it was, without wind or rain, so he wished he knew of someone who might be needin' his field burnt and prepared for next season.

"Your daddy got to looking at the field across the way, where Mr. Giesle farms and he's already got a devil's fork in it for ol' Mr. Giesle. So, he says to the sharecropper, 'See that field over yonder? It's still kinda tallish, but it's ready to be burnt. You can do it in your rotation, and then come up t' the house at the top of the hill to get your payment. The name's Giesle,' he says."

Beryl cringed and put her hands to her face. "No-no-no-no, Mama. He didn't!"

"Yes. He did. That's your wicked daddy. You just don't cross that man. An' if it comes back to haunt him, I may come stay in this big house of your'n permanent-like."

"I have that dental surgery coming, Monday. I was hopin' you'd stay an' help the first day or two."

"Plannin' on it, sweetheart."

"Also, the dog days of summer are on the doorstep. Two childr'n in this heat will be too much for me, Mama, if'n I'm in pain. So, why don't I send Laila with you when you go this time. Let her spend a bit of time in Saint Joe to remind Daddy of his responsibilities. I'll keep Coalbert here to help me."

"I'd like her company, of course. That'd be fine." So, Mrs. Sanders stayed through Wednesday seeing Beryl through the bad nights when the blood risked running and choking her from the vacancies of her mouth. Then Grandma Sanders packed a bag for three-year-old Laila, and she went to stay with Grandma for a time.

The day her dentist performed the crime of removing all of Beryl's teeth, Coalbert was dropped by Bertie's. Grandma Sanders came to fetch him when she was leaving. He promised to check on his mama's needs each day, and the sight and sounds of her sobered the boy for life.

Not only were his mama's jaws and lips swollen, but her eyes were swollen, and she just kept leaking water from her eyes and drooling from her mouth. He brought her bowls of water, washcloths, and took away bloody pieces of tissue and gauze to the burn pile. He sang to her, rubbing her back when she'd let him. He couldn't understand a single word she spoke, which was the worst thing.

Beryl didn't know which had been more painful, the pleurisy or the removal of her teeth.

Within three weeks, she got her new teeth, and Coalbert seemed fascinated by their awful beauty. When she put them in, her face filled out to normal. When they were out, he learned to listen carefully and began to understand her lisping, but she noticed her son hung his head to listen rather than looking her in the face.

Ten days after her teeth were fitted, Coalbert began walking to work with his mother, the newly shriveled, extraordinarily quiet Beryl. There, he sat quietly looking through architecture magazines, glancing sideways at her when she spoke, and drawing his own buildings on paper.

The men talked to the boy in passing, and he listened to them converse about land rights, easements, and legalities arising in the courts. Gospel singers of all kinds would tour the southern churches and whenever she heard of one of them coming to Western Grove or Saint Joe, it didn't matter which church they were coming to, Beryl would be sure to pull the children along to the services. She even crossed the race barrier to stand outside of a black church to hear Mahalia Jackson sing to Thomas Dorsey's songwriting and playing. Mahalia spoke slowly between songs describing how she sang at this and that jubilee, at funerals, and at revivals all the time. At the political events and jubilees, she confessed that she counted the heads of all those coming in to make sure she was paid fair-n-square. Otherwise, she said, "I'm a fish and bread singer, meanin' I support myself with housecleaning and cooking for the rich folk. Nevertheless, glory be to the Lord, as I've dedicated myself to singing up the word of God and sweet Jesus whenever I can." She swore she'd never sell out to those tempting devils of record promoters seeking to capitalize on the talent and inspiration given to her by God Himself.

She felt so uplifted by the church life and kind church friends, Misses-Proper-Hudson decided she practically lived for good country preaching and for the gospel music that came from the souls of the afflicted. It was because the face of God kept looking down upon her that she kept reaching up and helping her children to reach up also.

At work, she listened to Billy Cotton's "Oh! How He Misses His Missus" with longing and repudiation all wrapped up together. The military parade music through World War II was always running in her ears; Ella on the radio, even the Glenn Miller Band, were always coming out her mouth. Still, nothing stood her soul up quite so full a cup as the gospel truth and songs of revival.

Songs like "Sit Down Moses, I Can't Sit Down," and "Will the Circle Be Unbroken" motivated Beryl to hope actively. Being busy on her home front to please Jesus and bring in the sheaves as souls from her own family became her aim. But when she heard her own husband happily singing a witty song called "Jezebel," it was hard for her to hear, and she prayed for her husband and for her sister Helen, who cared nothing about shaming their family name.

One thing that comforted and confounded her in the same thought was that there would be a trial in heaven, and everyone would one day stand for judgment of their earthly deeds.

INVISIBLE CHILDREN SPIED AT THE ASYLUM

When Grandma brought Laila home next time to visit, a Sears mail order catalog of clothing and household goods became the subject of dreams in the Hudson household. Everyone voted on their two favorite outfits, where one was for immediate use and one was to grow on, and Coalbert got an extra set for school, "because he's a roughhouser boy," said Beryl. She felt she owed him.

"Jim says he has a bone 'ta pick with Dorjan," Mama Sanders said quietly to her daughter.

"Oh? What about?" Mama had never spoken to her like this.

"It's just that the barbers were paid 'ta visit the asylum, meant 'ta cut the hair of some o' them out there, and Jim saw a young man the spittin' image of Dorjan, said they could'a been twins, Beryl!"

"What's that?"

"And Jim said the boy saw him starin' at 'em, and so he asked the boy what his name was."

"And…?"

"Well, he said it were Theo Hudson." Lugilla let the news sink in. "He had a job there—he wasn't insane or nothin' like it. He ran the store for those who lived there."

Beryl still said nothing.

"Jim told him he knew his brother, Dorjan, that he was married 'ta you and had children. And the young man said he knew that because Dorjan comes 'ta visit him ever' so often, and there's one of the sisters who writes 'em."

Beryl's eyes peered into her mama's face. "I'm guessin' that must be some family secret, Mama. I don't know."

"Well, the boy said he was a toddler when the old folks died. None of the brothers or sisters could take care of 'em 'cuz he was so wild and unwieldy, so they hauled 'em off to the asylum, and he grew up there. It's his home."

Coalbert returned to school. Laila went back home with Grandma Sanders and continued helping her mama smile on weekends, if not helping her talk. Beryl, feeling deeply betrayed and at a loss for any happy things worth speaking about, continued working.

When Beryl finally asked Dorjan if it were true he had a brother living at the asylum, he only said, "Hey, you know what I heard, Beryl? An invisible man married an invisible woman...and the childr'n weren't much ta look at neither! 'Taint that a riot?"

Beryl's loss of her teeth meant the loss of a dentist, too. She began speaking of him as the man who took her teeth. Maybe he meant to scare her into taking the children for cleanings more regularly. She didn't know, but once her teeth were fitted, she never set foot in that dentistry again.

Beryl's dignity as a wife and mother was reduced to nil every night as she removed her new teeth from her gums and put them in a small bowl of water. The monkey on her shoulder chided her that she was wanted less than any woman in Arkansas.

Why had nobody told her to expect a loss of appetite for beef, unless it was ground into casseroles? She also had trouble eating a ham steak unless it went through the meat grinder. Then, there was the feeling of being less beautiful than ever, practically ugly. Her reflection in the mirror soured her stomach as the last thing to envelop her before sinking to sleep.

It was only her two new tailored collegiate dresses from the Sears catalog that kept her chin up. She was so glad to have chosen this new style, though she'd never graduated from high school. Seeing her children were happy enough also provided her comfort every morning. "Lord of mercy!" she exclaimed in praise all set for work.

A GREAT *FROST* IMPRESSION

One foggy winter's day, as Beryl walked to the surveyor's shop, she prayed desperately with each step for a woolen coat. How would she ever get one? Her gloved hands, hat, and thin woolen dress weren't doing the job. Up ahead, town structures loomed as ghosts, and her own spirit identified with the faded, disbursed scene.

A hole had opened in her once plucky hope for a large family, a fine motor car, and for Coalbert's future college fund. This was particularly because she had caught her sister Helen winking at Dorjan before Thanksgiving dinner. Then, when Dorjan took his seat, Helen ran her hands over his shoulders and massaged his neck without shame before Beryl's shocked gaze. Helen rolled her shoulders at her sister and pouted, daring her to do or say something in the way of challenge. That knowledge was what keeping her eyes open had earned.

Beryl spoke up. "Dorjan, husband, please come and carve this turkey, will you?" She hadn't known what to say then, and she still had no idea how to broach any confrontation. She lacked power and opportunity. In that moment of revelation, being betrayed by not one but two loved ones, it felt like a pair of knitting needles piercing her chest. Seeing the two thoughtlessly knitting an accessory story to her own carefully knitted hopes caused an interesting unraveling, a powerful unhappiness; Dorjan recklessly tinked back the sleeve on her well-knitted love for him and their family's future.

Oh, she'd seen Helen's sultry eyes looking at other men, other than her own sweet husband, Homer, but it had never occurred to Beryl that Helen would stake a claim in her Dorjan.

Her fingers found the shop door and tried to open it. A pretty woman was waiting for her, laughing and hopping on her toes in the frosty entryway. Beryl's gloved fingers continued to fidget with the lock. "One moment." She bit off her glove and managed to insert and turn the key.

"What a beautiful hat pin you have, miss!"

"Yes, thank you. My sweet sister gave it to me."

"I notice that you are underdressed for the weather, miss."

"Yes, I suppose winter dropped in without warning me." Beryl cringed at being caught off her professional edge by a client. "May I help you?"

"Just making a payment." She waved an invoice quickly. Inside, the woman paid her bill and left with the sound of the bell.

Within the hour, a young man entered, well-dressed, carrying a woolen coat over his arm. "Hello, miss. My dear Renee met you earlier when she came to pay our bill."

"Yes?"

"You remember?"

"I remember. How may I help you?"

"She sent me over with this winter coat to propose a trade."

"Pardon me?"

The man extended his arm with the long brown coat. "It has all its buttons," he said nervously. "My Renee says she would like to propose a trade of this coat for your hat pin if you are willing."

Beryl's thin lips parted in astonishment. She had hoped for a brown wool coat to match her hat. Glancing at the coat hanging from the man's hands now, it appeared the hat could have been manufactured with the wool garment in mind. She stood carefully and walked around her desk. Then, she opened the front of the coat. The bronze silk lining appeared to be without fray or stain. "Why would she do this?" She turned and put her arms through the sleeves. The man held the coat for her.

"She's taken with your hat pin, miss."

Beryl's eyes gleamed when she showed the long, shiny hat pin to the man. It was the one piece of finery she owned. She removed it and handed it over. Bertie wouldn't mind such a trade. She personally understood Beryl's desperation.

It hadn't been easy for anyone farming in the Ozark valley since the flood of 1927 where the water laid on acres of land well past the entire planting season. Then, of course, the Depression hit Arkansas hard, and a drought prevented planting the next season. Finally, political divisions became polarizing between sharecroppers and tenants. To meet someone who was seemingly unscathed by all of this, who also had the gall to initiate a clever trade, felt like a miracle to Beryl. She just knew Bertie would understand. "Thank You, Lord Jesus, thank You!"

When Dorjan arrived home, Beryl was stashing her woolen treasure in the wardrobe.

He sauntered up to his bride and touched her hair. He kissed the back of her neck. He turned her toward him, and he used his manly caresses to woo his wife to love. Beryl wondered whether she had misread the signs her sister and husband had sent.

They carried on and off like this for months, Beryl wondering if she should ask Dorjan whether he was being faithful or messing around with her sister, Helen, whenever he was working near Ponca City, Oklahoma. Did Homer know?

Whenever rainstorms happened, Dorjan either had to stay home while funds grew low and, food became scarce, or she had to trust him to go where the sun was shining and work was available, but where was Helen?

"What about Helen?" she whispered through tears when they were finished one morning.

"You can't trust that woman. Sisters or not. She's nothing like you. Doesn't know the meaning of loyalty. You are the only woman I love. A quality woman. The mother of my childr'n. She can rot in hell with her antics. She's a reputation, now. Poor Homer. How can he live with the woman?"

Dorjan went on and on, blabbing and blaming Beryl's sister, feeding his wife bitterness as though it were a love letter. There was no denying what had happened, and there was nothing poor Beryl could do about it now.

Until next Thanksgiving, Beryl would have to survive the flood of betrayal, and the new political divisions in her family arguing about who owns what, and the scythe of the Great Depression. The face of Renee smiled brightly in the forefront of Beryl's mind. "I'll be Renee, unscathed, and willing to trade up."

Dorjan's snoring stopped. "What'd that, baby?"

Beryl's nausea began almost immediately. It was like her husband had fed her moldy fruit. To combat her demons, she began to smile more at work, and chat more easily and more knowledgeably with her boss, and with his employees and clients. She picked up the *Wall Street Journal* every morning and after the misters had read it, she picked through the pages during lunchtime and brought it home for evening reading.

I CAN NO LONGER *SEER* THE PLACE TO AIM FER

Plain Beryl was on a mission to find a way out. Bettering her mind, she learned about China and South America, the stock exchange, tax issues, and Bonnie and Clyde. She listened to the company radio quietly and learned that unions were looking for new laborers in California.

California. Now, that was a place to aim for.

That winter, Bertie, who was already weakened from lack of protein, contracted an unknown illness. When Beryl, now heavily pregnant, arrived, Bertie was clutching her side, moaning, writhing, and screaming in pain. Beryl administered her leftover pain medicine, the Acetanilide the doctor and the dentist had given her, and she washed her face with warm cloths. By Saturday evening, however, her sister's eyes grew dim and her breath was gone.

Beryl, in shock, wept inconsolably as bereaved of her beloved sister as were Bertie's own husband and children. Grandma Sanders, through her tears, promised to care for the children like they were her own.

The good Lord isn't blind, and He isn't deaf, and so Mrs. Sanders had to assume that He didn't err in plotting and planning for her children to survive the great flood and live during the great stock market crash of 1929 ushering in the failing economy in Arkansas, more than most other states of the Union. She did everything she could to help her family members and their children survive. But, when her daughter Bertie caught the illness, she could not sustain her life, and the funeral brought the whole family low.

"We have to share and share alike," she said firmly, not looking at any one of them, but grasped the hands of those seated on either side of her on the church pew that sad day. "I can't bear burying any more of my childr'n', or their babies, do ya hear me?"

She reckoned in the beginning of the Depression there was nothing she could do about her hardworkin' boys being jilted by businesses who were jilted by banks going belly up. Several of her children had already moved back north to find work nearby her remaining Fowler family, roots being in Ohio. Some of the girls sought work in neighboring cities and states. There was no one left who could help Bertie's family.

Laila came home to celebrate her fourth birthday, home on a permanent basis due to Grandma Sanders needing to cook for Bertie's brood. Laila had turned into a bit of a snob from all her spoiling by Grandma.

A BABY CRIES BECAUSE EVERYONE SEES HER SHORTCOMINGS

Bertie Gail was born February 26, 1936. Beryl's own mama was the midwife despite there being a new doctor's office in town. With the women in the family spread thin on chores, Dorjan ordered his wife to quit work immediately.

Seven-year-old Coalbert, with black curls falling over his green eyes, leaned into the crib, falling in love with his baby sister. He cuddled her in her pale, knitted wool gown and tucked in the quilt like swaddling clothes when she cried. The white islet quilt had been made with devotion by Bertie's family during the pregnancy and was handed over reverently as a sacred last gift.

Laila liked baby Bertie, but she felt the heat of competition when she saw Coalbert so gingerly holding their sister.

"Did you like helping Grandma, Laila?" asked Beryl, spreading love in her direction.

"Yes."

"Tell me about it, darlin'."

"Grammy tol' me to sneak his money from his coat pocket, and I tried to, but he caught me, so's I ran up the hill and he caught hold of my leg and grabbed the money back."

"I'm sorry, darlin'. You're just a little girl. Your daddy says, 'A man's gonna do what a man's gonna do,' but I'm sure you laid the fire of God over Grandpa's conscious anyway. Grandma was glad to have your company."

"She had lovely flowers in her garden, Mommy. All colors, and I would pick 'em and she would put 'em in a vase and water 'em. She says we need all the colors of the garden for the best bouquets and to remember that for life, too, Mommy."

"Did she? Well, I didn't know she felt that'a way. Goodness. Grandma sure takes that 'love everybody' from the good book seriously. Doesn't she?" Beryl wasn't at all sure what her mama was trying to say to Laila, but she felt it went too far for a little girl to absorb.

When her fast-talkin' joking Dorjan came home sucking on cigarettes and describing one of his horrific stories of blacks shooting whites or whites lynching black men, Beryl's own conscientious concerns fired up, but she was just a woman with her three babies to look after. It was okay to aim for a full bouquet in life, but there was never going to be a guarantee for every color of the rainbow. Even the turning of the seasons taught you that.

Everything turned shades of brown and orange, and eventually slate gray. Beryl, by now, had become used to buttoning her lip.

Her acute desire to flee her marriage was a fearful thing to master. She just couldn't stand the idea of her sister sleeping with the children's father. How would they ever explain it to them?

Once a week, she'd walk into town, arms full of children, and find all the discarded newspapers, catalogs, and journals to bring back for reading. Both Coalbert and Laila were in school now, taking good care to walk home together. Beryl was free to read and dream of gallivanting into the stream of progress and out of the dearth of Western Grove, Arkansas. She picked through any bit of information on jobs in California. Whenever Dorjan was home, she'd read him the tidbits, never asking for anything, just planting seeds.

She cut paper dolls for the girls out of the rest of the newspaper. If she saw a slogan, she'd cut it out also and ask Coalbert if he'd heard of it in school and what he thought of it.

"Gimme some of that leg of lamb, baby." Dorjan grabbed his wife and squeezed her hamstring. More than ever, Dorjan seemed insistent on her sexiness when he was home, but Beryl couldn't abide his kisses. She guessed that the sisters, Rachel and Leah, those the biblical Jacob had married, surely felt the hatred she and Helen felt between them, always jealous.

"Dorjan, we need a new mama pig and a brood of chicks if you intend for us to stay put. We need meat, and Coalbert's old enough, as is Laila, to feed chickens and pick up their eggs."

"We 'taint no farmer Joneses, Beryl. Coalbert will grow up to be a carpenter like me."

"*If* Coalbert grows up, you mean." Beryl hadn't meant to sound ominous, but she often felt the fingers of the boy's starvation clawing at their porch steps. "I went to visit our neighbors, James Garland Ferguson and his wife, with Coalbert, little Bertie, and Laila, hoping, just hoping that they would offer the childr'n a small cookie or a piece of bread, or just anything. But, they never considered how hungry they might be, and I was too proud to ask outright. I'm goin' to find us a pregnant sow and an ol' milk cow somehow."

Dorjan suddenly snored, breaking into his wife's tragedy within disregard.

Beryl had heard of ostriches putting their heads in the sand and ignoring the plight of their offspring, but it was exceedingly difficult not to smother her husband with a pillow that night. "Oh, dear God, help us. We are weak, but You are strong."

HATTA-GIRL

That year, a sewing shop opened in town. Beryl went to browse the new Butterick dress patterns and ask questions. The fabrics ignited her imagination.

"Would you like to learn to sew?" asked a trained saleswoman.

"Yes, ma'am, I would."

"We hold classes several days of the week, and you can try out the sewing machines here if you'd like to buy a pattern."

"Where did you learn to sew these garments?" Beryl peered around at the lovely items hanging on the walls and positioned in the large showcase windows.

"Oh, my dear, I came from Harrison where we WPA workers made clothes in sewing rooms and taught adult education classes. I thought, '*why not combine the efforts for women and teach them to sew?*' So, here I–we–are!"

"Aren't you a welcome addition to the community!" Beryl's voice was faint, but also full of wonder and relief.

So it was that Beryl learned to sew baby outfits, children's clothing, and even a new suit for church. The more she sewed, the more she longed for her own Singer machine.

One day in early spring, Beryl gathered her courage and brought her newly cleaned and pressed woolen coat. "I'd like to make an offer to trade this coat for a sewing machine." There. She'd blurted out her mission.

The manager liked Beryl and appreciated her situation. "All right. I believe I could make that trade."

"Oh, I'd be so grateful!"

"But I have a request, also. When you get compliments on the items you make, I'd appreciate you giving us a word of reference for the lessons and sewing machine, patterns, or whatever seems reasonable."

That was how Beryl Sanders Hudson turned the gift of a hat into a brand-new sewing machine.

With these provisions, she kept her children fed and clothed, and learned to sew for all the practical needs of her household. She caught herself smiling more often at the family's future. Dorjan even teased her about singing little songs and ditties while she worked. She was stuck lately on Irving Berlin's newest, "Blue Skies."

DON'T *SWEATER* THE SMALL STUFF

When Bertie Gail was old enough to ride a trike, Coalbert teased her into racing on the family's wraparound porch whenever the fancy hit him. Laila would stand on the back of Bertie's trike and help their speed by pushing the trike forward like a skateboard. Coalbert always gave them a head start and then took off riding his own half-sized bike, winning every race. One morning, little Bertie was especially determined to beat her brother, and she pedaled her heart out. When Coalbert swerved around the bend, he bumped into Bertie and Laila, felling the sisters off the porch into the bushes.

Bertie jumped up with her hands on her hips and shouted, "I tol' you, brother! You was goin' too fass!" She chased him and kept saying it while Mama cleaned her scratches and on until dinner was served when Mama told her to hush up now. Everyone snickered, and years later whenever Bertie Gail got irritated with anyone in the family, someone would put their hands on their hips and lisp, "I tol' you brother! You was goin' too fass!"

About the time Bertie turned three, little Lou came into the world. The favored cherub prize was pinned onto someone else's dress. Baby Lou wore the infamous unruly Hudson curls right out of the womb, but hers were glossy blonde.

One day when Bertie observed everyone cooing over Lou's arrival, she decided to take a long walk alone down the path that led her brother and sister to school. She meant to explore what was to be her future with them but standing there in the path was a German shepherd as tall as a horseweed.

Bertie turned on her heel and ran. A minute later, the dog ran her over, scratching the back of her leg with one of his claws. She sat up and watched the blood spurting, then she picked open the wound to see how it looked. Understanding that her leg needed attention, she struggled to her feet and marched past the grist mill, past the cotton gin, and on to town. All thirty pounds of little girl came to the new doctor's office and pounded on the door. A kind nurse washed off the blood, and also washed quite a lot of dirt off Bertie's grimy limbs to boot.

The doctor put two stitches in her leg as she told him about the big dog chasing her. They smeared some ointment over the wound, put her feet on the ground, patted her back, and pushed her toward home. Properly, she said, "Thank you, very much."

It wasn't until her next bath that Mama got an earful of the full story, meaning, how Bertie Gail had walked to town to visit the doctor when everyone was paying attention to her baby sister Lou.

At Christmas in 1941, the family with four beautiful children piled into Dorjan's shiny spring green Chevy Special Deluxe Fleetline and drove to the Saint Joe's Christmas play. The family sat with Mr. and Mrs. Sanders at the town Grange while the animals of the Christmas manger paraded onto the stage, pulled and prodded by determined actors tugging ropes and collars. It was the first time the children experienced the traditional story of Christ's birth.

Ten-year-old Laila, six-year-old Bertie Gail, and three-year-old Lou wiggled and jumped to see the flighty angel characters and the shepherds, Mary and Joseph, and the baby. Bertie Gail wanted the star to take home. Nine-year-old Coalbert wanted the horse. Everyone experienced the Christmas story live and vibrantly. That was the first Christmas any of them really remembered.

BEING LOYAL TO A *FAULT* CAN'T CHANGE THE LAY OF THE LAND

Lugilla was achy more'n ever in her backside.

It was probably from the nursing and midwifery work, but it could have been due to the dressing of bodies for funerals. She always told people she was tired in her backside due to her habit of bed jumping in Western Grove with the grandbabies. This talk-about open attitude of hers proceeded to chat up her new maid when she decided it was time to hire help.

Precious, a negro from across the state of Arkansas, was a woman with a grown family of her own, a woman whose husband had died many years ago. Precious was all made of tact and business when she cleaned Lugilla's house and laid out dinner for the Sanders. She sometimes used her hand to swipe away all Lugilla's interrupting chattiness. This reflex tempted Lugilla to tell just one more story or ask just one more question.

"Mrs. Sanders, ma'am. I am not your friend. I am not your companion. I am your maid, and I'm a needin' to keep to the schedule here, as my strength'll fail me. Neither you nor I will like the outcome much."

Lugilla had never been spoken to like this before, except maybe by Mr. Sanders. Her presence had always brought out the kindest, most grateful conversations from others. She was the community's local hero, and no one, not even if they diverged from her manners or treatment or omissions in a service offered, ever dared put Lugilla in her place for fear that the next time she was called, she took her time.

She sat silently for a few minutes considering this. She decided to stop following the maid around her house, distracting her with girlish talk.

Lugilla's song welled up in her throat. She began to sing "Just a Closer Walk with Thee" in her dusky alto timbre. Pretty soon, she heard a strong soprano harmonizing. Precious might not be much for personal confessions and chatter, but she seemed to happily join in as she wiped down the kitchen surfaces.

Over the weeks of singing and respecting each other's situations, Lugilla and Precious knew a bond of something had strung their souls together. Lugilla enjoyed toting special gifts from the café or women's store for Precious.

One day, she broached the question, "How did your husband pass, Precious?" She handed her maid a cup of tea.

"Ever heard of Elaine, Mrs. Sanders?" Precious took the tea and sat down at the table.

"Can't say." Lugilla placed the teapot in a handmade cozy on the table between them.

"Well, it's where I'm from. It's what happened to my strapping young man. I'm not sure you want to hear it."

"Try me."

"It was after the Great War, ma'am. Our people in eastern Arkansas going ta starving. We was being taxed and underpaid by the tenants us sharecroppers was working for. No winning for *us*."

Precious took stock of the look on Lugilla's face to gauge whether she might continue.

Lugilla nodded, ready to hear more.

"This was Phillips County, ya know. One farmer refused to give his sharecroppers an accounting. Another farmer stole the entire crop and all of the proceeds leaving his sharecroppers stripped of wages. Widout a rightful wage we'd soon be done living. Another farmer kept his sharecroppers slaven' on the fields or in their cabins and nev'a allow' 'em to move about. He lynched one of 'em he caught on the road coming in from town just to show his workers who was boss-man. That one man was the love of my life. He was getting supplies for me when my youngest was born."

Lugilla found her chilled hands shocked her warm face. Tears welled and spilled down her rosy cheeks. She felt the fear of touching Precious even for comfort in the moment. There was something, maybe self-defense, maybe a bitter root, in the story and who could blame her?

"Listening to me wail, my neighbors decided to hire an attorney for a writ of complaint about the lynching and unfair treatment of sharecroppers. There had already been meetings about forming their own union, so they went to formalize their intentions. He agreed to help."

"Oh, my. My! That's wonderful!"

"You have no idea, missus. Soon, two white men came out to burn our cabins, and our men with guns shot 'em down."

Lugilla couldn't stand where this tale was headed.

"You sure you never heard this?"

"No!"

"Well, the white men came back with vengeance on us and murdered over two hundred and thirty innocent people, some women and chil'ens, too."

"Sweet Lord. Just because you wanted fair work?"

"Just."

Lugilla's gaze drifted over her compact one-bathroom home, the one which she often felt imprisoned by. She glanced at her older model car sitting on the gravel in the front yard. She looked over her comfortable but aging furniture. "I'm sorry. I – I have no words!"

"That's right. There are no words for such a thing. I've been on my own, helped by my chil'en ever since. We hid in the woods, after which we started o'r and came up here north. Not north enough, but we came with those friends that survived and we've managed."

Lugilla's fingers reached to Precious' hand, but Precious slipped her fingers from the table and placed them in her lap. "I hope you understand, though I trust you and you've been good to me, I cannot call you my friend – prob'ly ever – because we are from two separate worlds, Mrs. Sanders."

Lugilla swallowed and tried to sip her tea. "I do. Believe me. I do. But do not hesitate to confide in me or say so if I'm not treating you fair like."

"One day on the other side…"

"Yes, one day when Jesus wipes away all tears from our eyes, we will be like Him and we will be true friends, I'm sure of it."

WHAT MEDICINE CAN BRING *HALF* TO THE SOUL?

Beryl's gaze drifted to the clouds. The softly moving clouds seemed friendly today.

Funny how homes stayed the same, except of course, they required repaintin', and steps replankin', and fences needed fixin'. Her house standing static against the fields reminded her of the ugly factory and grain silos, the unremarkable shop silhouettes greeting her approach to town when she'd worked in the surveyor's shop. All flat and immutable, time standing still. How small her life felt settled next to the bleak Ozark hills in winter.

Although years had passed, Beryl's favorite wintery memory to nurse the bile of the Great Depression was the time when Dorjan's sister came to visit from Chicago with three children. It was just after the last pig ran away and the cow ran dry.

Dorjan hadn't been home to greet his sister – most likely he'd been hiding from being jilted out of his wages once again – but his sister sauntered inside the family home anyway with her children whining behind and dragging their luggage over the grass, up the stairs, and through the door. She made herself at home.

"I won't be any problem for ya, sister. We even brought our own food. But, ya must know, this home is just as much ours as it is my brother's. It was supposed to go to all of us, so I thought we should come down to take a look at what's rightfully ours, leastways, to share a bit."

The problem for Beryl was the sharing of her poverty. Her home was invaded by her husband's sister who was uninvited and overtook her children's bedrooms, the living room, and the kitchen. Beryl and the children had nothing to eat, much less to offer others, and his sister didn't share anything they'd brought along.

Her children's eyes. Their moist lips.

She often felt inconsequential in the world.

It was only the sunrise and sunset, the clouds steadily moving overhead that provided her with the perspective of God's long brush-like movements on earth. A history, an accounting, and miraculous interventions were moving along at a steady pace. Even if she couldn't see the changes, changes were certainly turning as the hands on the clock turn. Someone was watching and ticking marks on a ledger.

"Dear Father in heaven, may the words of my mouth and the meditations of my heart be acceptable in Your sight, my Redeemer."

FRINGE SHOWING BENEATH A HEMLINE IS A DOWNWARD SLIP

The ol' sour apple juiced through Elsie's teeth as she picked up the framed photo from her mother's tallboy. She had never liked this portrait of Grandma and Grandpa sitting side by side as a photojournalist had formally posed them for their newspaper's notice. The event was the couple's fiftieth wedding anniversary.

It was an advertisement for divorce by every estimation.

Grandma, fortunately, had learned to be jolly again in her later years, and that was the person Elsie remembered and worshipped.

"Mom, why did you frame this picture? Grandma wasn't happy here, and neither was Grandpa. It was supposed to be a big celebration but just look at their faces. Why would you save it?"

"Dad had been sick with cancer. He was in pain. It was the last photo I had of him."

"Grandma told me once that she'd forgiven him the eternal seventy times seven, but I don't think forgiveness looks good on either of 'um. It pains me to look at her."

"I know, but she was caught up with the whole family's expectations by then. Coming up on fifty years, It was probably just another rite of passage she had to make it through, by then. They were throwing a fiftieth celebration. You remember going down with me?"

"I couldn't have stayed with a carouser."

Gail grabbed her daughter's arm. "You don't know how lucky you are to have found a good husband, Elsie. You don't understand what other women have to put up with. Sometimes, they get out, but things don't get better, they get worse!"

OAKLAND, 1945

IN DIRE STRAITS, WE HEAD STRAIGHT TO THE OCEAN

The good Lord answered Beryl's prayer when Dorjan came home next. On the cusp of the rainy season, when tufts of moisture hung from invisible threads in fairytale skies and announced, "I have a will 'ta move 'ta the land of Hollywood and the 'burgeoning coastal developments,'" like he'd read that phrase in a magazine. Then, he pressed on the horn in case she hadn't heard his hollering.

"I want a piece of that action, baby," he said. "I can run my own company. Reckon I know how to do just about anything in construction, hey, why not?" He grinned as he rolled out of the driver's seat. He smacked his thighs in a rhythm and did a fancy two-step. "The sun's always shining. There's bound to be work for me till I have no more need." She went to hug him. "Lickety split, we'll be going west with the childr'n's school break," he said.

That's just what the Hudsons did. They left their free-of-charge huge, white house to the older brothers and sisters, taking brother Dennis along in the backseat with the four children.

Coalbert sighed. "We're just gonna leave the house like that? For someone other'n us to occupy, Dad?" His heart was laying in that big white house with the wraparound porch.

"Small thing. The place is tainted. It 'taint yours and it 'taint mine."

"I hope we get an indoor toilet, Mama!" Laila shouted.

"Your daddy's set on getting all the new things where we're going to." Beryl felt the childish giddy that her children displayed in packing. Her only sadness, and it was a well of sadness, was leaving Mama Sanders. Daddy could take care of her for a while, but she wasn't getting any younger. She told her mama, "I'll make sure we come for a visit every single year, and we can telephone each other too, so you will call me if you need me, right Mama?"

"Of course, of course!" Mama smiled of happiness through her tears of loss. "Things will be so much easier without all of those rascals to look after now," she added.

The Hudsons moved into a 1950s California bungalow on Jones Avenue across the street from a school with a baseball field and basketball hoops on a concrete pad, and the kids used it for roller skating. They'd come up with fanciful dance moves.

They lived three years there across from the school, where Coalbert, Laila, Bertie Gail and "Baby" Lou fastened on their skates with so much gusto and space to practice, they began dreaming up full dance routines on their skates bowing to the imaginary audience after a leap or a twirl or a couple's skate. Perhaps a talent scout would see them practicing and take them to Hollywood.

Bertie Gail attended third through sixth grades at the elementary school. There was a play yard supervisor who habitually invited Gail to play sixth grade ping pong. She became the champion of the tournament. She also learned to play Rummy as well as other card games there.

Basketball attracted Coalbert, but he wasn't much good at throwing hoops. This California appetite for sports was a new thing for the teen boy, but he hung back with his friends and let them lead in that area. He was more concerned with learning his daddy's trade. Dorjan was busy managing a crew and building the Oakland airport, terminals and all.

Because traveling on airplanes was a thing of the future, Coalbert felt his daddy held a kingpin stake in the world of California and beyond. His heart pumped pride like orange juice from a carton. He hung on to his daddy's bravado in recounting stories of the construction's dilemmas and the colorful decisions his daddy, as foreman, made in the building progress of the Oakland airport. Why, the airport practically belonged to him.

"No, you're wrong about that, boy." Dorjan chuckled. "'Taint what ya' do, it's how ya' do it, that counts. 'Taint my place. Belongs to the government. It's my job and I do it the best I can. We have ourselves a home, electric lights, and flushing toilets cuz of it."

Having a built-in bathroom was the greatest delight of the Hudson family, yet in effect, everything Dorjan touched seemed to bring home new inventions, new tastes in fruit and vegetables, new appliances like a toaster and a blender, new matching kitchen goodies for the girls and Beryl, and new tools for Daddy and Coalbert.

Coalbert began learning the construction trade from his father. He prided himself in seeing the respect Daddy's crew showed him. Hearing the men revere their boss and obey his direction engaged Coalbert's own hope to be like his father.

Though Beryl was never a vain woman, but almost frighteningly serious, an interesting thing transpired when she first viewed the film *California* in a movie theater with her girls. The movie, starring Barbara Stanwick, turned Beryl's head in such a way that she became a life-long fan. Barbara was a tough, not flimsy, gal. Her features reminded Beryl so much of her dear sister, Bertie, in fact, she looked a lot like the image in Beryl's own mirror.

Every film the actress starred in, Beryl made sure to go see it, whether she went with Dorjan, walked into town with the children, or managed a stolen ticket all by herself.

She began to use a bit of make-up, just lipstick and eye pencil, and she went to the beauty salon to have her hair fixed occasionally. She had always been careful about nice dresses, but now, inspired, she bought herself pieces of jewelry to update her dresses to accessorized outfits, with a black onyx bead set that included a bracelet watch, and a string of lovely pearls for her neckline.

Dorjan came home from work one evening, surveyed the face and figure of his wife and declared, "California looks good on ya, Beryl!"

True to her word, even though she didn't yet have a driver's license, Beryl visited her mama once a year. During the year, she kept a list of all the things relating to her new home for explaining to Lugilla. At first, Dorjan drove her to the bus depot, and she took the coach cross country. It was the most interesting and most miserable tour of the southern states she could imagine.

Over the next couple of years, the whole family returned to Western Grove by car during the rainy season. Then, in 1947, with the news of the United States Air Force gaining a Chief of Staff, reports of safety regulations in the newspaper, and airports for civilians, travel by aircraft tempted Beryl. In the heat of August and September 1950, she had Dorjan deliver her to the newly completed Oakland Airport where she stepped into her first airplane and flew to Little Rock.

Dorjan was as proud to show her around his handiwork in the Oakland terminal as Beryl was proud of him.

"You know, taking the train down south would'a been jes fine, darlin'," Dorjan said, "but I found the conductor had subversive *locomotives*, so now we's got ourselves an airport where'n we can trust the pilots. They're making too much good plain *sense* to ever come out'a the clouds."

"Pilots makin' plane *cents*, you say, mister? Even the railroad's new ticket prices for luxurious first-class comfort can't bring 'em down?"

"You nailed it, baby. Their *train* of thought is derailed. They's no match for them jet engines to power you home."

Husband and wife shared an intimate giggle and a formal goodbye kiss.

AN ONION, CHEESE AND *SPITINIT* OMELET, ANYONE?

Docking in Little Rock, she hired a day car to drive into Saint Joe for three whole weeks to spend with Mama and Papa Sanders accompanied by her new favorite singer, Merle Haggard. She respected him in a similar fashion to her lifelong admiration for Mahalia Jackson.

It was that flight home to Arkansas that seeded an intense patriotism in Beryl's heart.

Secure in her mama's embrace, she rattled on about the thrill of flying, the beautiful airport practically built by her husband, the frights and mechanical rattles, a kind stewardess on the plane, and the terrific view of every American farmer's lands passing beneath her window, and even the Mississippi River. Lugilla's heart kept leaping at the wonder of life seen in her scrawny daughter's fatted flesh, her creamy skin and silken hair, above all, her chatty happiness. "Good Lord! Thank You for blessing my girl!"

"Got it better than Hazel Walker's Arkansas Travelers!" Papa Sanders shouted.

"Papa! Why have you moved your barber's chair into the living room? Goodness' sakes alive!" she cried.

"I already own this home. Why should I pay rent at my age? My friends keep coming cuz they know'd where I live, baby girl. Pay no mind to this here chair."

"Pay no mind?!" Beryl looked at the chair and at her mama who was turning toward the kitchen. Beryl followed. "How do you live with a barber shop in your front room, Mama?"

Papa had lost his hearing, and though he was an avid conversationalist, he often missed the details.

One day, Beryl was waiting for her father to finish barbering a friend's hair in the Sanders' living room, when she accidentally eavesdropped on their conversation. Her papa, making noises about troubled veterans living on the streets of Saint Joe, cited mental health disturbances coming from World War II, while the gent in Papa's chair made predictions of stormy weather and cursed a hack of an insurance salesman going door to door. They got along fine for a full 20 minutes—one swearing about a salesman and the weather while the other gabbed on about the remains of the war.

Unable to stop her giggling, she rose to move into the kitchen. "What's got into you, Beryl!" her papa swatted her backside. "We have a guest, here."

When Beryl flew home, she implemented some ideas and strategies for gaining an even better life for her family. When she found a new 1030-foot home, one with a detached garage that Dorjan could turn into a studio apartment for Dennis, the family prepared to move.

What Beryl didn't know was God had used their first placement in Gail's life to anchor her.

The elementary school attended to the notion of separation of church and state by providing a flexible hour during the school day wherein the children could attend a place of worship of their own choosing and obtain religious training. In Gail's case, she chose to attend a class being held at the Evangelical Free Church down the block. That church set about teaching the children Bible verses for as long as the opportunity was afforded to them. She memorized, "For it is by grace you have been saved through faith, and that not of yourselves; it is the gift of God, not of works, lest anyone should boast. Ephesians 2:8 and 9."

Always one to reach for the proverbial carrot, Gail further loved to compete in an honest challenge.

The church offered a crown for a day and special treatment to anyone who could memorize the most scriptures and challenges that semester. Gail won by memorizing whole chapters of the Psalms and everything else the teachers or her own home church offered. She won that crown for a day and thrilled at the special treatment she earned. Seeds were planted, sprouted, and moved into her heart and mind. The verses she memorized would not be dug up.

San Leandro, a suburb of Oakland, would become the new Hudson home, just in time for Gail's junior high years. The new house also had easy access, with a straight shot across the Bay Bridge, into San Francisco.

Beryl told her husband, "A benefit of moving to San Leandro, is the church, Oakland Assembly of God Tabernacle, within walking distance. You won't have to drive us!" She prayed a prayer for back up. This proximity was exactly what she'd been seeking.

Dorjan, much to Beryl's surprise, agreed to everything. Every Sunday morning, Dorjan could hear the church bells and on cue, would scold his wife and children, "Childr'n, your mama's goin'ta walk with you to the assembly, so's I can have an hour of peace 'n quiet."

Nodding, Beryl scooted her four young ducks out the door. She began to encourage the children to find friends there, but her children had strong accents to overcome before they would assimilate into the fast, elegant society of Californians.

In no time, the town of San Leandro became home.

Dennis was happy to move into his own newly finished and mildly furnished garage space. Beryl, though fond of her husband's brother, nevertheless thought he lacked initiative and seemed to live off her family. There was nothing to be done about Dennis, so she leaned into the "upwardly mobile bug" and took a job at the Del Monte Cannery to help pay bills.

Then, her own brother, Leonard, who had cultivated a taste for country traveling, also developed the habit of alighting in sunny California with her. She breathed freely when he was gone for days, even weeks, but then he'd open the back door, plop on the sofa, and tell her children wild stories while she made dinner for the entourage.

Soon, Beryl discovered through eavesdropping on his stories, her dear brother had acquired her papa's taste for gambling houses.

Everybody loved Leonard. They sat around him as he explained how he always wanted to have a nice ring, so he'd saved his money and picked up this one with a ruby, flashing it for the children to admire.

"You must have a bundle, Uncle Leonard!" Laila laid her head on his shoulder.

"Nope. I only had a bundle, one time, my dear, but that doggone, fresh wife of mine drained me dry whilst I was defending our country, and when I got home, she'd disappeared." Beryl paused to recall that cheat of a wife. Her brother's heart had always betrayed him. He was too good-natured to see a fox staring him in the eye.

Beryl needed to keep him out of her teen children's crosshairs so she explained that he would have to bring them dinner if he wanted to stow away on the family sofa. That was how he could contribute.

Dinner terms helped to detour Leonard's habit a bit until one day she heard him explaining a scheme to the children. "Now, Coalbert, I'm serious. You get your mama to take out a life insurance policy on me, so that when I pass, you kids will get a windfall."

Gail spoke up, "We don't want you to die, Uncle Leonard. We want to hear your stories. We want you to live."

"Now, you don't understand what I'm getting' at girly…"

"That's enough, Leonard! Come set the table for us!" Beryl shouted.

PILOTS IN A HURRY SHOULD TAKE CRASH COURSES

Though it was sunny in California, the clouds and haze from the sea often poured inland and kept Dorjan's workers from getting sunburnt. "Just enough sun comes out for a woman to sew a pair of sailor's britches," he'd say.

Kids at school mocked the Arkansas accent of the Hudson children and called them "hillbillies" and "Okies" even though they were from a neighboring state to Oklahoma.

While the girls tried to eradicate their accents to fit in, Coalbert resented this mocking. He swore to return to Western Grove as soon as he graduated from high school because he was determined to find a pretty girl back home. He was willing to wait another year. "Why is your brother so stuck up?" Gail's friends asked.

The year *No Highway in the Sky* was released, featuring James Stewart and Barbara Stanwick, the point was not lost on Beryl. Though her government presented itself as protecting the lives of its citizens, there were many varied private interests confounding this new invention of public flight. Given the sweat on Jimmy Stewart's brow as he tried to save the passengers and ground the plane for mechanical difficulties, she just knew she would have been an unwitting victim in the story.

She decided to take the train home to Arkansas in the future or take the whole family in the family vehicle where they could safely pull off the road in the event of a mechanical failure. It would take her years before her faith in flying was renewed.

Laila's friend from Western Grove, a boy named Warren, wrote a letter asking to come visit her family and look for work. He did that, but in following through, he found a young woman whose fire for cars, movies, fun, and beaches drove him crazy in the pants. Before he took his first job in a bowling alley, he asked Laila to marry him.

She was very young, but her parents couldn't talk sense to her. She and the young man, Warren, eloped. They found a judge to marry them and proceeded to find an apartment of their own.

Laila fell pregnant immediately, even before she cracked the spine on her own *Better Homes and Gardens* cookbook, but the notion of beginning a home intrigued her, so she learned to cook and bake, along with soaking her dreams like olives and celery in her evening drinks.

Bertie Gail, who insisted on dropping "Bertie" completely because it sounded "hillbilly," loved the bowling alley. She loved the movies. Hillbilly or not, she loved the dance hall, and she had the twenty-inch waist, the shiny black curls pinned back or tied with ribbon, and the arching eyebrows of Elizabeth Taylor.

She introduced herself as Gail with a dazzling smile and a handshake. She drove the San Leandro boys crazy with her casual, reluctant charm and willingness to try anything once. She was also a good kisser, so Bertie Gail, affectionately nicknamed "Gail," found that she was never short of weekend activities.

The sisters, "Baby Lou" and "Gail," were allowed to go on double dates, but not to *go steady* with any particular boy. That suited them just fine.

Sweet high school boys trying out their new wheels asked the girls out to the Oakland dance hall, and whoever was asked first insisted that her sister come along as a double date.

The couples sought out any opportunity to go a little further into the romantic, bustling city of San Francisco. The ballroom in San Francisco was so glitzy and large, filled with exciting big band music to claim their feet and scintillating bodies, it became the only thing interesting for the sisters and their dates to do.

The Glenn Miller Band was certainly fine and dandy, but Gail loved some of the jazzy Negro bands that were especially fun for dancing. She loved their rhythm. Upstairs, there was a bar, but she didn't go drink like Laila. She told her little sister, "You know those people who go upstairs to drink don't have half as much fun as those who stay on the floor and dance." She always wore nice church-type dresses to dance in. Stockings with a garter belt were the norm, not casual pedal pushers. Sometimes Laila would come downstairs to catch up with her sisters' lives and boyfriends and see how Mama and Papa were doing, but Gail no longer felt close to her older, more worldly, sister.

Gail bought herself a used car, born in 1936 just as she was, a classic Ford, with rear lights that looked like insect eyes bulging from their antenna. It was rusted from the sea air, but it got her back and forth to school and to an appliance store where she'd taken work as a shop attendant.

She was afraid to drive the car across the bridge, so when she and Baby Lou wanted to go out, they'd go to the Oakland Sands Hotel where the Sweets Ballroom held equally fancy dances with the likes of Duke Ellington and Count Basie. "I swear! Swing dancing's in my blood!" Gail hollered at Baby Lou.

"Oh, me too!" agreed her toe-tapping sister.

Dizzy Gillespie and Frank Sinatra became huge calling cards for boys and girls to meet up, have a great time, and then go home.

Laila dropped by the house one weekend with a round belly the girls had never noticed before. "You are drinking too much, Laila," Gail stated with concern.

"Silly, this isn't a drinking belly. Sister, this is what a pregnant woman looks like!"

The girls wanted to touch Laila's belly and asked her an abundance of questions, most with answers unknown to her. She enjoyed the attention for a while, but then declared, "Hey gals, I don't have much time to enjoy my freedom, and I'm simply dazzled by the Latino bands at the Sands. Won't you come out with me tonight?"

"What about Warren?"

"Oh, Baby Lou, Warren doesn't see the charm in it all. What a drag. That's why I came to ask you two."

That night the girls were introduced to Tito Puente's Latin jazz. Lou agreed with Laila about the sexy, new vibe. Laila leaned heavily on a strange dark partner whispering Spanish nothings into her ear. Watching this, Gail became disconcerted for her pregnant sister. She managed to haul Baby Lou away from the growing interest of the evening, but Laila insisted she had a ride home.

Baby Lou and middle sister Gail had yet to experience the goodness or faithful heart of someone of the male gender. They were hungry for love and were too naive to realize that some boys were born with two faces, one to buy a girl's affection in a heartbeat and another to make them pay for the short sale.

IN BOUNTY AND BOOTY, THE GIRLS ARE *TRICK*LED PINK

One night at the Oakland dance hall, listening to Willie Bobo, Gail met a lovely Navy man, Petty Officer First Class Bill Carroll. He asked if he could call on her, and she agreed.

On their first double date, Bill and Ernie met the sisters in Oakland and drove in a vehicle shared by three Navy chums to the San Francisco amusement park.

Another time, the boys drove the four-lane highway as fast as they dared in their shared old Chevy, and then walked the girls slowly through the fish market showing them foot-long giant crabs, the trawlers in the harbor, and strings of long silver fish lined up ready to sell in the fisherman's stalls.

Pretty soon, the other boys fell off the radar, and the handsome Navy man with the kind brown eyes and minky-fawn crewcut, became Gail's new steady.

At sunset, he showed her to the lookout station on Telegraph Hill and explained the use of it overlooking Golden Gate. They watched boats in the broad waters and snickered at cars parked on the overlook. Then, he surprised her with a seafood dinner at Fisherman's Wharf. The entire evening, Bill spoke to the waiters and other customers with his best faux Italian accent. His good humor and romance provided slices of heaven to a girl ready to leap. Petty Officer First Class Carroll, decked out in his Navy suit or in plain clothes, was now the only man within Gail's sights.

Gail began making deals with Baby Lou so that they could both sneak away after work. Meeting Bill, even if it was only for a heart-to-heart conversation about their childhood memories or their beliefs and what they wanted in life, felt intoxicating. When Gail wondered whether he would meet her parent's approval, Bill assured her that he sometimes went to a church near the base and believed in Jesus Christ as his parents had raised him to. These were miracle-making words to Gail.

Dorjan's hackles were raised seeing that his eldest daughter had already lost her best prospects to someone he was not fond of, and his other two girls were now dating young men he'd never before laid an eye on. Where did these boys come from? He questioned the girls about every date, every boyfriend, and set ten o'clock as their curfew.

It was the smallest slip up that would inform him of the worst in his teenagers.

When Gail overstepped her curfew, she often found her exhausted father had gone to bed, but he'd left out a foot stool for her to trip on or placed a pillow on the ground to make her stumble. "Is that you, Gail?" She'd hear him calling.

"Yes, Dad."

"Okay. Get to bed now. You woke your ol' man up, so now you're grounded!"

"Okay, Dad."

When the same thing happened to her sister Lou, she called their dad a devil, but when it happened to Gail, she giggled and felt tender toward her father who was trying to make her accountable for her actions.

Bill decided to treat his gal to the new Sky Tram on their next date. Gail leaned into Bill's side and took advantage of his intentions. When they landed, Gail asked Bill what church he went to. Nervy on the most controversial subject of their church, she admitted that she couldn't speak in tongues and didn't believe like the others did that it was a sign of salvation—

Interrupting her, Bill laughed and agreed.

"You better keep that opinion in your back pocket, though, Mr. Carroll! Speaking in tongues is very important to my mother, though I guess Daddy wouldn't care a whit."

Two months later, Gail brought Bill home to meet her parents, and Beryl, a nervous mama having heard so much about the gallant Navy boy, served up her best pot roast with onions, a heap of buttery mashed potatoes with Gail's favorite gravy, and boiled carrots for Sunday dinner. Before dinner was served, they sat on the porch and made homemade ice cream together. Gail sat on the ice cream bucket while Bill churned—abiding the flirting of Baby Lou and worldly Laila, though married with a baby.

The Navy boy couldn't care less about the two sisters because he was busy pouring ice cubes and salt into the bucket soon hidden again under Gail's skirt.

Coalbert, the working boy, accompanied by his cute girlfriend, Ivy, wasn't going to be outdone by a crew cut. He started making pig squeals and then said, "Come on, piggy, I wanna kiss you!" This was the story that humiliated Gail the most. She hated when Coalbert told stories from their Arkansas childhood.

"What's with him?" Bill looked at Gail.

Coalbert took over and explained how Gail had fallen in love with the baby pigs they had bought to ward off starvation in Western Grove. "She'd run chasing them through the mud and shit, 'Come on, piggy, I wanna kiss you!'"

Gail got off the ice cream bucket and walked into the house. Bill laughed and stayed on the porch with Coalbert and the sisters, shooting the breeze and catching up with stories to embarrass Gail.

After dinner and chocolate ice cream sundaes, Bill asked Dorjan for Gail's hand in marriage. After Gail's father snorted, he grinned sheepishly. "She's a nice looker, my girl, Bertie Gail, 'taint she?"

"Yessir. Nice in her heart, too, sir. I love her. I'll treat her real nice, sir."

"Okay then. Go ask her. It was real good of you to consider my opinion there, boy."

Gaining both parent's blessings, Gail accepted Petty Officer Bill Carroll's ring and proposal with a yearning and delight she'd never known. She bought an antique wooden shipping chest, painted it white, and began saving fine linens. "My hope chest" she called it. Finally, she bought her three-quarter length lace bodice on satin skirt wedding dress and began looking at wedding announcements.

THE LAST THING I'LL NEED IS A *CASKET*

The call came from one of Bill's best friends.

"Ernie was driving over a bridge in the afternoon sun, and coming off it, Gail, he missed the turn. Bill was sleeping in the backseat, and when we landed, the car was smashed up. We thought we were lucky. But then when we finally got out, we looked into the backseat and saw my seat had crunched into Bill's. His elbow went through his stomach, Gail. The rest of us made it out alive, but Bill ... not Bill."

Writhing with grief and disbelief, Gail insisted on seeing his body. The Navy boys took her to the morgue and stood with her, supporting her as best they could. "Why? Why? Why?" Gail's anguish hollered at the mortician and at Bill's friends. None of their explanations brought back life to the man she loved. Unable to let the tragedy pass, Gail and her beloved's friends piled in a car and took a road trip to southern Colorado to attend Bill's funeral. There, she met Bill's parents.

Through tears, she told them about Bill's wonderful dates, the way he talked, the things he had introduced to her, and the way she loved him. "You are just the finest folks to have something so awful like this happen to you. I don't understand it." She hugged Bill's pale mama and stalwart daddy and she visited with Bill's sister who was married to a man in a wheelchair. He had been injured in World War II. He had no arms. He drove a car and fed himself with his feet. Bill had mentioned the brother-in-law's autonomy—despite his disability—with respect, but Gail saw that his sister still cared for her husband, and the impression of mutual respect stuck with her. "To think we had to meet this way..."

The U.S. flag on the coffin, the folded flag given to Bill's mother, the taps played so solemnly, and the minister's dedication of Bill's soul to God felt surreal. Gail was undone and unwilling to move through the loss that she could barely comprehend.

Everything about Bill's family seemed ideal and sweet, except that they had slipped through her fingers. Gail's grief extended beyond the loss of her Navy man to the loss of joining such an ideal ranching family that worked together with the rugged, purple foothills of Colorado on the horizon. She knew she would never again see these parents, this pristine ranch, or this future.

Back home, unexpected episodes of anxiety and depression surprised Gail. Her hands would shake at work and she lost all interest in social outings with girlfriends.

Finally, at the urging of just about everyone, Gail accepted a date to go dancing. She and her date were on the road to the Oakland ballroom when someone ran a stop sign and hit their car. Riding in the passenger's seat, Gail experienced surviving a car accident firsthand. She called her mother to come get her and began shuddering with nerves. Afterward, she started biting her fingernails to alleviate feelings of panic.

The thought entered her mind that God was mad at her and intended to keep her from marriage and becoming content and happy.

WHAT A DRAG

Beryl drove her ailing daughter to the family doctor. It was a rare visit for the healthy family and Gail sat even more anxious in the exam room, clutching her mother's hand. Her doctor prescribed smoking as the cure.

Gail detested the smell of her father's Camel cigarettes, and everything associated with a working man's drags. "Suit yourself," replied the doctor.

"Gail, honey, why don't you distract yourself by learning to sew. It will give you something practical to do with those fingers of yours, and you'll have a handy skill for when you have your own family one day," offered Beryl. It was the first hint of having a family in her future that Gail had heard, and it came from the authoritative lips of her righteous mother.

Gail had watched her mama sewing for the family's needs throughout her childhood. She nodded, deciding to learn to sew her own clothes.

One evening, when she was sewing a skirt for dancing, pushing the material under the needle, the machine needle went through her index finger. No one was home because Mama had taken a job at the Del Monte Cannery. She began rifling through her parent's bureau drawers for medical supplies and found Dorjan's Camel cigarettes. She decided to open the bottom of the package and pull one out.

Hearing Uncle Dennis rambling down the hall, she dropped it. He helped her find some iodine and a band aid. Gambling problem or not, she liked her slightly built, introverted uncle and she was glad their paths intersected. When she couldn't look, he washed her hand, poured on the stinging solution, and wrapped her finger with a bandage. She owed him. Thereafter, she was the one to defend Dennis whenever she sensed he was on thin ice with her mother or curiously stared at by house guests.

When he was gone, Gail recovered her daddy's cigarette, lit it, tried it, but didn't like it. That didn't surprise her. She sealed up the package again and hid them where she'd found them.

One daunting day when even the leaves of the lemon tree drooped in the heat, a boyfriend offered to share his cigarette with Gail. "Have a drag, sweetheart. Nothin' wrong with them."

She took a drag on the sexy Marlboro brand cigarette and found it did indeed calm her nerves.

Soon, she was hooked. She and Lou began going out again and living up the California life as they imagined it looked inside the Elvis Presley movie set.

Gail asked her friend Joan to the house for a sewing experiment. She explained she'd seen a glossy skirt a girl wore on *American Bandstand* and wanted to try to make that skirt for herself. Together, the girls cut out a skirt pattern in very thin plastic and sewed it onto another skirt, but when it was done, Gail realized she didn't like the stiff, shiny effect after all. She gave the skirt to her friend for being willing to help. They shared a seat on the porch, and a cigarette, talking of going steady, waving at the boys driving by.

BIRDS MAKE TRICKY ESCAPES WHEN THINGS GO A*FOWL*

After graduation that spring, Gail went roller skating with Lou. On the way home, Lou told Gail that she'd met an Air Force man who asked to take her out. Giggling, she explained how she laid down the house rules about being Pentecostal and their parents' requirement that boys would need to go to church with them before she could date them. Gail laughed. "Was he handsome?"

"By far the best-looking guy ever to ask me out!" Lou giggled. "You'll meet him."

Richard Finch, the Air Force technical draftsman on leave from his base in Phoenix, Arizona, decided as soon as he looked at his bedside clock that he had time to go check out the church that cute girl Baby Lou said she attended and perhaps meet her parents. Tender memories of his grandma tugged at him, like a gentle angel on his shoulder, reminding him that there was a good God and Savior watching over him, and perhaps he should take in a worship service on a Sunday morning, though it wasn't the approved Sabbath day.

These two thoughts, a pretty girl, and his grandma's smile from heaven being more than enough motivation, sprung the physically beautiful Airman First Class out of bed and into the shower.

Arriving, he stretched his long legs from his taxicab. He ran his fingers over his buzzed crew cut and entered the California church. That's when the spitting image of Elizabeth Taylor hurried across the foyer, with a wide smile, fleshy red lips, a flash of dark eyes under sparkling curls, and a be-damned figure. A tailored hemline over the black heels seemed to embrace shapely legs in a flirtatious hip hugging manner. A bomb went off in his chest. Richard's lips moved and he heard himself utter, "That's the girl I'm going to marry."

At first Baby Lou didn't see it. So happy was she to see the airman again from the dance hall, she immediately took his arm and led him into the church. There, Richard, Lou, and Gail sat together on the same pew near Beryl Hudson, but Richard kept leaning into Gail and speaking to her about his questions and observations. He smiled politely at Lou but gave her nothing more in the way of attention.

Gail flinched when she felt Richard's shoulder next to hers. She noticed that he stood very close, and he sang very well, so apparently, she deduced, he knew the church hymns from somewhere, but her heart was dead to this man and his fine-looking tan. Besides, he seemed to be ignoring her sister, and Gail just felt awkward. After the service, she excused herself quickly and walked home to Lark Street with a cigarette.

Richard saddled up to Baby Lou and her family and of course, was invited to the Hudson family Sunday dinner, which he couldn't refuse. Even Mama and Daddy saw he only had eyes for Gail. Gail enjoyed her fried chicken, potatoes and gravy like always, but then she asked to be excused from the table and went to her room.

"What's up with your fancy-pants sister, Baby Lou?" Richard motioned with his thumb.

"She's lost her fiancé this year, Richie. She isn't much fun anymore. Do you want to go for a walk?"

Richard's heart fell into the drink. But he mustered courage and agreed to a walk in the park. In the sunshine, he plied Baby Lou for the whole story about Gail. When they returned, Lou slid down the hall, knocked on Gail's bedroom door. When she answered it, Baby Lou told Gail there was someone at the door who wanted to meet her.

Gail came into the living room where Richard stood at the window. What a cad!

Lou said, "Richard, please meet my sister Gail. Gail, meet Richard." She spun on her church heels and went to her room.

"Honestly!" Gail declared.

"I can't help it. You are truly the most beautiful girl I've ever set eyes on. I was just asking questions and Baby Lou told me about your Navy man and how your heart is still broken. What a rough break. There are more fish in the sea, and I'd like to prove it to ya. Really, all I want, Gail, is for you to let me write to you. I'm going back to the base tomorrow, and I'd like to know that at least you'll accept my letters."

"Well, you know where I live now, don't you? I guess I can't stop you from writing." Gail wasn't going to give this guy an inch. "Safe travels, Rich. Thanks for joining us for Sunday dinner." With that she opened the front door and ushered Richard out. "I have a mess to fix with my sister now, you realize."

Richard leapt off the front porch with a holler. Waving goodbye to Gail, he thought, *"It isn't the guy who gets to the starting line first who wins the race. It's whoever finishes first that counts, and I'll be the winner, sorry chum."* When he got to a corner grocery, he used the payphone to call a taxi back to his pal's place.

"Howdy, Brent, you wouldn't believe my luck of the draw today, gee-whiz! Maybe going to church is the best dating pool ever created, thank the good Lord!" Bumbling Brent, whose admiration for his clever, gorgeous friend never ceased, pumped Richard with questions. Brent had a stutter and wore thick glasses, but the two clever boys who met in high school mechanics remained confidants.

NO *CHARM*, NO FOUL, OR MAYBE IS AS MAYBE DOES

The first thing Richard did when he arrived back at his quarters at Luke Air Force Base in Phoenix, was start a letter to Gail explaining his rank with the airman's two stripes. He suggested she could tell from his square penmanship that his job was that of a draftsman.

Richard continued writing regular letters to Gail until his next leave, at which time he hoped to have real talking points with this gal and find out where she stood. Only one return letter came for all his effort, addressed to "Rich." He wanted to tell her that he was being considered for a leadership promotion. He'd throw out the hook.

He had no idea how long Gail's limbo could last on account of grieving Bill, or what exactly marked the gulf between them. Her heart was unmoved. She continued to go on dates with others biding her time until another love appeared.

Beryl chided Gail's strange way of reading and tossing away the letters from Arizona. "Rich is a very nice catch, dear. You are going to have to marry someone soon, and it would be better to marry someone as besotted as Richard is with you than waiting for the same kind of infatuation as you had with Bill. As long as you have Bill on a pedestal, dear, no one will compare. You're just going to have to have a little faith that when someone loves you like Rich does, your heart will follow eventually."

Gail was more interested in buying a shiny 1957 Ford convertible, a Sunliner, making its debut that fall. She'd been chugging across the Bay Bridge from Oakland into San Francisco in her twenty-year-old rusted-out Ford, a classic 36, but it was an unflattering old geezer. Just last week, while trying to climb the hill where Joan lived, the rummage-sale-on-wheels stalled halfway up the grade. She'd been forced to coast it back down the hill looking through the rearview mirror the entire way. After parking, she hiked back to her friend's house in high heels.

For a good year, she'd served the Ford Motor Company well in accounts payable; now her boss notified her to tag any one of the beauties coming in the next shipment, any that she thought she could afford with her raise.

Today, the jet black and cream convertible pulled up her spirits with the same ease it had climbing the San Francisco hill to Joan's house.

Over a breakfast of cinnamon sugared milk toast, Dorjan laughed at his daughter's ability to fall in love with a car and toss away the letters of a perfectly good U.S. Airman. He had never lost a great love and couldn't understand what was holding his daughter back from another man's offer. "Shoot! At least get to know the man. He got the military in his favor and everything else I hear a gal likes, Bertie Gail!" Dorjan pointed at his daughter. "What about those cars he fixes? He'd be handy, so you won't go n' starve, girl. That's all 'at matters."

"Maybe, Daddy."

"You know what they call a bee that can't make up her mind?"

"Really, Daddy. Not now."

"A maybe." He chuckled and pinched her cheek.

When Daddy left the breakfast table, Gail took a piece of paper and listed out Richard's good qualities.

He was persistent. All the girls thought there was an extraordinary physique on him, and a glowing Olympian smile. He had neat, squared-off handwriting. There was also his mechanical talent. He apparently could fix the motor on any car. He had drawn her detailed pictures in some letters, mentioning with pride this hobby. Her family liked him, and he was a church boy.

She was surer than ever that it was her own brokenness that caused the dissonance in her feelings for Rich.

The next letter she opened told her that Rich was scheduled to go serve in Saudi Arabia, halfway around the world! Gail immediately called her friend, Joan. "Wanna go on a road trip, darlin'?"

"Where to?"

"Oh, just down Highway 1, see the coast, and inland a bit to Phoenix and back…"

"We're going to check out your new beau, aren't we? You rascal!"

"Maybe. I'd like to show the showoff my new convertible and see what that guy's really about."

The two girls put in for a day's vacation, hightailed it down the highway and over to Luke Air Force Base for a whirlwind weekend.

Rich was taken unaware, a small affront. It presented him with the conflicted feelings of being flattered by the girls' visit and angry at the sassy, unyielding young lady who wouldn't bother to put pen to paper who showed up full of brass in a top-notch Ford, a brand-new convertible no less! He licked his parched lips and held them in a tight grin, irritated but flattered. And what was he supposed to do with two girls now?

"What were you doing, anyway? Are we bothering you?" Gail flirted.

"Just twiddling my thumbs, like always," Rich returned, cat-like.

Taking in the stares of his chums, stares for his lucky attention, Rich decided to take both girls out for a burger and Coke before they turned and left town.

The whole time, he chided Gail for the thirty-seven unanswered letters he'd written, caressing her shoulders as he hung onto her stories of the spinning events that brought her into his embrace.

"So, I couldn't believe my luck when I was able to qualify for the Sunliner—Aw, Rich," she finished, "I just came to tell you that I'd write you if you don't want to be lonely halfway across the planet."

"You will?" He perked up like a deer in the headlights.

"Yes, of course. You deserve a chance." She winked.

In the same whirlwind as the girls arrived, they departed.

It was now Gail's turn to be writing Rich, not knowing whether he would receive her notecards. He wrote back like a lazy man. Oh, he was full of interesting news about the middle east and his longing for her. "You are the girl I dream about"—His letters, however, were far less frequent.

WATCH FOR POGO'S ABOUNDING SCHTICK

In February of 1957, Rich earned his next leave to visit Gail. The news did the glad job of making Gail's choice sure.

She offered to meet him at the airport and watched curiously as he stepped off the plane wearing his casual blue airman suit.

"Nonstop?" Gail asked.

"Of course."

"How does one get off a nonstop flight, Mr. Air Force, if it doesn't ever stop?"

Rich stopped and looked Gail over. He didn't get her joke.

"You have luggage?" she asked.

"Yes. One case. Over this direction." He took her arm and led her down the corridor.

"Have you ever lost your luggage?"

"No. I haven't flown commercially much."

"I hear you can sue the airlines if they lose your baggage."

"Oh?"

"Yes, but there's no guarantee that you'll win your case." Gail skipped in front of her boyfriend and laughed in his face.

"What are you talking about, girl? I have no intention of suing the airlines."

Gail's teasing ceased. Rich obviously had no sense of humor. At least not her kind. Sobered, she let him take the lead.

He seemed casually confident throwing his bags in the back seat of her convertible, then asking if she'd like to go to the lake to let him give her a ride in a rowboat.

"I've taken the afternoon off, expecting to spend it with you, Mr. Air Force, so yes, I'll go along with you this once."

The afternoon air was full of warm caresses on their sun-licked arms driving to the park. Then, Rich picked a rose, handed it to Gail, and took up the oars. She stepped into the romance of Richard O. Finch's world.

"How is officer's training going, Richard?" she asked.

"Oh, I should know any day now. My chain of command lost the papers, but they've been found, so they'll let me know when I'm starting very soon."

"You mean you've been to Saudi Arabia and back and still no training?"

He rowed silently through the lake and began to describe his most recent travels through Germany and Switzerland on his last leave as they followed the wake of ducks and geese. "You and me are going to have to visit those places together, someday, Gail. I took so many photographs! I have some good ones to show you."

"Yes, you sent some interesting ones. Of course, I'd like to hear more about them." Over on land, the park's flower gardens provided a lovely evening of succulence, almost mystical. Gail laughed radiantly and enjoyed being wooed.

Rich let Gail drive to the Showboat, where he hoped they didn't require dinner reservations for servicemen returning from active duty. He read the map and pointed to where she needed to turn, and she felt safe.

Passing through Chinatown, Rich ordered, "Keep going along this road straight to Jack London Square, babe. We're eating on the wharf tonight."

Sure enough, a table in the corner window was open for a swordfish dinner special under the influence of the Dick Lane Trio.

Gail's stomach swished. She was giddy that Richard knew how to make her happy.

Over dinner, she told him about the list of his assets that she had made from the letters he'd sent. She apologized for not giving him much hope, but it was because she just needed time, and she told him that they had the blessing of her parents. They liked him, even loved him, she said, making his heart beat rapidly.

"What do you want in married life, Gail?" he asked.

She hadn't given much thought to her future so she said, "I just want a man I can respect and a dozen kids to herd!" Her beautiful smirk and jostling shoulders aimed to flirt with him, yet her whole response made him feel sick. Maybe it was a case of bad seafood.

His neck tightened at her ability to joke about so many kids. He knew nothing about raising children. His own experience hadn't been stellar. He'd pretty much raised himself and his little brother, probably ruined him.

He chuckled at her joke and decided that this was a topic they'd have to discuss when the wedding was out of the way. Besides, what could she do about it without his approval?

Before they took off from the wharf, he escorted her, arm in arm, around the plaza and finally knelt on one knee producing a velvet black box, and inside were tiny diamonds in a row planted in a gold engagement band. Grinning up at her, he asked if he had finally managed to win her heart. When she nodded, he slipped the ring on her finger.

"I agree to marry you, Richard, and I trust you. Thank you for such a lovely evening." It was all very pleasant and businesslike, but when he bent to kiss her, they kissed some more. She was absolutely sure of her choice.

"What a beautiful, tender neck! What a lovely perfume! I am the luckiest man alive," he thought.

Gail's friends were eager to meet Rich, but also very surprised at the proposed union. They made comments like, *"How did you land that god-like looker?"* and, *"Is he any good at kissing?"*

After shopping for dress patterns one Saturday, Gail and her best friends, Joan and Norma Jean, examined their choices. Rich stood erect on the side, almost formal, even after the rest of the family arrived.

"Aren't you exhausted, Richard?" Gail asked.

"Not much," he said. "Just twiddling my fingers."

Mostly because Richard described the fact that his papers were being processed for officer's training, Gail didn't feel too bad when her fiancé's leave was cut short, and he caught a return flight to Luke's Air Force Base. "Schedule the church for a June wedding. That'll be my next leave." She'd already managed to secure the date.

With her parents talking up her marriage to a quality young airman, she knew she'd have a lot of help planning the landmark celebration and reception.

Beryl telephoned Lugilla with the happy news. Lugilla told her daughter that she was hand stitching a quilt that should be ready for the wedding, and if not a gift for the wedding, then perhaps in time for the arrival of Gail's first baby.

"This year when I come visit, Mama, we can work on that quilt together! Ifn it's not finished by the time the baby comes, I'll finish it on my sewing machine."

"Oh, no you won't, daughter! This quilt has to be handmade. I want Bertie Gail and her children to have somethin' from me, special like, to remember me by."

That set Beryl's mind to thinking, too. She found a pattern for a Dutch Girl quilt and set about learning to cut and piece it together on her own free time. One of her children's children would want that from their grandma. The legacy idea appealed to her as most of her mama's ideas did.

Rich's letters were fewer than before, strangely, but there were quick phone calls and promises to be realized.

In Gail's earnest love letters, she sent photographs of herself, and her family, outings with her friends, and she tore out pictures of recipes and household things she liked and wrote about all of this to Rich. She also began asking questions because she realized how little she really knew about Rich, not even a hint about his parents or whether he had siblings.

During one of their phone calls, Rich answered her question about his religious upbringing telling her that he had been raised for a couple of years by a grandmother in Oklahoma, and she was a Seventh Day Adventist. When Gail asked her mother what a Seventh Day Adventist was, Beryl assured her that he was a good Christian, even if he wasn't a Pentecostal. "You'll just have to show that boy how to let loose." She laughed.

In one of his letters, Rich told Gail about his younger brother, Luster. He was a stepbrother really, because Luster was born of another mother after his own mother passed away. He assured her that he'd take Gail to meet his family in San Diego when he returned.

When next Rich arrive in San Leandro, he teased Gail for being "packed and ready to move to Phoenix as soon as the ink dried on that marriage license." Her beautiful curls made her look all the more exuberant and *"for goodness' sake, she's chatty!"* he thought.

"Do you have a scarf for that hair?" asked Rich as he opened the door to his soon-to-be bride's sleek convertible. Giggling, she tied on her scarf, kissed her mama, and donned her new, glamorous sunglasses.

Riding down the coastal highway to San Diego, Gail relaxed in the wind and enjoyed the gorgeous beaches and coastline. Her whole future lay ahead. She grabbed Rich's hand and kissed it. As the morning sun began to burn Gail's face, Rich became more and more withdrawn.

Stealing a glance at her beau, she noticed his sagging cheeks and pursed lips. *"'Going down to San Diego' seems to be working on him somehow,"* thought Gail shaking her pretty shoulders to allay the nerves.

She moved closer to ask a question, but he moved his hand away to turn up the music. *That's odd,* she thought, but let it go.

Rich drove through a suburb of San Diego, and onward to the outskirts of town. He pulled her Sunliner into a gravel yard lacking a paved driveway, and when he opened her passenger door, he stood looking ahead at the tiniest trailer she'd ever seen.

When no one appeared to notice the sound of their car, Rich knocked on the door and introduced Gail to Dick Senior who motioned them inside. Rich's stepmom, Carmen, and his dad sat at a kitchen table only big enough for the two and motioned for Rich to take his girl and sit on the sofa.

"Well, Junior, tell us about your grand gal!"

Gail's sunburnt face accompanied her parched throat, but no one bothered to offer her a drink. Shocked, and finding it a little creepy that Rich's parents lived in a 16' x 12' trailer, she greeted the couple quietly and then asked about Luster, Rich's brother.

Dick motioned to his son, "Let's head outside, Junior. We can pick up some burgers to go and let the women folk talk."

A little panicked, Gail graduated to the tiny table opposite the plump, scant-haired Carmen. Carmen's mousy colored hair was coupled with narrow eyes that blackened when Gail asked for a glass of water.

"Oh, sure, hon. Help y'rself. The glasses are above the sink on the left there." Again, there was silence, and still no response to her question about Rich's brother. She was about to try a different tack after downing a glass of water, when Carmen interrupted, "There's iced tea in the fridge if you'd like some, and I'd take a glass myself, kiddo."

When Carmen waved to the fridge, the flesh under her arm wagged. After pouring, Gail took a better look at her plain housedress and slippers from behind.

The young woman obediently brought back two glasses of iced tea to the table and sat looking around the room, a trapped animal behind zoo glass. She'd been taught to compliment her hostess on at least one thing when entering a home, but there was nothing more than curiosity in her paneled surroundings.

Carmen must have noticed Gail focusing on a row of dolls kept on a high shelf around the perimeter of the living room. She kept them in their original plastic containers. "Dick traveled during the war and sent these to me from all over the world. They are my treasured souvenirs."

"Oh! They are beautiful, and so interesting. I can see that they have different costumes…"

"The thing you should know about me, kiddo, is don't ever cross me. I never forget and I never forgive."

"Oh! Oh, okay." Stunned, Gail nodded and acknowledged this warning and immediately wondered if her marriage decision was as good as she wanted to believe.

"So, tell me about your mama and daddy, then."

Gail talked about living in Arkansas, trying to find common ground with the step-mom of her groom-to-be.

Saved by the sound of Rich's car parking in the gravel and the doors slamming, she abruptly stopped her soliloquy in anticipation.

With a knock on the trailer door, Rich and Dick Senior entered bringing a sack of burgers and fries with a palate-pleasing variety of shakes, two strawberry, one chocolate, and one vanilla. Gail waited for everyone to choose whatever it was that looked good, and she took the leftover burger and shake.

"Gee, I'm sorry. I should have warned you about my folks, babe," Rich said as they followed the highway back up the coast. When Gail offered only a weak smile, he added, "I should have told you that I am the bastard child of my father. You'd probably want to know that.

"I was the product of my mother's affair with Dad in Oklahoma City during a time when Carmen and Dad were broke up. She's part Cherokee Indian and she never got on with the religious folks around home. I know she can be a handful. Oh, you noticed?" Rich felt a giddiness about the shock he was delivering to the classy girl at his side. She could use a reality check.

"Well, after I was born, Dad apparently couldn't take the crying of a baby and bashed my head against the wall above the crib to make it stop. I'm kind of deaf in my left ear because of that. So, my mother kicked him out. Dad went back to Carmen, his true love, and she refused to stay in the same town as my mom and me. So, Dad took her way up to the shipyards of Washington during the war, where he worked till the end of it. We then moved down to see what all the fuss was about in California."

"What about your mom and you?"

"Well, let's see...I remember my mom must'a lost hope in Oklahoma City. I can recall waiting for her in the car while she went in to have a few drinks with whatever guy was buying, and then earn a few greenbacks for a little more effort.

"After a few years of being knocked about because she had a bad reputation in Oklahoma, my mom thought she was dying." Rich looked to see if Gail was listening to his barrage of words. "She was sickly with TB and a heart problem. She always seemed to be sick as far as I could tell. Anyway, Mom took me up there to Washington with a brother I no longer know. She toted my older sister, Mary, from another man up there, too.

"I remember standing by her side as she begged Dad to support us, but he refused, calling her every name in the book and threatening her to stay away." Rich's jaw clenched and the car swerved around another on the motorway. Getting back into his lane, he finished. "Finally, she took the train down to Los Angeles to lay us all at her sister's doorstep where she died. I was eight."

"She died when you were eight years old?"

"All I remember was that my aunt couldn't take me and my sister. She kept my younger brother, and he grew up with her. My sister went to live with a preacher and his wife in Texas somewhere. My granny accepted me back at her place, and that's where I got my religion."

His voice changed to a more tender tone and the Ford slowed to join in with traffic when he described living with his granny in a tiny house with a white picket fence and a big garden.

"Every night she read me one of the Proverbs and something of a story from the Bible and then she prayed with me. It was the best memory of being a kid I have."

He said, "It was only after my granny heard rumored 'round town that Dad was coming to take me back to live with him and Carmen that she put me on a bus and sent me up to a boy's school in Kansas to hide from him. I was about ten or eleven then, and Dad came and found me and brought me to live in California. The trailer where you just saw them? That was where he and Carmen settled."

"But you and your brother and them couldn't possibly have lived in that small trailer!" Gail challenged.

"No. No, we didn't. They had another one out back. Luster was just a kid when I came to live with them, and they put us both in the other trailer with a couple of beds, and that was where I basically raised my little brother."

"Oh, my word, Rich. Where is he now?"

"Dad said Luster's been drinking a lot lately. He's still a kid in his last year of high school, and he just needs to find himself, but Carmen is not at all happy with her favorite child. So, he's 'on the outs' right now or he would'a loved to have met you. He kind'a worships his big brother. So, if he would'a laid eyes on you-"

"Stop it. Stop it, Rich!" All of this information, all that she had seen today was too much for Gail to absorb.

She felt creepy sitting next to this desperado talking wild about everything bad and hopeless all at once. "I need some time to think about all of this." Kids at school had called her family Okies and hillbillies, but they were a far cry from the meanness in that trailer.

"If you want to stop the wedding, darling, just let me know now. I mean if my past is too much for your pretty head." He waited a minute, then added, "Geez, Gail, I knew I was overreaching and that you'd want all the best things, but I promise to do my best to please you, if you can be just a little patient."

Gail's tears swept off her cheeks and chin into the wind. They drove in silence, except that Rich put on the big band tunes that kept young lovebirds thriving, the sensuous horns and violins that labeled them both idealists. When she arrived home, she jumped out of her door and said, "Thank you, Rich." She curtly turned away from her own car, letting herself into her parents' front door. "I'll call you tomorrow."

NEVER TRUST *ATOM* BECAUSE HE MAKES UP EVERYTHING

The sunshine and scent of honeysuckle streamed through her islet curtains, awakening Gail to a happy, fresh suspension of other facts.

She resolved to put away the day before. It served to make her feel she and Rich were actors in an Alfred Hitchcock film, perhaps *Rebecca* or *A Shadow of a Doubt*. It just wasn't so.

Now, laid out safely in her P.J.s, her rational mind assured her that Rich was not a bit like his parents. He had a future. He had multiple talents. He was ambitious.

Gail jumped from bed to call the Ford Motor Company. She put in her two week's notice. Life was moving on!

During this time, Beryl approached her daughter on two separate occasions trying to explain the difficulties with the facts of life as she knew them, but the awkwardness of the subject matter embarrassed Gail. She said, "Mama, I know, I know. Shush, Mama. I don't want to talk about this."

"*Laila didn't have any difficulties with her rite of passage, so why should I?*" Gail reasoned.

The day of the wedding, Gail turned radiant. So many of her mother and father's siblings came, filling every space of the house. Having saved the gown she'd purchased for her wedding to Bill, her twenty-three inch waist slipped back into the quarter length gown, and her mama and Baby Lou were nervous chambermaids.

Gail worried a bit about the cold sore on her lip. Doggonit. Why did she have to get a cold sore on her wedding day?

Since her hair and nails had been done at the beauty shop that morning, all that was left was to make it to the preacher at the Oakland Assembly of God on time. Daddy drove her with Mama in his new red and white Ford Fairlane.

This was a wedding to make them proud.

Sweating at the front of the church, Rich smiled his happiness to see the doors finally open. Dorjan and Gail began the father-daughter wedding steps on the red carpet to the front.

On one side, Gail looked up and grinned at Joan and Norma Jean. She greeted her groom, noticing his moist baby blues. He gave her the satisfaction that he felt all his dreams were coming true. Behind him, the figure of his awkward best man, Brent, jittered on a nervous knee. He adjusted his glasses and smiled. Gail had only met Brent once, and though she didn't consider him a likely match for her husband, his wife seemed very nice. She knew they'd make friends.

Rich's younger brother, Luster, offered a smile of wonder, glowing proudly behind Brent.

After the ceremony, they crossed arms and carefully fed a piece of white wedding cake into each other's mouths to the music of cheering and applause. Rich's charm when he shook hands with the guests and accepted their well-wishes assured Gail again of her good favor and choice of husband.

Luster was a tall boy for his age. He gave Gail a boyish hug and said sheepishly, "I think you are a goddess. My brother married a queen." Gail smiled gratefully and gave him another hug. "Don't be a stranger, okay?"

Handfuls of rice showered over the couple with a perfect sendoff from the stone portico of the church. Rich's waiting rental, a gleaming black 1954 Customline, a classic ride, complete with a chauffeur, welcomed the bride and groom who paused just long enough for professional photographs.

At first, the clanking cans attached to the back fender made Gail laugh, but on their way out of the parking lot, Rich told the chauffeur to pull over where the two men pulled off the noise makers, leaving only the giant white letters "Just Married."

The chauffeur and formal getaway car was mostly a photo opportunity so that they could pick up Gail's car and allow her to change into her going away suit. The suit, which was lovingly tailored by her mother, awaited Gail in her room. They stopped at the quiet Hudson home, and Rich ran around the car to help his bride disembark with both train and veil in hand.

Uncle Dennis, carrying a pile of gifts to open, waited at the door.

In short order, a feeling of overwhelming happiness enveloped the couple as they drove an hour up the early June coastline to Monterey and Carmel-by-the-Sea. There, they checked into the honeymoon suite as Mr. and Mrs. Richard O. Finch.

Rich proudly escorted his finely suited bride into the dining room where they ordered two steak and lobster dinners overlooking a sunset vista. When it came time to establish the bill, the waiter refused, making it known that someone had picked up the newlywed's tab.

Sadly, Gail hadn't planned her wedding date well. At least that's what Rich sputtered in so many words when she appeared from the bathroom that night in her negligée only to inform her husband that her period had started.

"Are you kidding me? Is this a joke? It isn't very funny if so. Did you purposely plan to do this to me?"

"Of course not, Rich. It happens to women all the time. Some women's cycles are so erratic that they couldn't possibly guarantee it wouldn't occur. I planned the date according to your calendar on leave, honey, and I didn't think twice about it. I can't imagine why no one mentioned this was a possibility. I'm horrified, honestly. Please forgive me?" She kissed him gently.

He pulled away from her. He couldn't account for the depth of animosity in his heart with the delay of the marriage's physical union. He felt tricked out of the best day of his life by his own bride.

Monterey Bay was gorgeous and romantic, but neither of them felt like honeymooners regardless of what anyone said to them.

"Why spend another day waiting around for a honeymoon that isn't going to take off?" Rich reasoned with Gail. So, in the morning, they left, and went home to pack up their gifts to move to Phoenix and set up home.

MORE TO THIS TIDY STORY AS IT UNFOLDS

"Here are your sheets, Mom, warm from the dryer. I'll make us some lunch while you fold."

Elsie knew not to do everything for her mother because getting her mother's blood to circulate would help dispel the swelling in her feet. She dropped the armload of laundry on the ottoman beside her mother's lounger.

"I can't fold sheets alone. Help me with these."

Of course. What was she thinking? Elsie turned to grasp a couple corners of her mother's queen-sized fitted sheet. "I need to relearn how to fold these things anyway."

Mother and daughter pulled and halved, tucked one corner inside another, and brought the ends together like partners in a square dance. Suddenly, Gail growled, "Oh!" Fed up, she grabbed the other end from Elsie and wadded the whole thing into a roll which she folded over in thirds. "I don't remember how to do these things! Just stuff them into the linen closet, will you?" She laughed.

"Okay. I was hoping you'd teach me how to do it."

"If you don't know by sixty, daughter, it's a bit late! Mom was always so good with linens. You should'a seen her linen closet. It was like the linen closets at Macy's, all lined up. Mom took pride in her housekeeping no matter what, but I just don't care anymore."

Elsie was noticing how she no longer cared about much of anything either. The proverbial rug had been pulled out from under her, and though she went through the motions of taking Gail's vitals, dispensing her meds and massaging her feet, they often had little to say to one another.

"Mom, why do you think the Bible says so often to remember this or remember that?"

"Does it?" Gail gasped, "—talk about *remembering*?"

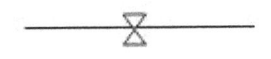

PHOENIX, 1957

WHY SO *PUNISHING*, MY DARLING?

For three nights, they slept in a lovely little hotel and walked around neighborhoods seeking places to rent near Luke Air Force Base.

Riding through the developing new neighborhoods and the older, traditional ones nearer downtown, the couple found one place they agreed upon, mainly because it only cost $18 per month.

"Will wonders never cease?" Rich whistled at the price. The cinderblock house was close to town and was less expensive than the brand-new apartments.

"It's only temporary," they told each other, until Rich's discharge from the Air Force.

Unpacking the car the first day, their unity remained thrilling while Rich and Gail moved into their small adobe styled apartment house in Phoenix, Arizona. Then, Rich visited the bathroom and came out commenting, "Gonna have to keep things tidy since the place is minuscule. Howdy! I've seen your bathroom back home, and I'm already having doubts about your ability to clean up after yourself, baby."

"What a thing to say!" Yet Gail nodded, and after taking a second peek herself, said, "All right. It is rather small, isn't it?"

Looking around the place's tiny spaces made her think of the term "utilitarian" because there was only one small bedroom with a hall bathroom right next to the entrance. The hall fed into the living room and kitchen diner. She only liked it because of the friendly front window, but it seemed fine for a starter home. After all, they'd only be living there until Rich received his discharge. Two years tops.

The next morning, after Rich went to work, Gail arranged their wedding gifts, mostly kitchen appliances and dishes, into cupboards. She was in a conflicted mood, both lonely and happy, remembering each of her friends and family members who had contributed to her household as she unpacked each piece.

After that, she decided to make her mother's favorite casserole with the few tins of peas, carrots, pasta, and beef they'd picked up from the grocery store yesterday. Humming, Gail removed her curlers from her beautiful chestnut head and put on her makeup to make the surprise complete for Rich's arrival from work.

She was setting the table for dinner when he came in and kissed her. "I'll just put these things down and be back in a minute." He filed his draftsman briefcase and overcoat into the hall closet, then decided to empty his bladder before he sat down.

"Gail! Get in here…now!" As he surveyed the bobby pins covering the single cabinet top around the sink, his military ire rose. Gail's pink and teal curlers were piled high on the back of the toilet tank, too.

Thinking something had broken, or maybe Rich had fallen, Gail hurried to obey. Only, it was his bony fingers grabbing her arm pulling her into the four-by-five-foot bathroom space to stand beside him that made her wince.

"What's this? Wasn't I clear enough yesterday? I told you not to leave your things out! Don't tell me you can't clean up after yourself. I had a feeling you weren't going to be much good at this, so I'm just going to have to rub your nose in it like a dog for you to be able to acknowledge your own mess! Now, get it tidied up before dinner!"

Gail's shock was palpable. Eventually, she swept up the bobby pins and found a container in which to keep them as she shuddered with dismay. She was a fool, rightly humiliated for not knowing to clean up after herself in such a small place. "I'm sorry! I should have known, and I just forgot or something." She should have taken a moment to do this little thing. Why had it skipped her mind?

With that small question, an answer crept to attention. *"You were unpacking and putting your kitchen together. You were making dinner. For your husband. You were fixing your hair and putting on makeup to please him when he came home. Then, you were distracted and went to set the table for dinner…"*

WHEN TIME IS HUNGRY IT GOES BACK *FOR SECONDS*

It helped Gail's desperate feeling of isolation to know she could call Coalbert, who had also just settled here with his cute new bride, and was already living just across town, if she needed him. She liked Ivy, so there was likely to be an instant camaraderie. With two siblings in Arizona, surely

Mama and Daddy would come for the holidays, perhaps in the rainy season, or by way of passing through on their way to visit Grandma and Grandpa Sanders. These were the thoughts in Gail's mind the next morning as she set about hanging clothing in the closets, putting linens away, and making up the bed.

When their neighbors came to introduce themselves, Al and Doris were a bright spot, inviting them to play cards together this weekend or next, or really any time.

That night, Rich and Gail tried again to have a romantic experience but were unable to succeed. Gail panicked to think that she and Rich may not be a good sexual fit for one another. The panic subsided into a general disquiet and disappointment after their third try at intimacy.

Punishing Gail for her unhappiness in his sexual performance, Rich told his bride a tale from Saudi Arabia, a tale which culminated in mutual hostility.

He turned on his elbow and ran his finger over her breasts as he revealed, "While I was at the base in Saudi Arabia, I was fixin' to take photographs in the marketplace when I was approached by two young girls who bid me to follow them through a narrow entrance. I went into a darkened room. It was scented with incense and spice. There was a cassock lying on the floor, a woven bed the Arabs use, surrounded by platters of spiced meats and fresh fruits."

Rich continued to arouse his wife. "After the girls fed me, they laid me down and undressed me and proceeded to give me an exquisite massage to please and excite me so that I couldn't help myself. I had sex with both of them and then went back to the base."

Gail leapt from bed and went to sit in the tiny bathroom, seething with grief and anger. Then tears began to roll down her cheeks. To consider that her husband was arousing her as he spoke of his betrayal made her want to jump into the shower. That he expected this kind of arousal from her in a culture so far flung, confused her. The fact that he was not a virgin and further, that he hadn't bothered to tell her this before the wedding, felt shameful.

Waves of rage washed over the building layers of regret for marrying Rich. The way he played with her in the telling of it!

His physical foreplay had readied her to try again, but now a sick feeling of remorse and hatred claimed her body. Gail stepped into the shower and steamed away her confusion, her disgust.

Gail wiped her tears and asked Rich to go sleep on the couch while in the same sentence informing him that she would be seeking counsel in the morning. She omitted saying what kind of counsel she would seek. She hardly knew herself.

Rich might have fought his wife on her request. Instead, in a fit of shame and excitement, he complied, all the while wondering how it was he could yearn to woo her and to punish her with equally conflicting tenderness and resentment.

The next day, Gail awoke to blazing Arizona heat already filling the house, a heat to which she was not yet accustomed.

Though she felt grossly defrauded by her husband, she was determined to rise above her ignorance of these physiological levels of marriage and be pragmatic about the thing. There was nothing she could do about the past, but there was certainly something she could do about her future.

With her husband gone to work, she decided to move out of the hollow space of her bedroom and drift toward the kettle and coffee in the kitchen. She rallied as she looked through a phone book. She would find a nurse to ask about the subject of sexual incompatibility.

At the doctor's office, Gail felt the heat rising in her awkward need to explain, but the nurse patted her hand and listened until she was sure she understood the problem. Then, she quietly and matter-of-factly helped Gail to comprehend that there was never going to be a physical incompatibility between men and women.

"From human biology and physiology," she said, "we know the genitalia is designed to fit naturally together no matter if the male is a little bigger or smaller in size. However," she explained, "a woman needs to relax and enjoy the process, so foreplay is normally practiced in the bedroom to arouse the woman. When she is enjoying the experience, she will naturally open up and experience a sensation of intense pleasure." The nurse said, "Foreplay is an exciting experience for both males and females, but sometimes a man needs to be taught to please his wife and not rush to please himself first."

Gail grasped that and immediately became indignant. Her feelings toward her husband and his demand to be serviced along with his verbal manipulation as if he were the only one in the encounter, left her breathless with fury.

The nurse explained many young men had never been taught by their fathers or doctors that pleasuring their wives would make both experiences more climactic, so Gail might need to help her husband however she felt she could.

Gail nodded.

Satisfied, the nurse pulled an illustration from her drawer to explain further that only foreplay was needed to help her accept the man's penis.

"Shall I call in the doctor now?"

"Um, no. I think you're right. I think I'll go home and try to work this out on my own. If I need more help, I'll make another appointment."

After Gail's appointment, she drove into the City of Phoenix to seek out whether there were any posts for retail work or office work. Gail's second goal, to find work, was highly influenced by her immediate disillusionment in marriage. Laila's unhappy marriage could happen to anyone, she guessed.

She knew that she wanted to meet her own financial needs in the event her marriage did not succeed.

The "Help Wanted" sign in an appliance store window felt hopeful. She was familiar with appliances from her first job at the Oakland Appliances store. Besides, what woman wouldn't be interested in the latest developments of household machines? She returned home with anticipation. She thanked God, thinking about how important this learning curve was to her. He must see her and care for her as she had been taught in all those years of church attendance.

When Rich casually asked her, over supper, if she would like him to help her learn to please him, she smiled. Yesterday, she would have taken his request as normal, but today, she invited him to learn to please her if he wanted her to love him.

"That's a hell of a thing! What do you mean?"

She simply served a slice of strawberry shortcake with a smile. Then, she quietly told him he needed to work a little harder for what he wants.

"My mom used to say that even an elephant in the room will stay unnoticed if you keep the lights off."

"What's that got to do with us?"

"Sexual intimacy concerns both of us, not just you, Rich. I am made differently than you are, so to be a successful husband, you need to practice being a better lover. I need to feel your love rising in me before I can physically accept it or return it. You know, silly me, I actually thought that maybe we were not physically suited for one another which is why I consulted with a doctor's office today."

"You did?"

"I was assured that there are no male or female parts in the whole wide world of human beings that wouldn't fit together. It is playing together and showing love that opens the physical gates to married love and there is a divine pleasure that sets humans apart from animals. So, you, my love, need to find the key to the gates of splendor. It's no one else's responsibility."

Education is the best offense, but it is also a fine defense.

He was surprised by her sudden candor and clever challenge. "Okay," he said. "Let's give it a try right now." That night, she had no problem becoming aroused. Rich and Gail spring boarded into a mutually pleasing sexual relationship.

Just after the phone line was installed and a phone number was assigned to their place, Gail made a phone call to her mom. It was the second week midweek into living in Arizona, with lots to tell about, but it proved to be a short chat. "Long distance phone calls add to a normal bill, my darling girl. It's sure to be the expensive surprises that men don't take kindly to. So," Beryl said, "phone calls shouldn't become a habit."

After that, Gail languidly relayed her news about the new job at the appliance store and finding their new home and meeting the neighbors. She'd earned this phone call.

Then, her mother conveyed some strange news. The Oakland pastor who had performed Rich and Gail's marriage counseling and ceremony had split with his wife and they had already filed for divorce. Rumors were running rampant. Gail listened to her mama's voice full of grief and confusion. She knew how her mother adored her pastor. How could this happen? The feeling of dread went much deeper in Gail's mind.

"Bertie Gail, there are bad things that happen in every marriage. Whenever you get two people from two backgrounds on the same wedding certificate, you're going to have to work things out. . .every day if need be. Lord knows, it's all about hearing the other one, and stepping into the headwinds."

That evening, while washing the car, Rich spoke to his neighbor Al, and took him up on his offer to play cards the next night. Gail invited Coalbert and Ivy over, but Coalbert said he was too tired to do things like that after working all day.

"Put Ivy on the phone, will you?" she asked.

When Ivy came on, the young brides compared notes on the family and the husbands, on Gail's new job and whether Ivy was going to go to work.

"Well, actually, no. See, I'm pregnant, and I'm having morning sickness an awful lot. I couldn't imagine holding down a job right now. Besides, Coalbert is doing well for us on his own."

"Oh, well, that's nice. I mean, well, congratulations to both of you, of course! That's exciting news!" Ivy sounded so tired! "If you need some help, please call me. I'll do what I can." Gail hung up the receiver. She felt strange. She sliced a head of lettuce for lunch seeing the wedge between herself and Coalbert's wife before covering it over with mayonnaise dressing.

The appliance store's bookkeeping position provided Gail with the gal pal she needed. Fran was a happy jokester and someone who loved to shop. She and Gail began to confide in each other and, arm in arm, slip out to go shopping and frequent movie theaters together when Rich didn't want to go, which was typical.

Having always longed for children and having made no particular effort to not get pregnant, Gail discovered in her second month in Phoenix that some things happen in due course. Cause and effect, she missed her period.

Though she had no morning sickness, she knew she was pregnant. Rich seemed happy to take this as a natural result of marriage, but it was Fran who helped her find a baby crib, clothing, bottles, and the stroller endorsed by the Good Housekeeping Seal of Approval. Being from the area, she had secrets to pull out of her sleeve, and Gail's genuine gratitude soon turned into a delightful momentum of preparation for the baby's arrival.

Her new doctor placed her due date in mid-March, exactly nine months after she and Rich figured out how to be intimate. The nurse gave her a knowing smile.

Rich pulled out his little notebook and jotted things down.

"What are you writing about?" Gail ventured.

"Well, baby, that's none of your business. It's just my way to keep the days straight."

Gail was impressed when Rich got permission from the landlord to turn a large bedroom window into a bookshelf and close up the exterior wall with matching brick so that they would have some room to store baby things. She watched him work in wonder. "Does my father or brother know that you know how to work with your hands?"

"Oh, I told them about a go-cart I built once when I was little."

"How little?"

"I think I was about eleven or twelve, just after we moved to San Diego. I put a motor in it and Luster and I drove it all over the place until we crashed it going down a hill."

"Was your father handy?"

"I don't rightly know, Gail. My father is the strong, silent type. I only know I have always had a talent for making things. It was something I enjoyed. I made end tables for my mom and I graduated from high school with honors in woodworking and tech, so I think it's just a gift I have."

"Good for us, then! Can you make a changing table?"

"Show me what it is and I'll try."

After Gail took Rich to the department store to show him what a changing table entailed, he bought some 2 x 3 studs, some wood sheathing, and some small screws. Then, he set about making a table for changing diapers.

While she was folding clothes in the same room, she mentioned, "Whatever happened to your promotion, Rich? Shouldn't we be celebrating by now?"

"I told you. They lost my papers and said they couldn't give it to me without the proper documentation."

Gail's fingers froze. She stopped folding. "How is that possible?" She was sure he had never explained anything of the sort to her.

"It doesn't matter. I only have another year. Then, we can get out of here, and I can get a real job back in California, maybe in electronics. I hear things are exploding in advanced technology in the U.S. I think I'm smart enough to find a place in the stream of things."

The young wife decided her husband had been practicing this answer to her in the quietness of his mind. She didn't believe a word of it, but what did it matter? She bit her lip. He was talented in many regards if not in leadership. Rich's charm affected so many people positively, it seemed her husband would be a natural leader. Was it due to Rich identifying as German on his applications after the war that caused prejudice against him or was it some other flaw? She went to the restroom to wash her face in cold water even as she flushed the dream for lifelong honor and privilege.

Perhaps, this was why Rich had mocked her when she pointed out a beautiful chandelier in a *Better Homes and Gardens* magazine. It sparkled in the interior grand entrance of marble floors and circular staircase. It looked the part of a fairytale, and like Cinderella, she pushed over the magazine under her husband's nose, laughing. "Do you think we'll ever be able to have one of these, Richard?"

He pushed it back with a broad grin saying, "The day you become my fairytale wife, you can have a fairytale light fixture and a winding staircase to go with it." He held her gaze with cruel, clear ice, a gaze from which she often shrank.

"Don't hang on the rope of animosity, Rich. It may break from the discord," she said.

Just after Thanksgiving, Gail walked into work, only to have her boss meet her at the door. Though he had always been nice enough, when he quietly walked her to the back office, an odd atmosphere surrounded him.

"Fran has already cleared out her personal items, young lady, and I want you to do the same. I assure you we have discovered what you've been up to. We won't press charges, but you are fired, young lady, and I wouldn't try to get another job in this town, if I were you."

Gail's hand found her desktop to steady herself in the shock of his abrupt words, being let go before the busy season of Christmas, of all things. Her boss' rudeness showed he was under the delusion that she and Fran had done something indecent together.

"What? What's wrong, sir?"

"You know exactly what's wrong, Gail, and I'm surprised that you have the gall, being pregnant with child, and with a husband in the U.S. Military!"

"I'm sure I have no idea what you are talking about, sir." She said this as she nervously gathered her few personal items, but when she looked at him, he merely held his hand toward the doorway and nodded.

When she told Rich what had happened, he stood at attention and simply informed her she would have to, "try to get another job. I appreciate your financial contribution to the household. Women are fighting hard for the right to equal pay, so let's see what you've got to offer, babe. Don't get discouraged now!"

Gail felt slapped across the face, though he never touched her. Her husband showed not a whit of concern with the implication that his wife had been accused of something, something disconcerting enough to be fired over, and he didn't show any feeling of sympathy for her predicament. Rather, a smile played around his lips. He seemed amused to know that she found herself in such a precarious situation.

During the two weeks following her loss of employment, Gail did apply to a few other department stores because, with all the window dressings announcing Christmas, she knew they would be looking for holiday help at the least. Yet, after filling out application after application, not a call rang, and no one hired her.

She telephoned Fran. "We're being black balled!"

"I know. It seems he's told the whole city something that he couldn't bother to say to either of us!"

Gail, though indignant, had to let it go.

Instead of working a job to save money, she decided to invite her mom and dad out for Christmas and invite Coalbert and Ivy over for a family meal. She bought new yellow curtains with white embroidered flairs on them and hung them throughout the house; she added matching throw pillows to the couch by cutting and hand stitching one of the panels of curtains into several squares. Then she decided to paint a wall.

She also busied herself clipping grocery coupons from the daily paper Rich left for her after he finished it. She bought a Christmas ham. She found new recipes for candied yams, pies, banana bread, and vegetable dishes. She bought a centerpiece for the tablecloth she'd been storing for such a celebration. She was already pleased with how the house would present itself, but the shame of being fired kept slapping her in the face.

Ivy might appreciate her decision to stay home, but how would she explain her change of circumstances to her parents after just telling them how much she loved her new job?

It was back to milk toast with cinnamon sugar in the mornings. Thankfully, Rich found a used black and white television set he could fix, so she was able to watch *I Love Lucy* on the couch with a cigarette in the afternoons. Lucy brought laughter into some of the common conundrums of life. Gail wondered at the woman who repeatedly mouthed a smart comeback and a brilliant idea to every little affliction a housewife could encounter. *I Love Lucy* was addictive.

Closer to Christmas, while perusing the daily paper, she noticed a local police announcement detailing the facts of an accountant caught embezzling money from several local businesses that year. One of the affected businesses was the appliance store she'd been fired from.

"There it is!" She shouted and waved the paper in a fist of victory. She first called Fran, who seemed relieved. Her second phone call was to the owner of the appliance store to tell him that he'd better stop his campaign to ruin her name and Fran's since the real culprit of the thieving had been discovered. Her old boss apologized and agreed, chuckling with a little embarrassment. Then, he offered her job back.

"Are you kidding, sir? No thank you." She hung up. It was time for a cigarette.

HOW *TEARABLE* A PAPER AIRPLANE THAT CANNOT FLY

Beryl and Dorjan stopped to visit Rich and Gail at their new digs that year on their annual trip to visit their families in Arkansas. Lugilla would ask how Gail and Rich were doing of course, and it was only natural to stop and deliver their Christmas presents, make a few observations, and share the meal that Bertie Gail had worked on so diligently before going to spend the remainder of the holiday with Lugilla. Daddy Sanders had passed away that year and Beryl didn't like being gone too long from her sweet mother, but Lugilla refused to move to California with them, so as was their habit, they left Dennis in charge of their home and spent the winter holidays with Beryl's mama.

Dorjan wasn't sure why his new son-in-law kept his little pad of paper in his left-hand pocket, with the retractable pencil, but he watched Rich take that little pad of paper out every so often and record items in it. "Never trust a man with graph paper. He's always plotting something," muttered Dorjan.

That day after his daughter's husband purchased gas for the car, Dorjan watched the record keeping ritual and decided to ask.

Rich explained that he could tell all kinds of things about his vehicle, well Gail's car as the case was, and even the state of the economy by simply keeping track of the cost of gas, the amount of gas put into his tank, and the mileage that tank of gas was able to motor through.

ELSIE & FINCH

Dorjan didn't know whether to admire the record keeper who'd been added to his family or just call the man odd for his dedication to recording small things.

Some people are record keepers. Lighthouse keepers, for instance. Weather keepers for the almanac. There are organizations with profound record keeping characteristics such as archivists for arts and history museums, research scientists, political biographers, and the recent Internal Revenue Service which could be up to no good, but what was Rich up to?

When her parents arrived, Gail seemed to be a nervous bride. Her smile was bright, and her baby bump was showing in her flowered shirtwaist dress with a flouncy skirt. "Just a minute, Momma and Daddy," she said, making an arc with her finger from the corner of a brown box on the floor toward the hallway. She intended to store the box under the couple's rollaway bed before they got situated in the room.

Dorjan walked to the hallway and asked what so many small papers there were worth storing. "Mostly gas receipts and grocery bills, some tax documents we'll sort out later in the year, Daddy. If I buy clothing, Rich wants me to save the receipts in here, too." She shrugged.

"That man is obsessed with the cost of gasoline. I'm not one to complain, but I've never seen anyone like 'em. Is he a government agent? You'd best watch your 'P's and Q's!'"

While Dorjan took a nap, Gail and Beryl partook in a Fanta orange soda in a tall glass with ice. As Gail confided her first months of marriage to her mother, she paused in thought. "Mom, did you ever pray about my marriage to Richard?"

Beryl shook her head. "Why, Rich seemed so ideal, honey. I just wanted my baby to be safely married, and he seemed right. I thought the Lord had provided, and I guess I really only prayed about you getting your heart around the idea—and of course, the wedding details. Did you, honey?"

"No, Mom. I don't believe I ever did. I hoped, I worried, and I wrestled plenty with myself, but it never entered my mind to ask the Savior whether I should marry Richard. I guess I thought Jesus was only interested in my eternal destination."

In January, Ivy had her little baby boy. Six weeks later it would be time for Gail to give birth to her first child.

Nearing Easter, Lugilla Sanders came into her house carrying her load of fresh blown and dried laundry. She always loved that smell. Her heart skipped a beat, and she set down the laundry basket, took a deep breath, and sat on her comfy plump couch. She felt a strange heady sensation of floating away, watching the things in her living room divulge themselves of meaning. In an instant, she was standing on streets of gold in the courts of the Lord. Birds were singing. Palm trees were swaying just like she imagined they did in California, and then she saw her Savior face-to-face.

Gail was called to her grandma's funeral in Arkansas, but she was closing in on nine months full of her child. She just couldn't.

Within the week, her sister Lou tried to commit suicide with an overdose of pills and was begging for Gail to come. Lou was living in San Francisco. It was warmer there. Gail couldn't refuse her baby sister's call. Though she could never get a straight answer out of Lou about what was ailing her, she did play the part of the nurturing elder sister, fetching food and water, washing Lou's clothing, and entertaining her with stories about her first two years of marriage to an Air Force serviceman.

"Did you ever fly in his plane, Gail?"

"Fly? Oh no. My husband is a draftsman, a measurements man, an engineer's interpreter, a plotter. Not a pilot."

THE MOTTO, "IF AT FIRST YOU DON'T SUCCEED, TRY, TRY AGAIN,'" INSULTS A FIRSTBORN

When she felt the labor pains, she called her husband. "Dagnabbit," he said. "I'm in the middle of a project on deadline! Is there any way you could call Ivy? Or drive yourself there? I'll be sure to pick you up in a week, baby. Call me if you need anything, okay?"

Baby Carlene was born right on schedule and came with a shock of yellow curls. Maternal love for her beautifully intricate treasure flowed into her nipples and into her heart and into her every thought. She longed to share this wonder with her husband and asked the nurse to call him and let him know about the successful delivery.

"Isn't he waiting in the stork room?"

"The stork room? No, I don't believe so. He had a deadline and had to work."

But Rich didn't show up that evening, or the next day or the day after that. By the fourth day, Gail's full heart began to shrink. Her postpartum hemorrhaging was better, but she was weak. She asked the nurse to put the baby's name as Carlene Ann on the birth certificate and to name Rich as the father. "Is he involved?" asked the nurse.

"What? Yes, of course, he's involved." *He's just emotionally unavailable,* she thought.

She telephoned her husband at work and left a message for the date and time he should make ready to pick her up. With a couple of days' notice, he should be able to clear his schedule.

Right on time, Rich stood waiting beside her convertible to welcome mom and baby in arms, a wide grin on his face.

The nurse helped guide her patient into the car and ignored the husband. Gail murmured and touched her precious bundle all the way home. When they arrived, she saw the crib, but wasn't yet ready to put her baby down.

Politely cooing at baby Carlene, Rich's pinched lips put kisses on her forehead. He allowed her to hold his finger. Then, his eyes filled with tears as a feeling of awe overtook him and he laughed with the mother of his child. Their miraculous new life sincerely surprised him.

"Well, tell me what you did for your week of vacation, baby." He said this as he sat on the couch and patted the space next to him.

Gail sat obediently. "I had a child, Rich. You wouldn't want to know about all of that. They do like to give a new mother and father some education for the arrival of a baby, though, things like bathing, holding, and safety precautions, and when to get vaccines, things like that."

His wide grin came and evaporated. "Okay, that's nice. I suppose you'll fill me in as needed?" Only he could feel the ebb and flow of the creek bed inside him, the cool clear water disrupting his muddy sludging soul.

"I suppose."

He began to realize that he was no match for his wife's technique of accommodation and avoidance.

"There are some handouts in the diaper bag if you would like to look at them. Oh, can you pass me my cigarettes, please?"

He got up and found the box. Tossing it over, he said, "Well, there are some jobs that have come down the pike, so while you've been away, I've been filling out applications and planning for our future. I also telephoned Brent to ask him to keep an eye out."

"Is that so?"

"He and his wife send their congratulations."

"That's nice. Coalbert and Ivy will be by sometime this week they said."

"Oh, you talked to them?"

She blew out a long, elegant cloud of smoke. "Of course. Mom and Dad called too, and I spoke with Norma Jean, and Fran, and Joan. In fact, I spoke with everyone this week except my own husband."

"They don't allow husbands in the delivery room."

"No, but the delivery was over within a matter of hours, and there's the stork room where men usually wait until the baby comes. Then again, I was in recovery bonding with our little one while we waited in the hospital for six more days, dear. It was so nice of you to show an interest."

Gail's sarcasm was not lost on Rich, who abruptly pushed himself off the couch. He said, "I've heard enough. I'm going to bed."

Gail changed Carlene's diaper and placed her in a blanket in the crib.

Around midnight when Carlene began to gurgle and whimper, Rich wheeled the crib out of their bedroom and into the living room and snuggled back under the blankets. When the cries grew louder and more incessant, Gail asked Rich to bring Carlene to her to nurse. When he didn't reply and didn't move, she stuck her legs out of bed and felt a rush of liquid leave her body. She was hemorrhaging.

"Oh, dear!" She groaned. "Rich, I need to get into the shower. I was hemorrhaging in the hospital, and they thought that I was better. Apparently, I'm not yet, so if you could call the emergency number on the brochure and explain to them what's happening and ask what's to be done, I'd appreciate it."

With the baby's fussing growing towards a tantrum, and his wife's blood all over their bed, Rich found the number and made the call.

"You are to maintain bedrest," he shouted into the bathroom. Grudgingly, he cleaned up the sheets, sprayed bleach and lay down towels for his wife. Then, he hugged his pillow to his ears. His hopes were murmured so loudly, "This can't be happening. I'm not going to live this way; I need my sleep!"— they felt like prayers.

When Gail returned to the room, she said, "I'm going to sit up in bed for a while. Can you get the baby from the crib and bring her back to me? Maybe I can calm or cuddle her." She carefully sat down with her back against the headboard and began to pile up the pillows.

"You are spoiling her. Babies should cry themselves to sleep."

"But she was sleeping and now she's awake. She needs me or she's hungry. Please bring her here."

"No. I'm exhausted, I've changed the sheets, and I'm the one who has to go to work in four hours."

So, Gail got up and brought Carlene into bed with her. In one fluid movement, Rich rolled out of bed and exited the room to sleep on the couch.

The months of crying and colic proved to be the worst part of being a new mother. It drove Gail to smoking more and eating less. Carlene Ann's little fists would curl up in angry balls, her face would redden, and her little legs would go stiff with tension.

Beryl telephoned to try to give hints and help that might work. "Gail, have you tried rubbing the baby's belly or holding her up to burp her?"

"Of course, Mom."

"Have you checked her for allergies?"

"I'm breastfeeding, Mama, what could she be allergic to?"

Pause.

"Well, I'm very tired, Mama, so I'm going to let you go now. Rich's fit to be tied. He says he's placing resumes around California, so here's hoping we'll be nearer to you by this time next year."

Rich took to sleeping on the couch like a cat since Gail insisted that Carlene's crib be nearby.

"You can let the baby cry herself out, you know," the cat snarled. "Doctors are saying that is the best thing to do, just let the baby cry herself to sleep."

"She's in distress, Rich. Somethin's wrong with her. I'm not going to leave her alone as long as I'm here to try to solve it. I can at least rub her belly or jostle her."

The next week, Rich brought home a spring-loaded basinet chair. "I found this at the center for recycled goods on base." The next day, he brought home a new rocking chair. "Now, we're talking," Gail said and gave him a kiss.

The next time Gail called her mom, Carlene was sleeping soundly, and as Beryl told her the news about Laila being hooked on drugs due-and-owing to being abandoned by Warren, and how she was afraid for the baby, Gail said hmm and hmm. "It's just terrible, Mom, really. But what can we do? I'm discovering that just because two people are married, that doesn't mean they see eye-to-eye on anything at all, and it doesn't mean you can make them behave either, so you just have to find a way to live with it."

"Bertie Gail? It sounds like you and Rich are having problems of your own."

"Well, nothin's perfect, that's for sure." But, she stopped short of telling her mom that Rich had not received his promotion which meant they were living on pennies, and with her having to stay with Carlene, she was off work, too.

"I'm going to bring this to the foot of the cross, and you'll see. Things will get better."

"Okay, Mama. I'm going to hang up now."

Beryl quickly packaged up the quilt that Lugilla and she had made for the baby's arrival. She'd been hand sewing the scraps, and Beryl was done with the late evenings she'd spent whipping and tying up the quilt backing to the front and then binding it for her daughter. It was time to finally pass the special heirloom along.

WINGING IT, BY PHOENIX RISING

One night, after fixing hors d'oeuvres for Canasta, Rich failed to appear at the card table.

A while later, Gail excused herself to look for Rich and Al said he'd look around outside. While Al looked in the garage and backyard, Gail found Rich in the bathroom taking a bath in the claw foot tub with baby Carlene.

Deciding to avoid the oddity, she closed the door behind her and said, "Please give Carlene to me. Did you forget that tonight is game night? Al and Doris are here waiting to play Canasta. Can you hurry and dress?"

Before he could answer, she carried Carlene out in a towel and closed the bathroom door behind her.

Gail not only felt embarrassed telling Al and Doris that her husband forgot their date, but she felt a little curdled when she considered why Rich would be taking a bath with their baby. Gail quickly rinsed and dried Carlene at the kitchen sink and put her into a clean onesie for bed. The rest of the game night "went off without a hitch" as Rich memorialized it in his pocket diary later, and to Gail as she pretended sleep.

Ivy and Coalbert agreed to a Saturday outing with Gail and Rich because neither couple had yet visited the sand dunes. The new families carried all their baby gear to the sand dunes along with blankets and a picnic lunch. They put out a blanket to eat on, and the two men walked off a ways to catch up.

Ivy offered the news that she and Coalbert were going to be moving back to Arkansas somewhere near the homestead so that Coalbert could start his own business with a chum back home.

Gail was going through the motions, politely congratulating Ivy, when she felt a bitter sting on her heel. Nobody realized that scorpions hide in the sand until Gail got stung. The party ended with a hasty trip to the emergency room. While they all waited for news on Gail, Rich placed a call to the newspaper.

Two days later, a man came to the door offering to buy Gail's convertible.

"I don't know what you're talking about. It isn't for sale," she said. When he showed her the advertisement on the folded newspaper, she told him he'd have to come back when Rich was home from work. "How dare you sell my car out from under me!" she shouted at the walls.

Then, she placed her own call to her husband, who said, "Look, we have to find cash from somewhere. It doesn't grow on trees, you know. I can buy a 1953 Opel. I've already checked the car over, and we can save the difference to move back to California."

"But, Rich, it is my car. I worked hard for that car. And you didn't bother to talk over your plan with me! Were you going to forge my name on the title? Sometimes it isn't where we land that's so awful, it's the way we get there that's killing us, don't you see?"

"If you can think of a better plan, I'll hear ya out, baby. We'll talk about it over dinner."

"Aren't you just one in a *melon*," she muttered. At dinner, Gail agreed to sell her car to save the difference for their move back to California, but she reminded Rich not to forget that these kinds of things are decisions to be made as a couple. Rich smiled to appease his wife and nodded agreeably.

FECKLESS, A CRAZY LITTLE THING COLD LOVE

Though Elsie had slip-slided her way to her mom's, neither one of them would be going shopping today. Gail's driveway was slick with sleet, and the rain had already turned to snow.

In the bottom drawer of her mother's tall boy, Elsie's fingers landed on a portrait of a young man. When she pulled it out, she recognized the Navy Cadet who must have been her mother's fiancé, Bill. She pulled out two more portraits of young men she didn't recognize, handing one over. "Who is this, Mom?"

Gail switched on her lighted magnifying lens studying the portrait. "Isn't he handsome? This is George. He wanted me to wait for him after he was drafted into the war, but I don't think he made it out. Elsie stared at the rugged, Italian face.

"Who's this one?" She handed another portrait over.

Gail bent over the face. Suddenly, she lurched backward. Her hand went to her forehead. "Oh! This is Lloyd Crocker, the love of my life! We were engaged at the end of high school. He was the nicest, sweetest boy, but I messed up."

"You? How did you mess it up?"

"Oh, he took me to a party at his friend's house and I started flirting with his friend for some reason, maybe to make him jealous; I don't remember. So, Lloyd took me home and asked for his ring back. He said he couldn't trust me. Oh, I was brokenhearted over him.

After I married Rich, Lloyd looked me up and we went for a walk. By then, he had a child and so did I. Oh, how I've regretted losing him. I hope he had a good life."

Elsie recognized her mother's feckless heart had never truly been rehabilitated. She could forget anyone if the next person in line seemed entertaining.

SAN LUIS OBISPO, 1960

A CAREFUL GUNNER CANNOT BE *DISARMED*

With the vehicle switch-a-roo done and pocketed, Rich began to make plans to move to San Luis Obispo for college. The Californian Polytechnical Institute was the place to be, but he couldn't find any available housing in newspaper listings or on the college housing board. He reasoned it was a land locked area so they couldn't expand like some suburbs do.

To hold them over, Dorjan offered construction work to Rich if they could make it to California. It was enough of a job to warrant the move, and something Rich knew he could handle.

"I thought you wanted draftsman work, Rich," Gail challenged. "Shouldn't you just wait for the right offer?"

"I'm as good in construction work as your father, Gail. I like that kind of thing, so if it gets us back to the vicinity of school, I'll take it, thank you kindly."

The couple did find an apartment in the land locked town after all. They were hired to be apartment managers with a living opportunity on the side. Gail agreed to do the cleaning and be the daily point person for the tenants. They could live in the small, white house attached to the apartment building. It was situated across the street from a large community church called Grace Tabernacle and on the other corner was a wide, welcoming park. She felt an element of safety and hope there.

They stayed for two years, Gail carrying baby Carlene around while she vacuumed the halls, interviewed potential tenants, and passed along management issues to the owner to resolve. Rich was available to fix maintenance issues.

When he was off work, Rich's head was hidden under the roof of the Opel when he wasn't washing and waxing it. He seemed to like it better than the convertible, and he laughed agreeably, saying it was because the Opel was a German made vehicle, and it was sure to last longer than the Ford.

As though the joy of being within driving distance of Mom and Dad ushered in a vision of the ideal home and family, Gail began to beg Rich for another baby. She prayed to God for a second little one and dedicated the baby to God's use if He would grant her heart's desire.

She decided to quit smoking. It was difficult. No one warned her that breaking a habit could be so hard, but she was determined to have a healthy baby and she understood, now, that her smoking might have been the cause of Carlene's colic. Even her occasional drinks were set aside for the goal of getting into physical and spiritual shape to rear a second baby. "I want to go to church again, Rich. There's no reason we didn't go in Phoenix, so let's find one we both agree to."

"There's one right across the street. I'll go there if you want to," he said.

Jack LaLane's television show invited her to get in shape with his daily half hour of exercises. Gail took the challenge.

When she offered to take on babysitting and help financially again, Rich agreed to help her make Baby Number Two. He told her he couldn't afford additional children though.

"You won't always be a student, Rich," Gail argued.

"But technology and computers are a risky way to make a living, baby. Nobody knows yet where it will go, and I don't know yet where I'll fit in. So, let's plan on two children."

Once again, Gail had the distinct impression that her husband was drawing a line, making an ultimatum without consulting her. Rich seemed to have forgotten her dreams and desires — the goals they'd shared together early in their courtship.

When Rich was hired by Lawrence Radiation Labs as a draftsman, he seemed pleased. He began working figures and timeframes and putting down plans for after graduation, but when Gail asked to see his plans, she realized he'd forgotten to figure in raises, whether cost of living raises or merit raises. Gail awakened to her husband's faulty architecture of their lives by omissions in logic and building his case without her input.

He seemed to have forgotten that progress comes with raises and that the whole world was calling for technological advances. It wasn't a risky business. It was progress, and why shouldn't they enjoy the landslide of good things to come with his work?

Elsie was conceived in the marriage bed, but for Gail, it was a long nine months of heat, apartment management, and babysitting other mother's babies before her little promise arrived.

No signs of Elsie's desire to enter the world were felt. Gail felt her belly might burst. When the ten-month mark on the calendar arrived, Gail's water broke. She called Rich and asked him to take her to the hospital. "It's coming!"

"I thought one of your friends was taking you, baby." Rich played coy.

"Fine. I'll find someone." With the hurtful exchange between them, Gail hired a taxi to take her to the hospital.

Elsie was born smack dab in the middle of April, in 1960, a month after Laila's daughter, Janey, entered the world. Six months later, the Internal Revenue Service changed the Income Tax Act setting April 15th as the due date for reporting individual income taxes. Since Easter was also often celebrated on her birthday throughout life, so began her habitual identification with the day of dread for what she owed or the day of salvation.

Gail felt an exuberant gratitude for an entire three weeks until the two front teeth in Elsie's mouth bit her left breast while nursing, clamping down on her nipple breaking the skin.

Elsie's two teeth became the tools of torture for Gail. Her breast became infected, and she had to cushion it with a pillow. Gail had never felt such pain. When the doctor lanced the infected breast, an entire cup of pus oozed out.

It was a little different trying to tote two babies around while vacuuming and cleaning out vacant apartments. Gail found a portable record player and some children's records, *Sing Along with Marcy*, to entertain Carlene in the playpen on the front porch, while she carried Elsie on her hip.

Rich and Gail invited other newly married couples to picnic on their grassy front lawn, occasionally, and Gail was able to make friends in the park while she walked Carlene's stroller and toted Elsie on her side.

Rich decided they should move to Castro Valley, near Cal Poly (California Polytechnical College) for the technical course work offered there. Completing it would put Rich into the job flow he wanted. As long as they could continue to attend Grace Tabernacle, Gail agreed the move was a smart choice. They could invest in a trailer, save money and have an asset to sell in a couple of years.

The couple purchased a single-wide, two-bedroom, one bath trailer, and Gail put the word on the grapevine about her availability to babysit. She tacked slips of paper into a cork bulletin board in the office of the trailer court. She also called their new church, Grace Tabernacle, to see if there were other mothers who needed a babysitter.

There was a pop out window in the hallway between the two bedrooms just large enough for the baby's crib, so the second bedroom could be used for guests, babysitting gear, and Rich's draftsman desk.

A couple their age also attending Grace Tabernacle was eager to accept the babysitting help. They'd become friends through the young marrieds' class already, and Nollie and Adrianna Tabor had a daughter almost exactly Carlene's age. Their daughter was named Coleen.

"Oh, dear!" Gail cried. "How will we keep the girl's names straight?"

Adrianna laughed, then confided, "We're trying to have another baby now."

Nollie's boisterous good nature won over Rich's reticence to friendships, "Hey kid, looks like we're both new to the area, and we're both trying to graduate from Cal Poly," Nollie observed. "Our wives seem to get along, so let's find something more to do than church and babysitting, shall we?" And though he seemed a bit of a playboy for being a church fellow, he loved cleaning and fixing boats. Rich latched onto him as much as Gail latched on to Adrianna's friendship.

After school some nights, Adrianna and Nollie began inviting Rich and Gail to the marina where they could eat seafood. Then, after church on Sundays, they'd go to the bay and race along in Nollie's speedboat, sharing boating stories and the mechanics of the vessel. They would then have snacks during sunset in the shallow channels where they would point out landmarks and tell each other stories of their youth.

With plenty to talk about among the topics of church, college, and the babies, the foursome decided to enroll in a new Christian Bible study together.

A woman in their trailer court also answered one of Gail's babysitting ads. LaShandra Hess had two children. She happened to work with Rich at Lawrence Radiation Lab in Castro Valley. The couples arranged that LaShandra could bring her children to the trailer for babysitting. She would then drive Rich to work.

Gail was so tired that keeping track of Rich's college hours and work hours was near impossible.

When he wasn't around, and the babies had been picked up, she often visited one of her sisters or her high school buddies, Norma Jean and Joan. Sometimes, she studied her Bible and meditated on the verses she memorized. One verse that seemed to anchor her soul was Philippians 1:6: "Being confident of this very thing, that he which hath begun a good work in you will perform *it* until the day of Christ Jesus." She didn't understand everything about it, but it spoke to her about confidence in Jesus Christ. The King James words made her slow down. They were like puzzle pieces presenting themselves to be studied and correctly fitted together.

One overcast afternoon, LaShandra's husband came to pick up the children. Then, he began coming more often saying that he and LaShandra's work schedules had flipped. He was sitting at the table waiting for Gail to ready his children, when he told her with a shaky voice that he knew LaShandra was messing around on him. Gail stopped packing the diaper bag. The man's distress had legs.

"Are you sure?"

He said, "Yes, I'm sure. I've even laid under the trailer skirting and listened to them, but by the time I could get out from under the trailer to confront the guy, he was already gone. I couldn't catch them."

Gail imagined the man lying under the trailer in the dirt and pebbles listening to his wife's unfaithfulness.

Her second thought was whether Rich was the one messing around with LaShandra, but beside her husband's irritability at her every comment, he seemed to still want sex with her. She suppressed the thought. Nonetheless, the two were still carpooling. It would be safer to find a real home that wasn't a cramped single-wide trailer with this volcanic heat broiling the life out of her by the time Rich arrived home every day.

On Wednesday evenings, Rich, Gail, Nollie, and Adrianna met with Jerry Deyong, an able Bible teacher who seemed fond of questions. Taking on the challenge of having four eager young Christians in his study, he explained a lot of Bible history and things about God that both couples wanted to know.

The couples became very close that year, so close that they decided to make each other the godparents of each other's children.

NEVER FIGHT WITH A WELL-ARMED OCTOPUS

Though babysitting was difficult, Gail began to believe in God in a much more personal way. With the Pentecostal church, she'd felt like a second-class citizen. It put her off religion. She'd hung in there only because of her mother's faith, but her beliefs hadn't become active or real until Gail prayed for another baby, and God changed her husband's heart and gave her another healthy pregnancy.

More than that, with the Deyongs and the Tabors, she could ask questions and pray in a community that supported her eagerness to learn and experience the Lord's friendship.

They chose verses to memorize together each week, and they laughed when they stumbled through them together.

Gail also prayed privately that her rage at Rich's snippy, condescending manner of speaking to her would stop. She was going to try to win him over with gentleness, keeping her differing opinions to herself. Of course, this route garroted any real conversations between them.

Her rage did quiet down, but with it, she stopped caring very much about Rich. He participated in most everything during those days, regular church and Bible studies, but nothing changed his behaviors. He still worked late hours and ignored her or talked down to her at home. She just didn't love him like she imagined love would feel. Her heart was pricked when she worried about her marriage. Maybe she wasn't doing enough on her side to woo him over.

With a goal of paying off the single-wide chomping at their heels, Gail agreed to babysit Adrianna's newborn, Melanna, and Laila's daughter Janey. Gail had her hands full when she agreed to babysit two other babies, plus the Tabor's toddler, Coleen, in her single-wide trailer.

One day, when two-year-old Carlene pooped, she removed her own diaper in private and set about using the poop to paint the walls of the hallway where Elsie's crib was situated. Gail assumed she'd been given a gift of quietness and rest that day until Rich appeared after work. Hurrying to the bathroom, he stopped short to find the artwork in brown tones fingerpainted all along the hallway. Of course, Gail was lectured for not paying enough attention to their daughter. During the argument, it came out that Carlene had become an obstinate toddler stubbornly at odds with Gail's smallest instruction. Of course, it was due to being in the terrible twos, she supposed. But Rich replied, "Now, you are going to blame your lack of management on a two-year-old?"

Washing diapers in the toilet made Gail's right thumb painfully useless. A doctor prescribed antibiotic for a staph infection. Gail's thumbnail, however, remained thick and ridged, a small deformity. Mourning her thumb was just the latest on her list of grievances, though. She no longer enjoyed her seventeen-inch waist, far from it. Two babies, a host of others to watch, added baby fat, stretch marks, and a lack of parties or dancing made her grouchy.

The second bedroom in the trailer was full of other mother's children's toys and playpens, diaper bags and blankets. The only fun the couple found together was when they joined Nollie and Adrianna on the boat or sat with them at church and chatted afterwards.

Laila kept putting off her childcare payments. Gail felt an animosity growing toward her sister, especially since Laila asked her to take in both Dale and Leona in addition to baby Janey. Was this a wise course of action to invite all three of Laila's children to the trailer when Laila couldn't seem to hold down a job?

Laila's older girl, Leona, proved to be a natural with children, and her youthful, nurturing spirit embraced even Gail's fragile spirit.

Sometimes, Mama Beryl would sweeten the pot by bringing over discarded baby food jars and cans of fruit and veggies from the Del Monte Cannery. Occasionally, she even paid Laila's bill and apologized to Gail on Laila's behalf.

The problem became obvious; either the fathers were deadbeats, or their mother was, and who could win, babysitting for parents like that?

Laila telephoned one evening with a hoarse throat to say she was very sick and wondered if Gail could babysit Janey for a couple of days straight, nights included? Gail agreed in irritation. Later, when she called her mom to catch up, Beryl's own irritation revealed itself. "Bertie Gail, please pray for your sister Laila."

"Why Mama?"

"Because she's got another drinking boyfriend and they left the children alone while they went carousing and gambling in Las Vegas. It's Valentine's weekend, you know."

It dawned on Gail, that this was Valentine's weekend, and she and Rich had no particular plans, not even a card, but here she sat in the stupid trailer babysitting Laila's baby.

"Mama, she brought baby Janey to me before she left. I have her. She's safe." It was hard to pray for a sister who didn't seem to care about her own children's welfare or using her sister.

"Bertie Gail. You cannot control what other people do. You can only bring your troubles to the Lord and let Him bring you comfort," Beryl said.

"I'm upset, Mama, because I feel used by Laila, by Rich, and by all the mothers who are supposed to be my friends but are using me to advance their own lives."

"Why don't you get a piece of paper and write down your blessings, Gail, because you'll see that there are markers of improvement in areas that you've prayed about. Counting your blessings will soften your heart."

Gail took her mother's words to heart. She sat down and wrote out the changes when she prayed and how she was able to stop smoking for her pregnancy with Elsie. Because she'd stopped, there had been no croupy second baby to tend to afterwards. Her husband had a good job and had managed to stay employed—unlike Laila and her boyfriends. Gail recognized that by babysitting, she was helping all the children in her care stay safe. Doing so was helping her make the double payments on the trailer home to realize the payoff very soon.

AS SECONDBORN, I PREFER THE ARGUMENT THAT GOD TESTED HIS THEORY ON ADAM AND PERFECTED IT IN EVE.

Rich came home from work one fine day just before Easter to inform Gail that he had applied and been accepted to a better job drafting systems for a power company formally known as Pacific Gas and Electric Company. They would be able to pay off their trailer almost immediately. To celebrate, he took Gail out to a glass-enclosed restaurant situated on the bay.

Then, he suggested, "I think I'd like to sell the single-wide soon. We could live a half hour away from Morro Bay, from this restaurant, in San Luis Obispo, and live a little more freely." The romance of Rich's hope was infectious and brought Gail waves of optimism.

She could imagine the family sitting at a table under the blue swordfish, getting fresh caught fish and chips, and with that image, she felt a promise of happiness.

On her first free morning, when Gail found herself alone with the car, she decided to take a drive to explore her housing possibilities. She noticed small family homes for sale, and when she found one on Madonna Road near a bluff where the landmark of Ramada Inn was situated, she scrawled the address 1230 in Rich's gas log booklet clipped to the windshield visor and brought home the details. There, she placed a call to a realtor to discover what it would cost to move. It had three bedrooms, two baths, and a nice backyard.

When Rich came home that evening, she had worked the numbers to show how they could sell the trailer for top dollar and presented how much it would cost to own a house with a garage and three bedrooms. "We could be the new owners of half past lunch Madonna Road, dear!"

"What's that?"

"You know, 1230 Madonna Road. Half-past-lunch!"

She was braced for a lecture, but Richard surprised her with a chuckle and his interest in going to look. His wife's happiness and hope tickled him; he congratulated her genuinely admiring her work.

All seemed right with the world when Richard was able to buy a home. He didn't know he needed this landmark of stability and achievement, but it served them well.

The two put their quick plan into action.

THE STAIRS ARE ALWAYS *UP TO SOMETHING*

Shortly after the move, Gail discovered that she was pregnant with a third child. While she was overjoyed by the unplanned pregnancy, Rich threw one of his childish tantrums accusing her of tricking him. He reminded her, "I'm still going to college, and in fact, I have two more years left. Did you forget that? What were you thinking? We've just bought a house. Are you trying to work me to death, just when we are finally making ends meet?"

His lecture and accusations went on and on, never asking for a conversation or a response, never admitting that there are always two people involved in a pregnancy.

Then, Rich discovered the power of silent treatment. He moved into the new spare bedroom for sleeping and stayed away from home as much as he possibly could. When he was home, he stayed outside while Carlene rode around the driveway on her trike. Standing outside the front entrance, he began to dream, and then he took out his little pocket journal and began to draw a design.

"What are you doing out here?" Gail called through the kitchen window.

"Designing a little waterfall for the entry." He grinned and pointed to where it would go.

Surprised, and being given a logical reason to forgive her husband's prolonged, silent isolation, she did so. A waterfall for the entryway would be seen from the kitchen window and would welcome their guests in a lovely fashion.

While she readied the nursery, painted, and gathered baby goods, Rich found lava rock, cement, plumbing supplies, and proceeded to build the rock wall and pool for the waterfall. Other than that, the two rarely spoke or planned what was to happen in the future in their new home together.

The family's new kitchen was a simple California bungalow kitchenette, a first family home with an eat-in kitchen space. The couple bought a new oblong melamine table to fill it. The table had a harvest sprig of wheat emblem embossed on four corners and a metal belt to celebrate the modern look of aluminum; it seemed to the harried parents that the table including six two-tone plastic chairs, was completely child proof.

When Elsie gagged on her peas and refused to eat them, she sat by herself at Daddy's order for an hour in the darkening room, and finally managed to swallow them without throwing up. The children ate oatmeal or Cream of Wheat for breakfast. They waited there for dinner every evening as silent arcs of electricity sprung between Rich and Gail. They witnessed Rich take a thin, cotton kitchen towel from the oven's handle, roll it up and snap Gail on her bottom and arm. Mommy screamed at Daddy and tried to slap his face. He stomped out of the house.

"I'm sorry girls. It's the hormones. I'm pregnant, see?" She didn't mention that she didn't like her husband snapping a stinging towel at her while she was cooking.

The couple carried on with their church going and the Bible studies, often held in their home, and one day Rich found and unpacked a box in the spare room that held a coffee tray displaying a brilliant blue butterfly collection under glass. It was one of his treasures from his happier days in Saudi Arabia. He decided to set it on the coffee table in the living room before the members of the Bible study arrived. Without a word between them, the tray became the geography for a cold war.

For weeks, Gail kept wrapping it in newspaper and hiding it away. Rich kept trying to unwrap and display the tray made of teak and glass with brilliant blue butterfly wings, pulling it out just before guests arrived, and Gail made it disappear. She hated the creepy thing for reasons that seemed subconscious and unmentionable.

Perhaps it reminded her of the two women with whom her husband had sex before marrying her. Inside her, there lay unbidden an inquisition about this experience.

The tray seemed to be a souvenir of her husband's Saudi Arabian treachery while engaged to her. She hid it, hoping to squelch an unseemly conversation with visitors that Rich might have been scheming, but the children spotted it and Elsie carried it in awe to the sliding glass doors, to the sun.

"Mommy, Mommy! See? Boo-wings! Boo-wings!"

Carlene grabbed the tray away from her sister's clumsy paws and examined it herself. "Ooo, beautiful!" She carefully placed it on the coffee table, expressing her wonder. Why wouldn't their mother like something so glorious as the blue butterfly wings?

Rich won. He grinned at Gail and put it back on the coffee table.

After church one day, Nollie asked Rich and Gail to come to lunch and then boating with him. He said, "Adrianna isn't feeling well, so I'd appreciate the company." Although Gail wasn't interested, the day being too breezy, she felt trapped in the car by the momentum of two men.

When they arrived at the lake, playful breezes had become winds whipping up the water. "Surely you two see those waves. You can't want to go boating on that. Let's continue this outing another day." This was the limit of Gail's assertiveness when Nollie replied, "Hey gal, any kind of weekend weather is fine boating weather for me, even the not-so perfect weather."

Rich shrugged. "It isn't like we're water-skiers."

He and Nollie prepared the boat, but Gail waited on the dock. She shook her head and said she'd just wait for the boys on the pier.

"I'm pregnant. I just don't want to go this time. Go ahead. Believe me, I'll be fine here." She began to sit down, but Rich caught her up by her waist. "You're coming. That's final. I'm not leaving you here alone."

The air grew tense between the male counterparts and herself, rising with the intensity of the waves. They looked at each other and adamantly refused to leave her behind.

"Look, you won't get sick on the boat." Nollie promised in the same cadence as Rich grinned at his wife and held out his hand to usher her onto the boat. "How many times have we done this, darling?"

Finally, she took his hand and climbed into the speed boat with Nollie at the wheel and Rich hovering next to him.

As soon as they pulled away from the marina, Nollie shouted into the wind. "Hold on, children!" The conspirators at the wheel never looked behind them at their passenger while Gail cowered in the rear holding her belly, getting a full beating of the waves.

Bounced around with no mercy, Gail held her belly and pleaded to turn back or to drive slower but the men ignored her pleas. After an hour that felt like an eternity, the men decided to stop gallivanting through the choppy waves and slowly puttered back to shore.

The next day, Gail, in excruciating pain, called Rich at work. He did not answer. He did not return messages. Gail screamed and cried most of Monday as she sat on the toilet and had a miscarriage there. Running in sweat and blood, she wrapped the baby boy in a towel, called a neighbor to babysit, took a shower, and drove herself and her dead child to her doctor who helped her cope with the finality and with the pangs of afterbirth.

Bereaved, she made it home, thanked the neighbor and headed to bed to sob herself to sleep.

Rich's arrival from work was followed by a rattlesnake response to the two children wandering the house without supervision. Finding Gail in bed, he berated his wife for her selfishness.

Gail announced the miscarriage to Rich. "I hope you're happy."

He shrugged and said, "I'm sorry about that. Comm ci comme sa. You win some, you lose a bunch. I guess I'll go fix spaghetti for the girls."

She turned over to look him in the eye. "It was a beautiful, perfectly formed little boy," she said with a tear-streaked face. Rich looked a little stunned at the news.

He heard his wife's voice dull compared to the coursing blood in his ears. "Yes, he looked like you. His curls, his lashes..." Maybe he would have wanted a son, but the wheels of his mind kept turning. *"There's always another night, another baby to be had when he's out of college, another son to be born when we're more financially stable."* "If you wouldn't have tricked me..."

"Into this pregnancy," she finished his thought. "And so, you think you have tricked me back."

He had no regrets about his boating plan with Nollie. It had all gone off without a hitch. It was calculated, precise, and carefully designed—straight from the mind of a draftsman.

Gail, morose and listless, grieved for her baby boy. She couldn't talk with Adrianna about their husband's suspicious boating escapade. Adrianna would reject the implication of any conspiracy, even though she admitted to knowing her husband's behavior was often blind and uncaring toward her in many regards, but she would not agree to her husband being a part of this. "Boys will be boys," she often said.

Gail imagined how the conversation would go: *"He would never! We have a third child on the way, ourselves! If you think I'd accuse him of such a thing, you have an overactive imagination! Nollie's finally making a decent living for us, what would I gain by asking him about your outing on Sunday?"*

Since Adrianna had already decided to ignore Nollie's infidelities in exchange for the financial security he afforded, Gail understood that there would be no ear for justice or mercy from her friend, Adrianna.

When she considered talking with her old friends in the light of day, Gail guessed that her mind must be overactive; no man would intentionally kill his own baby; no friend would willingly aid and abet in such an evil scheme. Gail decided she needed to get out of the house and visit her mother.

But, when she went with her two children to visit Beryl about the miscarriage, it was like her mother's mind couldn't absorb such a malicious act. Not from Rich, the handsome hero who had saved her daughter from becoming an old maid. It had to be a coincidence. Not from the handy, talented son-in-law who was the church goer and good provider. She hushed Gail's accusations, and hugged her close, telling her that God would provide another child when the time was right and that she should never say such things to anyone ever again if she hoped to reconcile with her husband. There would be no justice.

SMALL MATTERS

Gail didn't know which was worse: separating from the monster she now believed her husband to be, dirt being slung everywhere in so doing, or living with him for her children's sake. How she regretted her lack of a college degree! Despite the wisdom of her elders, Gail felt at a loss in dealing with betrayal or envisioning her family's future.

Her mom had shared a stack of family photographs, telling tales of the difficulties each one faced in a verbal history, things no one talks about openly nor usually records. Notes were penned on the backs of the images in Beryl's unmistakable eighth grade, phonetically spelled scrawls. Trying to decipher these notes spawned an unfamiliar gnawing. Though she could put sentences together much better than her mother, she would fare no better in this modern age having to raise children without a husband. She'd have to grit her teeth, somehow, and stick it out with Richard.

She left her parents for home on Sunday afternoon, almost as distraught as she had been driving there on Friday afternoon.

The sun was low in the winter sky. It was an exceptionally beautiful coastline with an evening mist of pastel peach lingering over the beach, and the pale sky with silver lined clouds hanging above her.

She had to move on with her life now because a miscarriage isn't a real baby, after all. There was no birth certificate. They hadn't picked out a name. She hadn't had a baby shower, so there were very few people to tell how it had ended. It wasn't something one talked about. Miscarriages happen. The horrible thing she suspected was just too terrible to frame.

It couldn't be true.

Suddenly, a big, black bird hit her windshield on the upper right corner and slid off, waking the dozing driver from an end that had claimed her first love. She gasped to see the approaching bridge and began to tremble.

Gail pulled away from the road onto the scenic overlook and turned off the ignition. She turned, looking back at her two sleeping children in the car. They could have died! *Oh, God! Thank You for sending that bird to wake me up! I have two precious girls to look after. I can't sacrifice their futures because of what my husband has sacrificed.*

She had another friend at church named Iris. Gail telephoned Iris and asked her to come over for coffee after the children were tucked in for their naps. Iris came. Iris listened. She commiserated with her friend about her grief and suspicions. Then, she prayed for comfort and safety for Gail and the children.

As Gail opened the door to the lovely sound of the waterfall playing into the front entry pool, Iris turned back to make another offer. "Look, Gail, you have office skills from your earlier jobs. There is no need to keep babysitting when you can find a job that pays better. Why don't I watch the children so that you can get a job you like, a job to get you out of the house, and maybe you can save some money aside for a rainy day."

Gail was speechless. It was such a kind and graceful way to say so much more than "I'm sorry." It was a true friend's offer to make good of a dead-end situation.

Pretty and practical, Gail's new job with an insurance salesman paid her well. Now, with Iris Castile as her babysitter, Gail could entrust her children to her friend, and earn her own living while saving for the next rainy day. From her fear of Richard, there grew a quiet defiance. She held back the full amount she was making at work from Rich and put her skimmed and earmarked dollars into a private bank account.

Iris had a son named Jeffery, Elsie's age. At three years old, Jeffery and Elsie learned how to play cowboys and Indians on the front driveway with little plastic figures. They colored together in the front living room and watched television when Iris allowed it. Gail had told Iris that Rich had banned television in their home, saying it was the devil's playtime, but she also trusted Iris' discretion.

The children ate sandwiches together for lunch. They snuck to the side of the house, eventually, to show each other why one is called a boy and the other called a girl. Carlene found them and tattled. When Mr. Castile got home from work, he spanked his son and took Carlene and Elsie home to Gail. Turning red, he apologized, saying he might as well confess before Carlene told her version of the story. Gail laughed to relieve Mr. Castile of any feeling of embarrassment or guilt.

In a fine mood one Saturday, Rich took the family of four to the glass-enclosed Swordfish Café on the wharf. A painted swordfish on the opposite wall kept Elsie commenting and asking about the size, color, and the fact that she'd never seen a fish with a sword for a nose. It was a happy experience. When they got up to leave, Rich left a tip on the table and three-year-old Elsie thought he'd accidentally left it, so she brought it back to him.

It was time to sell the 1953 Opel. After all, it was now 1963 and Rich was struggling to find parts for what ailed it. He put their car in the newspaper for sale. When a couple of men came knocking at the door, Carlene reached up and opened the door. The adults were in the backyard. One of the men introduced himself as being interested in the Opel for sale. Carlene offered in her most business-like tone the list of all the reasons her daddy wanted to sell the car. "Oh, yes. The tires needed replaced, and my daddy keeps workin' and workin' on it, but he can't get any more parts for it."

"Oh? Why's that honey?"

"Because that car is an old model and they aren't making it anymore, so they can't get parts for it. He gets really mad."

Just as Gail noticed what was happening, she called for Rich to attend to the buyers, but the two men began laughing and waved goodbye to little Carlene. "We think we'd better go look at a different car now. Thank you, little darling!"

When Gail became pregnant again, she was gainfully employed by the local insurance brokerage with a kindly man as her boss who understood the difficulties of a young mother with children. He entrusted her with the secretarial letters to clients as well as the bookkeeping, but he would allow her to leave the office when one of the children was sick or needed to be taken to the doctor.

Though she didn't lead her husband on, he still occasionally wanted his sexual rights with his wife. When she hid her next pregnancy for as long as possible, going about her routines, Rich eventually noticed that his wife had grown new girth and had again conceived. His anger was erratic and wild. "I told you I don't want any more children!"

"You know where babies come from, right?" She leveled a glare.

RUSSELL, THE NAME OF THE MAN IN PAPER TROUSERS

On a fine July day of gently blowing coastal breezes, Melanie was born.

Her father used a fine-pointed paintbrush to put the finishing touches on a painting of a sailboat paint-by-number on an easel. He and his painting were pleasantly shaded inside his garage beside his new motorcycle and the new 1965 Oldsmobile. He refused to drive his wife to the hospital. Otherwise, baby Melanie was warmly welcomed by the nursing staff, and of course, Melanie's mother and grandmother. Soon her sisters, Carlene and Elsie, would fawn over their little baby sister.

Gail, having driven herself to the hospital again, snuggled with her new little babe, and signed the birth certificate naming her newest daughter Melanie. Rich was nowhere to be seen, even though her stay was merely two days this time. When she drove herself home, he didn't come to greet her. She entered the house with her child in her arms and said, "Again, you couldn't be bothered to visit your wife or your newborn in the hospital. What a fine man you are."

He said, "I told you I don't want more kids. I haven't changed my mind."

Maybe Carlene sensed the tension between her parents. Maybe it was due to their absence and being cared for by a babysitter. It wasn't clear why she packed her little doll's suitcase and ran away from home just before she turned seven. She walked out the door, to the sidewalk, around the corner, and crossed a major highway when the "walk" sign lit up.

The little darling was smart enough, however, to think through her prospects. While the adults followed her in cars and on foot, she returned home, resigned. Rich and Gail were searching their friend's homes for their daughter as Gail told the story that just last week Carlene had decided to stand with her nose in the corner rather than apologize for biting the girl next door. Even when she lost her bladder, she preferred standing in the corner than to offer an apology. Returning home, Rich and Gail found their daughter sitting on her bed. "Why did you run away?" they questioned.

As in a premonition made by her six-year-old self, Carlene said, "I was going to run away, but I decided to run away when I get older and have more money."

Gail found a new and better job as a girl Friday for the concrete/masonry company. Her boss wanted her to type and make business deposits and keep his books. Her work included talking with prospective clients and conferring issues they had with the design, the product, or the results and payments owed to the boss. Sometimes her boss paid her just to shoot the breeze with him. It wasn't flirting, the man just needed a listening ear.

IF YOU LOVE CHRISTMAS THIS MUCH, JUST *MERRY* IT

After Thanksgiving, Rich and Gail went to the department store, Macy's, to buy the newest display of the 1966 Christmas season: a popular silver Christmas tree, a Chatty Cathy doll for Carlene, and many little gifts for their other children.

When they brought home the tree, Rich set about pulling three delightful tinsel tree pieces from the box. He dressed it in blue lights with Gail helping to wind them around the tree. She had put on a Christmas record and Carlene and Elsie were invited to hang ornaments after the blue string lights were plugged in twinkling with wonderful effect on the souls of the family. It was the most beautiful thing the children had ever seen. Gail complimented Rich on the decorations. The twinkly lights and delighted children softened her spirit. Rich popped popcorn and sat to absorb his very own idyllic family scene, hugging his wife close. Later, when the children were carried to their beds, as individuals romantically inclined, they celebrated.

Grandpa and Grandma Hudson spent Christmas morning with Rich and Gail's little family. They cuddled, play wrestled, presented their own presents and Dorjan told stories trying to convince the children that Santa Claus had delivered the roller skates, coloring books, dolls, nighties and underpants. Next, a fancy turkey dinner with the horribly sweet potatoes Mommy cooked were offered on wedding china to all the guests.

The record player dropped Christmas albums one after another allowing Nat King Cole, Frank Sinatra, Bing Crosby, Ella Fitzgerald and Johnny Mathis to fill the holiday house with pop Christmas love and Santa Claus tunes. The day was layered with idyllic moods, tastes, twinkling colors and unremarkable conversations to make the hours unforgettable.

That Christmas, the nearly five-year-old Elsie was given a particular gift. It was from her mother. As soon as she saw it, she needed to have it explained to her. Elsie had sucked her thumb from babyhood through her grown up train adventure with Mrs. Paul, and beyond. Cousin Janey sucked her two middle fingers, so Elsie felt justified. But then, Mommy praised her cousin Janey for putting the sucking of her middle fingers behind her and growing out of her babyish addiction.

Why she suddenly began pressuring Elsie, who comforted herself with her thumb and the silken border of her blanket against her upper lip at bedtime, she couldn't imagine, but it put her mother and herself at odds. Why was it so important? She needed to see her cousin firsthand to confirm the rumor.

As a Christmas present to Mommy, one that she'd asked for during the season, Elsie tried to comply with not sucking her thumb one night. It proved too difficult. The longing for her silky piece of blankie consumed her. Her habit offered her a singular pleasure. She wasn't hurting anyone. Now, for Christmas, her mother offered her a small box with an ugly wax thumb inside. Mommy explained it had juice inside it when she put it over Elsie's thumb that night.

She told her daughter, "If you keep it on all night, my dear, then you can break it in the morning and drink the juice."

When that bit of Christmas comedy broke open during the night, it only served to annoy both the sticky little girl and her mother.

Gail tried a rubber wrap that she could strap on, but Elsie unbuckled it and continued comforting herself. Then her mother found a bitter ointment she painted on her daughter's thumb. What would she try next? Bedtime with a blankie and thumb was her favorite time of day.

I HOLD TO THE *NAUGHT*Y IN ANY TUG OF WAR

By springtime, Rich had designed a play area for the children and their guests by way of a patio the size of their home. He hired the concrete and mortar company his wife now worked for.

Gail's boss agreed to pour a backyard patio that extended the length and width of their sunken backyard in the shape of a piano. The patio, being overshadowed by a higher house, was enclosed by a comely brick wall with draping honeysuckle vines and a host of buzzing bees. Other succulent xeriscape spikes and whorls covered the topsoil. All the neighbor children and children of friends and family would play in the sandbox and ride their bicycles on the back patio while their adult guests enjoyed barbecues and ice cream socials.

Buoyed, Gail said, "You know why we bought the kids tricycles instead of bicycles?"

Rich looked at his wife, and her girlfriend who said, "Because they aren't old enough yet?"

"No." Gail laughed. "Because bicycles can't stand on their own. They're *two tired!*" She raised two fingers and made them cycle.

The pun rolled by Rich, but Gail's girlfriend furrowed her brow and finally laughed. "I got it. Hey, do you have some condiments for the burgers and dogs, Gail?"

"Sure, what would you like?"

"Relish today. I'll ketchup tomorrow." The silly women chuckled.

That year, the California weather was perfect. Fruit blooms filled the air with oranges and honey. Rich seemed happier and more content than Gail had ever known him. He had taken to riding his motorbike to work each day. He described how feeling the wind in his face and noticing the respect people gave him when he pulled into work or college on his bike "tickled" him.

Rich came to check on Elsie lazing around in bed one morning and asked what she was doing. "Whistling, Daddy. How do you whistle?"

Elsie had seen people whistle with two fingers in their mouth, and she had seen a friend in kindergarten whistling proudly. She was jealous. She practiced pursing her lips and pushing out air. She even practiced with two fingers in her lips. But she just couldn't get the pure sound of a whistle to come forth.

Richard helped his daughter into a sitting position and kept working with her until a pure sound came out of her mouth in one straight tone. Elsie couldn't yet change the tones up or down the scale, but she was showered with victory hugs and proud applause when the sound finally eked out.

By the time she caught her dad's attention again to display her new whistling skills, she was able to move the tone here and there on the scale. He laughed in celebration with her at first; he whistled a little tune for her himself. Then, he said, "Whistling women and cackling hens always come to no good end."

"What do you mean, Daddy?"

"My granny used to say that. It means that women shouldn't waste their time whistling because they'll come to no good end if they do." He laughed and walked away.

With that, Elsie's bell-ringing victory for learning to whistle was silenced. The child had practiced for hours only to earn a curse from her father's lips. She was torn now, between her dad's opinion of girls who whistle and her own pleasure of whistling.

"Dad! I promise I'll stop whistling by the time I turn into a woman!" she hollered.

MAMA DESERVES AN ANGEL CAKE, BUT SHE GESTATE

Gail found herself pregnant for the fifth time in their marriage. Stunned, she defended herself. "I didn't know I could get pregnant while I was still nursing a baby!"

Rich again withdrew in anger, blaming her. His ideal family size for his middle-class salary was now in peril. Nevertheless, the pride of their house accomplishments beguiled them into routine hospitality, working in unity to provide their friends and family with the most enjoyable holiday lunches. As imperfect as their marriage was, it seemed better than the marriages of most of their friends and siblings.

Gail saw the upside to being married to Rich. She thrived in hosting parties and began to claim a reputation of excellence in hospitality.

That summer, Elsie's attention was focused on the entertaining storytelling that 5-Day Club offered children when Gail invited the organization into her home. The neighborhood children were told about a tidal wave that breached the shores of an island named Haiti. The people ran to the tallest hilltop, but most of the inhabitants were wiped out by mudslides that came secondary to the tidal wave. One little girl was rescued from the mud. She prayed to find her parents and the missionaries helped her locate them. The missionaries helped the doctors as aids and nurses for the wounded islanders, and they helped contractors build new homes until life began again.

Elsie learned that all of this was because Jesus Christ, God's Son, loved the islanders. She heard Jesus was born as a human baby and He died for the sins of everyone on earth so that there could be peace with God.

The storytellers explained that this message was one for the missionaries' own lives and also for the islanders' lives when they entered into the kingdom of God.

She peeked and saw Carlene and other neighborhood children raise their hands during the prayer.

Next Sunday in her Sunday school class, Elsie's teachers handed out pictures of heavenly angels to color. While she colored the angels, the teachers explained there was a perfect place of light where God lived and reigned from His throne. They asked the children if they would like to live with God and His angels in the city of gold and light one day. If so, they would need to raise their hands and accept Jesus' death as payment for their own sins. Elsie wasn't sure about her sins, except maybe her obstinate thumb sucking and her whistling, which was sure to ruin her. But she did know that God was powerful and that He loved the people of Haiti, and He also loved her. She was sure of this because she felt His love. He lived with the glorious angels and wanted her to live with Him. She raised her hand and said she wanted to accept Jesus' sacrifice and she wanted to live eternally in heaven with God.

Afterward, from the middle seat of the Oldsmobile, Elsie sat forward and told her parents about her desire. Both of them seemed happy. Each of them asked her more questions and congratulated her. She wasn't sure why they were so happy, but she felt glad.

Leona came to stay with Rich and Gail at age fourteen because Laila could not manage her daughter. She complained to Gail that Leona was rebellious and uncontrollable, but Gail did not remember Leona as being that way. After Leona began to live with Rich and Gail, she offered more information about her mom pushing drugs, doing drugs every day in the living room, and she also claimed there were men who came over and tried to feel her up.

When Leona complained to her mother, Laila pawned her off to the nearest relative. Dorjan refused to take in another child, so it fell to Gail and Rich to help, since they were the closest.

Standing next to her new baby sister's playpen, Elsie listened to Leona cooing over the pretty baby. Their reverie was suddenly shattered when Rich approached Leona from behind and ran his hands over her breasts and buttocks.

Leona cried out and ran to her room, slamming the door. She immediately told Gail she was going to go home if she had to hitchhike because Gail's husband made her nervous. It wasn't that he was as bad as her mom's boyfriends, Leona added.

Shaken and concerned with what Leona wasn't saying, Gail packed up her niece's belongings and dropped her off at her parents' home. "Dad, you have to keep her. She is being taken advantage of by Laila's boyfriends and we can't keep her with three babies of our own." With that, she closed the door and went home.

Rich seemed skittish, avoiding her more when she returned. What had he done?

He was hardly sure what had occurred himself. In the afternoon light, he had mistaken the teenager for Gail. There was no explaining it now. What was done, was done. His wife was so disgusted, that she moved all his things into the spare room and locked herself in the master bedroom. Rich went along with the bold move of matching boldness for boldness, putting on fake smiles for pretentious ones.

There was the approaching Cal Poly Open Campus Day of 1965. He left Gail home with the baby and took Carlene and Elsie in hand to show them the school campus for a special Homecoming festival for alumni and new students. It was a bright, happy day, and as the new music of "The Elephant March" soared through the air being played by a small band, the children skipped along and marched beside their daddy. Mommy was nowhere nearby.

HIS LITANY OF LOVE, NESTED ARROWS IN A FULL QUIVER

It was Christmas 1967 when Kaida Beryl, named for both the feeling of wild victory and for her grandma, was born just sixteen months after her sister Melanie, grasping the heel as it were. By this time, Gail was as finished with childbearing as Rich was with despising her for it. He went to the doctor and received a vasectomy. No matter the pain or discomfort, there was no way Gail was going to get her dozen children out of him.

While the baby slept, Gail made her first three daughters matching red velvet skirts in preparation for a small performance at Grace Tabernacle. She bought three flouncy white blouses adorned with lace and made Swedish styled suspenders for each outfit. They had already learned a pretty little Christmas song she'd taught them, "Away in a Manger."

Even the three-and-a-half-year-old Melanie linked arms with her sisters to the platform. The pastor introduced them as the "Stair Step Children" because the girls were exactly one head above the next. The trio stood there astounded to see the audience staring back. Melanie belted through the lyrics, mimicking her sisters. When they sang, people in good Christmas spirits, chuckled and clapped.

Afterward, the pastor stood and prayed for a long time, a prayer that ended with "And all God's people said—"

"Amen!" Elsie shouted, wanting to hop off the stage as soon as possible. All the people laughed again. It was such a good experience for Elsie that for many years after, she kept baiting the girls to sing together at church, bribing or threatening them when the others had no interest to perform.

At just about the six-year mark, when Rich, a frustrated family man, had his graduate diploma within his grasp, a missionary came to preach at Grace Tabernacle. The missionary implored people to consider several opportunities for ministry. Rich, officially a graduate in business operations, decided to apply for the job of Business Manager. "Working with people scares me, but I'll be great with schematics and accounting."

Gail encouraged this opportunity. Becoming a missionary might surround the couple with godly leaders and thereby purify them of their sins. Perhaps a mission compound would increase Rich's desire to grow in the Lord. She had begged him to consider leading family devotions, but he was not interested. This idea of a spiritual calling hooked Gail.

After several personal interviews, a recommendation from their church, and a background check, Rich was hired to be the business manager at Fields Mission Corp., away across the United States. The headquarters was located in Pennsylvania.

The family needed to pack up the house they'd grown to love and sell it.

Rich offered to sell his motorcycle and rent a moving company to move the family beds, their washer and dryer and a heavy box of tools. He'd just crashed on his cycle and his ankle had been seriously sprained. "Anyway, I know I won't need it where I'm going to be serving the Lord. That bike will have no place in Pennsylvania at my new job." He shrugged off the final loss of being a young adult as a rite of passage.

"I'm sure God has nothing against motorbikes, Rich," said his pastor, "but your supporters might appreciate your personal sacrifice." Rich didn't tell him that his stepmom had fronted the cash for moving due to his cycle being in the shop and no longer being worth the original trade for the movers.

Gail ordered a souvenir of their lives in California, one for her parents and one for her own family's keepsake in the form of a family photograph.

The photographer came to the house but Elsie, who was dressed first, walked down the street to play with the neighbor's child. She was being very careful about not getting her dress dirty in the sandbox, like Mom asked. "And be home by ten o'clock!"

"Okay, Mom."

What's ten o'clock to a kindergartener who doesn't wear a watch? When she was late, her dad came to grab her by the wrist and tote her back to the house for photographs.

There were some men at the neighbor's house next door lounging on the tailgate of a truck, drinking beers. When she and Rich passed by, they asked Elsie if she had ever tasted a beer, and she didn't know. Rich stopped a moment, and one of the guys gave her a taste of their beer. The guys and Rich shared a laugh as they asked, "How long does she have to wait, by gum?" and, "What kind of a father are you that you haven't introduced your girl to the good stuff yet?" Rich laughed and led his daughter back home.

Elsie felt the whole photography thing was stupid and boring. "Why?" she kept asking. She didn't like being positioned, or fake smiling, or waiting for the flash. The adults kept pulling her thumb out of her mouth. The image the family settled on was one where everyone was smiling except a pensive Elsie who was biting her lip, waiting for the photo nonsense to conclude.

PHILADELPHIA, 1965

TO THE COUPLE WHO GOT *TIDE* DOWN, *SEAS* THE DAY

Gail collected the boxes and packed up all the family's belongings. She hired a U-Haul trailer and suggested Rich buy travel insurance in case anything went wrong. After all, they would be traveling from San Luis Obispo with four children in the reverse bumper seat of the Oldsmobile, with a trailer and all their earthly treasures pulled on a trailer hitch behind them. With Kaida being less than a year old, and three other littles, it could be an excruciating cross-country trip all the way to Philadelphia, for everyone.

Rich had a gift of organizing so that he was able to pack all the rest of the family's furniture and boxes into the smallest U-Haul and buckle it to the trailer hitch at the back of the family car.

Rich laid moving blankets at the base of the moving trailer. He diagramed a place for everything and proceeded to use the other family blankets, pillows, the couch and cushions as buffers. However, he forgot to buy insurance, or so he said when his lack of action became regrettable.

Off they went with children crying, orange juice sloshing, and crayons melting in the backseat.

When Rich asked for the orange juice, Gail reminded him that he'd put the snacks in the rooftop container. Rich stopped the car and opened the container only to see the sticky orange juice had spilled under the suitcases. An argument ensued about whose fault it was.

Gail found a station on the radio to avoid talking. Patsy Cline sang "I Fall to Pieces," and the Highwaymen sang "Michael, Row Your Boat Ashore." Roy Orbison sang, "Crying," and Rickie Nelson sang "Travelin' Man" soothing the couple's nerves.

Days later, crossing the border into their new home state, Rich felt the station wagon jolt. Checking the rear-view mirror, he said, "Thar she goes! Dam, dam, damnit!" The trailer had slipped off the car and seemed to be going backwards toward the cow pasture beyond the fence. He watched it ditch itself finally in a cow pond.

The idea of self-determination seemed incredibly silly to Gail in the moment. Look at this reward for thinking we could turn a new page for ourselves. She covered her face and wept.

"Oh, God! Oh, God, help! We're finished before we start."

THE OPPOSITE OF DE*FEAT* IS A SHOW OF HANDS

"You win some, you lose a bunch." Rich said. He, Gail, and their children, without a clean change of clothes to their name, moved into the gate house of the missionary compound.

The historic façade of the mission's gate house, part stone, part masonry, greeted the family with a smiling portico adorned in neat cedar shakes. White pillars supported the roof. Awed children entered their grand, new home to see a wide staircase with oak trims, leaded glass windows, a magnificent dining room, shining bathroom, and large bedrooms. This was to be their very own mansion.

In the upstairs window seat, they could look down to see two weeping mulberry trees framing the portico in the front yard.

Every night the gates were closed for protection, but the family connected with their neighbors and didn't know why the mission gates were even used. The children used their now rusty bicycles to ride the compound freely looking at the expanse of lawns, a true castle-like mansion where missionary families on furlough lived, and several smaller homes hosting staff members. The entire estate was manicured with rows of squared-off bushes.

In the back of the castle, a magnificent beech tree shaded the acre over which it spread its roots and regal branches.

The middle of the estate featured a shimmery pearl, a swimming pool to welcome family play.

Rich's idea of mission's work changed. Why, he'd landed his high calling straight from college! His duties included office management, caring for missionary funds and budgeting the costs of operations.

Having lost most of their belongings, the missionaries came around to offer donations to dress the family and fill their home with comfortable furniture.

In many ways, the impression of old wealth swirled gracefully about the family. As coastal and beach oriented as everything was in California, this place felt lifted from a European fairytale.

Cicadas buzzed through the night that summer, and the children found mysterious empty shells of the giant bugs hanging from the tree trunks to play with.

A nice man next door gave them sheets of copy paper to draw on or use for paper dolls. He brought over used carbon paper to amaze the children showing them how to make carbon copies of whatever they drew.

Outdoors, Carlene and Elsie strung blankets across a laundry cord and used it to perform plays, jumping from behind the "curtains" to perform their parts. Adults who would humor them sat in folding chairs and applauded.

Each child learned to dive in the swimming pool, except Kaida, whom Mom protected. The musky rich scent of lilies and Mr. Lincoln rose beds perfumed the humid air.

On sweet summer evenings, sing-a-longs occurred on the huge circular patio, filling the atmosphere with beautiful melodies, spiritual truths and comfort. Sometimes a missionary preached or told stories. One such story involved the Arab punishment for stealing.

Chills swept the audience as a missionary from the Middle East described how a Muslim child stole bread and had his hand chopped off by a machete as punishment.

Another man showed slides from the Congo where several of the missionaries had been slaughtered by a radicalized African tribe. The pictures were bloody, and the children probably shouldn't have been allowed to see them, but in the presence of so many believers, the gates of safety assured them of God's overwhelming presence.

Rich jotted some notes about the missionary stories in his pocket journal. Maybe he could use them in a letter home.

Sometimes, under the ancient shade of the front lawn linden tree, fragrant with sweetness, the community enjoyed a birthday celebration or a picnic to welcome new missionaries into the fold or commissioned others to be sent to unevangelized fields.

The hospitality that Rich and Gail had enjoyed together in California continued as perhaps their one united strength in Pennsylvania. In the large, lavish, and old-world dining room of the gate house, furnished with a china hutch and sideboard, a small secretary near a bay window, and a pocket door for privacy, lay the perfect setting for dining with no encumbrance to the couple's talent for entertainment. There, they welcomed guest speakers and missionaries needing refuge and friendship.

Rich told the story of their arrival at the mission, especially when he watched the trailer unhitch and roll into the cow pond until the children memorized it. He'd point to the hutch and place settings arranged on the table and say, "How all of these dishes survived without a scratch is still a mystery to me, and yet Gail's sewing machine was strewn about in a million pieces."

Gail flinched every time she heard this and determined to buy another machine as soon as possible. What mother could survive without a sewing machine?

It was easy for the Finch family members to ask questions and fawn over the interesting array of visitors, and Gail enjoyed cooking and baking, even if she didn't like the cleanup. Again, the children hung onto every word of the strange stories and perspectives expressed during those evening meals.

THE EASY BAKE OVEN DIDN'T GO TO COLLEGE BECAUSE SHE HAD NO USE FOR HIGHER DEGREES

One of the requirements at the mission was everyone there would take a turn giving a teaching or a devotional or preach. The rule also applied to the women. Gail saw a poster with her name on it before long.

She panicked. Gail felt incapable of presenting even a devotional, especially in front of people she saw as her spiritual superiors. She was not a speaker, she was not Biblically trained, and she hadn't even attended college. She just couldn't do it. The director insisted that she comply. When it came to be her turn, she stood and read a Psalm and then sat down. She didn't know what else to do. The director called her aside and told her that he sensed a spirit of rebellion in her.

"When men and women are married and they offer to serve the Lord together, they both need to be spiritually fit for their capacity."

"But I have four children at home, what can I do?"

"There happens to be a Bible college in town. Maybe you can take a night course through them."

Gail began taking night courses at Philadelphia School of Bible one evening per week. In the next two years, learning the Bible became the happiest and most freeing times of her week. For this weekly date, she hired a local babysitter who, being a freshman in art school, would draw pictures to entertain the children. She was especially talented at making leafy borders on the page of her artbook. Elsie worshipped her artistic babysitter and tried to emulate drawing the same kind of vines and leaves.

Elsie and Melanie liked to tear apart the couch and make forts with the cushions and dining room chairs in the living room beside the fireplace. There, hiding under a blanket, they'd tell each other stories and sing songs.

While playing one day, their mom came in to sit by the fireplace. The girls peaked out when they heard her crying. She piled her hair onto her head with bobby pins. When she realized the children were in their fort she moved to the kitchen to cry.

Elsie followed her mommy to ask what happened and Gail said it was so hot that she had been wearing sleeveless blouses, but a woman from the mission had come by just to tell her that her shirts were violating the mission's dress code.

"I'm not allowed to go sleeveless. It's just so hot and muggy! How can sleeveless shirts be considered scanty dress?" she wondered aloud. She had just been cited by the board for "wearing immodest clothing."

As conservative as her mother's church had been, and even in their six years at Grace Tabernacle, she had never been told what not to wear. Now, how was she to buy a new summer wardrobe on their limited salary? It was back to digging through the missionary barrels for her.

WHEN YOU GET *POOLED* IN

The pool at night told a different story. The best time to swim was after the sun went down when the air outside was colder than the pool water. Lamplights popped on with a mystical welcome. Adults shared the pool and with the surrounding garden lights glimmering over the surface, it offered enchanted respite for missionaries and staff members playing water volleyball in the evenings.

Laughter, teasing, and friendly competitions comprised the new backdrop of the Finch's homestead.

If the children grew cold, they'd wrap themselves in towels and run into the change area, where they could go through the hall into the castle basement and up to explore the hallways and empty bedrooms in every one of the four levels of the castle. Yummy smells from the kitchen always tempted them.

One night, while the adults played pool volleyball, the director of the mission playfully pushed Gail's head under the water, but something tickled him into holding her head under for a while. She thrashed and kicked him. He let her up. She gasped and splashed the man, then climbed out of the pool and wrapped herself in a towel. She looked at Rich to say something.

Catching his eye, he shrugged, grinned, and volleyed the ball. *You win some, you lose a bunch*, she imagined him saying. Rich was never going to be the kind of man to defend his wife.

For a short time, Rich decided to please his wife, and comply with her pestering to lead family devotions. He read the children a Bible story every morning for a week, and then they all knelt in front of the couch and prayed their prayers. Gail, however, was not informed of his new tradition. While the children bonded with their father, Gail made breakfast. She suddenly appeared one morning to call them to the table only to find she had interrupted the rest of the family's prayers during devotions.

"You wanted family devotions, so you're getting family devotions," Rich quipped. That ended family devotions.

Across the street, Carlene and Elsie most often played with the Woodley children. They lived in a four-story house. The children played easily in their rickety wooden garage attic, climbing up the ladder and snooping through slats, as well as hiding in the corners, and spying out the window. They would even form figurines with homemade playdough in the sunroom, the smell of which intrigued them as much as their braided creations with the stuff.

Carlene and Elsie's favorite game at the Woodley's took place in the back yard trees. Tag or Red Rover took up hours after school, and Mom made friends with Mrs. Woodley who needed help wallpapering the four-story stairwell. Always spunky and full of ideas, Mrs. Woodley had six children and a huge home to manage. Mom climbed up and down the ladders, pasted, folded and unfolded wallpaper for Mrs. Woodley because she felt such a unique bond of confidence and friendship with her.

Gail soon confided that she felt honored and delighted to be hosting a particularly well-known teacher who specialized in family matters. She told Mrs. Woodley how excited she was that he would be having dinner at their home and about the many things she'd already learned from the man's teaching.

With an out of the ordinary request, Mrs. Woodley asked if she could come meet him that night. Gail invited her friend for dessert. When they were given a bit of privacy afterwards, Mrs. Woodley asked her questions and came away from the dining room beaming. She had met her Savior that evening.

GULLIVER WANTED TO KNOW THE ALTERNATIVE TO ADULTING. SO, I SAID, "JUST *KIDDING*"

School itself was only around the corner and up the street past black iron fences, rose gardens, shady woods, and stone walls hiding other magnificent homes.

The first-grade art teacher assured Elsie that she could make no mistakes in art. But when Elsie did make a big mistake and began to cry, her teacher showed her how to fashion it into something new and beautiful.

The children lined up to move from Mrs. Getty's reading room to the snack room where Nabisco Triscuits with cartons of milk were served on child sized dining tables. They lined up again to move from the lunchroom to the library.

To please her teacher, Rich helped Elsie learn to print her letters better by modeling his own squared-off draftsman's script. Elsie learned to mimic the neat letters and greatly pleased her teacher.

Carlene had a teacher who treated her with contempt for being a wild haired, free-thinking, California-speaking Gentile. She couldn't feel a sense of belonging at the school so long as the teacher kept correcting her every "drawer," "egg," "orange," "creek," "water," "soda," "supper and dinner," "rubber bands," and "sneakers" mid-sentence.

She also endured a sharp learning curve for new words like shoe fly pie, Quakers, Amish, jaw breakers, being snoopy, what a crick was, a hoagie, and many geographical places or civil war sites in the state of Pennsylvania. Carlene did not take kindly to being mocked or rebuked on a regular basis. She dug in her heels. She also decided never to treat people that way.

If the teacher had taken time to engage her new student's personality, she might have been surprised to find that Carlene was quite the little eccentric who enjoyed different cultures. Instead, when it came time to pass or fail the fourth grader, she gave her pupil a written tongue lashing to warn the upcoming teacher of her obstinance and reticence to learn.

Rich worked in the office across the drive, and over a stone path through the dogwoods and apple blossoms. Gail worked as the chief cook and housekeeper, though Carlene and Elsie's chores included washing dishes by hand every day. Carlene usually washed while Elsie stood on a stepstool drying them and putting them into the tall upper cabinets. Rich also swam with them on Saturdays, rode bicycles with them, and read books to them.

IF YOU WANT A PRIZE FOR DOING ABSOLUTELY NOTHING, HERE'S *ATROPHY*

Camile became one of Gail's friends. Her only friend at the mission, in fact. Camile was an elegant woman from Canada and her husband was well-respected, so it was an honor when the Finches were invited to their Thanksgiving dinner. It was a welcomed day out.

Gail felt that she could talk about any practical matter in grooming the children or spiritual matter impacting her marriage or in the mission community with Camile. She helped her process her tangled thoughts.

The children yammered for pets, but no dogs or cats were allowed, much to Gail's relief. She took them to a local pet store and allowed them to pick out turtles and fish. Within a few months, the turtles had died. Nobody had really learned to care for them or been held accountable. Strangely, the guppies began to multiply in the little fishbowl. They were having babies. Then, as quickly as it began, the guppies disappeared.

When they went back to the pet store to ask why, the fish handler laughed. Oh, when the mother guppies have their babies, you have to remove them and put them into another bowl. If you don't, the mothers will eat their babies.

Elsie, upset by the thought that a mother could eat her babies, she went home and poured the bowl of guppies into the toilet. Dad said they would be released into the creek if she did that. She didn't know what happened to them, but she didn't care.

When Carlene arrived home from school before Elsie, she got the first pick of the snacks, and that was reason enough to race each other home. One day Elsie arrived to find that there were no snacks remaining for her. She asked her mom for crackers, but there were none to be had. Carlene had already gone outdoors to play without stopping to gloat. Elsie felt jilted.

Rich came home and pulled out his pocket notebook to write a note. Elsie, sitting at the kitchen table pouting finally garnered his interest. She told her father what happened.

He came and stood over her. "You may as well get used to it, darling. Life is not fair." He left her to absorb the fact that he could not, and would not, help her balance the injustice.

One terrible Tuesday on the walk home from school, Carlene was talking to herself about her teacher when a man sitting in his parked car asked her if she wanted a ride home, but when she looked in the window to say "No, thank you," she saw he was playing with something in his lap. With the intuition of a child, she ran around the corner and into her house where she described the experience to her mother. Gail called the police, but the man was gone and couldn't be apprehended.

That Christmas, the couple held a parent conference fielding what could be done for the kids' presents. They simply couldn't afford store-bought presents, Rich insisted. However, Gail told Rich that she could sew bean bags, and he could build a bean bag toss from fiberboard and paint it. That would be the kids' joint present.

CAPTURING THE CROWN MAY COST A ROYAL TOOTH

After their first-year anniversary at the mission, Gail decided to add her own style of ministry to the mission's agenda for women. She embarked on a creative course of Bible training for her children and the neighborhood children. Her youngest recently proved to her that even toddlers could learn to sing scripture or memorize important verses. Kaida could quote Psalm 100 from the day she turned two years old.

So, Gail set about offering the children who lived under her roof, and those visiting them, a silver dollar for quoting Psalm 23, Psalm 100, and Psalm 1 by heart. A silver dollar was a beautiful and unique coin, a great incentive for the girls and their friends. Each of the children accepted her challenge to them, and many of them committed whole chapters to memory.

In the older girls' respective fourth and second grades, they learned two things.

First, Carlene and Elsie discovered they could ride bikes in a new and different way. They could stand up on the rear fenders of their rusty two wheelers and steer by slight changes in balance. Perhaps the handlebars were rusty, but it was great fun acting like they were acrobats in a circus. Occasionally, Dad would join them, and they'd ride bikes throughout the neighborhood, and on to the corner store where they could buy giant jawbreakers to lick off colors in layers over a few days.

One colorful autumn day, Rich bundled the nearly three-year-old Kaida on the bike behind him. He explained that she had to hold on tight as he strapped her to his torso, but almost as soon as the group took to the street, Kaida began to scream. He thought she was frightened, so he kept peddling, but when she kept screaming, he stopped to see that his daughter's heel had been eaten away by the spokes of his bike. She had lost her shoe! It was up to him to take her to the emergency room and watch over her as her foot healed.

Second, Elsie and Carlene found that they loved to climb up the old beech tree shading the back of the mission estate. The two Finch girls and the Woodley children all enjoyed climbing in the tree, seating themselves on the top branch in a row, peeling leaves, throwing bugs, and talking about their lives. One day Carlene told her sister she had heard a crack in the top arching branch, the one they all liked to sit on together.

The implications of this news didn't fully register in Elsie's mind as the next time she went climbing alone, the branch gave way beneath her. She fell sixty feet to the ground, tumbling over two other large branches on her way down.

Someone inside the castle heard the branch crack and the crashing fall of the limb through the underbrush. Looking out, he saw little Elsie lying under the branch. "Call an ambulance!" the man shouted.

The attending doctor told Elsie's parents to keep her in bed for a couple of weeks while the bruises and bones healed. He said the other branches that broke the fall most likely saved her life.

This tumble from the tree became a defining moment for Elsie. Not only did she learn to live with a deformed pelvis and clicking hip when she walked, she also thanked God for saving her life and wondered whether He had saved her for some reason, perhaps to do something special and purposeful someday. From that day forward, she would look for her special life's purpose.

SHE HAS A HUNCH ABOUT WHAT CAUSES BACK PAIN

Their mom took care of Melanie and Kaida, studied her Bible, sewed the children's clothes, and retailored clothing she found in the missionary barrels. She coached them to memorize scripture, and entertained visitors for dinner. She baked cookies or made other after school snacks available. Occasionally, Gail dusted the windowsills, hoovered the carpets, mopped the oak floors, and dusted the staircase. The children experienced their parents acting in unison when they walked to the castle for sing-a-longs, to the pool for an evening of pool volleyball, or attended church.

Another tiny fracture happened in the Finch's future at the first freeze of their second year in Pennsylvania. While Gail was stepping out of her back door, she slipped on the ice and fell down the steps. The emergency doctor told her and Rich not to worry as she'd likely broken her tailbone, but when she had serious trouble walking and going to the bathroom, she was ordered to bedrest. This was fine with her because she could barely move without excruciating pain.

Rich left his wife alone. He decided she was playing him for a fool. He did not bother to check in on her for her bathroom or dietary needs until she proved to be incontinent.

Gail only had to pee the couple's bed one time for Rich to realize that it was not to his advantage to ignore his wife entirely. This tailbone injury had taken a turn for the worse and Rich still railed against her for milking attention. How was he supposed to hold down a job and babysit the children?

He nevertheless cooked canned goods for the children in the absence of their mother, took them to see where he worked, and strolled with them along the estate boundaries. What else could be done?

When Gail was able to walk, a month or so later, and slowly resumed her household duties, she decided to pay a visit to the director of the mission. She was desperate to repair her marriage and to find counsel for how to live with Rich in unity.

She couldn't explain what she was missing. Was it food or clothing? No. Did Rich help with the children? He did as much as any man did, her friends and mother assured her. It was the feeling of danger that seeped from him in his silent treatments, in his presence lying next to him in bed, as though living at the mission was the only physical barrier protecting her from abuse.

She had the distinct impression that she had misplaced a thing called "happiness." She'd lost her merry self somewhere in Pennsylvania. She didn't recognize the tired woman she'd become there. She didn't dance and couldn't as she'd grown plump around the middle. Her back pained her every day just to sit down or stand up. She used to love going to the theater, but according to mission rules, the theater and movies were off limits.

She felt a palpable jealousy when she saw a couple's simple caresses, kisses, back rubs, or hand holding. Envy stabbed her heart when seeing a shared "knowing look" between the missionaries telling their stories over dinner.

Whenever she tried to discuss a note of personal importance with her husband, he made a crude comment or lectured her for some sin he perceived in her motivation for talking. Even the joy of watching her children at play had leaked away. She felt numb.

She voiced her complaints and a request for marital counseling as best she could in her meeting with the mission director, it came out that her husband worked 18 hours a day but didn't get paid overtime and that he never prayed with the family but left that spiritual training to her. She mentioned how she felt Rich's seething undercurrent of anger was fixated on her and she mentioned his lack of care for her while she was laid up in bed.

The director carefully jotted notes saying he took her request for marital counseling to heart.

Gail was given a date and time the following month in which to bring her husband and come to a board meeting. In the meantime, the director advised the couple to visit a Christian counselor who could give them a personality test where they could get counseling.

He advised the couple to drive out to a cabin property owned by the mission's doctor located on the inlet and enjoy a weekend away.

There, a little boat awaited the family, and they all hopped in. Only a mile offshore, the boat's engine sputtered and choked. Rich dove into the water several times to find and fix the problem. When he was successful, he turned the frightened family back to the dock. The children dug for clams and caught crabs with their dad and enjoyed the fireside, but at night, the family was bitten by bedbugs.

They drove home blotchy and itchy the next day.

Rich said he would not go to any counseling, but the testing intrigued him. Gail set up the appointment.

TOURISTS A *DOOR* THE SIGHTS IF NOTHING *RUINS* THE VIEW

The director advised the family to take another weekend together visiting Amish country. Again, they piled in the car and drove out to a farm where the girls watched Amish children doing chores and petted a monstrous horse while it was being fed. It was their first time seeing a living horse. It towered above them.

When the children were absorbed playing a game, their parents noticed the simple contraption stealing their complete attention. The marbles were collected from a box attached to the base of the game, lined up at the top and discharged down a zig zag funnel like a river winding down a mountainside. The children could grab from the spout at the bottom of the funnel and feed them back to the top to watch them go down again.

The parents analyzed the value of a souvenir like that and decided to purchase it seeing that all four of the children's hands competed to grab the marbles even as they played together in happy unison. It was the simplest invention, and mesmerizing. It became a prized possession, for it was a free and effective babysitter offering hours of distraction with miles of entertainment.

They enjoyed a tour of the Amish town and museum and saw handmade quilts hanging on walls, blacksmiths clanking on metal pieces with their hammers, and they ate hot cinnamon-spiced ice cream.

On the way home, Melanie's eyes were as wide as her scoop of ice cream. "Why do they dress old-fashioned?"

"They're just different from us," answered Carlene. "Do you like horses?" Carlene asked her little sis. "Yes, aren't they beautiful? I wish I could have one."

"Don't give it a second thought, my dear. It ain't gonna happen." The front seat had spoken.

Melanie asked why the Amish rode in buggies pulled by horses instead of in cars. Kaida echoed her sister's question, "Yes, why?"

Dad said the Amish believed in simplicity and hard work.

"Your dad would fit right in except the Amish also don't believe in electricity or motors," Mom quipped.

Dad switched on the radio, and they drove the winding country roads all the way home distracted by music.

Another weekend, Dad took the family to see the Liberty Bell, bolted together after it cracked, and the Hershey Chocolate Factory. They spent another couple of hours at the Gettysburg battlefield and learned about Betsy Ross making the United States flag, and Lincoln's Declaration of Independence. When they came home to the mission, they studied the stone walls around their house and the Woodley's clapboard house looking for bullet holes from the Civil War until Dad said "You won't find any holes, girls. These houses were built after the war."

CUFFLINKS AND HANDCUFFS ARE HANDY BRACELETS

When Rich and Gail visited Dr. Bryant, to sit for their personality tests, he reviewed them and called them back asking the couple to sit down.

"Rich, you have a fine mind for tactical, mechanical thinking and doing. Gail, you do too, but not like Rich. There is nothing wrong with the way you process life. The real difference I see between you—and this is very troubling to me—is that Rich is off the scale indifferent to people, to conversation, and working with others. Now, Gail, you are off the scale the other direction, very sociable, very friendly, very spontaneous. To you, life has no value without warm relationships. Rich, you are task oriented, and that makes you a great employee. You could be a great leader if you saw the value in other people more, but I'm not sure you can change without concerted work."

"I'm not interested in counseling."

"Yes, I gathered that from our first meeting." The counselor turned to Rich's wife. "Gail, being people-oriented, you mapped so far from your husband that I must tell you, I see no future for your marriage. Your husband will always despise you for not working hard enough and for trying to connect in a meaningful way. He does not enjoy conversation and sees no purpose in teamwork."

"What?" she gasped. "You are supposed to be a Christian counselor! With God, nothing is impossible!"

"Yes, but God doesn't force His way into places where He is not welcome. So long as Rich believes he's doing fine on his own, your marriage will continue to break down. You cannot love a lamppost and expect it to love you back."

Gail broke down in tears. The counselor handed her a box of tissues. Rich stood, shook hands with the counselor, and avoided the crux of the problem by saying, "You heard the man, Gail. Ain't no how. Ain't no way. Let's go."

The counselor had one more parting word. "Rich, if your loved ones do not feel loved by you, you don't love them." He paused. "That goes for you, too, Gail. As difficult as it is when you feel unloved, you need to keep loving those in your charge with courage and faith as you are able."

The next time the mission board convened, and the couple summoned, Rich watched as the director called Gail to stand before the board members. "Tell them what you have told me," said the director. She was mortified to be put on the spot without warning. How could she set forth her marital complaints with her husband sitting there? Gail's hopes were dashed. It felt like a trial.

At the end of the confrontation, with both Rich and Gail trembling, the director stood and made a recommendation for the couple to be given three months to sort out their problems and continue their mission employment or Rich would be terminated.

"A house divided against itself cannot stand. You are our gatekeepers and our office manager. Our missionaries deserve every stability we can afford them and, right now, we don't have the confidence that you will be able to fulfill your responsibilities competently if you are traumatizing each other."

Rich, of course, was furious. Gail had borne their dirty laundry into the light and in front of the men he respected and had strived to impress. Perhaps Dr. Bryant had sent his own report to the board? He didn't know. He knew Gail had humiliated him.

As he laid into her, seething quietly so as not to disturb the children, there was a knock at the back door. One of the board members stood outside and offered Gail a box of candy. He said he was extremely sorry for the way the situation was handled. He ended his visit by saying that he would keep the couple in his prayers.

Rich pulled out his journal and began to jot down a few notes of analysis.

Gail's already shriveled soul felt ripped apart, her spirit was strewn in pieces, without a surgeon to put it back together. Finally, after a sleepless night, she came to her senses and asked the Lord to be the surgeon. Only He could put her wreck of a marriage back together, and only He could sew her spirit back into her with a will to live.

MAYBE THE WAR *DEMOATED THE* CASTLE

This being their second Christmas away from California, and still as poor as ever, Rich made another spectacular proposal to Gail. To him, the idea seemed poetic given all the drama his children had already endured. He pulled out a piece of paper with a drawing and a list of items.

"Look, I don't want to throw you for a loop. We can at least make it through Christmas. Let's try Dr. Bryant's suggestion of teamwork. I'll make a wooden box with a window for a puppet theater, if you can make the puppets and the curtains."

Delighted, Gail agreed. Her husband had redemptive surprises that always made her question why she doubted his devotion to the family. She loathed the confusion clouding her judgment. Her husband's absence of everyday concerns caused a desperate haunt. Yet, his suggestion was creative and doable.

Being used but unseen had driven her to suspect everything Rich did. Nevertheless, she accepted her duty in faith. "For the eyes of the Lord run to and fro throughout the whole earth, to show Himself strong on behalf of those whose heart is perfect toward Him. Second Chronicles 16:9," she quoted aloud.

Christmas that year proved to be a huge success, despite the clouds. The theater box with moveable curtains and paper mâchéd finger puppets awed the children. They had a unique present they could never have imagined. They could ask their friends to help them make up stories and play with the puppets, or they could invite their friends to watch and be the audience. Christmas gifts, really any gift if it is clever and made with love, does not have to be expensive.

In mid-February, an older man, round and balding, knocked at the front door. When Gail answered, he said, "Uh, where should I park my car?" Gail felt like she should know the man, but she couldn't place him. "There is a driveway around back." The man parked around the back of the house where the children had put on their plays, and again, he knocked at the back door.

"Hello?" she answered.

"Where's Junior? Did I catch you at a bad time?"

It dawned on her that the man was the children's grandfather. Rich's father had driven across the country to visit them without his wife. She invited him in to sit at the melamine kitchen table, where a small white radio played music interspersed with news items.

"Carlene, go across to the office and get your father. Tell him his daddy's come to visit."

Elsie crawled into another chair at the table and listened to the man's pleasantries. "Elsie, this is your grandfather, from California. He's come all the way out to visit you, honey."

"Me?" She liked him.

"Well, all of you, and your father of course. How is Carmen keeping?" She turned her attention to Dick.

"She ain't sick, she just don't like to sit in a car for so long. Do you happen to have coffee?"

"Yes, I'm boiling the water now." She took down a mug and piled a heaping spoonful of coffee crystals into the cup, poured in the boiling water, and stirred. "Do you take cream?"

His ruddy hands reached for the mug, "Ah, no, miss. Too many years on the docks to care about cream."

Rich came in the back door, shook hands with his father, and sat down across from him. Gail moved into the hallway to give them privacy, but she listened with one ear. Why hadn't Rich bothered to tell her they'd be having a guest?

"Have you seen the house?"

"Nope. Just arrived."

"Well, it isn't ours."

"Okay."

Dick sipped his coffee. "Four little ones, is it? Your girls?"

"Yep, Dad. I don't know how we're gonna get back."

"Ain't no reason you can't love a woman like that. Kids are happy, you got a mansion to live in. Good coffee…"

"You tired, or do you want a tour of the grounds?" Gail heard the door open. She suspected this visit was meant to be her hint that they would not be staying at the mission. Had Rich asked his father for help with the move?

Rich and his father were not close. The many years of neglect and abuse Junior suffered at the hands of his dad had severed any opportunity of fondness to survive between them. Yet, here he was, visiting.

Luster, due to living in the off-set trailer with his brother, had grown to idolize his brother and vilify his cruel and isolative father. Rich once witnessed his father picking up a bike Luster was seated on and throwing it across the grass. The two mechanically minded males, Dick and Junior, also vied for mechanical excellence.

Now Dick had a singular aim in visiting his number one son. There were words of apology and moments of setting things straight between them. A wad of cash was handed off toward the expenses of the upcoming move, and there was a promise made that Rich would continue to watch over his stepmother. She had found a place near Denver, Colorado, to put up a new trailer where she would live next door to their best friends, Leo and Marge Friend. Rich then agreed to set up a home nearby.

Dick packed some gift boxes from Rich for his stepmom in his car after the weekend concluded and he'd said his goodbyes. No further understanding was offered about the mysterious visit from Rich's dad until two weeks later when a phone call came from Carmen; she informed him that his father had died.

COLORADO, 1968

A FAMILY DISASTER IS A DISORDERED EASTER

On cue, Rich packed up the few family belongings and strapped them into a roof-top carrier on top of the Oldsmobile. A warped maple tabletop was the largest item, so he used that as the foundation supporting the trunk. He thought he might be able to salvage it someday.

Everything else they'd enjoyed over the past two years belonged to the mission. Their church and the few friends who had learned about the trailer and the loss of all their worldly goods coming to Philadelphia two years prior had tried to make tax deductible contributions to the mission to be given to Rich and Gail so that they could replace their belongings, but the mission's policy was to pass along and pay only the salary of its staff and missionaries. Special gifts were deposited into the general fund. A surly and despondent father gathered his children and their small suitcases into the car intent on leaving the mission with barely a goodbye, but at the last minute, he saw Gail's face of horror at the back door. "If you want to come along, get in!"

Gail opened the passenger door and carefully backed into the seat. "Where are we going, Rich?"

"You never mind that, baby. You're either coming or you aren't."

She shut up and closed the door.

Before the warming car began its escape, running toward the family from the Woodley's house across the street was the spunky Mrs. Woodley with a bowl of fried chicken in her hands. "You can't go off without something to remember me by. You kids be good to each other now. I'll miss you, Gail."

Off they went down Freed Road to PA 36, Gail's tears streaking her face, and on to Highway 76, stopping only when the children begged to go to the bathroom or began arguing and crying for food.

"I still don't know where we're going, Rich. 'Mind letting me in on your little plan?"

"Plan? I have no plan. I have no job. I have four children that you tricked me into raising. You can come along for the ride and find out for yourself where we wind up."

Rich made a beeline from St. Louis, Missouri south to Oklahoma City. He said it was to look up family gravesites and some old friends.

Carlene asked, "I was born in Phoenix, right?"

"Yes, you were."

"Then, why do you have friends in Oklahoma, Daddy?"

"Funny thing, Carlene. My life didn't start with your life. I've had my own life long before you were born, and much of it was right here in this town."

The children, hot and sweaty, looked out the window at the strange surroundings. They didn't dare complain. Their mother was in no mood for more questions. "I don't know. I don't know," was all she said.

As the children sat in the car with their mother in the parking lot of a stone courthouse, Rich went inside. There, he asked to speak with a judge, someone he'd known in his childhood. The man's name was Judge Wilson. Rich grinned and greeted his old friend, giving him a name they both recognized, and in time he asked about the judge's sister named Noeleen. "Was she my age or a year older?"

"When were you born, '35? Well, I reckon Noeleen's the same age as you, Rich." He rocked on his feet and folded his arms. "Oh, she's married and has three children now. She lives just over off Grand Avenue. Why don't you pop in for a visit?"

"Eh, not now. I have to pull into Denver by tomorrow, and I have my whole family with me, but I have roots here, and strong feelings pulling me back. Perhaps when my mother passes, I'll come on back to Oklahoma. Tell Noeleen I say hello, will you?"

With Plan B dashed, Rich accepted his concession prize and moved up the interstate toward Denver but not before he showed the stone sundial on the lawn to his children and explained how it worked with the movement of the sun overhead.

"Why did we stop there, Dad?" Elsie asked. She felt the place was wild and foreboding, not at all to her liking compared to Philadelphia. "I've never heard of Oklahoma City."

"I wanted to show you the sundial." Rich said.

Gail wasn't the only passenger who suspected there was more to the sundial than met the eye.

It was the summer of 1969, when the Finch family, such as it was, began to travel north to Roberta Flack's voice singing, "The First Time Ever I Saw Your Face" followed by Simon and Garfunkels' "Sound of Silence." This time, it was Rich's tears staining his face.

When six lost children, some much older, pulled into the driveway of Carmen's new house, she gave them Christmas gifts she said she'd been saving them for the children.

Melanie and Kaida received a nursing bag with mock instruments for healing. Elsie received a game called Operation and Carlene received a makeup tote with a compact and fingernail polish. They didn't recognize the stout woman in the housedress, why would she give them gifts?

Carmen took Rich aside to explain how his father had passed away the month before.

The children played until nighttime. They moved to a hotel and then the family drove off again toward California the following morning.

Rich spoke to the rearview mirror. "I need to look for a place to live and see about work. I need to take care of my mother. But, in the meantime, you and the children can visit your family in California."

In California, the aunts and cousins welcomed the family with open arms. Lou, as soon as she set eyes on Kaida, fawned over her. One day she laughed and said, "That little girl is going to be a heartbreaker!" It was a prophetical moment, but not in the way any of them thought.

They ate Grandma Hudson's fried chicken and mashed potatoes with gravy in a round robin fashion, and for breakfast, they had grits, eggs, and toast. Laila introduced them to avocados at lunchtime, and Lou carted them all off to see *Oliver!* the new musical.

Elsie sat with a ghost of loneliness in the back seat of her grandparents' vehicle. Cramped and on the edge of the seat, she tried to enjoy her boisterous sisters and cousins singing, "Food Glorious Food" and "Consider Yourself" from the new musical they'd seen. Looking out the window, she also sang, "Where is Love?" to the memory of her dad.

REPEAT REJECTIONS, A RANGE OF ROCKY *TRAILS*

Dorjan lost his temper at Gail's family camping in his living room. "I can't afford to raise another family. We did it, and you are goin' ta have to find your'n way, girl. That's all."

Gail, in abject poverty and dependent on the men in her life, ever after had trouble forgiving her father for cutting her and her children off without a bit of wisdom or even a tank of gas while he continued to keep her Uncle Dennis safe from all the world and had Lou's family staying on.

Gail decided to visit her old church where she and Rich had worshipped for six years. The church had supported them in the move to Pennsylvania and then continuing at the mission. She drove up to the church and got out of the car. Perhaps she could counsel with her pastor.

Her pastor was standing on the lawn, watering it. When she saw him recognize her, he backed away from her and sprinkled the hose toward her. "You stay away from this church, woman. I want nothing to do with you!"

Gail backed away from the pastor, got in her car and drove along to the next block trembling where no one could see her.

But God her Father did see her.

"Help me. Help me!" she moaned. "I've lost my way with four young children to raise. I have no way to provide for them, Lord. Even my pastor rejects me! What could the director of the mission have said to him?"

She wasted minutes wondering whether her reputation, her Christian agency no longer intact, would prevent her from getting another job if Rich was going to abandon her. As she rehearsed life, her heart hardened against Richard, the mission, and the church as she knew it. There, in the parked car, a foamy resentment also pooled for the children strangling her. She confessed all this abject brokenness and begged God to rescue her.

Personal mortification was the key that unlocked Gail's tree of knowledge that not all Christians are sympathetic or helpful in times of crisis.

It seemed Rich fully intended to leave the lot of them with Gail's parents. Coalbert, however, now living back in Arkansas, learned about the situation on a phone call with his parents. "Your sister Lou is already staying in our guest room with her two small children," his father complained. "If you can think of any way to 'elp 'em, Bertie Gail, I mean, feel free."

Two weeks into Rich's abdication of his family, Coalbert hunted him down at his new job, called him, and told him to pick up his own damn family from his parents' house. Did Rich think that his father made enough money to support two divorced daughters and all their children?

Rich answered, "We're not divorced."

"Well shit or get off the pot, brother. You can't leave them there. You'd better figure out something."

Rich felt so soundly upbraided by his brother-in-law, a man's man he'd followed after as a pal in Phoenix, that he immediately rented a beat-up two-bedroom railroad house in south Denver for his family. It had no lawn. It was the cheapest thing available, but it had a chain-link fence for safety. It was safe enough from everyone but him.

As soon as he brought his family to their new home in Colorado, Gail turned to him and said, "I'm going to find us a real home."

"Go ahead if you think you can do better," Rich challenged.

The children felt frightened and vulnerable in the empty old house. The children outside talked wild and leered at them.

Gail read the papers and began driving her husband to work. She followed all the leads until she found a new development in Northglenn. The house was situated half a block away from a Baptist church and three blocks away from a brand-new elementary school. In the other direction, a junior high would welcome Carlene. The ranch house was only a two-bedroom spec house with wheat fields staring it in the face a block to the west, but Gail challenged her husband. "I found the house. It has an unfinished basement, but you're clever. Go ahead and finish the basement for the girls, and we'll have ourselves a home."

Rich bought the pitch, and within a month, based on his new salary in the computer programing department of Electric Service Company of Colorado, the family moved into their new home fitted with a church and the right schools on the shoulders of the block, a house just their size.

For nearly a year, they lived out of boxes for dressers, but the warped maple table rescued from the cow pasture became their new dining room table. Soon a couch and two chairs filled the living room. They'd make do.

In the Northglenn house, Gail made good for about three months, just long enough for Rich to build out two bedrooms and a small bath for Carlene and Elsie to share. The rest of the basement space was divided into a playroom, where she ended up putting her mother's sewing machine, and an unfinished laundry and utility room.

Her back continued to cause significant pain and dysfunction. When she could barely move, her new friend, the pastor's wife, took her to a chiropractor. That doctor began to treat her, but realized there was a crushed disc and vertebrae, both of which had failed to be diagnosed after her fall in Pennsylvania.

The doctor helped Gail back into the friend's car and instructed her to go directly to the emergency room. More tests were done, and Gail was admitted to surgery.

Rich's own stepmother, Carmen, who never before visited the children in their own home whether in California, Pennsylvania or Colorado, now stepped in to cook and care for the children until Gail returned from surgery.

Carmen plucked a chicken in the kitchen sink the first night and mocked the children for never having seen a dead bird before or a cook plucking off the feathers. They clung to the wall, watching the barbaric reality. "Never thought about it?" She yanked a handful of feathers off and tossed them into the trash. "This is where your roasted birds come from, at least it's what they look like before they're cooked, sillies." She took a butcher knife and whacked off the head and feet.

There was no telling where she had found the bird. She also cut up yards of pig's flesh and made salted pork rinds for them to eat like potato chips, first scraping off most of the stiff black hairs. She made pozole and introduced them to hominy.

The children missed their mother, but Carmen and Rich refused to allow them to talk about her. Their meals were cursory, but the food kept them alive. Cereal in the morning and some dish they'd never seen or smelled before, in the evening.

When Rich failed to come visit his wife in the hospital, the nurses refused to allow her to return home until she was well enough to walk and function on her own.

Carmen had good reason to fulfill her vow of dirt when Rich detailed his account of his wife's troublesome public reproach at the mission. Carmen had always taken offense at Gail's fancy modern dress that turned Rich's head with such power it converted her stepson into a churchgoer.

In her heart, she preferred him being on the outs with religion. She mostly hated Christians, but this opportunity was good enough reason to introduce the children to a dose of down-home reality.

When Rich collected Gail from the hospital, she limped badly, moved slowly, and clenched her jaw in residual pain. Her doctor's discharge instructions ordered a limit to lifting and driving. However, with Carmen shoved off, Gail would have to cook for her family and hug her children, shy and reticent from their mother's month-long absence.

WITH SURGERY, THE PATIENT HAD A *CHANGE OF HEART*

During a hospital phone call, Beryl offered to come help her daughter for the first couple of weeks. Gail remained tightlipped toward Rich, telling him as little as possible, not that he was asking.

The first night home went along quietly because she went to bed after greeting her children, but the next evening, seated at dinner, Rich observed his ten-year-old daughter's new bust out top, frizzed hair, and made-up eyes. "Do you really want to look like a hooker, Carlene?" he asked.

In that moment, Gail's patience for her husband reached critical mass. She flipped the water left in her glass at him.

He pushed away from the table and stomped from the house.

The next morning while she carefully made breakfast and lunches for the Finch children, Rich dragged in a bucket of water he'd left out to freeze overnight. In a fluid movement, he tossed the cold shower over his wife's shoulders, the counters, stove top, and kitchen floor. Then, he ran out to his car warming in the driveway and peeled away to work.

Hearing the screams and the slamming of the back door, the children ran to the kitchen and gasped.

When they asked what happened, Gail wouldn't say. Thinking it was funny, like a pillow fight, the children began to laugh. No one else had witnessed their father's cruelty. Gail began to cry fiercely and limped to the bedroom to change.

"It isn't funny," she said looking each of them in the eye.

They tried to help clean up the water. "Can you remake your sister's lunches, Carlene, dear?" Gail asked. They were a little late to school that day. What had Mom done to deserve that?

Not knowing the extent of the drama to come, it fell to Gail to drive to the airport and pick up her mother. Under lambent rays of silver lined clouds, she watched the sun drop through her rearview mirror, turning a sea of sky lavender and tangerine, finally hiding the ball of light under the indigo peaks of the Front Range, her new home. In the forty-five minutes of silence, she collected her nerves, calmed by the sounds of the highway and the beauty overhead. The Creator's sign language shouted His voice and expression of creativity and sovereign hope without speech, words, or sound. She wondered who else was seeing this message around the city.

A few minutes later, forgetting herself, she picked up her mother's suitcase to place it in the trunk, and when electricity shot through her back, she immediately regretted it.

The children were thrilled to see their favorite grandma waiting for them after school the next day, but when the women pulled out a cot for Rich, leaving it in the living room, the children grew frightened and went to bed. Beryl and Gail retreated to the master bedroom, talking in hushed tones.

Late at night, Rich tip-toed into the house, passed the cot, and turned the knob to the bedroom where he found Beryl peeking out of the covers next to his wife. She trembled to think he might fling her out of his bed. Instead, he retreated to the cot where his pajamas were piled with a blanket and slept there. In the morning, he took the cot with him, and didn't return for weeks.

The next evening at dinnertime, a grandma took the seat where a dad usually sat.

Carlene recounted her day saying, instead of watching Gilligan's Island, she watched an Elvis Presley show about two racing competitors and laughed describing the girls sporting big hair. "Grandma, Daddy won't let us watch such shows, but I know you like Elvis."

The children were nervous about her retelling the story line throughout dinner, but Mom didn't seem to care. Grandma said "Elvis Presley is a good Christian boy who's just lost his way, but Jesus will bring him back. He has a song about walking with Jesus by the sea of Galilee. I have Elvis' record with all his gospel favorites and mark my words, he's just tempted by all the sins of Hollywood and has backslidden. I just know he sings those gospel songs from his heart."

When everyone was silent about her opinion of Elvis Presley, Gail said to her mom, "Rich doesn't allow us to watch much television, and certainly not Elvis Presley."

Elsie complained, "My favorite show, *I Dream of Jeanie*, is banned by Dad, but I sometimes sneak it when no one is home." Melanie said she loved *Bewitched*, and Daddy won't let them watch magic either.

Grandma asked, "What do the children do when they are home alone, Bertie Gail?"

"We ride bikes through the wheat fields and down the hill to the river. We have a bike path we can race on with hills and jumps. We ride with our friends."

"And we dig for crawdads," Kaida shouted.

Melanie said, "Me and Kaida go down to the creek and find them."

"How far is the creek, Gail?"

"Oh, it isn't too far, maybe a mile. Our neighborhood is very safe, Mom. The kids don't have to cross any major streets to get there."

Elsie added, "I practice walking around the split rail fence, Grandma, and now I can walk the whole way."

"How impressive."

"Yes, and I also liked to play with the Howards. My friends, Amy and Cindy, and I can climb the ladder into a fort that Pastor Howard built with Shane."

"Shane's his teenage son, Mom," Gail filled in the gaps, "Our pastor's family lives on the top of the hill."

"There is nothing wrong with these children, Gail."

Elsie didn't know how to describe the fort further. She liked the smell of wood, the mystery of coming up through the trap door, and the way she and the girls played cards on the deck, dangling their legs over the side, looking at the clouds rolling in over their growing neighborhood.

"Grandma, I like to call the neighbor children together on the porch and tell ghost stories because I can scare them to pieces!"

"My-oh-my!"

Elsie didn't mention that she'd been thinking of quitting that storytelling because she'd grown afraid to go down the steps into the dark basement to her own bedroom alone. Her imagination had gotten the better of her.

SEE DANCERS ON POINTE COMPETE IN THE BALL ARENA

On a day when she was desperate for grocery money and paying an electric bill, Gail opened her mailbox to find a check from the IRS. Their tax return had arrived! Rich had left her destitute by removing all the money from their bank account. She couldn't keep borrowing from her mother.

"Mama! Get in the car." Beryl complied. "I have our tax return! I'm going to go cash it at the bank. I can pay you back, buy groceries, and pay the utility bill."

"You don't have to pay me back, Gail. Let's get those layaway items so the kids are set for summer, instead." Strewn rose petals fallen onto a path kept coming to Beryl's mind. What could her small gifts do to reverse the demise of her daughter's rose garden?

Colorado summers usually included grandiose, but very short thunderstorms in the afternoon. Beryl and Gail drove carefully through the flash storm. They'd enjoyed picking up the layaway items and shopping other blue light specials down at the K-Mart store. Gail, in a happy mood, allowed Elsie's friend to stay for dinner. A new potato fry called Tater Tots was served.

Everyone had seconds, leaving only one tot in the bowl. In the middle of the cheerful dinner, the lights went out for just a few seconds, and when they turned back on, both Grandma and Elsie's friend had their forks in the last Tater Tot in the serving dish. "I guess we found something we all like!" proclaimed Gail.

It had been two weeks without a peep from Rich. Gail still had no job, no income, and no cash. "You'd better call an attorney, Bertie Gail," Beryl advised. "Rich won't pay you a dime unless he's made to."

She was right.

Gail contacted an attorney through someone at the church. She intended to file for a legal separation with the bit of Beryl's savings given on the sly. Mother and daughter were sure the Bible said God hated divorce, and they knew how church people generally treated divorcees as second-class Christians.

"I'm sorry to inform you, Gail," the attorney advised, "it would not be worth your money to file for separation. If you only have this much, we may as well use it to file for divorce. You'll have some weeks of separation that come before the divorce, and if things can be mended in that time, fine, but if not, you won't have to pay for my services twice." Gail agreed.

The papers were served to Rich at his place of work. Of course, he was furious. She had one-upped him again.

He couldn't believe his religious, impoverished wife had it in her. He didn't, however, fight with the petitioner's statement naming Gail as the sole caregiver of their children.

The petition included no finger pointing. With no specific accusations needed, Gail's attorney named the cause as "irreconcilable differences." Rich personally answered her petition by checking the same boxes she had checked.

He hadn't calculated for the children's care came as another surprise. Maybe he could argue against the amount, but how?

In the meantime, at Gail's follow up on her sacral area, the surgeon put her back in the hospital for a small correction to her first surgery. It was only a weekend stay, and Barbi Howard offered to keep the younger two children at her house.

Rich, eager to show himself a faithful guy, took hold of his two older girls' hands and walked them to the Baptist church at the corner while his wife lay in the hospital. He sang in the choir, as did Elsie in the soprano section, and was about to escort the girls home when a child came running into the foyer to alert Rich to the fact that Kaida had been hit by the wooden swing at the Howards' house on the hill. Rich, with Elsie and Carlene trailing, went to see Kaida.

She was lying in the Howard's master bedroom with both of her eyes swollen shut, black and blue with a cut to make her proud. Her nose looked flattened to Elsie, who, sickened, backed away.

Kaida was shaken, but well enough to describe how she had forgotten to get out of the way of the swing after she jumped off it. It came crashing back into her face.

Barbi Howard had already called an ambulance. When it arrived, Rich was expected to sign for the transport and treatment. Instead, he told the driver that his wife was the sole caregiver and that she was laid up in the hospital. The driver called the hospital to request permission to get authorization from Gail for transport and care for Kaida. A nurse at the hospital had to wake Gail in the recovery room so that she could speak on the phone and give her authority to treat Kaida.

A CANDLE QUITS A JOB WHEN IT FEELS *BURNED OUT*

Finalizing the divorce, three months later, the petitioner's attorney reiterated his requested amount for child support. "The amount is determined by statute and notice was served upon the father. It has not been objected to."

Without a glance at Rich or Gail, the amount of child support was signed by the judge.

Given the unspeakable emptiness of her marriage, and the humiliating effects of it, Gail intended to keep her divorce quiet at the church, but the church was comprised of a small family of believers, mostly from the neighborhood.

News spread. The women gathered around to hear Gail's story, but she said, "The most difficult thing for me in divorcing Rich was the decision to act. The rest is tenacity."

She had nothing to lose.

Little did she know she'd lost a landslide of treasures already.

Carlene doted on a little blue parrot the family kept near the sliding doors to the back yard. It could say its own name, "Pretty Bird." The pet belonged to all the kids, so Gail said, but Carlene mostly took care of it. She felt it really belonged to her. When Gail couldn't feed the family, she also couldn't afford to feed the bird, and one day, looking for something to satisfy it when the millet ran out, she found another grain spilled under the sink. She didn't really read the box; she just saw it on the bottom shelf and took a little scoop for Pretty Bird. The grain was rat poison.

When Carlene saw her bird lying on the bottom of her cage, she didn't listen to her mom's excuse. Her mom was a murderer. "I hate you! I hate you! I want to go live with Dad!" she screamed.

Gail believed her daughter would eventually forgive her, but that day never came.

TRAILING LACE IS NOT ALWAYS A *SLIP* OF A STORY

After the divorce, Rich developed a difficult breathing condition with a prolonged cough. Since basic training, Rich always carried a cloth hankie in the back pocket of his pants. It became more and more handy as his coughing grew habitual. In his annual physical, his doctor diagnosed him with asthma. For a healthy man, this news came as a blow. It felt ominous, like some sort of divine judgment, but the doctor assured him of the marked improvements to asthma medicines. He should be able to continue with his life without much interruption.

During the next two years, Rich only felt free when he sowed into his own dream of piloting an airplane. Being able to take flight was top on his list. It was the part of his Air Force experience he most envied and always regretted. Now, he would become a real airman, and no one could stop him. To fly above the earth would be like flying above all his problems, and indeed, that was exactly how he felt earning his instrument license.

When Carlene's eleventh birthday rolled around in March, he collected her to take her to dinner. When Elsie's ninth birthday rolled around in April, he took her on a special date to see the Ice Follies. Gail didn't withhold the kids so long as Rich paid child support. She got herself a decently paying office manager position and deftly handled invoicing, purchasing, customer complaints, and bookkeeping.

Being divorced himself, Gail's boss was kind to her. Being a man, he quickly became besotted with Gail's lovely form and talents. Hal did not at all worry that she would become an invalid. Gail was quick on her feet again.

Hal lived in an apartment complex with a pool. He often invited his new assistant's family to come watch television and eat tacos or spaghetti. One time, he invited them for a pool party. The children found Hal's food choices to be new and delicious, and they of course, looked forward to the pool.

Until they heard screaming.

While they were eating, Kaida had wandered off and fallen into the pool. Having never been taught to swim, she was drowning, sinking to the bottom. Hal jumped in and saved her because he knew how to do heart compressions and resuscitation.

As grateful as Gail was for everything Hal gave her, including the feeling of queenliness and confidence, she searched her Bible and couldn't find any permission from the Lord to remarry. It just wasn't to be, so she resigned her job and let her friend from church know that there was an opening.

While Gail was working, the children became latch-key kids. They could get into the backyard gate and open the back sliding door to enter the house, but no one would greet them. There were no cookies baked, no snacks, no mother's arms to greet them and ask about their day, and they knew their dad would not be coming home after work.

Elsie picked up a habit. When she walked on the neighborhood sidewalks, she began avoiding the cracks trying to measure her steps to do so or jumping over them. When riding in a car, she also began clenching her jaw and teeth together counting the passing mile markers, street signs, and traffic lights for no apparent reason. Anything vertical that interrupted the horizon had to be clenched. She annoyed herself, but she was powerless to stop it. She also began having asthma attacks and migraine headaches.

When asthma attacks or migraines happened and her mom was not at home, Barbi, the pastor's wife would come down to the house to comfort and care for Elsie.

VOLCANOS ARE RUDE *INTERUPTERS*

Rich forgot to celebrate his two younger daughters' birthdays that year, but he remembered Easter baskets filled with neon raffia and the best candy the girls had ever tasted. He also remembered to take them to his work's family fun day at the local amusement park, and to the lake for the Fourth of July Independence Day celebration.

Rich began singing in a choir from his work. Music had always felt like mental, emotional salve. He had often been told he had a nice baritone voice; now was the opportunity to learn to read notes while getting free voice lessons. He brought his children to his holiday concerts.

As though Rich aimed to recapture the lost events of his own childhood, he escorted his children to the circus and the Vienna Boys' Choir, and, when *Fantasia* came to town, he took them to see it too. They went to dinner afterwards. *The Sound of Music* was next.

The idyllic singing family made Elsie weep with envy. She knew her family was broken forever, and she would never have such a fairy tale ending. The German problem completely escaped her, because the only thing that mattered to her was the love story and the children who learned to perform together in heavenly harmonies.

When Rich looked in the barber's mirror, he told himself that he was in no way at the end of his romantic options. He knew exactly where he could find a supply of available women, where he had first found Gail, at a local church.

He chose an exceptionally large city church, where he could get lost in the mix and not be sorted out by anyone who knew his past. He'd just go and look around.

Both Carlene and Elsie favored and idolized their father. Comparing their mother, who seemed flat in personality, to their father who had been the one to play in the pool with them, ride bikes with them, and take them on trips. They simply felt a closer bond.

Now, they longed for any new adventure he offered just to be with him. One outing was horseback riding on a narrow trail through dry grasslands with a girlfriend from his church. Another outing was cherry picking with his singles group. Rich's girlfriend from church didn't last long—much to his daughters' relief. Rich sought out other girlfriends. When their dad took them along on his dates, Elsie wondered whether she and Carlene would ever fit into a new family.

Carlene said Elsie had better get ready for the judge's question though. Courts were asking children their preferences of parents these days.

Elsie agreed with Carlene. If the divorce court judge asked, they would say they preferred to live with their father.

"Of course, you will, Elsie."

Doubts overwhelmed Elsie. She didn't want to break up the sisters. She didn't want to hurt her mom, and her mom was willing, no, was insistent, she would raise the children. Didn't she have them living with her? Dad could have taken them. Although she longed for her father, something did not add up.

She prayed that this choice would never be asked of her. She wanted to stay with the majority of the family, in their house, at their church, and at her school, with her friends. She had seen her father's apartment once. It was colorless and cold, empty of comfortable furniture or a television. It felt like she was visiting an alien.

Then again, her father had just given her a stuffed animal dog from Radio Shack. Inside the belly a radio was hidden. Hadn't he given her the perfect gift? She felt his love in so many ways.

The two younger daughters were too much of a liability for Rich, who making excuses, left them behind with Gail.

This game plan did not stop the younger daughters from yearning for their missing father. His preference for the older two became a fine torture the younger siblings endured.

BURIED ARTIFACTS ARE *HILL AREAS* TO DIG THROUGH

Children are blind to the suffering of a parent, especially when one is trying to be discreet and the other is ducking.

Both Rich and Gail, hid from their emotions because neither could afford to face them, much less express vulnerability to another whose loyalties, counseling skills, or level of education were unknown. Hiding in the concrete aspects of "getting through the day" granted strategic progress for daily food, shelter, medicine, education, and a savings account. Just putting one foot before the other granted time to quiet the—fear? What was this crushing sadness? The fear of failing—? To voice the landmark events of their lives would cast shame on each of them if they were honest. They couldn't face the past.

Gail never intended to limit or defame their girls' father because she believed a child deserved access to a father, and Lord knows, Rich had given them so little time as it was, that anything she could do to encourage their relationships seemed a good aim. Gail failed to comprehend the same thing applied to herself.

Her children physically needed her presence for emotional bonding and enjoyment of daily life with her. What kid wants to grow up and face the rest of life if there hasn't been deep affection and goodness shared already?

Gail was no good at tutoring or helping her children with math homework as Rich had been, but she did pretty well with spelling and geography. Only a couple of issues—preoccupation and distraction—bored holes in her quality time with them at home.

Gail penned a third letter to her best friend in Pennsylvania, the one she'd had so much fun shopping with. If she didn't hear back from Camile this time, she planned to pick up the phone and place a long-distance call. Some people just weren't letter writers.

Busy trying to provide for all the "shoulds," their educational and medical needs, Gail couldn't see that her children were oblivious to equal opportunity, or a perfect and comely appearance, or a college fund. They just wanted the undivided attention of a parent to giggle with, ask questions of when they needed to talk, and encourage them to learn something new, or to cuddle with them.

When Gail toted her children to the store, she often left the younger ones in Elsie's care saying, "Wait here girls, I'll only be gone a minute."

Her minutes became "mommy minutes" because they were mostly fifteen minutes short of an hour. The girls would roll down the windows, open the doors for ventilation, and try to find something to play or talk about. Boredom usually turned to squabbles as Mom danced to the rhythm of the ragged cart inside K-Mart.

One bright morning while shopping the blue light specials, Gail found a perfectly good pair of tennis shoes to fit her youngest daughter who had been begging for them. Kaida excelled in gymnastics and all things sports. Gail bought the shoes with only a tinge of worry.

Back in the car, when the delighted little girl opened the shoebox, she screamed. "They're green! Mom! They're green! I can't wear these to school!"

Gail rubbed her daughter's back and tried to reason with her. "They were the only shoes that I could afford, and they're the only ones in your size. They're cute!"

"No, they aren't. I won't wear them. Take them back!"

"If you want tennis shoes, you're going to have to wear them. I can't afford anything else, and there's nothing wrong with them."

Kaida left them on the dining room table and went away crying bitterly.

To Gail's knowledge, her daughter never put on the shoes. When she began to feel guilty, she went searching for them in Kaida and Melanies' bedroom closet. They were not to be found on either side of the closet and neither did her search for them produce them from under the girls' beds.

"Where are your new shoes, Kaida?" Mom asked.

"What shoes?"

"The green ones?"

"I don't know. They're somewhere."

The green shoes never did reappear. Thinking how funny this mystery was, Gail decided to write a letter to her friend in Pennsylvania.

Elsie began to remember that Kaida had asked her to make some sandals out of a pair of her shoes. Assured that she had found the shoes and was given permission, they'd spent an entire afternoon cutting the leather with their mother's sewing shears. Although they worked for hours, the shoes, now shredded, were not turned into sandals.

"Don't tell Mom!" Kaida looked them over for a final judgement. She threw them into a bag and then into the garbage can on trash day where no one would find them. The girls' failed attempt at shoe remodeling was never mentioned again.

WHY DID THE ASTROPHYSICIST LEAVE HIS FAMILY? BECAUSE HE NEEDED *SPACE*

The neighborhood was not comprised of the wealthy. It held no civil war history and no stone buildings. The local church and two schools were made of cinderblock and concrete. There were no trees in any of the neighbor's yards. The air was not woven with the fragrance of seasonal blooms.

If it weren't for the wonder of learning, and the hay fields to play in afterward, Elsie's disdain for Northglenn might have been complete.

The beauty of life was gone. Any nurturing or affection Elsie had felt from her parents was a thing of the past. She was sick to death of life's disruptions.

To find more time in the day with her children, Gail moved the television to the master bedroom where all the children could lay together and watch a show before they moved to their own bedrooms to sleep. Then, the children would take turns staying in her room with her so that they could be near her.

The grace she found for herself in that simple, restful choice became an enjoyable memory in the hearts of her children.

The choir director and pianist at the church also had four children, and they welcomed the opportunity to help Gail by watching her girls while she worked at the office. After school, they would use their house keys to get into their own place and wait for their mom to come home.

Elsie, though three years younger than Rainey, the babysitters' daughter, became enthralled with Rainey's stories, magazines, and especially her ability to write songs. Carlene should have been the more likely friend by age, but Elsie loved the musical aspect of this family and especially Rainey. She talked about Rainey as her idol, and she took her part in her reported woes.

The children often spent long hours with the pastor's kids, also, owing to their ages being about the same, and the proximity of the Howard's parsonage a block away.

Whether together or apart, the children raised hay forts to the sky out of oblong bales bound in twine. They watched tornadoes in the distance from the swing set in the backyard, the nearness of danger dancing on the edges of life swinging to and fro with their own far-flung ire. They also finagled from their mother a dog from the pound.

They called the mutt "Bandit" because of the white and black spots over the body of the mutt culminating in a face mask. Before winter, this little straggler was given a doghouse by the back fence for shelter, and Dad visited his children long enough to string up a light bulb in the doghouse gable.

Gail refused to allow a dirty dog into her house. Even on very frigid nights and days, there was no exception.

It was Bandit who came running when the children crawled over their stockade fence after school to get to their own back door. It was Bandit who comforted them when they were locked out and peed on themselves. It was Bandit's tilted head and scruffy ears when they needed to cry or tell their stories to someone. The children took turns caring for the small dog.

One week, it rained steadily, and caused a pond to grow by the back fence. Then, came an unexpected freeze. The next morning, when Carlene went out to feed the dog, little Bandit was frozen stiff. This was the second pet in a short time to die from neglect or ignorance.

Losing Bandit was a tragedy the children again blamed on Gail for keeping him outdoors in the freeze.

One evening when Elsie was bathing, her mother began yelling at her sisters outside the bathroom door. She began to wheeze and unable to expel the air in her lungs, she panicked. "I want my dad! I want my dad!" she cried between gasps.

Gail, distraught with Elsie's breakdown, telephoned Richard and handed the phone to Elsie as she towel-dried her daughter and plopped her into bed.

To bring her empty-hearted daughter comfort and to fill the void of having lost the dog, Gail agreed to let Elsie adopt a cat. Cats, she explained, were clever and preferred living outdoors.

In the quiet of the evening, a rattled Gail dialed her friend in Pennsylvania, her elegant, sweet confidant. Right then, Gail needed a listening ear. Some things were worth the price.

When her friend picked up, she began, "Hello Camile. I haven't received your response to my last letter, so I thought I'd just pick up the phone. How are you?"

Camile quickly interrupted Gail. "My dear, I don't want to have you waste money on long distance calls. I may as well tell you now that we have never been friends. Our mission director asked me to be your friend and see if I could help you. Well, I obviously failed, and now we couldn't be living more different lives. I do hope that you can find someone nearby to befriend you. Is that okay, Gail?—Now, I must go to bed with my husband. It's two hours later here. Okay? Goodbye, dear."

THE AMOEBA FAILED MATH CLASS BECAUSE HE DIVIDED RATHER THAN MULTIPLIED

Chewing his cud at work, Richard understood his leaving the girls to their own devices hadn't been his brightest hour. Switching his tail at bothersome flies, he also recognized his pastures were no greener.

A family reputation mattered more than he at first imagined. Maybe he should have tried harder to dispel the bickering of his offspring, tried harder to control his household like a man. Lesser men than he at the office spent time in the lunchroom comparing dates with their wives and endearing squabbles with their teens. The beasts seemed contented with their burdens.

A year into the divorce, Rich realized a ready-made, healthy, and good-looking family waited for him. Since Gail was not going to be an invalid after all and had refused to marry a man trying hard to engage her, he decided to woo her affections back.

"My mistake, Gail, all of it. I should have fought for you and the kids."

Wisps of a confession wrapped tendrils around Gail's hands.

Not surprisingly, Rich's change of mind did not include a blessing from his stepmother. Her opinion of her stepson careened. He was weak.

When the children went to visit Carmen in the trailer, she welcomed them but didn't cuddle, never made them a meal, and she couldn't rise from the table to play or give them anything to entertain themselves. She didn't offer them so much as a glass of water. They stood in awkward silence on her enclosed patio on a Sunday afternoon and listened to their dad and grandma talking. She spat their mother's name and glanced oddly at them.

What their mother had done, they couldn't say, but they feared showing a particular loyalty to her in this trailer, and they lack the wisdom to inform them differently. After all, it was their mother who had sent their father away.

Poor Melanie, the blondie princess, had to fend off Kaida's sporting competition toward everything from riding her bicycle faster, jumping higher, keeping the hula-hoop up longer, or getting the attention and friends that Melanie wanted. They screamed at each other like incessant winds across a prairie even though they shared a bedroom.

To try to comfort her sisters, Elsie would read bedtime stories to them, help with dishes, and help set the table. She thought if she could be good enough for everyone, other sprigs of kindness might bud.

With an irritability born of exhaustion, Gail shouted orders through the halls at her children to vacuum, dust, finish their homework, or sit down for dinner. These were all normal, expected activities, but her tone of voice kept the children hiding in anxious alert. At other times, they adopted a defiant "who cares" attitude until she hunted them down and grabbed their arms.

There came a time in the fall, when Gail took issue with something being taught at the girls' school. Seeking to influence the principal, she invited Mr. MacPherson to dinner. He honored the whole family one night by coming. The girls felt special, not knowing that Gail had something to discuss with him. Over the table, their mother was able to confer both her appreciation for him by telling him how much her girls loved him, and also some of her concerns about their curriculum.

He responded in a gracious manner. He gave each of the girls a small necklace pendant.

The pendant was shaped like a globe, and a band around the middle read, "Do unto others as you would have them do to you." He explained that it was called "The Golden Rule" and it was taken from Matthew 7:12 to explain the importance of the Ten Commandments. With this mini Bible and history lesson, he took his leave, but he left behind a stellar impression.

Gail tried hard to provide life-long advantages for her children. She found a job working for Home Interiors, a job where she could make her own hours, even it if was mostly evening work, and as such, a job where she could give welcome advice in home décor to other ladies.

Since both Melanie and Kaida needed glasses, Gail duly provided them. She became an avid shopper of K-Mart's blue light specials and their layaway plan so that her children never lacked clothing or school supplies.

An Olympic size swimming pool lay only a bike hike away for the kids in the next school district, over the open fields and a tall hill for them to climb, but Gail allowed them to ride there together any summer day they liked. It was one decision they each had to agree to before any of them could go. The prize of diving into chilly blue water and swimming for hours was as good as any motivation to agree.

Gail longed to sort out her girls with well-placed words of wisdom, but she was unsure whether children of that age could understand wisdom. Besides, she mused, she had so little to give. Was it a problem of nature or nurture, her girls' bickering? She suspected it had less to do with their desires to subdue one another than to assert their own identities. It seemed pointless to explain that they bounced off one another because their father had abandoned them. There was no foundation, or walls to define them. She could hardly corral her wild offspring into everyday civility.

If Rich had stayed, the soulless weight of the lies her girls struggled under would not be weighing them down. Who were they? Why did they exist? Who was the boss? Why was no one ever home to nurse their wounds? No use wishing otherwise, whatever was defining them these days, she preferred it to having the handsome glowering face of her ex at the family table and in her bed.

Was the face she showed them any better?

What she couldn't give them in timeless wisdom or selfless hugs, she could provide tangibly.

Carlene was old enough to attend the youth group, which included junior high school children, so whenever the invitation was extended, Gail allowed Carlene to go roller skating, go ice skating, play baseball, and attend special functions. Carlene was ahead of schedule, pounding the door to become a seventh grader and move along to the neighborhood junior high.

LIVING IN A VOID IS *NOTHING* TO BRAG ABOUT

Elsie was a well-liked, happy girl when she wasn't feeling sorry about her missing father. Her inborn idealism and soft heart prevented her from accepting the situation they had been dealt as a permanent situation. She could make it better.

Elsie rebuked Carlene when she began going boy crazy, and not coming home after school, and sassing their mom, but she was frightened of the already matured Carlene. So after she said her piece, she locked her bedroom door and hid out of the way until things simmered down.

She tried to help anchor her mother who swung from happy-go-lucky to simmering fury on an hourly pendulum. She set the table for dinner, baked desserts, and watched the younger sisters after school, trying to talk everyone into being their better selves while staying out of trouble herself.

Elsie corrected Kaida and Melanie who shouted back, "We don't have to obey you. You aren't our mom!" No, she wasn't, so trying to discover what made her life unique, she attempted to be mature about her lot and think what her parents might do given the situation.

For a child, Elsie's ability to absorb the significance of Bible stories was notable. Much to her Sunday school teacher's chagrin, Elsie corrected errors as she saw them until one teacher began talking right back to her. Humiliated, Elsie saw the error of her ways. Nevertheless, she kept remembering that her life had been spared for a special purpose when she fell from the tree back in Pennsylvania and escaped the curse of rabies from the shrew she stole out of the cat's jaws. There must be a calling on her life. She would attune herself to find it.

Welcomed at the home of Pastor Howard, she often joined their family with a reprieve from her own. There, Barbi made chili dinners or sandwiches. After eating, the pastor, or someone in the family would suggest a game of catch outdoors, or a game indoors, Monopoly or Canasta. Why couldn't she have been born a Howard?

She felt most free when she sped over the nearby bike hills and made successful jumps on her hot pink Stingray. Otherwise, she could tell ghost stories to the smaller children in the neighborhood. Life was pretty good without much oversight.

Haunting Elsie was the guppy mom who ate her babies, and she wrote a poem about it in her third grade writing class as it related to her mother. She tucked the poem away in her diary and hid the key, but every night she brought out the diary, unlocked it, and wrote about another day's events, her successes, her questions, her prayers, and her heartaches.

She'd been brought up to understand that lying, hiding, and deceitfulness were all pretty much the same thing. They were wrong, but she just couldn't bring herself to tell her mother what frightened her most about their future, *"about the guppy mother eating her babies,"* this, she preached to herself. *"It would hurt her badly."* Besides, it was only a nagging fear, not reality, and shouldn't she honor her mother? "Thou shalt not lie" was in the same Ten Commandments as "Honor thy father and mother." So, Elsie kept her diary and her poem of premonition well-hidden.

TO THROW A PARTY OF THE PLANETS, YOU MAKE *SPACE*

Surprising them all, Rich began "dating" Gail again, taking her to fancy restaurants and out to movies. One restaurant was located on the Denver airstrip, where they could eat and watch the airplanes take off and land. Another was Baby Doe's Matchless Mine with a twinkling skyline view of the city. Rich's office building was especially pretty at night. Anyone on the highway could see the whole top floor lit up in rotating primary colors of yellow, red, blue, green, even purple.

Rich didn't believe in dancing, he said, so there was none of that, but Gail's faulty back had limited her natural inclination anyway. He took her, instead, to El Rancho, a lodge style restaurant in the foothills, and he tried to have mutual conversations with her. He wanted her to leave their home in Northglenn and move into his two-bedroom apartment until they could find another home, but Gail said she was satisfied with her home, the kids' schools, and the little Baptist church that had come to mean a lot to them.

She wouldn't budge.

Rich also wanted her to approve of his love for flying.

Approaching Rich's instrument certification flight, when he had accumulated enough hours, he asked Gail along and she agreed to go. Rich's cloud jump was a defining hour to test their resolve and jostle their nerves.

Piloting Gail over farmlands cut into acres of circles and squares, a tapestry of deeded wealth and industry, he flew her up the rocky ravine and pointed out El Rancho along the highway beneath them. When they turned back, Rich flew under a cumulus cloud that suddenly sucked the airplane into the cloud leaving very little control to the pilot. His wooden attaché case filled with books and their jackets in the back seat, became weightless, flew up, and hit the roof of the plane. Rich, cussing furtively, struggled to regain control of his floundering wings, and finally did so. He brought the plane onto the runway and parked, sputtering in disbelief.

Gail's heart was in her throat, pounding wildly, but she remained calm in mind and spirit.

When Rich finally said, "Man-o-man! I thought you'd be screaming, and you weren't. I'm impressed," Gail answered, "The Holy Spirit's words came to mind, 'Even the winds and the waves obey my voice. Peace be still.'" She also raised her head and looked evenly into his eyes saying, "I've never been one to frighten easily, Rich. You should know that."

He was beginning to believe it.

The following week, Rich accompanied Gail to her church where people came and shook hands and welcomed him back. He read an announcement in the bulletin that said the church was looking to start a men's chorus or a men's quartet. It captivated him. The children felt proud and extremely happy to sit between both their mother and father during the service.

An official marriage proposal came with a letter, offering Gail the opportunity of a lifetime. The letter said not many divorcees get to be reunited with their husbands. She simply had to agree to his certain conditions:

1. Rich will continue to budget for his hobby of flying;
2. Gail will live within a budget of fifty dollars per week for groceries and other family necessities
3. Gail will keep her girlish figure
4. Gail will be a submissive wife and obey Rich
5. Gail will continue to work to supplement their needs
6. Rich will build a two-car garage and breezeway as Gail asked for, including a workspace for her home interiors job, and
7. Rich will take Gail on date nights once per month.

As the proposal was written, it felt like a contract rather than a bond of love, but Gail considered what was best for the children, and she was beginning to believe that she could live with this new and improved version of Rich.

She asked Rich whether he would also be willing to help with the chores on weekends, allow her to work if she wanted to—although her working had never been a point of contention—and maybe he could also convert their garage into a dual-use living space.

In her mind, she'd been designing a sunken living room with a bay window and a fireplace in the lower half, with a formal dining room in the upper half.

The challenge excited him. He agreed.

She forgot to ask him whether he could find space in his heart for his two youngest daughters.

Rich planned an extravagant honeymoon for them flying away to California in his Cessna airplane. He asked Carlene and Elsie to accompany them because there was an available back seat. He taught them to read the instrument panel and steer the plane with their feet.

On this occasion of their second honeymoon, Rich and Gail took their two older children to the Grand Canyon, to Disneyland, and to visit his college friend, Brent Landry and his family. Their pastor's family agreed to care for the two younger girls.

When they returned, they brought gifts and stories to Kaida and Melanie, but the damage was done. The two younger girls would never forget or forgive them for being left behind on such a tremendous occasion.

COWS HAVE BELLS BECAUSE THEIR *HORNS* DON'T WORK

Rich became a new man when he and Gail reunited.

He built that dining room and sunken living room for his family out of the old one-car garage complete with a fireplace boasting indigenous stone and a beautiful mantel. Then, he set to work building a two-car garage and breezeway. Elsie climbed up the ladder and helped her father pound roofing nails. Roofing with Dad wasn't like the chore of vacuuming.

The garage was so big, Rich added a storage workroom for Gail's Home Interiors business, because she excelled in this sales position.

Rich took over Sunday breakfasts creating a new tradition of rice pudding with raisins, a dish everyone loved. He marveled at the dishwasher in the house and showed the children the best way to load the silverware so that the knives didn't cut through the cutlery basket. He also expected the plates and bowls to be stacked in line with the others, not spread out willy-nilly.

He taught the girls to scrub the pots and pans, and when they couldn't manage to scrub them clean, he would go at them until they shone spotless.

Little Kaida, now eight years old, saw nothing very important about loading the dishwasher as her father taught her. Elsie would correct her sister's mistakes and lecture her on her daddy's behalf when he wasn't around, but Kaida laughed and regularly left her older sister to her own devices.

It didn't escape Rich's notice that Kaida took after her mother with a mind of her own. The muscle in his jaw pulsed whenever he watched his carefree youngest doing most anything.

At an early age, the one thing they most obviously had in common was Kaida's desire to play the violin. Rich also loved the violin. So, when Kaida needed to rent a violin for orchestra class, her daddy went with her and learned about tone, strings, and care for the instrument. He didn't like to hear her screeching to reach the notes, but he understood that this was part of the making of a musician. He often tried to fiddle with the instrument himself now that he knew how to read notes.

Elsie shared her dad's longtime devotion to the romantic tunes of the forties, fifties, sixties and even the seventies' love songs of the folk-rock variety, which he kept the living room stereo tuned to. But Elsie struggled in her piano lessons to reach proficiency.

Kaida, on the other hand, could pick up any piece of music and master it within a few hours. She had more giftedness for mechanics and finger dexterity required of a musician than Elsie had. Nevertheless, Rich continued to resist his youngest daughter and her natural talents for the classics. He favored teaching Elsie how to listen to the harmony line in the music, and how to sound out where the alto line went in the chord progressions.

Rather than listening to Kaida practice her violin, Rich preferred picking up Carlene from the shopping mall.

Rather than listening to Kaida's stories or picking up Kaida and Melanie from school events, Rich preferred Elsie's fascination with his men's quartet. Toting her along to practices felt joyful. Hand in hand, Elsie would skip along next to her long-legged, handsome father, going wherever he happened to take her. He often took her to Dairy Queen after her school concerts where the two of them would celebrate with a banana split or a fudgy peanut parfait.

Elsie persisted in her piano lessons, even though the songs assigned to her weren't interesting to her. Playing scales was the most boring thing in life she could imagine. Mom and Dad both assured her that musical scales and piano lessons were fundamental to all music.

The more that Rich avoided Kaida—pigeon-holing her as her mother's sprite—the more Kaida pined and schemed to gain his attention. Rich's youngest was evermore as clever as her father, and just as much a rascal. People would put Kaida's name before Melanie's when they referenced the younger sisters because she was the dominant child of the two. It disturbed Rich that he had met his match in his own child, but he usually kept his wrath in check.

Elsie began picking up neighborhood babysitting. While collecting her pay from her next-door neighbor, the lady asked, "Do you think your father is a nice man?"

Elsie quickly nodded and asked the lady what she meant. The lady said, "Your father was sitting at the kitchen table when our cat jumped up on it. I was stunned when he grabbed our cat and threw him across the room! I was so shocked. It just made me wonder if he loses his temper with you girls like that."

"Oh, I've never seen him get angry. Not with me anyway."

"Well, I guess a man can like some and be enflamed by others."

Disturbed by this exchange, Elsie walked home lost in the tension between loyalty to her dad and encountering a new truth about his temper.

EXPECT THINGS TO GET *BEDDER*

Rich began working at another family's home, building their basement as a work of charity.

"Where's the money coming from?" Gail questioned.

"Don't you worry about that," Rich answered.

Gail's heart twitched like a frightened rabbit, readying to leap. "But, you're making our family live on fifty dollars a week, Richard, even at Christmas, and here you've found the money to build an entire basement for charity work?

Rich's charity work of building laundry rooms, installing bathroom cabinets, and building other items for families in the church, put him in good standing with their friends.

The year that Rich was commissioned by the church board to frame in the basement level of their church building, Elsie went along to watch the miraculous interior develop and to learn to pound nails into studs. Her goal was to pound them only three times each, the way her dad did.

Eventually, she got the hang of pounding nails, but she was nowhere as rhythmically accurate as her father. "You're a showoff, Dad!"

"You think so?" He laughed.

They hung the insulation between the sixteen-inch spaced studs together, and then hung the drywall after Rich installed the electrical wiring and patched in the boxes.

Elsie believed her father to be the most talented man on earth. He could do no wrong.

She didn't know that her opinion did not align with the pastor's.

The pastor, however, kept an eye on Rich's behavior since the day his wife began explaining the dynamics in Rich and Gail's household. Gail had mentioned her worry that Rich was reverting to his old ways of avoiding her, not talking with her about family needs or budgets, and spending his money however he wanted.

Barbi confided in her husband, "Gail says she needs to work because Rich only gives her fifty dollars a week for all the children and the food and clothing. She says she trusts Elsie to babysit and has to trust the Lord to watch over the kids while she's away. She can't afford to be heavy handed with their whereabouts in her situation."

"That doesn't sound right. Look at the expensive work he is doing for so many others in the congregation. Flying lessons are not a cheap hobby, either. He isn't treating his family right."

Barbi and Gail remained close friends, though by comparison, Barbi kept her kids nearer to home and limited their escapades. She also did not work away from home.

The pastor also took flight lessons and was just short of Rich's hours logged in flight. Thinking a flight excursion could be a means of bonding with Rich, who now sang with him in the church men's quartet, the two men agreed to go up together on Rich's next scheduled flight. Rich, for some reason, did not offer or allow the pastor to take control of the Piper airplane. Instead, he kept the pastor as a passenger during the entire flight.

Rich began dozing during the half hour sermons at Far Horizons Baptist Church. Gail would nudge him awake whenever she heard his breathing become heavy. She made excuses for him, saying he was so tired from being overworked and his new asthma medication, but she wondered whether her husband had any desire to learn and grow spiritually.

When he responded to an invitation to teach Sunday school, Gail thought better of him.

Rich took on the role of teaching fifth grade boys and girls, the class Elsie was in. She was eager to learn from her dad, but she easily became disappointed at his humorless manner. She still adored him but decided that perfection didn't have to include teaching skills.

WE LIKE VOLCANOS BECAUSE THEY'RE SO *LAVABLE*

Looking much older than her age at the end of seventh grade, Carlene would tote her radio on her shoulder, saunter down the avenue in her hip huggers, and flirt with the workmen and older boys slamming out the steel school doors after school sports. A never-broke mustang, she would sass her mother from very early on.

One morning, Carlene's sarcasm and disrespect peaked. Gail shouted at her daughter, "You, young lady, are out of control!" Carlene, in turn, pushed her mother into the open dishwasher. Gail grabbed Carlene's arm to steady herself, then slapped Carlene's face bringing the girl to the floor with her.

Carlene screamed for her dad, then sat on her mom which is what Elsie saw when she came running from her basement room. Her mother managed to turn Carlene over on the kitchen floor. There she was, screaming and hitting Carlene's mouth with a wet dishrag until Rich also came and pulled her off, separating the two.

Only a week before, Elsie had come home from school to see Carlene eating a celery stick and a pickle while she was talking with a friend on the phone. Elsie began pestering her to get off the phone so that she could call a friend, just quickly see if she could ride bikes.

When Carlene refused to acknowledge her presence, Elsie reached up like she would take the phone from her sister's hand. Carlene twisted and glared at her. "Bug off!"

"I need to call Franny!—Your ten minutes are up!—Get off the phone!"

Carlene grabbed the phone and receiver but ended up pulling the whole phone off the wall.

When Elsie and Melanie began to laugh, Carlene took a knife to their faces and threatened them. Of course, they told their parents what happened.

Carlene was grounded for a week, meaning there would be no after school walks, no church youth group events, or any other activities for her with friends.

That night, Carlene scooted her bed under her basement bedroom window, opened the slider, and managed to climb out. The police were called, and when they found her, she was making out with a boy on the lawn of the junior high school inside the construction fence, listening to "The Loco-Motion" by Grand Funk Railroad on her radio.

The police returned her to her family, but there was no change of heart. She remained cold and aloof toward all of them. While grounded in her bedroom, she played Joni Mitchell, Harry Chapin, Elton John, Carole King, and Helen Reddy to comfort herself. She was warned if she played the music too loud, she'd be grounded another week.

Gail researched her options to help rebellious children. In doing so, she discovered there was a Christian girl's school near the Gulf Coast where Carlene could go. It was similar to a boarding school. She spoke with Rich about it.

The next time Carlene acted out, Rich took a couple of days of vacation time, put Carlene and two suitcases into the car and drove her to boarding school. She was angry and talked about her mother's evils toward the family trying to change her daddy's mind. When the ten-foot fence surrounding the boarding school's compound came into view, she became enraged. The shock was complete when she noticed that none of the girls were wearing miniskirts or looked hip. A sullen resignation took hold.

Frizzy haired, she sat with clenched fists and folded arms, feeling unbelievably betrayed by her beloved daddy. There were bars on the windows and a surveillance system around the compound. She was trapped. In the office, her dad signed contracts and paid for the first month's rent.

"Now, you stay here a month, young lady, and see if you can enjoy the experience. If you get a good report and want to come home after that, I'll come get you. If not, then you'll stay for the full year." She wept in terror and begged her father not to leave her, but she knew she'd burned all her bridges, and she knew she needed help. She resigned herself to give it a try.

When the first phone call home was provided to her, Carlene sounded like she'd found something to hold onto. The school's music program embraced her. She'd made a best friend. She was memorizing all kinds of scriptures, learning to cook, and excelling in the eighth-grade coursework. She told her parents she loved them and thanked them for bringing her to the school. Then, she asked if she could stay the remainder of the school year. Rich and Gail agreed. They were thriving on the peace and happiness of being together again, and not having a back-talking teenager to contend with.

I WORRIED THE BALL WAS GETTING BIGGER, THEN IT HIT ME

Throughout fifth and sixth grades, in Northglenn, Colorado, Elsie became an avid reader. In 1971, She read C.S. Lewis' *Mere Christianity*. She read *The Hobbit* from J.R.R. Tolkien's *Lord of the Rings* series. In 1972, she read the *Screwtape Letters*, Hannah Hurnard's *Hinds Feet in High Places*, and John Bunyan's *The Pilgrim's Progress*. She also read a few Harlequin Romances.

One of the most interesting people to her in church was a woman who sang in the choir behind her in the men's section, a woman with a sultry tenor voice, a woman who said she made her living writing novels. Elsie begged her to tell her the book titles and longed to read one. The woman's pretty smile cocked to the side as she said, "Your parents wouldn't appreciate me if I did that. These are not the kinds of books a girl like you would like."

As the sun streamed through the one small, dirty window of her basement bedroom, while Elsie lay on her bed thinking over what had happened in her family, she realized she was clenching her fists. Why was she clenching her fists? She had no answer for it, but she opened her hands and placed them on her stomach, trying to relax.

In sixth grade, Elsie bonded with a female youth leader who reached out to her on a regular basis, listened, asked meaningful questions, and prayed for her and her family. The youth leader also discovered a Christian camp in the mountains for Elsie to attend. Rich and Gail sent her and Melanie to a week of summer camp. Kaida was too young, but the following year, she could go if the girls liked it.

Kaida argued that she was smarter than Melanie and got better grades and it wasn't fair that she kept getting left out of all the fun.

Gail said she'd make it up to her and she did. While her other daughters were gone, Gail instilled the confidence of a goddess into her youngest, telling her how smart she was, how much talent she had compared to the others, and how athletic she was. She took her shopping for books and clothes and then out to eat. She allowed her to go to the skating rink and then set up a movie date with her dad.

Visiting a church friend at their farm after camp, Melanie became enthralled with a Shetland pony. When her mother told her to come along inside to play with the others, she said she just wanted to stay outside and watch the pony.

The pony bit her. Then, it kicked her in the head. From inside, they heard her scream, and scream again. The adults went out to find her crying, and her head bloodied. The family cut their visit short because the next stop was the Emergency Room. Yet when Melanie attended camp, she signed up for all the opportunities to learn about horses and to constantly be with the horses on trail rides, on hayrides, grooming and training horses, and at the end of the week rodeo, she endorsed camp whole-heartedly to the rest of her family.

A sad thing about summer camp is that there are at least ten months between the week-long summer camps. A lot can happen in those ten months.

That fall, when the family was all together at dinner, Melanie mentioned, "When I grow up, I want to be a truck driver." She kept talking about big rigs she'd seen and what a truck driver could see and do. To change the subject, her mom asked, "What else are you interested in, Melanie?"

Melanie sat on her hands. "I want to play the drums."

This subject seemed no better. "Why the drums?"

"I don't know. I just like them." Her face lit up.

To imagine her buttercup of a girl at the drums or sitting in a rig at the truck stop, astounded Gail. No one understood where Melanie's ideas came from that evening. She'd never mentioned them. She'd never shown an interest in rock music or even the school band. They didn't encourage her.

Gail shook her head and sipped her Kool-Aid. Questions seemed pointless.

When Melanie spoke to her dad, he said, "Girls don't itch to do boy things, Melanie." Everyone felt relieved that he'd been the one to say it. "Howdy, on my salary, I'm sorry to disappoint you, but I couldn't afford a set of drums, iff'n I wanted to." Rich's Oklahoma accent always slid into words of irritation.

"Whose turn is it to clear the table?" Gail asked.

Rinsing the dishes, Elsie prayed for a sense of humor to lighten the atmosphere at home.

With her dad back home, Elsie began to overcome her secret compulsive counting and clenching teeth through a similarly secret four-fold approach. It was just something she did, and she didn't like doing it, so she took a strident look at it. Elsie's Secret Four-Fold Approach: a) She recognized it was an odd and imprisoning behavior and she wanted to be free; b) she prayed about it in her distress; c) she realized that breaking up a thing she liked could be needed for a variety of reasons, i.e. concrete walkways need stress lines to maintain quality and mile markers and traffic signs are important cues for travelers; and d) she turned it off, distracted herself, and turned away whenever she realized she was doing it.

A friend of the family invited the three kids over to play tetherball. The game grew more and more competitive until finally, the pole set in concrete weighed down by the tethered ball fell on Melanie's head.

After her concussion that year and the next, Melanie struggled with her teacher at school. Although she was given Gail's full support academically, she failed to thrive.

Otherwise, the winged Finch children enjoyed many happy hours at the neighbors' houses, around their dinner tables, up in a fort, on the hill standing with a blanket in the wind learning to sail and jumping off swings. The baseball field, planted in the Howard's backyard, provided for many summer youth activities.

I'D RUN THE WORLD OVER AND WIN THE LION'S TROPHY IF I DIDN'T HAVE A TEAM OF *CHEETAHS* AFTER ME

Being the oldest child left at home that year, Elsie was appointed babysitter for her two younger sisters. Kaida and Melanie argued, berating each other continuously, parting like a river at the Continental Divide to flow in opposite directions. If they weren't bickering about closet space, shoes, or clothes, it was about the bikes and friends the one was stealing from the other.

All this wrangling, hitting, pulling hair, hiding things from one another, and challenging each other's statements, was above Elsie's ability to manage. Her little sisters' screams and cat scratching drove her batty.

Since her parents had designated her the chief babysitter while both of them were working far from home, Elsie resorted to becoming a "drill sergeant" in her demands to distract the two.

"Sit down!" She'd put them in different rooms, making them play alone.

One afternoon, she unhooked her dad's belt from her parents' closet and startled them in their room. "Turn over, both of you!" she ordered. When they did, she spanked both of her sisters as if she was a parent, but her nerves only allowed for two swats. She was frightened that she would get into trouble herself, and she really didn't want to hurt them. She just wanted them to shut up.

It worked. An amazing quiet filled the house.

A defining moment occurred when Gail caught Elsie throwing marbles against the wall, teaching her sisters to bet on them for nickels and dimes. Her mother towered over her, warning, "You know, I had an uncle who was addicted to gambling. It might be a genetic thing, I don't know, but I'd watch that, if I were you."

No one was as addicted to the beautiful cat-eyed marbles as Elsie. Her sisters snickered and went outside to play with their friends.

In the sunlit breakfast room, Elsie gathered her glass orbs and stared longingly at the glorious sun-kissed striations in the marbles. If there was a danger in them, it was her attraction to their essence, not the gambling. She hid them in a safe box where she could take them out and look at them whenever she liked. She wished there was a way to glue them together or string them along the window so she could stare at them in sunshine.

When Grandma came to visit next, Elsie interrupted a conversation between her mom and grandma to show them a tap dance she had devised in her sandals. She saw the grins turn to surprise and then to smirks as they watched her perform.

"I want to take dance lessons, Mom!"

Both women barely contained themselves. Her mom said, "Honey, you don't have the legs for dancing. I know you like to, but it isn't the same thing as performing. Why don't you find something else you want to do?"

"Like what?"

"Like playing with the dog or riding your bike? Aren't you writing a story? You can finish that. I saw you had some mermaids you were drawing hidden under your bed. Why don't you go draw something?"

"Mom, I want a guitar. I want to learn some John Denver songs."

"Okay, well, let's wait for Christmas, dear. You never know what will happen."

That year, Elsie made all her gifts for each family member and her friends. Some turned out better than others. Kaida especially loved her small decoupaged treasure chest because Elsie had found pictures and words representing who Kaida was and what she loved. Kaida adored her sister Elsie, deeply, for seeing her and praising her this way. For many years, she would bring out that little chest to remind her who she was and why she would never hurt Elsie.

THE POETRY WAS IN THE POET'S *WREST*

> Music, like a mother's kiss,
> a place of bliss in worlds estranged,
> oh, that life could feel that way, every day,
> where even the dissonance is binding and the nest of it,
> belonging.

In Elsie's sixth grade year, Rich led the youth choir at their church. About ten of them sang the songs from camp, new hymns and old, and Rainey's mother played the piano. Since Elsie idolized her father, she wanted to impress him, and what better way to do so than through their shared musical experiences?

Every time a solo was announced, Elsie offered to audition for it. By the fourth audition, and having already been assigned the solo parts, she was brought up short.

Rich stopped the music, asking all the children to sit down. Then he told the story of an egotistical little girl who wanted to have all the attention. "Ya'll, pride comes before a fall. Pride is one of the things that God hates." He went on to say, "Harmonies are what make a choir beautiful. Children who wait their turn to be promoted will go a long way, but those who are itchin' to steal the glory for themselves will be brought down."

His lecture was so recriminating of his daughter, that all the children looked sheepishly from the corners of their eyes at Elsie whose tears began to fall silently. Then Rich said to the choir, "Ya'll are dismissed."

He picked up the sheet music left in the empty seats.

In shame, Elsie headed for home without her normal fatherly escort. Face burning, she sat on her bed in her basement bedroom, trying to think over what she had done wrong, and how it had been misunderstood.

She could see where her passion might have been mistaken for pride, but this was her beloved father. He knew her! He shared this gift and love of singing with her, and he had betrayed her love for him and made a mockery of his own daughter in front of the entire choir.

There was a pair of fingernail scissors laying on her dresser, the same dresser where she had first experienced an answer to prayer. She took up the scissors and started cutting her wrist. She wanted her dad to find her bloody and lifeless. That would be his reward for his hateful treachery. When she began cutting her flesh, she remembered that God had answered another prayer in this very space, and she realized she didn't want her life to end; she only wanted to punish her father. So she stopped cutting and began to cry out to God.

She heard her father come down the stairs and turn on his Peter and Paul folk music, then Art Garfunkel came on. He was searching for a specific song. Then, a knock came on her door.

When she didn't answer, he opened it and came to sit beside her. She hid the scissors under her thigh, but she refused to look at him. In that moment, she hated him as long and wide as the oceans fill the earth.

Then, he began to cry. "I'm so sorry, my dear," he said. "I don't know what came over me. That is not how I feel about you at all. You are very talented, and we both love music. I was wrong."

She continued to stare ahead toward the wall. His apology to her was one thing, but he had humiliated her in a very public way. She was sure her friends had gone home to tell their parents about the drama that had unfolded that evening. Then, her dad said, "I'm going to have to apologize to the entire youth choir next week. I did you wrong, and I'll do that because I never want to hurt you again."

With that full apology, they both began to cry and hug each other. Young Elsie forgave her dad as far reaching as clouds can cover all the sins of the earth.

The next week when the choir gathered, Rich, true to his word, apologized as wholeheartedly to them as he had to his daughter.

He was again her hero.

She wrote a poem.

"Make me humble, Lord, when I've got it all together,
when I'm confident and free, put my confidence in Thee.
In my living, let me find You there, for comfort,
strength and care.

Let me never blast upon them in a confidential air.
For it's when I'm tired and lonely that I need a friend
in Thee,
not an arrogance of spirit born of passion born of me..."

The poem ended with her intent to glorify Jesus, not herself. She bound that poem with some of her song lyrics and other writings into two books for her mom and her dad.

IT ONLY MAKES *CENTS* TO SAVE YOUR DIMES AND QUARTERS

Christmas inspired creative shows of affection. Gail figured out how to buy Elsie a decent beginner's guitar. It was a K-Mart special from the music department, which she paid on for several weeks. She also laid away a pair of boots and coats for each child including clothes, dolls and games. The way she did this was by working at the Jackson's Turkey Farm.

Every year, the holidays called for tons of turkeys to be delivered to restaurants and shopping centers for Thanksgiving and Christmas dinners of, well, almost everyone in America. When a local family discovered how they could capitalize on the season, Gail learned to pluck turkeys for six weeks prior to Christmas morning so that she could get whatever each of her girls yearned for.

Elsie filled the remaining winter months playing her guitar at every waking moment, trying out new picking strategies, plucking rhythms, and strumming techniques. She wrote songs and learned cover tunes. She and her friend, Rainey, sang together in harmony as did her friend up the block, Debbie.

That Easter, a choir came to perform at the church and Gail's brush pulled through the knots in Elsie's curly hair, made a part, and braided her locks in style to attend. When the agony ended, all that remained was dressing and helping to dress her sisters in their K-Mart special Easter finery.

As it turned out, the three girls in the women's trio stayed at Rich and Gail's house in each of the three girls' bedrooms. For the three Finch girls, it was as if they'd each been given their own Easter basket of sugar chicks to pluck, taste, and muse over for later comparisons. One of the college women was also named Elsie and she encouraged the young teenager about her musical hopes. She even agreed to be her pen pal. Elsie took this as a sign. The only thing that interested her was the wisdom she heard from the Bible, usually found at church or camp, and putting it to music.

By the end of Elsie's sixth grade year, she knew she wanted to major in music at the same Bible college the women's trio hailed from.

A TAXING DEDUCTIBLE

The next year, Gail and several of the other moms at her church formed an educational charter of mothers determined to provide core curriculum to their children. A carpool schedule formed to take the children to a new school promising to teach only traditional, basic education and curriculum.

Gail wasn't going to risk what happened so dramatically in Carlene's life to happen to her other daughters at the hands of a public junior high school.

Elsie felt jilted as she yearned for a role in the music program at the public school. She'd attended a couple of holiday concerts there and she'd taken up some lead singing roles already in her elementary choirs, but off to the castle on the hill and into private education she went.

The school, housed partially in an old sandstone castle, smelled musty. The grand staircases creaked, and the boiler knocked and squealed. It was the closest thing to the mission in Pennsylvania she had seen or experienced in Colorado, and she loved it. They offered art, music, reading, and chapel with interesting speakers.

Elsie ran towards her ride after school and realized she was clenching her fists as she ran. She stopped and shook out her hands.

Gail's stress levels never seemed to resolve. She often screamed at her children, ordered them to cook and clean or pick up the house after their homework was finished. She usually came home from work too exhausted to do anything more herself. One day in her tangle of distraught thoughts, she shouted at Elsie from the top of the stairs and then, threw Elsie's guitar down them.

Elsie, shocked and angry, gathered her guitar, opened the case, and screamed back at her mom. She back talked only long enough to hear her mother running down the stairs.

Gail picked up a cushion from the couch and began slinging it at her daughter from one side and then the other. Elsie toppled over and crawled away to her room.

Happiness was still a long way off when Carlene, who had accepted the nickname "Murkie" arrived back in town.

Just in time to join her sisters at the private school on the hill, she came back as a serene picture of the Mona Lisa with languid curls, not frizz. She spoke with a Texan drawl, and she quoted scripture as readily as she said anything else. She sang songs with her sisters and took the younger ones in hand as they walked together as sisters. She was happy to get on the bus with her siblings and join them at their new private school.

She was transformed.

Then, Murkie asked her mother to take her shopping, but it wasn't to K-Mart.

At the sewing store, the newly-minted Murkie spent an hour or more looking through patterns to sew new clothes by. Gail at first believed the patterns she picked were a joke and tried to dissuade her. These were no ordinary patterns.

Murkie's choice in patterns featured long flouncy skirts, frilly aprons, slinky vests, side buttoned bodices and bonnets, and hats with feathers. Whatever fashionistas might see modeled on a Vogue runway or perhaps worn by a rock musician in costume, were within her sights.

She accepted a full, double Vogue challenge to make luxurious, vintage outfits and to wear them with fishnets or hot pantyhose.

While away, the Texas preacher had drilled the girls at his boarding school with sermons decrying the cheap and deplorable garments sold by the fashion industry for one aim only: to turn girls into a sexual commodity. "Sexy is as sexy does," he shouted. Girls didn't need low slung necklines and skimpy skirts. God had created their bodies naturally unique and wonderful.

The more Murkie considered her own sexuality, the more she realized the preacher was right. It was the woman inside the garment, how she moved her body, and how she wore only a bit of mascara and a smear of lip gloss, could spin a man's head around.

She'd been carried away from home wearing miniskirts and hip hugger jeans. Hereafter, she made and wore Vogue costumes no one had ever seen a living teenager wear.

She also instructed everyone who tried to use her given name that she would only answer to Murkie. People were to call her "Murkie," not Carlene. She was a new person.

As aggressively as she flaunted her personality prior to leaving for boarding school, her new projection of individual sensuality excelled it. Elsie, in awe of her sister, discovered a new idol. The idol intimidated everyone with her avant-garde ways and her absolute opinions. She not only turned everyone's heads, but she also returned sweet smiles for their adoration.

Murkie's inclusiveness and welcoming effect were offered with an air at arm's length. After all, it was she who had been sent away from her family and friends for nine months of discipline. Returning to the family held psychological and physiological implications. She presented herself fresh and set aside in her individuality to all who knew of her disenfranchisement.

To save face, she decided to live above the others, untouchable and airtight, never to be vulnerable again.

Murkie took a volunteer job after school at a place called Ridge Home. It was an asylum of sorts and her job was to spend time with the residents, talking about life. The residents intrigued her so that losing one of them from time to time broke her heart.

"You're a little young to be working at a place like this," said a staff member. "What do you like about it?"

"It's better than being home." She said this with a demure smile.

Her beauty, her singing, the swing in her high heeled step, her sewing talent, and her sense of style, alarmed Gail, and shook Rich to his ankles.

While their daughter's tight, curly locks with runaway frizzes had been the talk of her junior high school friends the year before, now her disciplined, silken hair made of nighttime orange juice cans, and lying elegantly over her shoulders and down her back, became the undoing of her competition each day.

A fine crust, as thin as a robin's eggshell, became the coat of protection over this red-blooded teenager. Murkie was now the talking point of all the teachers at the Finchs' private school as well as the cloistered students of her ninth-grade class. Who was this girl? Even the upper classmen took note.

In the fall, the private school's staff organized a Halloween event and invited all the children to a party in the basement. In the mystery of blustery autumn leaves, fun costumes, and bobbing for apples, the children were won over. Private school could be exclusive, but it also held a certain mystique. Murkie stood with her back against the hallway wall, encircled by avid and curious young men.

Youth outings at city wide Youth Corp events opened Elsie up to a new genre of Christian music called "Jesus music." Sometimes Murkie would join in on these events, but often, she was away at work.

Since Elsie stood in as the eldest daughter while Murkie had been away from home, she realized she still had no elder sister to lead the way. She needed her courage to search out her own interests and figure out how to go forward.

Musical dramas offered by The Jeremiah People redirected Elsie's attention by cleverly penned and acted vignettes. These were designed to help teens think through church traditions, comparing them to deeper truths. Then, the harmonies and lyrics of 2nd Chapter of Acts felt like the voice of God breaking mountain cedars. Elsie encountered The Jesus People and Lamb introducing young people to Jews for Jesus, and at camp, everyone was singing the songs "Pass It On" and "For Those Tears I Died" by the traveling minstrels who appeared on the Denver auditorium stage at Youth Corp events.

As winter fell into a deep freeze, Elsie, and all the students at the castle school, her sisters included, learned to ice skate on the pond overlooking the city of Denver during gym hours and recess.

After school, in winter's dusk, beneath the glow of a setting sun streaming through the naked black limbs of surrounding trees, Elsie would sneak a few extra minutes listening to her skates scratching the ice, spinning, singing, and ice-dancing until she was forced to find her seat in the bus going home.

At Christmas, all the Finch girls received new ice skates as requested. For a time, Elsie twirled and jumped gracefully, her imagination chock full of what it could mean to join the Ice Follies, Ice Capades or compete in the Olympics.

A *DEFEETED* MARATHON RUNNER

While the school's rule—applicable to young women by having them kneel to ensure their skirts fell not more than two inches above the floor—could not touch Murkie's costumes or her soul, the boy who moved into Murkie's world did.

On the bus ride home, he joined them. Throwing his coat over the top of Murkie's head, he would use it as a shield to kiss and fondle her delightful form.

The older boy was the son of one of the staff members at the school, so when Murkie and her sisters disembarked the bus, he'd wave to his girlfriend and ride back to school elated, full of imagination. The boy's name was Foreman, and he was determined to marry that girl.

Elsie would race home, fists clenched as she ran, pondering this new liaison of her sister's. Everything about the youthful affair made her feel tense.

Rich and Gail chalked up the attachment to teenage hormones, but when Gail tried to speak with Murkie about "making out on the bus," Murkie smiled sweetly and quoted, "Judge not lest ye be judged."

Soon, both Foreman and Murkie passed their driver's license exams. Foreman courted Murkie by driving her home from the castle in his old Cadillac and taking her to work at the nearby Fashion Bar. What he did while she was earning her wage, no one knew, but he often collected her from work in the evening and deposited her on her doorstep safe and sound.

When summer came, Murkie became even more guarded. She saved money for her marriage to Foreman by working a full-time job at Fashion Bar. She grew into a more acceptable sense of style made in polyester and nylon while working there, but she also augmented her fashion sense by experimenting with Meryl Norman cosmetics from the store next door. The clinician took a liking to Murkie. She listened and talked with her eager new client as she taught her how to use eye pencils, blend eye shadows, and use lip sticks, face masks, and blush.

"My mom never wears anything but lipstick. She can't teach me about makeup," Murkie confided.

To everyone's surprise, often their shock, Murkie began to show up to school, work, church, and other events, with a heavily made-up face created to imitate a china doll.

At the beginning of eighth grade, Elsie realized her tenth-grade older sister lived in a world so different to her own, there was no point in shadowing her. Elsie had her own interests. Right now, those interests didn't include any risk of a serious boyfriend. She just wasn't ready.

Instead, Elsie asked the pianist at the church, Rainey's mom, to help direct a children's cantata. She agreed. Elsie called all the little children up to sixth grade and had them audition for roles in a musical called *A Boy and His Fish*, a story about Jesus multiplying food for the multitude of people who followed Him, making enough food for them all from one little boy's seaside lunch.

The play was fun, and the children all seemed to enjoy acting and singing their parts. Walking home from the children's music practices in the autumn air felt invigorating. Putting on the play was one of the most joyful experiences she remembered. The feeling was similar to how riding her bike and standing on the back fender, steering it by balance alone, had felt in Pennsylvania. Elsie tasted musical success, enjoyed the children, and loved leading their performance.

She knuckled down to learn her bar chords on the guitar, rhythms, and finger picking. She wrote her own songs every week, but she also learned to play "The Rose" the way Bette Midler performed it, "Grandma's Feather Bed," "Annie's Song," by John Denver, and Gordon Lightfoot's "If You Could Read My Mind." Musical emotions began to entangle her teen soul.

YOU HAVE *SUITE* DREAMS WHEN YOU STAY IN A HOSTEL

Two years after Rich and Gail's second honeymoon, a band snapped across the easy way things were rolling.

Affections abruptly changed.

For unknown reasons to Gail, Rich came home late one night as mad as a cut snake.

She was sitting on the bed looking over a painting. It was working out that a mother-daughter art class was perfect for creating bonding time with Elsie. She held it up to show it to Rich, but he knocked it out of her hand and proceeded to violate her. Gail had endured countless offenses at the hands of her husband, but this was rape. Despite her resolve to be "the submissive wife," this breach was unforgiveable.

Nothing was said of that night, though Rich's rage was satiated.

His wife, however, suspended any effort to find sympathy for Rich ever again. Though he managed to put out of his mind what he'd done, Rich would pay for that betrayal and abuse.

The truest thing about reconciliation, both Rich and Gail learned, is that it requires a fundamental trust to forgive, and a willing, tender heart.

Rich failed to understand why this reality mattered. He had used up his dedicated residual from the perfunctory marital trust fund.

Murkie lasted two years at the private school working toward a June wedding, a date she and Foreman had set. Foreman's parents were not only staff at the private school, but his father was a traveling preacher. Foreman had grown up more religious than Murkie, so when his parents expressed some concern about him marrying "a girl who looked like a prostitute," their opinions became just another wedge for Foreman and Murkie to dislodge.

She explained the china doll look to Foreman's mother and tried to cook for his father twice. Nothing she did changed their impressions of her. She really felt unwelcome in their home.

Cookbooks began to pile up in Murkie's bedroom, as well as kitchen design books, and books on marriage, as though a uniquely good marriage could be dictated through the pages of someone's platform of fame.

As she processed these books, she came out of her shell with Gail long enough to explain in detail everything her mom was doing wrong. In the kitchen, she needed a prep area, a storage area, a pasta making area, a sanitary meat prepping area, and a place to display bone china.

From her marriage books, Murkie instructed her mother how to be more submissive, and how to wear saran wrap to greet her husband with exciting sexual encounters. When Gail tried to engage Murkie in conversations about real life, Murkie smirked or rolled her eyes. She was having none of her mother's story.

She had never become especially fond of her mother, and just to make sure her mother understood, she kept Gail's contributions to her wedding at bay. She made comments like, "I don't think so," "That isn't my style," "Not cool, Mom," and "I've changed my style, haven't you noticed?"

Gail contributed to her eldest daughter's wedding by buying her own mother-of-the-bride outfit and sitting in the front row. Though Rich took pages of minute notes, he basically footed the bill and sat next to his wife during the wedding. Nothing more was required of the Finches.

When Murkie married Foreman, she was just the age of emancipation, yet lacking a senior year of high school. Who needed it?

She'd learned there was a GED test she could take instead of completing high school, and she intended to take it.

Murkie threw away all her old underwear, earrings, and necklaces, and started her marriage like a virgin rose ready to bloom in spring.

At seventeen, Murkie found a new job selling furniture and became a highly successful saleswoman. Who needed college with a talented handyman and a strangely beautiful and industrious young woman working together? Because she could easily support herself, Murkie skipped her last year of high school and sold furniture full time. No one knew who stole whom away, or who rescued whom. It was a mutually agreeable future the young lovers entered, even as they crossed the threshold to adulthood.

Foreman worked at the local college for a year before they moved to Lake Charles Louisiana, where he found work at a refrigeration plant, and took the training courses necessary to earn his certification. This bulked up his career with a little plumbing and a little electrical information tucked into his work belt, along with theories of refrigeration.

Soon after nineteen-year-old Foreman and eighteen-year-old Murkie began attending county auctions, they bought an old farmhouse being auctioned from the back of a moving trailer. They had it moved to a plot of land outside of Lake Charles. They installed the house on top of a stone foundation. The height off the ground served to protect them from potential floods.

Like clockwork, the young couple then set up their own home interior design business, using their new home address as the base of operations.

Murkie decided when she started selling jobs for Foreman in their remodeling business, that her given name would better serve her for interior décor. "Murkie" presented a problem, so back she went to the name on her birth certificate.

She was able to find many customers by winning a booth space in a flea market, and because she worked in a flea market, she also became an avid bargain hunter like her mother.

Her china doll makeup made her presence searchable and recognizable, gathering customers with awe, while Foreman's talent and work ethic installed her designs for them to a high standard. Carlene did the books. They proved to be a good team.

Since Foreman was a meat and potatoes boy, he failed to express thanks, interest, or appreciation for the gourmet meals his bride concocted from her stash of cookbooks. The newly married woman couldn't have been more surprised, often greatly offended, by her husband's disinterest in her own attention to detail or hard work in their sweaty Louisiana kitchen.

Immediately, the wife absolutely stopped cooking.

Foreman, in order to fill his belly with anything more than prepackaged snacks, was forced to take his new wife out to dinner every evening or learn how to cook for himself.

While Carlene bought unique items to furnish her own home, she also thought of her family members. She bought what everyone thought were extravagant gifts for Christmas such as blanket racks, cuckoo clocks, gems, and jewelry. She was also never short of decorating advice. She stepped into the big sister nurturing role as best she could from Louisiana.

REPLACEMENT THERAPY, PSYCHOLOGY FOR KIDS OUT OF ALIGNMENT

Back home, things were getting dicier by the day. Rich's asthma became worse. He kept notes of especially poor allergy days, and the days when he felt exceptionally well. His chronic self-absorption had soared to new levels of self-protection and outright narcissism.

His attitude toward his remaining three girls drilled down to surliness for the youngest, obtuse dismissiveness toward Melanie, and careful attention to Elsie's needs.

One wretched night when Kaida snuck home after dark, Elsie heard her father yelping, "You're fixin' for the whooping of your life, little girl! One whoop for every one of the seven hours you stayed away from home without letting us know your whereabouts!" She rushed to the kitchen in time to see her dad pulling Kaida out from under the dining room table, carrying her wiggling and kicking like a cougar to the bedroom. "And, one more for running!" She heard him laying on the belt leather.

Having witnessed the horrible scuffle, Elsie wept outside the door, crying, "Dad! Stop! Dad! Please stop."

Illogically, Rich relaxed around Elsie, trusting his emotional safety to her. He continued to share his music and talk about the folk groups with Elsie. He talked about singing at the church, her own youth group experiences, and music. He held her hand going to the church on the corner, and back, and he took her out to celebrate with ice cream after her concerts. While Elsie basked in her dad's favoritism, she also felt sorry for her sisters. It was awkward when they expressed their frustrations from his neglect and compared their experiences to hers.

After a year or so, Elsie's adopted kitten became almost feral, because of never being allowed to live in the house. She would feed and water the cat, but she became wild and roamed the neighborhood. One night after Rich came in from work, he asked Elsie to follow him outside. They sat on the back stairs.

"Elsie, I saw your cat running across the road this morning when I left for work, and a car hit it. It ran into the neighbor's bushes over there, and tonight, when I went to find it, I could see it had died in the bushes. I'm so sorry. There was nothing I could do."

"Where is it?"

"Um, I had to bury it, honey. You wouldn't want to see it."

Elsie wept and let her dad hug her. This was the third pet she'd had that had died in these few years. Somehow, she didn't believe his story. Had he been the one to run it over?

"Do you think you'd like another kitty?"

She didn't want to risk getting another one. "I'll be headed out to college in a couple of years. Who would take care of it then?"

Rich breathed a sigh of relief.

Meanwhile, on his weekends, Richard acted out the role of hero for those church attendees needing remodeling projects. Rich responded well to being seen as everyone's champion, but he continued to have difficulty maintaining a family man's everyday honor.

All the girls loved different aspects of camp. Now, Elsie was old enough to be a counselor on camp staff.

At the conclusion of Camp Week, the bus dropped off all the campers at the designated spot for their parents to come and collect their offspring. When Elsie had worked all summer, she arranged for her mom to pick her up from the typical bus stop. As the camp bus rolled into the distance, Gail was still nowhere to be seen. Elsie realized she'd simply been forgotten. Her mother could manage her job and her sisters just fine without her. It was a landmark feeling, signifying what she meant to her mother—that she could forget her daughter for hours. Just before dinner time, Elsie's phone message came to Gail's attention. Only then did Gail realize she was missing someone.

Into the car, she raced past the K-Mart, over the railroad tracks, past the Jolly Rancher Candy Factory, and into the church parking lot to collect her isolated daughter.

"What am I, Mom, a wallflower so that you can forget me?"

"No, honey, no. It's just that there is so much drama going on with the girls' school and sports and everyone else, that I just forgot. Don't be so sensitive."

Elsie became incensed. If her mother had just said, "I'm sorry. Please forgive me," she would have, but those were not the words that came out. Nor did the words her mother chose bandage the ever-present consternation at home now topped by the odd feeling of being a thing to be managed.

That year, Elsie learned to drive. With her wheels spinning, she was gone at Youth Corp events or camp as often as possible.

She also drove herself to voice lessons. On the way to her classical pedagogy, she'd play the radio. The thing that most caught her interest was a new Christian rock station in town playing Petra, Silverwind, Bryan Duncan and Karen Lafferty. None of these voices figured in the sounds she was being told to practice vocally.

She kept her conflicted observations to herself because her friends in musical theater listened to James Taylor, Styx, John Denver, The Doobie Brothers, Kansas, the Eagles, and Foreigner while at the same time, getting their voices trained by the same teacher, or one like her, for the school musicals. Would the college she had applied to be teaching this kind of music?

Two ministries had been pivotal to her teenage life. Youth Corp's campus life clubs with their youth directors and Bible study groups had nurtured her everyday application of faith and kept her challenged to help her family and school friends as best she could.

The camp directors, Robert and Pim Kordios, became secondary parents to her. While camp employed her on a volunteer basis, it provided her with the unseen and rich benefits of deep friendships and her mentors cultivated a heart for service.

She would sit and listen to new Christian albums with their family, and eat home-baked desserts. When she worked on weekends, they would occasionally take her to churches where Robert Kordios spoke, and she would offer special music with her guitar. On the way to wherever they were headed, Pim, in the front seat, would read Luis L'amour books aloud to Robert. It felt ideal.

SEWING FINE GARMENTS REQUIRES A *SEEMLY* RIPPER

During Elsie's high school counseling session, she found she could double up the courses required to graduate a year early, so she signed up for what was needed.

Realizing how fast time flies, Gail, in her spare time, got busy cutting and sewing garments, special garments for Elsie. She wanted to send her daughter off to graduation parties and then off to college in style. No one in her family had ever gone to college. She felt proud of Elsie and wanted to celebrate her. To this end, she'd purchased a beautiful, muted plaid to fashion into a dress suit for Elsie. She tucked and pleated not only the skirt, but also parts of the jacket. It turned out tailored and handsome, a classic outfit for her idea of traveling or for classes in a private college.

When Elsie laid eyes on the formal suit tailored just for her, for the woman she was becoming, she felt a love emanating from her mother's arms and hands, a love she'd longed for her whole life. Her mother's hunched back leaning over the sewing machine in half light, and the dedicated furrowed brow spoke to her of sacrificial love. Her mother had been thinking, even planning for her! When she curled her hair, and tried on the outfit, she asked her mom, "Am I beautiful? I feel beautiful."

"You are, honey. You are very beautiful."

And she was.

Gail's eyes misted over not only for her success, but also for the memories of how her own mother had tried to sew her nice clothing as she was growing up. Of the girls, Elsie resembled Gail the most, and the image in the mirror took her aback.

The next outfit Gail tackled, was a formal party dress. Elsie's dark dancing curls would look gorgeous lying on the shoulders of this bright yellow silk. Yellow was the color for the season, for those who could wear it, and Elsie would surely pull it off. Gail prepped the tiny pleats for the bodice and backed the pleats with stays. The trim along the neckline, the tailored quarter moon cap sleeves, and the elegant bow hanging down the back all added to the garment's exquisite elegance.

Elsie shied away from the lemon, but the material and splendid form of this dress had to be tried on. It became her exactly as her mother imagined. When graduation finally arrived, it mattered little what the other girls wore. Elsie felt the best dressed gal among them, and certainly the most loved. It was a feeling that bolstered, and eventually, carried her through her first two difficult years of college.

During the work week, assigned to the project of computerizing the entire Front Range emergency energy system, Rich spoke the language of high-tech robots.

A black board in a darkened room covered an entire wall which modeled the Front Range electrical grid. It showed which geographical areas would be affected during an emergency such as a flood, blizzard or tornado. This was done by lighting up each block affected as he installed rolling blackout programs and computer designs to help first responders pinpoint emergency areas needing attention. This extensive boardroom was backed up by a room full of wall-to-wall computer towers. Rich excelled in computer programs.

Elsie saw all her father's successes firsthand that year because she took every possible opportunity to hang with her dad.

The thing that disturbed her about conversations with her father was his many references to the evils of the world. He would often say, "This ol' world is headed for hell in a handbasket," "The Lord is coming soon," and "The evils of the age are a sign of the times." Yet, Elsie couldn't agree with all of Rich's slogans. She hoped the best for her friends, her family, and especially for her own future. Maybe Dad knew certain details about the world that he protected her from.

The main reason she could hang out with her dad and have lunches with him downtown, was that her mom worked long hours to finance Elsie's orthodontic braces. The younger sisters needed glasses, but Elsie's teeth were crooked.

Gail aimed to make all her daughters as flawless as possible. After Gail found an elderly orthodontist just a few blocks away from where Rich worked in Denver, the couple worked together to bring Elsie's ill-fitting teeth into alignment. If Gail couldn't take her to her orthodontist appointments or pick her up, Rich could. He would hold Elsie's hand walking through the streets of Denver feeling like they were on a date.

WHY DO YOU BRING ME TO THE VALLEY IF NOT TO *VALLEY DATE* ME?

One night, several musical couples and friends of Rich and Gail's came to have a choir sectional practice in the Finchs' basement level where Rich had built a family room winged by Carlene's old bedroom and Elsie's bedroom. He felt confident singing, standing in the middle of his own handiwork. This was home. He pointed out passages in the music for the baritones to work on and mentioned where he noticed the sopranos squealed in the high notes.

Gail served cool drinks, coffee, hot chocolate, and warm brownies for dessert. Then, she sat in one of the chairs in the practice circle and began joking with the singers. "Be careful singing the Hallelujah chorus when you're drinking hot chocolate. It may be too hot to Handel."

The pastor laughed. "We shouldn't be eating these warm brownies either. Doctors are saying America has millions of overweight people, but I think they have only reported round figures."

The practice halted, and soon, there was one pun flying after another until everyone rollicked in laughter. A tenor said, "We need help solving this discordant harmony here, Gail. Can you tell us how much treble we're in?"

"I don't know. It isn't my aria of expertise. I'm only here because I heard you were singing an opera, but where's the soap?" Gail kept up with the men in her clever comebacks and one-upmanship. Rich, completely surprised by his wife's social intelligence, picked up the paper plates and cups and hid upstairs in the kitchen, wondering about this woman whom he'd systematically ignored. He hadn't really sized her up lately, and his mistake overtook him.

What especially irked him was their ever-serious pastor shone in the fun himself to the extent that he and Gail one upped each other as the quickest punsters of the evening.

As he came down the stairs to corral the choir practice into focus, he heard Gail say, "One of my girls plays her piano lessons religiously. The other one has a different rendition. She keeps banging her head on the keys. She's learning to play the new way, by ear."

"That's enough of a coffee break, musicians," he said. "We need to get through the B section tonight."

Everyone groaned but agreed. Somehow, after all the laughter, the musical issues ironed themselves out more quickly than expected.

Still avoiding a real conversation with the pastor about the things eating at him, Rich's motto became live and let live concerning the pastor who would have looked after his parishioner's soul, had he been given the opportunity.

Rich watched for the man to have a misstep, since he was the object of worship for so many. He knew that Pastor Howard kept studying his theology and had recently begun to offend some of the church members. Rich felt a secret glee when the pastor's change in end-times doctrine challenged the Board of Directors to act.

There soon came a time when a trustee of the church moved during a business meeting for a members' vote on whether to let their pastor go. The vote was practically split.

Secretly self-righteous people, including Rich, who didn't want to be introduced to things they disagreed with, felt Pastor Howard should leave the church. They managed, narrowly, to vote him out.

The shamed pastor realized very soon after being ousted that houses in the Denver area had increased in price so much that he could no longer afford to buy into the market. Their many years of service at the Baptist church and living in the church parsonage had in turn left him without a job and profoundly homeless.

The church body could not find a better, kinder pastor, and one day the building was sold.

To many, it felt like divine judgement struck those congregational members judging the man who had spent the better part of his life teaching and pastoring the community. Others shrugged off the crumbled church, attributing its demise to economic anomalies. Why chalk it up to anything in particular?

There were plenty of Baptist churches in the Denver area to slip into.

ANYONE WHO IS RICH IN THIS WORLD BUT NOT GENEROUS TOWARDS GOD COUNTS SHORTCHANGE

Just when Rich felt he'd successfully rid himself of his nemesis, Gail effectively removed him from the playing field.

This is how it happened.

On the evening news, Kaida and Gail saw a report detailing the problem of Denver's growth in the transportation industry causing a vast brown cloud of pollution. According to the pilot and cameraman shooting the cloud, viewers could see the wind and weather fronts keeping the poisonous air pinned in the northern part of the Front Range.

Gail pointed out the amazing image of the brown cloud cover to Kaida. "I see that everyday driving home," she said, processing her thoughts. "I'm beginning to understand that this isn't good for you or your dad, or me either! I've been getting allergies when I never had them before."

Gail tried to talk with Rich to explain that maybe they should move their family down to a safer, southern suburb of Denver for his ailing health, her own new allergy problems, and Elsie's asthma.

He just shrugged. "Elsie's fixin' to go off to college next year. She'll have to breathe all that Chicago air anyway."

Gail also researched school systems to discover an area with the highest rated school to serve her two youngest children—providing they could buy into the area. The move wouldn't affect Elsie's life so much, but perhaps Gail could save the younger two from allergies and asthma. Who knew what other lung diseases threatened the Finch family's health.

"Gail, I'm not really interested in moving south. Look what we've built here together! It's a corner lot. It has quadrupled in value." Rich tried to put the move on hold.

Yet in the Finchs' reality-sized Monopoly game, Richard's game token had lost value due to previous decisions made poorly. Gail's own game piece easily overtook and surpassed him moving steadily around the board. When Rich and Gail sat in their individual corners and looked over their real estate and personal assets, she was moving on, while Rich was stuck in the center of the board behind bars.

Rich only realized his devalued position when he jotted down his grievances with Gail in his pocket notebook:

- He barely spoke to her anymore only because she refused to submit to him as the Bible instructed.
- He had encouraged Gail to fend for herself by getting a job and she'd become a savvy sales and businesswoman who could scrimp and save her pennies much better than he ever could. She hardly needed him.
- Thankfully, she hadn't become an invalid after all, but now Gail was more daring and beautiful than ever.
- In her maturity, Gail frightened him by her creativity, with a new confidence and knowledge.

- He faced asthma causing him to lose his clarity of voice
- He also developed a vision problem, a black hole, that caused him to lose his pilot's license.
- He hadn't taken his wife out on a real date in years. His favorite haunt, the restaurant along the airport runway, had burned.
- He regretfully no longer used his prized camera to capture the family's best moments.
- He'd put all his effort and money into renovating this house, and while they'd made a good design team years ago, she wanted him to turn his back on it and move the family away.
- Though he'd managed to redeem himself in the eyes of the folks at their church, he'd never found a way to discredit his wife for her sins or get back at her for humiliating him.

Elsie, still very involved with camp, traveled over snowy mountain passes every weekend, even in winter and spring, to work away from home at family camps or science lab, every men's retreat or mother-daughter event. She went to the mountain to work in the kitchen and play janitor. She'd come home in time for school with her imagination pumped. What did the Lord have in store?

What awaited at dinner upon her arrival one night was far from what she imagined. Her mother declared her intent to purchase a new home far away from the family digs. She had learned the most favorable neighborhoods were situated an hour from the neighborhood the children had grown up in, from Elsie's high school friends, from their church! The sullen resignation on her father's face clearly displayed his own spin on the move.

She went to talk with him privately.

"I've been diagnosed with a hole in my eyesight and can no longer fly my airplane," he said. "All my labor on this home is being discarded. Look around! The sunken living room, the dining room, the renovated basement, the breezeway, and garage, all my work on the church basement renovation, your mother has tossed it all aside. She won't listen to me."

Elsie stood silently and let him hug her. She had no comfort to offer.

"As for your mother, 'Fool me once, it's on you, fool me twice, it's on me,' as they say."

He turned inward to lick his wounds, as her mother searched for houses outside of the city's smog, and the old absenteeism of her father's behavior returned.

Elsie decided she couldn't abide another year of the pendulum swinging at home. She couldn't wait to go to college to prepare for a place in ministry. She took extra classes and graduated after her junior year.

GREED AND INSECURITY ARE BOTH STORAGE PROBLEMS

Though Rich and Gail were no longer on speaking terms, they managed to pull together as Mom and Dad to bring Elsie to college, two states away. The last gift Gail gave to her daughter, was a warm woolen, three quarter length coat, for the Chicago winters. "You know, you are the first of my family to go to college. I'm so proud of you, honey," she gushed.

Gail couldn't help herself, "I'm like the sun. I didn't need college to shine a thousand degrees in all directions." She felt bolstered when both Rich and Elsie laughed.

Elsie hugged both of her parents. She thought the world of each of them, and they were certainly not lacking in class or intelligence, either one of them. "Thank you for everything, Mom and Dad. I'll do my best."

Things were not so easy returning home. When the entire family moved into Gail's new home in the southern suburbs, Rich immediately set up a single bed in the unfinished basement for himself to the shock of all the children. His passive-aggressive message? "Good times are over, folks." He put out the "closed for business" sign announcing his absence and sullenness for the remaining two children at home to absorb. Any excitement the younger two had been feeling toward the move, evaporated.

Rich and Gail's tattered banner of enmity was no longer folded with the other linens, no longer hidden on the closet shelf behind closed doors where no one in Northglenn could find it, neither neighbors nor church members. In the southern suburbs, they began raising their declarations of personal causes openly, parading the war banner over their home to see how it felt in the living areas, then retreating it into silent, hostile corners.

In the well-fitted house they'd shared in Northglenn, Richard—the trailer trash boy—had made good. There, he had set his past behind him and rested in his handiwork. He'd arrived. They had nothing short of magnificence to show for their fitful marriage there. He'd been proud of Gail for making tailored curtains for the house, and blinds for the kitchen. Their plush celery-green carpet still glowed with luxury, especially with Gail's Home Interior's gold mirror hung over their couch…he may as well stop dreaming. The house had sold to someone who had long salivated for it, even before it went on the market. They might not have been lovers anymore, but they were getting along well enough under the same roof.

These days, he felt his health ebbing, and knew he'd never be able to build out another home to nearly the same specs. At least, he was in no mood to try. If she was willing to throw it all away and start fresh, he wouldn't be her burden bearer, her fixer-upper, or her dream weaver. If she was a modern woman, he'd be entertained watching her roar for her keep.

Rich and Gail were no longer able to hide their troubles. It was just as well none of their concerned friends could see them now.

Rich casually painted the interior of the house when he was off work, more to contemplate his options, save some money on the side, and take the scare out of his daughter's bedrooms, but he didn't want to touch the exterior siding. Their last home had been red brick. It had been customized in a luxurious ranch form, a one level L-shape winding around the corner lot.

The new house was a two-story tract home. Rich was split down the middle trying to decide whether he should stay and try to build a new life as offered by Gail, or whether he should throw in the towel.

The irony was not lost on Gail that she had moved her family to a subdivision called Ironton. When the couple found a new church down south, the clencher in realizing her mistake in timing was Rich's grim jaw with his snippy, cutting words on the way to church together, and Gail's silent tears. They were going through the motions, but there was nothing left inside for them to build on. Their lives had fallen on hard times.

Rich told Gail, "Look. You've always been into real estate. I'll give you three months to get your real estate license, and then we can conclude this marriage for good. I will never be able to please you with all that you are aiming for in fancy houses and the best opportunities for the children. I've done my best, and it isn't good enough."

It seemed whenever he opened his mouth, he wound up cursing his wife or his children or sabotaging himself. As long as he continued to do so, there would be no phoenix rising from the ashes.

He also told a story spun of the truth to his friends at work and their mutual friends at Far Horizons Church. When Gail's friends stopped returning her calls, she began to understand what Rich had done, but not clearly.

He had, in effect, finally succeeded in painting his wife as a greedy, ambitious, and worldly woman who thought their former neighborhood was running downhill, implying that she intended to discard her friends and aimed to move up in the world. When they said Gail had called them for a lunch date, or just to chat, he laughed and said he was surprised.

Gail took Rich at his word. He wanted out. He refused to try. She no longer felt there could be any form of a Christian marriage when such tit-for-tat animosity existed.

SOUTHERN SUBURBS, 1985

IN A DOG-EAT-DOG WORLD, HER DOG WORKS *PRO-BONE-O*

Gail found and applied for a real estate certification course during the time that the state economy was at its lowest point in history. Admittedly, she was interested in selling houses. The oil companies were crumbling, and homelessness was at its height. Not knowing any of this, she prayed constantly, working her way through each of the courses on real estate contracts, real estate law, and real estate sales techniques. Gail's first real estate deal was the wraparound mortgage she worked around her own home.

Opportunities to sell houses in the beginning were scarce. She worked in a highly competitive office environment.

Two important lessons came at the time her first sale on a house paid out. First, she realized that payment on sales commissions was not immediate and second, being in sales meant her monthly income could never be certain. She would have to save the bulk of her earnings from a home sale until another house had sold.

Of course, Rich was late with child support if he paid at all.

In the checkout line at Walmart, the woman ahead of Gail fumbled with her sack and dropped a couple of items on the floor. Gail picked up an item and handed it back to the woman.

"Oh, thank you. I've got to stop dropping things. I guess I'm feeling a little rushed these days."

"I noticed it was getting out of hand." Gail smiled at the woman and chuckled.

The two laughed and continued standing at the front of the store chatting. When the woman discovered that Gail was starting a new career in real estate, she spoke seriously.

"I like you. I'm recently divorced myself. I have a rental I don't want and a house that I don't like because of the memories. I'd like to sell both of them and find a new place. Can I call you?"

It was an answer to prayer for Gail to get three sales in a couple of months. Still, she regularly had to address her feelings of panic and trust the Lord to provide.

In court, receiving a final judgment of divorce, the judge ordered Rich had to pay child support until the children turned twenty-one rather than the typical age of emancipation, eighteen.

Rich told his friends, Gail, and even his children, that the judge only sided with Gail because of her tears at the hearing. "She's a master manipulator." Telling his side of the story, Rich explained, "My attorney stood and argued, 'Ain't no precedent for this man to pay until the children are twenty-one, Judge!' But, the judge said, 'I'm setting precedent!'" And Rich pounded his fist on his hand just like the judge pounded his gavel on the bench.

This meant Rich would have to pay child support for Elsie even though she was now in college.

It only took a moment for Rich's pulsing jaw to set. He reared back saying, "I can't pay that child support."

His attorney said, "It's an order, Rich. You must comply."

Rich turned and walked out of the courtroom.

Although there was no deadbeat dad law in Colorado, and though there was no way for a parent to enforce a decree for child support, Rich fumed with defeat. For all his years of biblical study, it did not occur to Rich to lean hard on God—his Provider—to find the means to support his children.

Instead, he seemed to take a particular delight in making Gail wait for her child support money.

He took pleasure in hearing her beg on the telephone. He'd given her three months to learn a trade so that he'd never have to pay spousal maintenance, and by his calculations, only two children would be counted in the decree, and only until they turned twenty-one.

With three more years of Elsie's college left, and now roped into paying child support for Melanie through college, if she went, and his last child, Kaida, he realized this divorce scheme of his wouldn't serve him as well as he'd calculated.

Punishing his wife soon became Richard's supreme aim, and where his children's needs fell in his budget of priorities, proved inconsequential.

Rarely in the same neighborhood anymore, Gail stopped reaching out to her friends from up north. Rich seemed to have overtaken her relationship with them. It was awkward trying to hold on to friendships that had been mutual to the couple. Besides, what would the women there understand of the pressures she now faced having to work long hours without any assurance of income?

This was life on the edge for Gail. It was only the fact that she felt God smiling on her that she could rise up each morning and function.

It was a partly cloudy day when Gail went to church feeling numb for all her efforts. Who would help her if she couldn't provide for the children? Where would her next sale come from? Did God see her struggles?

Feeling new resolution to seek the Lord's plan and clinging to a strand of hope that might come through a good message, Gail listened to the Sunday school teacher speaking, only a little disappointed that the lesson was delivered by a young unmarried man. After all, the teacher couldn't have much wisdom as he was still single; he couldn't have much knowledge either, as he didn't even have a biblical education.

She studied his handsome face, a kind face, and understood he had good intentions. She looked at her hands and finally at her Bible text with a small remaining prayer in her heart. He was just telling the stories as he read them. There must be something plainly spoken in the text for her to hear today.

Ben taught the class at Belleview Bible Chapel because he was being equipped by the elders to find his gifts of service, and he was determined to do his best.

He said, "If a man takes your cloak, give him your coat as well," when Gail suddenly felt that God was telling her to not compel Rich to pay child support. Afterward, she asked Ben if that was right.

He said, "Oh! I don't know about that!" But that particular Sunday, Rich showed up on his motorcycle and was waiting for his ex to come out of her church.

"Here you are, madame," Rich said, pulling out a check from his leather cycling jacket.

Gail told him, "Why don't you pay child support on time? You make good money. How hard can it be?"

"I can't help it," he quipped.

"I think you are enjoying it," she answered frankly. "You know I can't budget without you being faithful in paying child support, and the children are suffering. I can't focus on work without knowing there is some basic provision, but you have continued to withhold it from me. I was praying about all this today, and I believe the Lord gave me an idea at church."

"Oh?"

"Rich, why don't you sign over the new house to me completely in a quit claim deed since we've only had it for six months anyway. If you do that, I won't ask you for another penny. Today the Lord told me at church to let you out of it, and this is the idea I got that seemed fair. He has promised to be my husband and He is going to take care of us. So, I won't make you pay any more."

"Well!" Was his ex really saying that he didn't have to pay any more child support? Rich experienced a moment of lift off, a moment of winning the gold medal in a surreal one off.

Gail, quickly reviewing her plan in her mind, knew that they had put their joint appreciation from their Northglenn house into the new house, and it would be like him giving his half of the value of that appreciation to her. If all went south, and she had to sell the house, at least she'd get all of the appreciation to float the family for a while. In this way, her life would no longer be tied to his.

She heard Rich say, "Will you put it in writing?"

Gail agreed. "We'll trade documents at the same time. You sign over the whole value of the family home to me, and I'll give you a notarized letter of release." At least she'd have an asset to start her life free and clear of him, and there'd be no money coming out of his paycheck ever again. Right there on his motorcycle, he agreed.

He stopped paying child support from there on out; though at first he thought he had won the lottery, afterward, Rich always said that she tricked him because, he had no assets or home for himself, no down payment saved, and he had to rent in Northglenn until he could build up his own credit to buy a home.

If Rich ever considered that it was God who was testing his father's heart and his own seed of faith to provide for his family, no one would know it. Had he cared for his children properly and humbly, perhaps he would not have forfeited the respect of his children.

Whenever Gail repeated this story, she said she had the distinct impression the Lord told her to release Rich from his dereliction of duties to her and the children. "It was as if God was saying, 'I will provide for you. I will be your husband. Trust me. Stop focusing on him.'"

Whenever she told this story to her children, however, she either forgot, or simply left out the part about trading the accrued value of their home for their father's monthly child support. In retrospect, she'd succeeded in anchoring her gain at the risk of her children's grocery bills being paid in an unsettled economy.

It supported their image of her being the hero, their ever-loving mother. Their father was the deadbeat. Yes, God was providing for them all through her work, but Rich wasn't the heartless deadbeat she implied.

A DOCTOR WITH NO *PATIENTS* SHOULD ACCEPT THE REALITY OF BEING LATE

It was an unseasonably warm evening in February the following year when Kaida's school crush took her roller-skating. His father dropped them off at the rink and told them when he'd be back to collect them. She hadn't told her mom that she had a date because she didn't have permission to date yet, being only fourteen. She reasoned her mom would be working through the dinner hour anyway on some real estate contract. If she got caught, the date would be worth the grounding.

Because roller skating had been a routine youth group outing at Far Horizons Church, she could now dance-skate pretty well. Already a seventh-grade flirt, Kaida, a naturally competitive girl in most anything, excelled in math, science, language arts, and boys. Her diminutive physicality also helped her to shine in gymnastics and track.

She skated energetically, looking like Dorothy Hamill, in her new haircut and short shorts. Her heart lurched whenever she felt her boyfriend's hand on her back or on her arm, holding hands in the couple's skate, and when he slid his hand lower, to her bottom. She reached up and gave in to the juices, kissing him passionately. The feeling that overtook her was surprising.

When the rink closed the skating session, she and her boyfriend moved outside to await their ride home. The boy looked at his watch and realized there was more time than they'd accounted for, so the two walked into the field to chat and kiss.

Before Kaida realized how defenseless she was, her pants were down and she was lying in a field with her boyfriend on top of her, touching her. "No! No! Don't! Please, don't!" But it had gone too far and he continued.

The pain wasn't as bad as she thought it would be, but the vulnerability, her loss of control, and the shame that followed, became daggers. He took her hand and pulled her from the field back to the parking lot where his father waited in the car. "You kids have fun?"

"Yeah, Dad. It was great!"

Kaida, breathless and speechless, said nothing until she was forced to give the man directions to her house.

When she used her key to open the front door, her mother met her with angry eyes. "Where have you been? It's late!"

"Forget it, Mom. I went roller skating with Celia."

"You need to get permission when you go out at night, and you know that. You're grounded. Go up to your room."

"Grounded for how long?"

"A week."

"Fine. What a jerk."

"Two weeks."

"Whatever, Mom."

There was really no way for Gail to enforce her disciplinary measures when she had to work, but when she didn't, she intended to make good.

Melanie had begun avoiding both Gail and her sister, Kaida. She slept around the clock in the new family home, in her pretty new bedroom. When she wasn't in school, she simply came home to her bedroom to sleep. Maybe she was doing her homework, maybe not. Gail was trying to give her some autonomy to figure things out. Besides, her daughter's absence gave Gail extra freedom and quiet in the evening. Gail was wrung out, operating her new business on fumes of a spiritual nature and she was, without real navigation skills in her new single-mother-of-teens world.

Sometime during the end of the grounding, when Kaida was doing homework at the kitchen table, and Gail was making beef stroganoff, Kaida said, "What would you do if I were ever raped, Mom?"

"What?" She stopped stirring and looked up from the stove. "I'd expect you to tell me."

"Then what?"

"We'd have to call the authorities."

"What would they do?"

"I don't know. Why are you asking?"

"I was raped."

"What?"

"Yeah, the other night at the roller rink. A guy raped me."

Gail rushed to look her daughter in the face. She sat down. "What happened?"

"I didn't go with Celia. I went with a guy from school. His dad took us and picked us up."

"You aren't allowed to date. What are you saying?"

"I'm saying that we were kissing, and then he started putting his hands all over me. I thought we were just making out, but he raped me in the field!"

"Did you tell his dad?"

"No."

"Why didn't you tell me?"

"Because you were already mad at me for breaking your rules. You grounded me, remember?"

"It sounds like you were heavy petting with him and led him on, Kaida. A girl can excite a boy so much that maybe he couldn't stop!"

"Mom, he raped me."

"Well, it's too late to do anything about it now. It's two weeks later! Rape kits must be done right away, and it's your word against his now."

"Thanks, Mom. Thanks for caring."

"Kaida, listen. You have to move on. You are my brilliant daughter. You can turn your life around and do anything you set your mind to. Shoot for the moon, darling. Forget that guy."

Gail felt helpless. She felt distressed. Her daughters were distancing themselves from her at the speed of light and she couldn't reel them back in. She didn't know what to do about this. So, she stirred the beef stroganoff, and scooped it onto plates. She called upstairs, "Come down to dinner, Melanie!"

"Okay."

The three of them sat down to eat in silence. When Kaida's silence howled like the cold side of the moon, she pushed her plate away. "I'm not hungry." She left the table.

IT WAS A CASE OF REEL TO REAL

Elsie attended college in Chicago during that first year of the Finch family dissolution. Prior to her move to college, her loyalties turned away from her father and she began to favor her mother because she'd been the one to keep the children. Though she couldn't piece her parents' puzzling marriage together, loyalty became a matter of practical deduction rather than sentimentality. On a scale of faithfulness and upright effort, her mother came out the clear winner.

Gail's handwritten checks to the college to underwrite her daughter's education, began arriving like a tithe. It was a matter of honor and duty since she'd traded out Elsie's child support. Elsie was grateful for all the help, even though she accepted a school loan and Pell Grant as well.

Where she landed because of her mother's aid, confused her greatly because she and her father had shared so much in the way of music and art appreciation. He was the one who walked her hand-in-hand from church, and took her with him to picnics, concerts, and the circus.

Her father had been an open book to her, and she with him. When she felt lost, she'd search for him in a crowd, and when he smiled at her, she'd be fine. While her father had treated her to special events and outings, her mother seemed stressed with the everyday routine of life. How often Elsie felt her mother forgot her. She didn't *see* her. Yet this evaluation of her parents as individuals no longer seemed to be about her personal sympathies. It was a family matter, a matter of Christian living, self-sacrifice and honor.

She now felt deceived thinking of her father.

Maybe she was a lowly pawn in her father's games, or maybe he needed her love. She realized there were others in her family who had suffered greatly by his refusal to show them love.

She prayed furiously for her father's salvation because by now, she was sure that his entire life had been a mockery. In her mind, she just couldn't reconcile that her dad could be calling Jesus "Lord" of his life and continue to damage his family; he had abandoned them twice without ever considering his kids' needs. What if they starved? What kind of a man did that? She was working in the college kitchen to pay her way through school, and she would call and ask her mother if she needed money, but her mother always said they were managing.

A friend noticed Elsie walking quickly across campus with her fists clenched. "Why so tense, girl?"

"Just thinking about my family. My parents' second divorce," she said. "It would be better for a millstone to be hung around a man's neck and he be thrown into the bottom of the sea than he make one of these little ones stumble." Elsie quoted this sentiment often to the Lord and waited for her dad's repentance or death.

Neither happened.

In her Survey of the New Testament coursework, Elsie studied the parable of the sower in Matthew 13. Jesus told this story. Seed scattered by the sower fell onto four different types of soil. Since there were four girls in her family, the number four stood out in Elsie's mind. Once from her car window, she had watched a tilling machine plow through a field as a flock of white birds swarmed around it. At first, she believed the driver of the tilling machine must be disconcerted by the number of birds rising and diving around him in violent flight. He must have disturbed the flock hiding among the dead stalks! She gradually realized the weaving birds were only looking for worms and seeds as the soil was lifted and turned.

In this parable, there was nothing inherently wrong with the seed, but the four types of soil greatly affected the seed's ability to mature.

The first type of soil was hard ground. The seed, lying on the ground, got snatched up by the birds immediately. The seed couldn't even sprout.

The second type of soil was stony. The shaded and watered seed was able to sprout but when it began to grow, it withered in the sun because there was no soil to hold the roots and the water for the roots drained away or evaporated.

The third type of soil was thorny. Although the seed was planted and found good earth to grow in, it could not compete with the thorns that overtook it.

The fourth type of soil was good, clean soil. It allowed the seed to plant deep, grow strong and produce fruit. Elsie became alarmed for her sisters and mother. They were facing hard times that threatened to quench their very lives.

She started praying hard for each of them.

A FAMILY *PI* IS NOT DIVISIBLE IN BIOLOGY OR PHYSICS

The morning sunlight streamed through the blinds, over the chair, and pooled on the bed next to it. Elsie plumped up her pillow and sat up to read Isaiah 45, where a verse indicated that God promised to show treasured things hidden in darkness to His children. She asked God to show her these things. Then, she read the verse in Isaiah 54 about God being the provider and husband to an abandoned woman. She called her mother.

States away, Gail had just read the same passage. The serendipity of this occasion felt like divine confirmation.

Her mother needed help after her father finally left the basement and moved back up north to an apartment in the town of Golden.

Kaida and Melanie were on their own so often because she had to wait for calls to come in at the office and was on call even during the evenings. She had to work the weekends because that was the most likely time customers held open houses and other customers looked for houses.

Over the telephone Gail told her daughter that she had released Rich from giving her child support.

"What? Mom? This situation just seems precarious for Kaida and Melanie. Why did you do that?"

"Honey, he was holding me hostage, and I was fretting so much about the child support that I couldn't concentrate on my work. I really felt God was telling me that He would be my husband and provide for you kids."

All of that sounded great, keeping Elsie going for the rest of the school year, but she keenly felt the ebb of her sisters lives like the tide growing further away from her. She never heard from them directly, and the things her mom told her did not seem wholesome or healthy. How could she help bring them back to shore?

Elsie had just been voted to be the new student body recreation and event director for her third year of college, but her heart was breaking for her mother and two sisters. She decided to take a year off from college. Though she was paying her way through college now, by working in the kitchen and by traveling in a singing ensemble to churches throughout the Northwest, she knew her sisters were missing the basics of being cared for due to their mother's long working hours and their absent father. They'd suffered for two years. She just had to answer the call of home.

A song from childhood haunted her that winter, "Let there be Peace on Earth"—*and let it begin with me* was the longing of her heart.

Sure enough, Elsie was met by two teenagers at home using coping skills at opposite ends of the spectrum. Melanie, always the quiet sister, now had occasional breakdowns. Gail assessed Melanie as secretly experimenting with boys and alcohol. Her grades were average or below, but a pastor she'd met at camp came around regularly to help her. She still loved the idea of horses, backpacking trips, and river rafting, all these adventures that going to camp afforded her, so there was hope. During that year, however, Melanie mostly went to her room after school. When Elsie checked on her, she'd be sleeping.

Melanie in fact kept Elsie at arm's length and told her nothing about the so-called pastor abusing her, as was her new boyfriend, a guy with whom she'd tried to be friends by acting like a tomboy. He preferred the girl. Then a trusted family member called the house and she found that when he was drunk or tired, he wanted to talk dirty on the phone to her. All these puzzling pieces, she kept hidden. If not the most ignored member of her family, Melanie didn't trust a secret to any soul with the last name of Finch.

A veil fell over Elsie's eyes as to how to help the other middle sister because of the disappearing goal line. Maybe she was too late. Still, she was determined to put a regular evening meal on the table and woo her back by just being there.

Kaida, on the other hand, gregarious as always, had two best friends with whom she invested her soul and athletic body competing in the school track team, buying high teen fashion, movies, gossiping, and drinking. She still played piano, and had learned to play guitar, but home was just a place to eat, sleep, and use as a springboard for her real life outside its walls. Elsie hoped to bring her back into the fold by providing interesting fun things to do together.

Kaida earned the highest marks in her education, and she sought out competition in every aspect of her life, openly ridiculing others less gifted, and competing with even her best friends.

The talent and quick wit, though sometimes caustic, impressed Elsie. Impressed her so much so that she felt inadequate to offer Kaida anything. Anything she could do, Kaida could do better, and she wasn't hesitant to prove it.

Kaida was infatuated with a boy from camp, one of the talented song leaders and kind staff counselors. But the more time she spent with him, the more she realized he only saw her as a camper to be inspired, not as a romantic interest.

During the school year, Elsie made meals for the family to take the load off her mother's shoulders. She tried to act as nurturer and counselor, but neither of her sisters wanted her religious input or advice. Discouraged, she took a job as a part-time waitress nearby and offered her time volunteering with a Campus Life club at a nearby high school.

Leading a solitary existence in a new town where she knew no one, Elsie played Christian cassettes and records, and practiced writing her own music on her guitar. She tried to run with Kaida, but decided that she couldn't "push through the pain of it" as Kaida advised. As Kaida introduced her to jazz, Elsie's interest in early jazz as well as choral classical music from high school and college grew along with her desire to perform in the evolving Jesus music genre.

Which genre would she land on?

One fall evening, Kaida failed to come home for dinner. Melanie and Elsie kept waiting to eat with her. Their mother was gone, preparing a real estate contract and showing houses to clients. Finally, Kaida stumbled into the kitchen and fell on the floor. She was out cold and apparently drunk.

While Elsie tried to wake her up, Kaida vomited and stopped breathing. The older sister called 911, and then called her father. To her surprise the ambulance came within a few minutes, and with it, a paramedic Elsie recognized as a co-worker from camp. Terribly embarrassed at the kind of emergency this was, she led them to the kitchen where they cleared Kaida's mouth and got her breathing again. Then, they took her to the hospital.

Gail met her daughter in the emergency room and eventually brought her back to sleep in her own bed after treatment.

Rich came after the paramedics left and walked upstairs to look after Melanie. When it seemed there was nothing more for him to do, he left.

The next morning was Saturday, and Kaida stumbled down the stairs with an embarrassed grin on her face. Nobody else grinned. Elsie had seen the worst of it and had been traumatized to think she might lose her baby sister.

"Whatever!" Kaida said, brushing off the alarm she'd caused. "You're an idiot."

"You're fortunate I was here, or you'd be a dead idiot, idiot!" came the retort. "You owe me a thank you."

"I don't owe you anything. Please stay out of my business. You think you're some big hero? I don't need you."

"Okay, girls." Gail interjected. "Let's just stop this. We're glad you're safe and sound, Kaida. Elsie was just trying to help." But Gail hadn't been there to see Kaida suffocating in her vomit or Elsie's panic not knowing how to help her sister.

Gail was a bit nonplussed that Elsie had called her dad before she had called her mom, forgetting that she was showing houses with clients. From there, the incident became a he-said-she-said memory in the Finch family history.

The animosity between family members continued to grow, so Elsie sought out the counsel of Robert Kordios.

Unable to control the tears, she told him all about the sins of her miserable family and how she would probably never be able to serve the Lord in music or as a missionary. Since her own father, a Sunday school teacher and pillar of their church, along with her godly mother, could not keep their marriage together, how could she ever be able to trust herself to marry someone and stick with it?

Anything she had hoped and trained for was now a moving target because her parents couldn't help launch or support her. They were barely hanging onto their own houses and the faith they'd held in such high esteem their entire lives.

She rambled on with the other difficulties she saw if she survived this.

With her private life in shambles, and nearly ready to graduate, she knew she was an unseen female preparing to serve in a male driven religion. She said she knew all the fences had been staked out for denominational territories, and when she examined them closely, there was no good fit for her.

Being a conservative Christian, there would be little room for her to find employment as a worship leader on one side of the fence. She also didn't fit on the other side of the fence due to doctrinal differences.

She said, "I sometimes think I'm going crazy. I've lost hope in finding any kind of purpose in the world because I can't even influence my own family members to think through their own faith or their behaviors. I have no power to influence anyone. Maybe I'm not credible.

I seriously feel crazy, and now, I'm a failure who is guilty by association because of both of my parents. I'm embarrassed to show my face in the church I grew up in. My siblings hate me..." she paused.

With a nervous giggle, she asked, "Do you happen to have a lifeline to throw to me? Something strong?"

Her friend and mentor patiently and prayerfully listened. In a stroke of wisdom, he quoted her a verse that she had memorized with her mother, "Elsie, I'm sure you know Philippians 1: 6: 'Being confident of this very thing, that He who began a good work in you will carry it through until the day of Christ Jesus.'" He also asked her to read a scripture her mother had taught her long ago when she had been afraid of the dark, 2 Timothy 1:7: "For He has not given us the spirit of fear, but of love and power and of a sound mind." He emphasized, "You're telling me you need a sound mind, Elsie. Well, do you know that none of these things happening to you right now are a surprise to the Lord? He knows far more about everything than you could possibly know, but if you stay in the Word, the Lord will help you stand on His firm foundation. You can stand there confidently against fearful possibilities, in the power of His might, and you can maintain a sound mind if you stay right there. Keep reading His word and telling Him what's on your heart, and He'll show you what to do."

The chains of death that were strangling her began to fall off. She felt physically free to grab ahold of the lifeline, this chord of substance she needed to save her. The Lord would not take her where His grace could not keep her.

Finally, Mr. Kordios turned in his own Bible to a passage that held significance for him, Ezekiel 18:19-23. It said:

[19] "Yet you ask, 'Why does the son not share the guilt of his father?' Since the son has done what is just and right and has been careful to keep all my decrees, he will surely live. [20] The one who sins is the one who will die. The child will not share the guilt of the parent, nor will the parent share the guilt of the child. The righteousness of the righteous will be credited to them, and the wickedness of the wicked will be charged against them.
[21] "But if a wicked person turns away from all the sins they have committed and keeps all my decrees and does what is just and right, that person will surely live; they will not die. [22] None of the offenses they have committed will be remembered against them. Because of the

righteous things they have done, they will live. ²³ Do I take any pleasure in the death of the wicked? declares the Sovereign LORD. Rather, am I not pleased when they turn from their ways and live?

She had never heard of this passage, but it told her that she was not defined by her parents any more than they were defined by her. Every person stood before the Lord and in His kingdom on his or her own two feet.

A LEAKING ROOF WITHOUT WALLS IS MOST LIKELY A CAGE

When Elsie went back to college the next year, she only had prayers left for her family, no more action. She didn't know whether her sacrificial year had been wasted or whether it had helped in any way.

Gail and Rich agreed the same boarding school to which they'd taken Carlene, would be just the instrument to help Kaida stop drinking and talking back to Gail. They hoped to pump some good Bible verses and social creeds into her. They imagined their youngest as a hungry chick opening its beak to a parent pumping nutrition down the baby's gullet.

The girl's home director had passed on, but the couple in charge was the same couple Carlene knew from her days there. When the parents talked over their plan with their eldest daughter, she agreed that it had been the best thing for her. Rich agreed to drive Kaida to the Texas boarding home for girls.

Rich called from work and asked Kaida to come out with him on a little breakfast date that Saturday. When he arrived, she skipped from the front door, a headband holding back her silken hair, and got into the car, giggling. All she knew was, her dad wanted to go for breakfast *with her*. Kaida had never experienced him taking any particular interest in her; certainly, he'd never asked to talk with her alone. Bathed in happy sunshine, she locked the door.

Unknown to Kaida, Gail had packed her suitcase. It claimed the space in Rich's trunk.

He agreed to take their daughter down, but when he returned, he billed Gail for the price of a one-way plane ticket for helping her.

Kaida's mouth filled with bile when she realized where the trip with Dad was actually going. She pled her case with her father, telling him about the rape and how her mother had done nothing which explained why she had turned against her mother and to partying. Her father, in fact, said he knew about the incident, and did not defend Gail, but instead turned the incident onto Kaida, saying, the floosy way she dressed and danced told boys that she wanted it.

Kaida felt such betrayal by both parents; she never forgave their treachery. "All Dad ever had to do was actually do what he said he was doing that day. I just wanted him to see me and listen to me and show that he cared for me. Huh! The only time he offered to do that was the day he took me to a girl's reformatory—for being raped!"

From there on out, it was never a boarding school, it was either "prison" or "girl's reformatory."

When Carlene approved of her parents' decision, she also got personally involved by calling and visiting her youngest sister, but many things had changed over the years. The couple taking care of the girls in the home lacked biblical authority and a thing called empathy. They had, over time, developed a particular cruelty in their disciplines and punishments forcing the girls to kneel silently for an hour or receive whacks with belts and rulers, forcing food or food deprivation as a punishment and removing privacy.

At their hands, Kaida did some mending, but she experienced as many evils as she did reforms.

RUFF DAY

When a parent drags the family through life like a bag of weights, children feel objectified. Conversely, when a parent chooses one child to be the balloon that lifts them high above life's responsibilities, the children feel that too. Elsie had experienced both treatments, and neither one turned out well for her relationships with her siblings or for her relationship with either parent. It was a no-win situation.

She was learning, when a parent's core energy is exhausted, there is nothing of substance to offer their children in the way of counseling, directives, or opportunities to equip them for their calling in life. Nurturing doesn't happen when parents are in survival mode.

Divorcees trying to build out a new financial foundation in patches, leave too many holes for their children to fall into. Some tripping and stumbling, even grown children fall into dusty holes where venomous creatures are housed. At a time when family members are least equipped to seek help, children will be stung by poor financial decisions, delayed by twisted ankles, and inherit bruised futures.

Melanie moved out of her mom's as soon as she graduated from high school and could get a job. When Gail offered her a new dress or outfit for interviewing, she refused. "I don't need those kinds of clothes to work in a car dealership," she said.

Mom was left with the newest family pet, a beautiful Irish setter, Reba, who required regular walking. Her breed couldn't be left alone for hours, but because Reba was left alone and was rarely walked, she began to use Gail's new white couch and chairs as scratching posts. She peed on her new white carpet. The doors became scratched, and with that, she coaxed Reba into her car and delivered the dog to the animal shelter without a word to the kids. One by one, as they visited or returned home, they noticed Reba's absence to their dismay. She had to fess up to her abrupt decision.

To each one Gail said, "You left Reba with me. She was your dog, and no one stayed home to care for her. I'm a businesswoman. I couldn't care for her. Reba wasn't my dog."

After the year of separation from her parents, Kaida also returned to her mom's empty house. Faced with the desolate news that Gail had taken her beloved running companion to the dog pound without consulting anyone, Kaida asked to live with her dad. He'd apologized for tricking her into the girl's home at least. Kaida could put her mother in her place, and she might even get to know her dad better.

Rich agreed having finally bought his own home in Golden.

"Dad, she's living like a queen in her all-white palace. She got rid of Reba, and Reba was my dog. Mine! Not hers. She knew how much I loved running with her, and I was only gone for nine months! She's a heartless bitch."

He didn't disagree.

When she moved in, Kaida discovered her father had at last furnished his place. He showed her the guest room. He'd turned his second bedroom into a computer room and a library set aside for his hobbies. Otherwise, she had full reign and could explore the place, the neighborhood, and make herself at home. The only rule in his house was that she went to church with him.

That was easy enough. She could handle one hour per week after all that she'd endured in her short religious lifetime.

At church in her first week staying with her father, Kaida met a Venezuelan boy, a handsome exchange student staying with one of the church families. When Rich came home from work one evening and found his youngest daughter in bed with the boy, he threw them both out of the house and told his daughter to find another place to live.

That year, Gail rarely called Elsie at college unless it was to tell her about earning trophies and vacations and new dining sets from her rare successes at work. The photographs snapped at her honor ceremonies showed a strong, beautiful woman. These became her treasures, saved in a special box.

When Elsie called to ask about Kaida or Melanie, Gail had nothing to tell. Elsie cried. When Elsie bemoaned the waste of a year at home trying to help them, and her lost touring opportunity in college because she'd dropped out, Gail said, "What are you saying, honey. you regret coming home? I can't imagine your sole aim in that was to help me or the girls. That's sentimental nonsense. They weren't the only reason. You worked and furthered your own opportunities with Youth Corp."

Her eye, cold to Elsie's heartache, was that of an ostrich who sticks her head in the sand, an ostrich who goes about foraging, forgetting her nested eggs, an ostrich who hopes a predator won't discover them. Yet the bird doesn't recognize them as her own responsibility to protect.

Gail said, "You have to let everyone live their own lives, Elsie. You have a bright future ahead of you." But Gail didn't know there were no options in music waiting for her daughter and she didn't ask. She assumed, certainly, a college education came with a recommendation and a key to open the secret sphere of a world.

With mounting animosity between her mother and father, Elsie felt she must choose only one of them to attend her recital and graduation. That person was the one who had constantly nurtured her talent and celebrated her concerts. Dad. Dad would attend and help her pack her things into his car after the ceremonies and bring her home.

Elsie's final week at college culminated in a recital of her best pieces. Throughout the year, she trained with an upright bass player, a violinist and pianist along with vocalists to back up her songs, some of which she'd written. She spent hours working on introductions to songs and writing program notes.

Then the day of the recital came, and Rich failed to appear. Her palpitating heartache continued throughout her performance as she looked into the audience hoping to see the face of the one person Elsie felt understood her love of music.

Two days later, Rich rolled onto campus asking the whereabouts of his daughter only to discover that graduation was that evening and he'd missed her recital. She hid from him in the student lounge, stoking the flames of her ire. He found his daughter and tried to douse her anger explaining that he'd simply gotten the calendar dates mixed up.

"What were you doing?" she asked.

"Nothing, honey. Nothing. I just didn't write the date down correctly."

"Dad, you could have called me if you weren't sure." She suddenly realized he'd never called her at college.

"Do you want to see the recital bulletin?"

"Yes, please." They were both crying.

Through his tears, the blurred titles of his daughter's music, her acknowledgements, and her concert notes met him in black and white, without tunes, timbre, or emotion. She'd dedicated the evening to him, but he hadn't been there.

That evening, it wasn't Rich's face in the audience that mattered at all to Elsie. Deflated, she said goodbye to her friendships, those who had family support, and those who had music careers waiting. As she crossed the stage, a group at the rear of the auditorium stood with a whooping ovation for doing her music internship in their community.

Afterward, while all the graduates took pictures with their parents, she realized her envy of other graduates' embraces and enjoying the plans their families were making to celebrate them.

"I was hoping to take a jaunt through the Black Hills on the way home, Elsie," mentioned Rich.

She sat in the passenger seat on her graduation laurels, dressed in some homemade college duds with a tilted French beret, feeling the full rite of passage from college. She was her own person now, though she felt like a gutted fish prepared to be eaten. She had leaned on a crutch that had broken and pierced her hand. Never again would she let it happen.

Rich sang along with his cassettes of old love songs, Billie Holiday singing, "Let's Call the Whole Thing Off," "The Very Thought of You," and Dionne Warwick singing, "That's What Friends are For," the theme from Alfie, and such cajoling her to warm up to him.

Her dad was a man in love with love. Rich, always the sentimental romantic, was a constant failure in the pragmatics of love.

Seeing the presidents' heads carved and sculpted on the mountain, took all of ten minutes. "Won'erful, won'erful," Rich said in his manner of admiring a thing. Then, he told Elsie to pick out a Black Hill Gold ring, and she did. It went a long way towards warming the chill between them. Wearing that memento, she could pretend her greatest letdown had never happened.

AS A *RIGHT* OF PASSAGE, ONE *WRITES* A CHECK

Her bank bills had been piling up in paper messes on her desk. Gail could no longer see the buttons and password boxes to fill in her name and secret codes. She finally called Elsie to help her pay these bills online.

"What's your ID, Mom? Is it your email address?"

"No, Honey. It's uppercase B for B-e-r-t-i-e, no space, H-u-d-s-o-n- with a capital H, and 36."

"No kidding, you went wa-a-ay back for that one!" Elsie typed in her mother's secret maiden name and the year of her birth.

"I had to be more careful than normal because you-know-who was trying to get into my account and knows my usual logins."

SIDES OF A SQUARE WORLD, 1986

YOU HIDE A HORSE IN THE DESERT WITH *CAMELFLAGE*

When Elsie landed her first real job at Youth Corp as a youth director counseling in a local high school, she asked her mom to co-sign for a loan to purchase her first new car.

Gail declined. "There is a proverb that tells a wise man never to co-sign for anyone because the co-signer becomes slave to the lender."

"I need a car to get a job. Do you think I'm going to jilt you, Mom?"

"Probably not, dear, but credit reports are based on the amount of debt one has, and also whether the payments are made on time. You are young and inexperienced. I have to heed the wisdom in that proverb."

Elsie wasn't sure how she was going to get the all-important wheels required for her job, so she asked her father. He immediately agreed to co-sign. He shrugged saying, "If I can't trust you in a ministry job made for you, then I can't trust anybody."

"Thanks, Dad." Elsie breathed a sigh of relief. She paid her loan payments religiously as she mulled over her first financial debt, the wisdom of the proverb, and the love of her father.

"Your mother has a funny way about money. I don't quite understand it."

"What do you mean?"

"Well, we had that great house paid off in Northglenn when she decided to move south. It was everything we'd ever wanted, and she'd had me build that breezeway and the garage and office for her, but she wasn't satisfied. She threw it all away and mortgaged herself to the hilt for a new tract home. Now, she's complaining about co-signing on a little ol' car for you."

The following year came with an opportunity to join a jazz rock touring band in South Africa—also through Youth Corp. When the idea was presented to her, it took her only three months to raise the required support, get a passport and visa, and put her bags together.

She sold her car to her sister, Melanie. She was out the door.

Gail packed Elsie's last letters in her purse so that she could open them enroute on the plane. After finishing James Michener's book, THE COVENANT, Elsie picked up her mail and began to open her letters. In one envelope, there was an interesting letter erasing her college debt. Apparently, a wealthy supporter of the Bible college had died, and his will allocated that his wealth help to pay off all the students' school bills who had earned a 3.5 average or above.

Elsie had struggled in college. She certainly wasn't the smartest of her sisters, and it really should have been Kaida who obtained a music degree. Even so, Elsie was persistent and compelled by her vision of serving in music ministry somehow, someway. She'd managed to graduate with a standing ovation from the Hutterite colony thanking her for teaching them music during her final year, but she also managed to eke out a 3.5 grade point.

The donor's will applied to her, and now she could start her music ministry free and clear of debt. Her happy heart praised God, even while it fretted from the ominous reading of James Michener's book hinting that there would be a brutal end to apartheid coming soon.

Perhaps her life would end violently in the next year. No matter, she trusted the Lord as she looked out the Boeing airplane window at the incredible sight of the fingers of the Nile River spreading below her. Life in the care of the Lord was too wide and too exciting to brood over how it would end.

Headed to a nation where so many people's race and culture splintered their worlds was more than unnerving to Elsie. Many strangers with fragmented puzzle pieces awaited her.

She didn't realize that she was jumping from the boughs of a splintered family tree onto a continent of trees uprooted, and trees pulverized to dust in many cases.

She was walking off the plane into the life of another city, more diverse than she'd ever known, with an open mic. She would also head to verdant fields with open mics. Her job in music and counseling awaited in school theaters and open-air quads. With Youth Corp, she was to help the youth of South Africa bind themselves up to seek a new future. She was to offer them biblical truth through inspirational jazz rock music, her own creative perspectives, and counseling them with the hope of reconciliation to God and each other.

She would be a drop of water in a drought.

During Elsie's first year abroad, Kaida got married to the Venezuelan boy, a foreign ambassador's son, though she and he argued constantly. Their relationship was so rocky they almost broke up the night before their wedding, but Kaida managed to walk down the aisle to claim him. Soon after, she gave birth to their daughter.

With the couple continuing to rage at one another, Kaida wrote a sad letter to her sister in South Africa. "You have all your choices still ahead of you. You got an education and now you are traveling the world. I got married and now I have a child and we're living on the third floor of an apartment building in the city. I couldn't be more miserable."

Gail helped Kaida and her husband find a small house in which they could begin their family and find some peace. The family did begin, but the peace always ran out the back door like an escaped cat into the wide-open fields as soon as the man of the family returned home from work.

Because the sisters had become pen pals, Kaida wrote another letter to Elsie: "I've stepped out of the frying pan into the fire. I cannot stand my husband, but now I have a child to raise. When I told mom that I was either going to kill him or kill myself, she decided to help us buy a home in the suburbs. I'll send pictures. By the way, I think I'm going to go mom's route and try real estate."

Gail's whole being was infused with new life at the birth of Kaida's firstborn. She honestly experienced springtime and a new purpose for living at Paige's birth. In a tangible, palpable way, Baby Paige's arrival provided Gail's existence with a new legacy, a new hope for redemption. Gail couldn't remember ever having felt so filled with love and goodwill, having the money to boot, to shower her graces on her loved ones since the day she'd fallen into Rich's trap and married him.

Memories of her own childhood cheerfulness came to mind and filled her with some unspeakable sensation of lightness and belonging, adding no parental liability for having to be the disciplinarian and bad cop of the family. She was simply and joyfully "Grandma," and she owned the role. She became Queen of Grandma-Land to Kaida's first child.

The only drawback to Gail's days at her youngest daughter's new south suburban home came when Kaida's irritable husband opened the front door in the evenings. The accusations, critique, and yelling would begin. He had no contention about Gail hearing the family disputes.

Gail determined to buy her daughter an older model Mercedes Benz and foot the bill for a real estate course and license as Rich had once done for her. She would help Kaida escape her marriage.

Not willing for her daughter to endure what she had with a husband who withheld not only love, but also funds for clothing and food, Gail began to supplement these goods whenever she could.

WHEN OUR HABITS ARE STRANGE AND OUR MANNERS DERANGED, THAT'S *OUR MORES*

There came one memorable phone call in South Africa from Elsie's father. He told Elsie, almost immediately, that the reason for his call was his mom, Carmen, had passed in her sleep.

This fact meant little to Elsie. Apparently, it was significant to her father.

"I'm so sorry, Dad. How are you doing?"

"Well, I'm doing pretty good, but I'm concerned for Luster, my brother." Elsie had forgotten that her dad had a brother. She'd only met him once out in a trailer in the desert. He had a new wife and a cat that lived in the top drawer of their dresser. This vague image was all she had of her Uncle Luster.

"Why do you feel sorry for him?"

"Well, he was her real son, you know. I'm just a stepson."

"Yes."

"Well, they were out of sorts with each other because he had an alcohol problem as a young man, so she named him as her son in her will, but then she gave everything to her neighbors who were her best friends. You remember them?"

"Yes, you meant that man and wife, actually named, 'Friend?'"

"Ah, that'd be them. She left everything to them."

"What? So even though you were over there all the time, she didn't leave you anything either?"

"No. Nope. Not a thing. But see, I wasn't her real son. I didn't expect anything."

"That's bull. Dad, you practically raised your brother for her! I can't believe she'd do that to both of you, but I always felt she was a heartless woman." The only figure Elsie could fetch in her mind of Carmen was that of a squat, immovably stolid form in a sleeveless housedress.

"A heartless woman? That's going a bit too far. She and my dad loved each other. You should'a seen 'em."

"I don't care. She's an evil woman. She's caused so much heartache, Dad. I'm so sorry for you but she can go straight to hell where she belongs!"

"Wait a minute. That's not a very godly response. She raised me after all."

"No, I mean it. She hated Christianity. Maybe that's why she hated Mom, for sure, I don't know, but you don't deserve to be disinherited." Elsie paused her wrath.

"I'm sorry. Dad, I've never been so angry in my life, and I spoke out of turn. I know people don't deserve hell just because they do mean things to their kids, but I just know she wasn't saved."

"That's not your call to make."

"You're right. It isn't. I'm surprised you are defending her, though, Dad. Really?"

"It isn't my call to make either. But, I'm surprised. I didn't know you hated her so much."

"Oh, I didn't before this. I hate her because I love you. She just gave me the heebie-jeebies. I just could never get close to her, and now I know why. There was no love in her." Elsie stopped there, because the torch she was feeling in defense of her dad would only be carried out in words that would further burn his heart. "I'm just very sorry for your loss, Dad, sorry for everything. Are you in touch with your brother?"

"Well, rarely, but I'll be giving him a call. That will be a good thing to see my brother again."

"Okay, well that's good. I won't keep you on this long-distance call, but I love you, and thanks for letting me know."

They said their goodbyes. Then, Elsie closed her eyes and had a heart to heart with Jesus, confessing her hatred and curses over Carmen's head, and praying for her father's comfort. She seemed to do much better singing and counseling others in Christianity than she could muster for her own family circumstances.

Elsie spent almost three years in South Africa Youth Corp, touring with a much-acclaimed Christian band there, known for its racial inclusivity and bookings to any venue, whether tribal, Afrikaans, English, coloured, Indian, or Chinese.

Near the end of Elsie's foreign missionary stint, Gail took a tour of Europe, something she'd won as a prize for selling homes, and dropped down to South Africa to visit her daughter.

Preparing Gail for her visit had been international news clips pocked with bombings and human carnage from the nation's political splits. The country spooked her. Though the Garden Route was exquisite in coastal beauty, her daughter was living in temporary housing. She kept her windows rolled up and the doors locked enroute to each destination, though she enjoyed seeing her daughter thriving in music. As best she could, Gail caught up Elsie as to each member of the family.

Elsie interjected, "Why hasn't Melanie written to me, Mom? Is she mad at me?"

"Oh, I didn't know that she hadn't. I'm not sure."

Melanie had complained to her dad alone about Elsie's deceitful gift of a car. She believed Elsie had intended to sell her the car, knowing it needed a new clutch. Rich failed to mention Melanie's feelings to Elsie.

Not knowing this had happened, or even how much the repair cost, Elsie could only guess why Melanie wouldn't communicate with her.

While Elsie was living a rich, musical life, learning about politics and the world at large, introducing kids to Christ, counseling them about attitudes, parental issues, life decisions, and apartheid, Melanie attended a year of Bible college herself, and promptly married upon returning home, but not to a guy from the college. Her husband was a younger version of Rich, it seemed, and this new edition of her father made Melanie happy. The two girls no longer understood each other.

When Elsie returned from South Africa, Melanie, a newly married woman, still refused to speak with her or even share pictures of her wedding. At the time, Melanie seemed satisfied with her husband and new job, and she carried herself well. She enjoyed buying jewelry and decorating her home.

Elsie believed her sister had come out of her shell and would settle into her place in the world. However, when Kaida mocked Elsie for not understanding what Izod and Polo shirts were, Melanie laughed. When Kaida called Elsie a nun, Melanie agreed. Elsie couldn't understand why her sisters treated her like a leper.

Finally, one evening, Elsie offered to take her sister Melanie from their mom's home to Melanie's new apartment where she and her husband lived. Elsie stopped the car along the way to ask Melanie what in the world was going on. Moths flitted through her headlights. She rolled down her window and gnats flew into the car, so she rolled it up again, bracing herself.

An awful conversation ensued. There was accusation and bitterness, apology and denial, mainly the issue of the car.

Then came the sisters' assurances to start fresh.

Elsie learned a lesson. Keep your line of communication direct and your misunderstandings short. If a wound festers, it will leave a trail of sweet misunderstandings for the ants to follow.

WHEN MY CAR GOT STUCK IN REVERSE, IT TOOK ME BACK

With a mother's pity, Gail invited Elsie to come live with her.

Elsie's intent was to live with her father. The brown cloud had all but evaporated from the north and west of Denver, due to political efforts there. It would have been safe, but her mother kept saying how excited she was to spend time with Elsie. She said, "I've decorated the large guestroom for you, honey. You can rest and take some time to decide what to do."

Rest sounded good to Elsie. She opened the door to her mother's guest room and stood in happy awe. Her mother's typical cleverness and casual elegance wrapped the windows and cushioned the furniture and the bed.

Having returned from Africa with a nickel in her pocket, her mother's opulent home also hit Elsie like culture shock in reverse. Her confusion was softened by the giant pink stars and freckled Asian lilies, filling Gail's front entry with musky fragrance. Elsie decided to accept the offer with an aim to finish her Bachelor of Arts degree at the Colorado College of Music.

Because Gail had visited Elsie in South Africa, there were people Gail remembered, people on which to hang Elsie's stories, but the effort to converse further was lost between them. Their first two weeks quickly filled with awkward attempts to speak about real life and faith with Gail and Kaida on one side of the table and Elsie on the other trying to locate an intersection between business and ministry.

Elsie observed the development of Gail and Kaida's mother-daughter bond with surprise. Their alliance became a bitter pill for Elsie knowing Kaida, in one of her yard sales had sold precious things belonging to Elsie without an explanation or request, a return of the cash, or an apology.

Gail and Kaida's yesterdays were filled with two babies, names of their mutual friends, clothing labels that mattered, places where they both shopped, and related real estate experiences.

Elsie, when speaking of her yesterdays, had a lot of explaining and backstories to build for them to make sense. The two women stared at Elsie, often vexed at the stranger.

Then, Kaida brought her friends over to meet the sister she'd only referenced since high school. They listened to her awkward viewpoints as gawkers watch an anteater at the zoo. Kaida also teased and mocked Elsie for not understanding fashion sense or the significance of labels.

Coming home to rest in the arms of her mother and sisters came with a pillow of porcupine quills. The next time that Gail and Elsie went out for lunch, Gail made it clear that she didn't want to go to this lunch or any lunch in the future apart from "going Dutch." She said, "I find it's awkward to do anything but go Dutch. One person always ends up paying more than the other."

Gail had been a generous person, and she still was, but she couldn't pretend she'd ever had an affinity for Elsie's goal of finishing her music major, nor did she now encourage her pie-in-the-sky music ministry. She'd been supporting her daughter's idealism far too long. It was time for her to grow up. Gail did not intend to continue supporting Elsie. She had to become an adult. Africa? The place seemed far away, so far-fetched. Almost uncouth to speak of!

Curiously, Gail also offered no compromising advice for Elsie as to where to reinvest her talents. She showed, by her suggestion of Elsie auditioning for the local dinner theater as a cast member, that she no longer agreed with her daughter's aims. Two years in South Africa were one thing but making it in America was a whole different world. Her daughter needed to get a grip on a business career, to get with the program here.

Shocked, these ill-fitting attitudes and new expectations became an offense to Elsie. Did her mother recall the girl she'd raised?

In fact, Gail had been so busy making a living in real estate while Elsie had been working in South Africa, that the engrossed businesswoman had only scrawled a couple of quick notes to her daughter over the years.

Now, the image of Elsie's divorced mother, remade, became clear. They lived in separate worlds. Gail's perspective of life had hardened to the practical candy making stage for survival and then melted to the sweet rhythms of happy success.

When her mother wasn't working a Sunday and the two attended church together, they went to the Salad Company with Gail's friends afterward. Gail treated Elsie as an acquaintance during these Sunday lunches. Gail's enthusiasm with musical dinner shows and party discussions spun at these lunches had at first sparked Elsie's happiness for her mom's happiness, but the way her mother kept talking about the shows, praising the singers, and lauding her customers' appreciation for such things while she courted them for real estate business, offended Elsie's dedication to evangelism. Gail's conversations left Elsie feeling second-rate, if she rated at all. Elsie didn't fit with the Sunday lunch group any more than with her mother's business associates though it was good to see her mother had found her stride.

When Gail bought nice pieces of furniture left after an open houses in new subdivisions, and gifted Elsie with two pieces saying, "If you like these, maybe you'll stop dreaming of touring the world. If you like these, there is more. I can give you more when you find a home."

Who was this career woman? The mother's heart had been mislaid in a strange pasture. Elsie felt her mother had traded true love in every sense of the idiom for the lure of worldly pastimes. Normally, she wouldn't have considered an honorable career dishonorable, but her new mother no longer understood her. She spoke a new language. Elsie couldn't comprehend it.

The evening Gail and her missionary daughter set out to see a film together, the film evoked deep distress in Elsie for third world and familial issues, while Gail took the movie date in stride as a night of interesting entertainment. A heated argument ensued, and Elsie packed her bags, feeling unseen and betrayed.

The argument highlighted Elsie's idealism and lack of perspective on the benefits of being American. Gail's argument came from her rooms of accumulated wealth, the housing market, and her redecorating savvy. From Elsie's perspective, her mother was clearly unconcerned about helping the real poor or funding Christian ministry.

So much had changed in so little time!

As noble as Gail's intentions may have been, Elsie saw her living a self-centered lifestyle full of divorced friends, real estate trophies and parties. No room remained for Elsie.

If any blessing was to be given, mother blessed daughter with the advice to finish up her college major by taking a few business and marketing courses and perhaps, follow in her own career path by studying for a real estate license.

Both these suggestions offered Elsie nothing but a view of spiritual apocalypse. "Mom, God may well be providing for you through this career. I see that. But changing my life course at this stage is unacceptable and feels unnatural."

I WON'T *TICK OFF* THE CLOCK

Spending time with her father after two years in Southern Africa and before her senior year of college allowed Elsie to see it was more acceptable to share a home with the parent whose lifestyle seemed less materialistic and unembellished even if his home appeared to be decorated by trolls. In her reverse culture shock, materialism was the great sin to avoid.

Rich habitually piled up books all over the floor and read some, but never dusted or cleaned his house. And, when he decorated, he used the discarded and broken items from her mother's interior decorating business rather than finding items of his own taste. No matter how he designed library shelves or plywood computer desks, his house looked ill at ease because it lacked the finishing touches. Elsie wondered at the difference between the beautiful house she'd grown up in, her mother's own beautiful townhouse and her father's dereliction of décor.

Elsie couldn't put her finger on what was wrong, yet there was something also askance with her father's religious dogma. He was gruff and judgmental. Those who agreed with him, equaled his view of American elitism. She found as much difficulty explaining South Africa's apartheid and her interest in contemporary Christian music with her dad as with her mom. Nevertheless, he booked her for a concert at his church, and she was appreciative.

He kept his living room stereo playing romantic themes. His favorite song was "Clair de Lune" by Debussy, but there were many records to choose from, like, Broadway musicals, classical collections, and records from the thirties forward. Elsie was listening to a 1930s record while perusing a book in Rich's dusty pile of books when she found a birthday card from her dad's old college friend, Brent. In it,

Brent told Rich he was sorry to hear about Rich's frustration with Elsie's arrogance.

When her dad came home from work, she held the card toward him. "Why didn't you tell me that my arrogance offends you, Dad?"

"I'm sorry, my dear. I shouldn't have told Brent anything. We were at a college reunion, and I told him about Gail and my disagreements and that you sided with your mother, which broke my heart. I shouldn't have dragged you into it."

"But, what about the arrogance?"

"Oh, well, it just seems that you think you are so smart with your biblical degree, smarter in religion than me or anyone else."

Elsie's mind went back to her sixth-grade bedroom when her dad's words to her friends in the church youth chorus had crushed her. This was the second time she'd caught her dad trying to make her a voiceless object for reasons unknown to her.

"Like I said, it was unwarranted, and I'll write to Brent right away to let him know I was wrong. Can you forgive me? Come on, I'll take you out for chinese."

That evening, he taught her the new computer processes of Word, how to use spell check, and his music tabulation software. "You can use my computer to work through the tutorials they offer. That should help you get a decent job." He slid out of his office chair and let her take over his position. From there on out, when he was at work, she could use his computer to practice her computer skills.

These were skills she could use. Her dad's pragmatic technology in the new world of desktop computers and secretarial office equipment could be useful.

One day relaxing on the back patio with her father after a job review, Rich told Elsie to be careful about ambition. He told her he would never be a supervisor in his own workplace. He said no every time they offered him a management job. He never intended to move up the corporate ladder. "I'm no good at telling other people what to do. See, people tend to rise in their career path to the point of ineffectiveness and inability, and I just want to keep programing computers because that is the language I best understand."

He continued, "That's why I couldn't get along with your mother. We spoke different languages."

Elsie applied at two temporary agencies and was immediately placed in a law firm using the software skills she'd learned from her father. Now that she'd finally found a way to earn money, she rested.

An interesting thing about living with her father was that he occasionally shared his stories. Rich explained to Elsie that his name had not always been Richard.

"Are you talking about your parents calling you Junior, Dad?"

"No, well there's that. I'm not actually a Jr. as in Richard Jr. I'm just Richard. They called me Junior like someone says 'hey, kid'. What I'm talking about is the day that my dad found me in Kansas at the boy's school—My name was Eugene."

"What?" Elsie frowned. This was the first time she'd ever heard that her father's name was Eugene.

"Yeah, ha-ha. See, my mom resented my dad for leaving us so much, that she started calling me Eugene."

"Why Eugene?"

"Well, I think it was after a guy she dated for a while, but maybe it was just to hide me from my real dad. See, he boxed my ear as a baby and made me partially deaf in one ear. Then, he ran off and refused to support me, and she figured she'd just hide me from him after that. If he couldn't find the boy named after him, then I'd be safe. Maybe she was sticking it to 'em a little bit."

Trying to wrap her mind around the confusion her father must have experienced, she said, "Go on. What happened?"

"Well, my dad and Carmen got custody of me from the school and from my granny because he had my birth certificate and a court order called a Habeas Corpus, which basically means he could collect the body from wherever he found it. I was the body."

"Oh, my word!"

"Heh-heh, yes, well, on our way back to California, we stopped at Carlsbad Caverns. It was a place where you could crawl into cervices and go down into holes and just kind of have fun like little boys like to do."

"Girls. too. I remember you took us there one time, maybe on our way to Pennsylvania."

"Yes, well, I saw this machine that could stamp out your name on a penny if you put it in there, so I put my penny in the machine, and it stamped out my name. I was playing with it in the back seat of the car when Carmen said, 'Whatcha got there, Junior?' I showed her my coin, and she said, 'Eugene? Who's Eugene?' 'Why, that's me!' I said, 'No it ain't,' she said. 'You are Richard after your father! Not Eugene.' Realizing the coin was worthless, I tossed it out the window, and I became Richard at age eleven."

Elsie was speechless. From there on out, she felt so sorry for her dad and later, with all the stories he told her about his childhood, that he grew up believing his mother was the town whore, things which he could barely admit even to her, she continued to make excuses for his behavior and inability to live up to everyone's expectations.

He told Elsie, "See, I was a bastard in the eyes of the world, and yet the Lord gave me a new name and a new life, such as I've made of it."

"I guess I've never understood a thing," she admitted.

After that, when any of her sisters or her mother said a disparaging remark, she became her father's defender. Not that she respected him any better, but that he had good reason for being unable to fit in socially. Every person standing in social judgment has a right to mitigating factors.

When Elsie found a permanent job working in reservations for an airline based in Denver, a major travel benefit was offered to her. Though the job was part-time in nature, the free flights and family discounts excited her.

First, she asked her father to join her in visiting Pennsylvania to visit the mission. He agreed. A stimulus of joy's molecules flowed and jumped to life doing things they both felt fondly of together, including planning the flight and the trip to Pennsylvania.

Elsie found going back to a childhood bigger-than-life memory, shrinks the reality. The corner store where they used to ride bikes to get giant two-inch jawbreakers was actually a tiny store only two blocks away. The estate with the castle on it and gate house, her father's office, and a couple other homes, were really situated on a mere five acres ferreted by a winding lane, intermittent gardens, a small pool, and one heck of an ancient shade tree. The tree from her memory loomed as large as ever

A wrought iron fence embraced the mission compound, and a kind lady let them explore and reminisce with her.

A STUNTED CHARACTER DOES NOT SEE GOD AS THE MOST GENEROUS, JOYOUS PERSON IN THE UNIVERSE

On a frosty Sunday morning back at home, after Elsie noticed that her father's car was missing all night, she touched the warm hood as they embarked for the Sunday morning worship service. "Were you with your new girlfriend, Polly, last night Dad?" He admitted it. An awkward silence fell.

Her dad must be lost. The handholding with Elsie from early adulthood even through high school, and college, was as strange as the way he looked at her when she stretched her arms in a yawn. He told her sexual jokes as readily as he told her political or religious jokes.

He made all kinds of excuses when he darted between vehicles and consistently drove over the speed limit or with his habit of driving up to the back of the car in front of him and riding it like a dog humping another dog.

Rich mentioned his great new relationship with two elderly sisters who often took up his time and fed him dinners. He had met the sisters at his church, being the song leader there. Elsie wondered if the women filled her father's real need for a mother.

Otherwise, Rich's social functions among his church friends seemed to occupy him, but a growing underlying rage with the world at large tempered his increasingly clipped conversations. Elsie either responded with nothing and accepted the eggshells of her father's life, or she forfeited a relationship with him.

Rich had developed a nasty twitch in his face and a constant cough. He habitually snorted back postnasal drip, much to her disgust. When they went out together, Elsie noticed his condition kept him blowing and wiping his nose and spitting into a cloth hankie which he saved in his pocket to later wash with the laundry. She couldn't wash her own clothes with his. The pointer on her germaphobia compass went wild fidgeting with neurosis.

When Elsie gingerly broached the subject of his health, Rich blamed Gail for the stress that caused his asthma.

Her once able, handsome idol of a father turned repugnant before her very eyes.

"Mom, Dad is killing me. He blames you for his asthma!" she said while at lunch with her mom.

Gail sighed, "That's a crude and ridiculous sentiment. I intended to find a family home south of metro Denver in order to get him out of the brown cloud of pollution. Why he insists on living northwest, in the thickest area of chemical poisoning, is a mystery to me."

"What are you talking about, Mom? You never mentioned that."

"You've seen it, certainly."

"As a matter of fact, I remember one time during that year I was home, I was not able to see the tops of the skyscrapers. I'd gone to visit Dad downtown, and I looked up into the sky and was taken aback, but I didn't realize it held any bearing on your move to south Denver."

"Of course, it did. And, as a result, I've had years of loss and regret. I'm surprised that you, being a vocalist, keep living with him up there."

This was the first time Elsie recognized the news that the brown cloud was lingering in and around her father's residence, where she had settled. Driving back to his home that evening, she saw exactly what her mother described.

Determined to move out of the socked-in smog as soon as possible, she accepted a friend's invitation to live in her townhome.

A CANNIBAL IS NEVER SATISFIED WITH BEING GIVEN THE COLD SHOULDER

Elsie planned another vacation, this time with her mother. She longed to create good memories with her again. They flew to Bermuda and rented a bed and breakfast together. They were led to their room on a winding path through a scented, overgrown garden.

Delighted, Elsie told Gail, "The humidity and the fragrance of this place and old-world charm of the garden house reminds me so much of Pennsylvania. Does it to you, Mom?"

"Do you think so?"

"Maybe it's the island version of old-world architecture. Gorgeous!"

"It is gorgeous, Elsie, and I know you have good memories of Pennsylvania, but I don't. I suffered living there, and if you remember correctly, your dad and I divorced shortly after leaving because he abandoned me emotionally there."

"Okay, I'm sorry. I can see that it was a poor comparison for you. Let's leave the past in the past, and just enjoy this time together, shall we?"

No cars were allowed on the island, so Gail and Elsie decided to take the driving test to each lease the popular mode of transportation, two-wheeled mopeds. Full of eager adventure, they listened to instructions on how to operate the cycles and how to stop them. Grinning, they donned their helmets and started their engines.

The first jaunt around the course went fine. They were getting the hang of it, but as they picked up speed, Gail lost control rounding the arc. She flew past the curb and tumbled down an embankment.

Gail was denied a license. She said she was happy to read her book in the garden and let Elsie explore alone on the moped. Their mutual adventure crashed with Gail's new limitations. As Gail's body turned black and blue, Elsie followed island maps to white beaches and a nautical museum featuring stories of the many mysterious disappearances of ships and airplanes inside the Bermuda Triangle.

Lush evening explorations to the end of peninsulas and beyond the end of the bus routes filled Elsie's ears with musical rhythms from island guitarists enjoying their front porches at night. Strains of contentment caught the tails of the humid air and rested on Elsie's senses.

Though their vacation was beautiful, Elsie felt the fracture of exploring the island alone while her mom stayed at the cottage. Elsie's guilt added to regret that she and her mother were not sharing or talking as she had planned. She kept motoring back from the beaches to check on Gail. She brought their meals to their lodge and told her about her excursions.

"I can't take that amount of sun anyway, Elsie. You go. I'm enjoying my book."

Though the island was intoxicating, the Devil's Triangle sucked the life out of the mother-daughter experience and would not part the waters to resurrect the shipwreck. Their relationship, ever-elusive, though amicable, was never close.

When she considered which parent would most likely bear her failures, confessions, or struggles, every time, Elsie returned to her father.

When Melanie's birthday rolled around, Elsie and her dad planned a party at a nice seafood restaurant to celebrate.

Rich took both of his daughters' hands and ushered them into the lovely restaurant where sentimental music filled the air. There, Melanie ran up the bill with glass after glass of beer, a second helping of crab legs, then a third, while blabbing nonstop about her friends at work and things that neither Rich nor Elsie could relate to. Her father hardly spoke, and Elsie counted the minutes before she could leave the fray. She understood so little.

Rich invited his girls over for Thanksgiving. He was having a party. This was, in itself, a strange concept. They'd never known their father to throw a house party.

The Finch girls each felt a gust of the north wind when, immediately after introducing Polly's two children to his own children at Thanksgiving, Rich informed them of his plans to marry his female guest. Mashed potatoes became glue in their mouths.

Rich's efforts to produce a blended family with Polly's children proved fruitless. His abrupt manner of taking what he wanted—without considering what he already had—hardly helped. Her children were about to graduate from high school, and his own were long gone. Also unsettling was the way Rich could find no blueprint for step-mothering and step-fathering adult children.

Rich's children saw the new queen of their father's house residing with her princess moon and orbiting planet son, and they didn't much like this stepfamily revolving through the Finch family universe.

One of them was always home when Elsie came to visit her father. There was a continual annoyance of stepmother and daughter keeping the hall phone busy, chatting nonstop. The chirping gossip and descriptions of items they'd just found shopping filled the house like a switchboard operation.

Maybe the children or the parents could have experimented with boundaries and respect, and some introductions to each other's lifestyles, but the stepfamilies were not to become one. Personalities were not a good fit for any level of friendship.

Elsie, making excuses, avoided her father's house allowing the new wife and children full reign.

Rich continued his habit of holding his daughter's hand whenever they went somewhere together. Going to dinner one night, he mentioned a girl at work who wore tight sweaters and shirts and stretched like that to show off her breasts when she talked to him. Now that he was remarried, she didn't want to hear these things from him. Yet he even spoke about different women at his church, not to honor them in appropriate assessments of their work. He spoke of them as being the reason he struggled sexually.

Elsie felt she was tumbling between the two alien worlds of her parents, tumbling down a crevice into a nether region. It was as though their own family held no sway in new decisions, emerging lifestyles.

Culture shock claimed her life for months, the effect of it possibly for years. Coming home proved there was no home left. She was not only out of the nest, so to speak, but the nest and the nest makers were lost to the elements of nature and time.

Elsie felt abandoned by her parents and her siblings.

She considered that God didn't say he hated divorce only for the sake of the spouses, but mainly for the sake of the children. A family is a village. Wounds, unhealable wounds, kept getting dirt rubbed into them. These sores created welts of odd behaviors, and perverse attitudes toward faith and God, toughening the skin of each girl.

CREATE *FISCAL* EXERCISE—BUDGET FOR BARBELLS

She was earning enough money to move into an apartment in Denver and pay expenses of a final year of college which she lacked for her four-year Bachelor of Arts degree. There was also a loan she was living off.

Elsie had a lot to learn about banking, budgeting, and spending. She was about to learn the hard way.

Getting into college and enjoying city life were her immediate goals—then perhaps she would move to Nashville or California, maybe even New York to find work. These ideas were being embroidered into her transitional lifestyle.

There is a proverb similar to a pun that aptly declares, "You make plans, but God directs your footsteps."

She made two mistakes in early adulthood. First, when she lived with her father, Rich co-signed for a revolving line of credit for her at his bank. Going to college, Elsie let the debt creep up by not paying the principal used every month. Then, one day after she was learning to live on her own, the bank called in the loan, and then threatened her with a collection process. Believing the bank was in error, she called her dad. He met her at the institution and listened while the banker explained the terms of the loan were only for four years.

What a surprise to Elsie who thought she could use the credit perpetually, like a credit card so long as she didn't max out the limit.

Rich further corrected her thinking, and then told her she would have to pay off the loan with another credit card and pay down that loan as soon as possible because "the interest rate will make you a slave to the lender." She obeyed him even though her college and new music business expenses seemed overwhelming. She also found herself a second roommate and subleased her new car rather than selling it outright, her second mistake. She bought a cheaper used car instead.

When the young man who subleased her car peeled away to New York and stopped paying, the loan payments again overwhelmed Elsie, and she had no car to show for paying them. The young man had cleverly found a way to enrich himself with a new car!

Again, when Elsie confessed her predicament to her father, he clenched his jaw but helped her. He bought himself a plane ticket to New York, visited the young man's supervisor at his place of work, and explained why he was there. The supervisor brought the young man out, made him turn over the keys, and before driving the car back across the county, Rich bought four new tires returning it to his daughter like an episode of Superman.

Incredulous that Rich would do something so heroic for her, a heart-bending gratitude and fondness was rekindled for him.

For Mother's Day that year, Gail asked all her children to bring over plants to plant. Elsie brought over spreading myrtle and pansies, a palate of them. But Gail didn't want to plant the plants herself.

"Did you bring your own gloves, darling? I have tools." She expected her children to weed the plots and plant and fertilize everything that day. She wanted someone to grill the burgers in the evening. The gift suggestion turned into a Mother's Day Tax as the hours wore on and everyone's joy turned to disbelief, then to dirty exhaustion.

"Ever think of hiring a gardener, Mom?" Melanie and Elsie teased.

"Yeah, Happy Mother's Day, Mom. Do you want us to work the entire 24 hours?" Kaida prodded.

"Well, if you can, I wouldn't argue," Gail shot back.

"*It isn't a gift if it is a demand,*" thought Elsie. "*I should write a lyric or a poem on that.*"

On her way home, it crossed the mind of more than one daughter, "P*erhaps Dad couldn't live with Mom because she was too demanding, too exacting, and never satisfied."*

A week later, Elsie wrote a little poem on a café napkin. Her roommate couldn't join her, so she ate alone observing other café guests in conversation. Couples eating in silence disturbed her and warned her to choose a mate wisely. She was lonely, but what could she do? Loneliness was better than getting stuck with a family of empty wells. It didn't matter how many buckets of water she poured into the wells of her family members, there just wasn't enough water to satiate their thirst.

Empty Wells
Empty wells, drinking in
drinking, drinking, drinking in
empty wells that never give
empty drinking wells that live.

While building music networks doing these activities, Elsie's circle of friends and contacts grew. Her need for a network of music and business connections far outweighed her need for musical success. While she'd moved back to Colorado because she yearned for her family, and while her family had abdicated their positions in her world, her heart would not allow her to move away again. Her relationships were growing by helping a small business network that promoted other musicians. It began to flourish.

Perhaps she'd found her niche in promotions.

One day, when Elsie complained of sore muscles, her dad put her on a bed and gave her a back massage which felt divine, but also intrusive when he worked her buttocks. She knew that he knew what he was doing. He'd often given her shoulder rubs that felt delicious, but in his presence, more and more, she left him feeling slimed.

She began to avoid both of her parents in the effort of trying to find her own way in the world.

On her way to work from a college course, Elsie found a little café in which to sit and have a quick sandwich. At a table along the wall, she noticed a Jewish father in his yarmulke bent over his food, speaking quietly to his son. The son looked to be about twelve years old. The father explained some issues about life to his son, touching his hand and the son's attention was clearly held.

Tears welled in Elsie's eyes as she watched the scene. A father who intentionally ate meals with his child in order to help prepare him for life was a precious commodity in her experience.

Oh, if she had ever brought forth the best in her father that way! If he had ever seen the need to take any of his offspring to meet wisdom in a lunchroom by speaking about everyday common issues they might face with wisdom. If he had offered his honed spiritual advice to political issues, humanitarian issues. If he had compared traditional views to modern dilemmas with them and blessed them by believing in their steadfastness to the vision! How might scripture have been applied by fatherly insight, should he have prepared his daughters for what they were facing now?

A WOODEN FLUTE WOUND UP IN THE TRASH BECAUSE IT *WOODEN* WHISTLE

Dan, Melanie's young husband, lost his job. He began lying to his wife saying, "I'm going to work," when he left each morning. Financial problems came next.

The tension between the two became a wall of silence. A man in the mechanics department of the Bible college where Melanie had attended began calling her. Then, he came down to visit her.

She slept with him.

As soon as she realized she was pregnant, Melanie filed for divorce and found a small apartment on her own. This was a wakeup call for Dan. He hadn't considered that he could lose his wife. He tried to reconcile with her over the phone, but she refused to see him. He apologized for lying to her. He found a good job and promised Melanie he'd never lie to her again.

Melanie listened to everything, but couldn't admit what she had done to him, and if she returned to Dan, he'd soon know. It was over.

There was no going back. He eventually moved back to Wyoming and counseled with a godly man who helped him do better. When he tried a final time to find his ex-wife, there was no paper trail. She'd disappeared.

Melanie confided in Elsie that she was pregnant from someone else, someone not her husband. The father was married and had a family. She didn't want to tell him. She didn't want to have an abortion. Could Elsie help her adopt the baby to a Christian household? Melanie was adamant that the adoption would only go through if it was to a Christian home.

Elsie agreed to help her because she knew of Bethany Christian Services, an adoption agency, and she also knew her best friend from camp days was unable to have a baby. The best friend had been married for several years now without a successful pregnancy. Melanie had met the best friend several times through camping experiences and thought the match was her best option.

The adoption process developed on schedule until the baby was born. Elsie's best friend and husband eagerly came to Colorado and booked a hotel, waiting for notification.

Notification never came.

Instead, Gail insisted that Melanie see her baby wrapped in the receiving blanket. After holding him herself, she insisted that Melanie hold her baby. When the baby cried, Gail told Melanie that she should try to nurse him one time before giving him up. Gail knew what she was doing. When Melanie couldn't resist, it became impossible to give him up.

The friendship between Elsie and her best friend was lost in the tragedy, but Gail showed no compassion or regret on Elsie's behalf.

Indeed, Gail felt no shame about what she'd done. She just couldn't imagine her grandson going to another family from another state where she might never see him again. She told Melanie that she would help her however she could, because she had also been a single mother. Melanie felt ashamed, nonetheless. She had not made provisions, nor had she planned to keep the child.

Melanie wasn't unhappy that she kept Richard. She loved the boy, but she named her son for her father and, simultaneously, resented her mother for her surprise maneuver. "You could have said that was how you felt, Mom. The adoptive parents waited for months for him, and now, you made me betray them."

"Aren't you glad you kept him?" Gail avoided the accusation.

"I'm not ready to be a mom, Mom! I don't have a nursery. They did. I don't have clothes or baby supplies–anything!"

Gail's last-minute action to prevent the adoption of Melanie's baby was the wedge that came between herself and Melanie and also between herself and Elsie.

Elsie may have excused her mother's act of blind love had Gail not kept her resolve hidden until the last moment, ruining the hopes and deep joy of an infertile mother and father. By doing so, Gail had destroyed Elsie's relationship with her best friend and badly damaged it with Melanie. Once again, she felt disloyal to one if she hobnobbed with the enemy. Yet, it was Gail's own lack of trustworthiness that caused a deeper, more profound despair in Elsie. Her mother's strength moved in whatever way pleased her, and others seemed not to matter.

Failing so badly, Elsie backed off from her family members.

Elsie thought, *"Life gets big, HUGE, sometimes, laying over you like a sleeping bear, a weight keeping you from running, walking, and finishing school projects. There is no bounce because you can barely breathe. Whether the sleeping bear wakes is completely random. Being morbid is the dread of what happens next."*

Elsie had outrun the lumbering bear of her family till now, but it had caught her.

Until her best friend, five years later, was able to enter a pregnancy study and successfully have a child naturally, their relationship floundered awkwardly. On the family front, Elsie's relationship with her sister was fragile, as was her relationship with Gail, who hid her feelings under the veil of careful, polite talk.

In a moment of painful clarity, Gail finally understood that she had encouraged Melanie to keep a baby she was unprepared to care for. Gail realized her coldly calculated actions resulted in the loss of two daughters' relationships. Even though she could not apologize to anyone for her manipulation, she began to buy diapers, blankets, bottles, and clothes.

When Rich heard that Melanie had named her baby after him, he panicked. In virulent rejection of Melanie and Ricky, he confided in Carlene a fright that people might think he had enjoyed sexual relations with his daughter, that this was the reason for her divorce.

Her dad's rejection made Melanie all the more adamant to win his care and attention. After all, she meant the name as a compliment, not a curse.

Though Gail promised to help, she was unable to babysit the boy during Melanie's work week due to her own business hours in real estate.

Being the catalyst of so much controversy and bearing the full responsibility for a little life placed squarely on her shoulders, Melanie determined to remove herself from her mother, and thus remove her son from Gail's grip. Her son would not be Gail's prize for deception. Melanie would not become her mother's dependent.

Carlene listened to the story from every angle, from her mother, her father, her sisters. She offered Melanie a hiding place.

One diaper bag and three suitcases later, Melanie moved to Louisiana, accepting her eldest sister's offer. She became office bookkeeper for Carlene's interior design business and for her new herbal natural healing business, also in exchange for free housing.

Carlene's perspectives on the Finch family, especially regarding Gail, were free of charge. She fed poison into her younger sister like she prepared oils and herbal remedies for those who asked.

Carlene and Foreman immediately got pregnant themselves, and when hormones were flying, Carlene ruled with the long arm of a benevolent dictator. Incrementally, Melanie began feeling indentured to her sister since she couldn't save any money to leave. Unable to get out on her own, and seeing that soon there would be a new baby needing the room occupied by Melanie and Ricky, she began to make emergency evacuation plans.

When Carlene's first baby was born, Melanie was asked not only to provide bookkeeping services for two companies, but also babysitting services.

The two babies, side-by-side, appeared as brother and sister, yet the gap between entrepreneurial sister and slave sister became more and more apparent to one of them. After a couple of dedicated years, seeing the dead-end situation for what it was, Melanie demanded a sum of money for settlement, packed up, and flew back to Colorado just as Carlene tumbled into depression and anguish over Melanie's outlandish accusations.

Carlene's emotional trauma stemmed from her decision as a business owner to not carry health insurance. In Louisiana, if a pregnant woman didn't have health insurance, her choices were to go to a midwife or a teaching hospital or take her chances elsewhere. Carlene opted for the teaching hospital. This meant, while giving birth, there would be a class of medical students observing and taking instruction.

Apparently, Carlene was not told or did not listen to the fact that teaching hospitals, by design, use patients as case studies with no privacy attached. Afterwards, she maintained that they had treated her "like a whore" and "the students had put their hands and fingers all over" her private parts.

Melanie, needled by this experience with her eldest sister, determined to work in a man's world from there on out.

When she qualified for Section 8 government-sponsored housing, she took a job at a car dealership in an environment where she surrounded herself with mostly men. When that job appeared to offer nothing more than minimum wage and benefits, she found a better paying job at a chicken processing plant in bookkeeping, also a job that mostly attracted male workers, though there were many immigrants as well. She asked Elsie to babysit, which Elsie did. Gail also helped.

Then Melanie, a fast learner, found a roommate willing to babysit for a share of the occupancy in the government issued house.

During this time, when Melanie disclosed anything concerning herself, she continued to assert that her child was not Dan's. Dan had betrayed her. Men were better companions only because they weren't women, but men were tools of common conversation, nothing more.

This marriage and the arrival of her first child developed her doubts about the relevance of sexuality at all. If human beings could only control their passions, they'd be a lot better off, she reasoned.

Melanie intended to make herself indistinguishable as female. Talking transmissions, oil changes, and career opportunities, she closely listened to male conversations. In her speech, bullets spit through pinched lips. She began wearing unpressed jeans, T-shirts covered by flannel shirts as her workday uniform, including Saturdays and Sundays. She stopped trimming or fixing her hair and she stopped dating.

She saw her father's absenteeism as being rational and logical, though Rich, the romantic, never would have agreed with his daughter. If anything, his romanticism was the thing that kept getting him into trouble.

When Melanie told people that because Ricky crossed his legs at rest, he was going to be gay, Rich did not offer a wise man's opinion. The females of the family rolled their eyes. For her sanctity of mind, she bought headphones to listen to her music without interference and also to make it clear that she could block out all the family noise.

Melanie slept in, got her mornings together slowly, and came an hour late to every invitation without an apology, or she offered excuses. She had two women friends, women who also deviated from traditional views of sexuality.

Much to Gail's chagrin, Melanie stopped communicating with her unless she was desperate for a babysitter. Instead, she formed a relationship with an elderly woman whom she began confiding in and calling "mom."

She gathered memberships to the local zoo, museums, and restaurant chains. She collected coupons for everything and organized them even if the discount was for a product she couldn't use.

She attended Gail's church for the food bank by acting the part of the impoverished single mother and underpaid victim, while those church members who knew Gail, knew her to be a responsible businesswoman who loved the Lord. Gail continued to praise the Lord openly for providing everything she needed.

Melanie's cunning ideas to distress and dishonor her mother continued while she smiled sweetly and worked the angles of neediness.

Who could hold a conversation with one who kept listening to ear buds wired into a shirt pocket device? The affront was as much visual as it was practical.

"No thank you," she'd say whenever her mother offered her a new shirt or new jeans or offered her son new shoes or a new outfit. The cuts to her mother's person seemed endless.

Rich accepted visits from his daughter and her child more regularly, but in private with reticence. When she asked for fatherly wisdom, he tried to share what he knew. He told her that if Ricky started masturbating that she should allow him to. His birth mother had taught him to masturbate, he said, and it was a completely natural thing for the development of boys. Melanie kept Ricky in bed with her until he started first grade, and even then, bed-sharing was the norm.

But, when Gail was able to see Ricky, she made the dates special. She bought him farm toys, small cars, Legos, and his favorite foods. She got down on the carpet and played whatever he wanted to play, and she gave him all the nurturing in her heart. She would often ask Kaida to bring over her children to play with Ricky so that they could all bond as cousins. She did everything within her power to be the glue her family so desperately needed.

Melanie, holding her mother responsible for forcing motherhood upon her, while she had been absent for much of Melanie's own childhood, consequently treated her child as baggage for the public eye, and especially with her family. Yet she loved her son and enjoyed his company in private.

She simply couldn't seem to muster the maternal instincts to dress him properly or bring him in blankets or with snacks to special visits. She'd often forget her son's sweater or coat in winter.

Her sisters looked on with growing agitation. Melanie didn't seem to know what nurturing looked like. When Gail invited her family to holiday dinners, their sister acted all the more conflicted. Sometimes, she didn't give him boots in winter because "he'll just grow out of them." Her so-called logic was illogical. Ricky learned to dress himself as best he could.

He was a happy, courageous boy, and industrious. At age two, Ricky learned to forage and feed himself by climbing onto a chair and then onto the kitchen cabinets to find prepacked foods in the upper cabinets that he could eat. The child had to compete with two ferrets that Melanie kept as pets; the ferrets also lived in her kitchen cabinets. Her house began to take on the smell of feces and musk. She lived in filth with her son and her roommate in a self-fulfilling view of herself as a loser, albeit a clever survivor living below the radar as a master manipulator of deals, benefits, and descriptors for charitable distributions.

For two years, Gail could not make good with Elsie. She wanted to chat. She wanted to mend fences and go shopping together, she wanted to show off the success of her latest diet. Couldn't Elsie just lighten up and let bygones be bygones?

Elsie wanted nothing to do with her well-heeled, trophy winning mother who had the power to usurp her daughter's choices and ruin intimate relationships. She declined the shopping excursions. Her mother was making none of the noises of regret. When she kept glossing over her winnings at her daughter's losses, Elsie tried not to think of her family members, especially her mom.

Distressed, Elsie finally picked up the phone to call her mother, asserting that maybe an intervention was appropriate for Melanie. She told her mother that she wanted to call child protective services, but Gail, though distressed herself, kept saying no. Gail was adamant. This tack was too invasive. The state foster care program was fraught with its own issues. She read Elsie some recent headlines.

Elsie backed down.

All they could do was continue to offer help from their individual corners. She, Elsie, and Kaida offered babysitting to Melanie, and friendship. The one, she happily accepted, the other she rebuffed.

Elsie and Gail's bond between mother and daughter began to sprout fragile roots. Elsie and Gail were the two who usually saw spiritual things in the same way. The main thing that bothered Gail about their relationship was that Elsie was not completely hers. Elsie would defend her father and occasionally Carlene and Melanie at the most unexpected times, while Gail saw her ex-husband as a fraud and a creep and possibly the murderer of her baby boy. Still, Gail trusted Elsie. And Elsie often asked her mother to help with different ministries and causes, which she did.

On her lunchbreak one day, Gail called Elsie to ask if she would agree to be the personal representative for her will.

Elsie said she'd think about it.

Finally, she agreed but only because it was the lesser of two evils. She told her mother, "I'm really concerned about the family dissention being more than I could handle, but of course, I wouldn't want my inheritance to be controlled by any one of my sisters. Could you just give it to an attorney or someone else, perhaps?"

In a few years, as the world turned, she would discover the outcome of this conversation.

PRESENT TENSE MAKES THE PAST PERFECT, A GRAMMAR LESSON LEARNED OF NOSTALGIA

When Mother's Day rolled around again, Gail called each of her children. "I'd like to do a repeat of last year's celebration. Don't give me a card or take me to dinner. I just want some pallets of flowers and ground covers for the garden. Maybe a row of bushes. I'm in the mood for spring, aren't you?"

The obedient girls knew to bring their gardening gloves and favorite tools this time. The little grandchildren played together as the adult girls spent the day prepping soil and planting.

It became apparent to Melanie, since her mother couldn't bear to be away from Kaida's kids for more than a few hours, that she and her son would have to take a back seat. Her withdrawal from her mother proved successful to a fault.

Elsie kept her distance from Gail because she'd caused the breakup of her best friend's adoption, thus breaking up her closest friendship. She also could get involved in the growing animosity between Gail and Melanie.

Carlene first encountered her mother's favoritism when she and Foreman began driving back to Colorado for family Christmases. Carlene's children were welcomed as the towheaded counterparts to Melanie's little Ricky, but Carlene couldn't get her mother to spend time individually with her children. Instead, she observed her mother doting on them in measure, but not in the way she seemed to need Kaida's children for nourishment.

Gail's plans and purchases were for Kaida and her children first; if she happened to find an item for any of her other grandchildren, they of course also benefited.

Carlene told her two girls, "I'm the eldest. I should get preferential treatment from my parents but watch Grandma's truly biblical switch in how she doles out affections." She told Foreman in their presence, "They get to experience what Jacob and Esau experienced and also what Ephraim and Manasseh and Leah and Rachel experienced: My youngest sister has beguiled the heart of my mother and supplanted the elder in the line of blessings."

Carlene's girls couldn't comprehend all their mother said, but as they watched, it seemed her perspective was true.

Gail and Carlene's relationship deteriorated quickly as each of them used three overused words in their communications, "you," "always," and "never," often with Carlene's daughters in the room. But perspectives of what was said, the timing of who said what, the catalyst, and the story omissions, were perpetually spinning tales.

Carlene said to her sisters, "You know what she told me? Mom said I deserved a strong-willed child because of what I made her live through." If someone listened to the one person's story, it seemed rational. Then, when the other person gave their side of the story, things changed.

Carlene refused to accept guilt for her preteen choice to leave her mom as far behind as possible. She'd kept her mother's nose in a corner since the family move to Colorado with her parents' separation.

She stopped seeing her mother or allowing Gail access to her children when she and Foreman came with their two children to visit family. Instead, she would stay with Kaida. When Kaida began mocking her by spinning stories of their times together, Carlene and Foreman modified their annual vacation destination to staying only with Elsie.

Elsie also sensed her mother's strong favoritism toward Kaida. It was obvious her other sisters' children were getting leftovers. Since she didn't recall how or why it began, she questioned the incongruencies and teased her mother. Gail flatly denied it. "Carlene's girls have two parents. Kaida's only have one."

"That's not true, Mom. They have two parents in town, plus a very generous grandma."

Gail felt a chilly draft more often between herself and three of her girls, but her response was to hide her spoiling of Kaida all the more.

She laughed, throwing it back at them saying, "You girls always loved your father more because girls naturally desire their father's love over their mother's. You'll wake up one day." Gail said, "Anyway, I hardly remember a time that Carlene didn't despise me." She also couldn't admit openly that Melanie withheld Ricky from her. It was too shameful and confusing.

Kaida bought her first home and Gail gave her the real estate agent's commission toward the down payment. "If any of you other girls want to buy your homes from me, I'll do the same for you," she promised.

Kaida shrugged at the huge financial gift saying, "It's about time, since Elsie has always been the favored child."

Elsie frowned and challenged the assertion, but Kaida cited, "Fact one: Mom took a job in order to provide you with braces. Fact two: Mom and Dad took you and Carlene on their second honeymoon and left us home. Fact three: Mom funded your college education. Fact four: Mom sent me to a girl's prison."

It took her breath away! Such caustic manipulation and comparisons succeeded in closing the mouths of both Gail and Elsie so that Kaida continued to enjoy her favored place in the landscape of Mom's world.

"You forget that I was there, Kaida, to see your uninhibited living, suffocating in your vomiting, and seeking your own pleasures in disobedience to Mom's rules." Elsie defended her mother's decision to send Kaida for rehabilitation. "Mom was at her wit's end, and she was having to compete for a living in real estate at the time when the whole state was in an economic depression. She had to work, and she couldn't hold onto you. Really, Kaida, can't you accept partial responsibility for what happened as your own behavior?"

Stuck in a defensive crouch, Gail would apologize over and again saying, "Well, I don't know. I might have done something else, but honestly, I don't know what. Please, forgive me? What more can I do now?"

It was a open-ended question to Kaida. She would pour herself a drink at these moments. She'd flip her hand at the apology and change the awful subject. Her relationship with Gail became rutted between their mutual desires to bury the past and offer the little grandchildren safety and privilege by protecting them in lovely homes and dressing them like darlings. Kaida's ability to guilt and grab her mother's attention and pick her pocketbook was quickly honed.

When Gail decided to move, Kaida also found a home in proximity to foster Gail's daily access to the grandchildren. They often conversed about issues facing the rest of the family, and they very often landed at the same conclusions.

Melanie decided she would rather become a lifelong renter than buy a home from her mother or compete with Kaida. She wasn't sure what she wanted or where she would land and didn't want to be locked in. Melanie couldn't trust her mother. Thinking it was a bribe, she sabotaged her own interests along with Gail's.

When suspicions increased between Gail and Kaida that Melanie's Ricky belonged to Dan, seeing as he keenly resembled Melanie's ex-husband, they schemed to get the youngster's DNA tested.

They located Dan living with a new wife in Wyoming.

Kaida called and wrote to him, sending him a picture of the boy. "If this is your son, would you want to know? We think he is. Would you be willing to do a paternity test and find out?"

Invested now in Promise Keepers, and devoted to his current family, Dan discussed his potential responsibilities with his wife. They agreed that he should do a paternity test, and if he proved to be the father, which they both thought likely, he would take an active role in Ricky's life.

The day came when Kaida invited the family to a picnic in a nearby park. Ricky was in her and Gail's care for the weekend, and Dan drove down from Wyoming to meet his son. He was pushing Ricky around in a child's plastic car, love filling his heart, hope rising, when Melanie arrived at the picnic with Elsie.

Neither one of them knew what had happened.

Melanie spotted what looked like her ex-husband playing with her son and stopped in her tracks, grabbing Elsie's arm. "Did you know about this?"

"Know about what?"

"Look who's here!"

"Who?" Then Elsie saw Dan and assured her sister that she had no part in whatever was going on.

"I've told them. Dan is not Ricky's father!" Her anger seethed, steaming through hurdles. "What are they doing? They have no right!"

The sisters approached the picnic table blindsided. Elsie sat down, waiting for the explosion and the explanations.

Melanie walked toward her son and lifted him in her arms. She faced Dan and said, "Hello. What's going on here?"

He told her what he knew.

She told him. "I never told you because he is not your son."

"But, his birthday, and the way he looks…"

"I know that, but he is not your son. I'm so sorry you've been conned into whatever Kaida and my mom are doing, but the truth is, I had a one-night stand when you and I were not speaking to one another. There is no way he could be your son because we weren't having sex. That's why I divorced you. It wasn't that you were unemployed. It was that our marriage was broken for so long, and I betrayed you over it. I'm so sorry."

Letting it all seep in, Dan shrugged. "I guess the paternity test will provide the final answer for all of us."

"The. . .what?" Melanie's fury lashed like a wildfire at all present. She stomped back to the picnic table to scream at her family. "How dare you! I know what that paternity test will say. How dare you?!"

Kaida shrugged. Some material is freakishly unburnable in fast moving fires.

"Well, you were so closed mouthed about it all, and Ricky looks like Dan! He's a mini-me of Dan, Melanie!"

"I don't have to tell you all my secrets. You don't have the right to them, and you don't deserve to know anything. You are a bunch of jerks. I hate you all. I can't trust you."

"Melanie, I didn't –" Elsie began.

"We're leaving." Melanie packed up Ricky's things and left the picnic with Elsie following close behind.

The paternity test confirmed Melanie's story, and as willing as Dan was to provide a father for Ricky, his services were thanked and dismissed.

"The sins of the fathers are passed down"...where is that verse again? When Elsie went to her apartment, she looked up the key words in *Strong's Concordance* and found it was the name of God that he gave to the Hebrews near the beginning of the Ten Commandments. That's strange, she thought as she read through it several times.

"For I, the LORD your God, am a jealous God, punishing the children for the sin of the parents to the third and fourth generation of those who hate me but showing love to a thousand generations of those who love me and keep my commandments."

Jealousy must have a different meaning than envy. God described Himself as being jealous about something. Was it righteousness? His own reputation? "Punishing the children for the sin of the parents to the third and fourth generation of those who hate me...but showing love to a thousand generations of those who love me and keep my commandments."

She saw two sides of God. Maybe He was a God of wrath, but it was clear that the wrath only extended to the fourth generation. Here, God was saying His love would extend a thousand generations to those who loved Him and kept His commandments.

"So, Lord, what happens when the parents of a family are so split? Grandma Lugilla's husband hated You, practically speaking, but she loved You and showed Your goodness to her entire community. Grandma Hudson's husband hated You and withheld love or help from our family, but she is the godliest person I've ever known, a praying, kind person, and so funny! Here, my father is a betrayer of his family, and I have no idea where he stands with You, and my mother seems more devious and selfish than I ever understood before, but I know You've blessed her and are caring for her. I don't understand if You are going to punish all of us and make Ricky and Paige and Grant suffer, too, or show Your love. Which is it, God?"

Elsie sat for some time contemplating what could happen, what her options were, what her sisters' options were, and how she might help them. It felt overwhelming. She put her head in her hands and wept. "I'm so sorry for our family sins, Lord. We had yet another landmark drama of them today, and who knows what harm will come from it?" She decided to take a long nap.

When she got up, she looked over the passage again. Pausing at the commandment, "Do not take the name of the Lord in vain." She considered it again. She'd always been taught that this referred to using the name of God, Jesus, or Christ as a swear word or euphemism. Now, in the context of her family's messes, she saw the word "take" as in taking on a label, or a branding. She thought of someone who puts on a coat or something to cover their nakedness. That phrase, for the first time, sounded more like, "Don't take My covering or label for yourself unless you live in Me and I in you."

It was a revelation.

NO LITANY OF LOVE *LIES* WITH A PLEA OF RELEASE

Melanie went home from the picnic defeated. When her rage and depression wore off to the point that she could think through the implications of her secrecy on Ricky's life, she decided to contact his biological father to see whether he would be interested in seeing his son or paying child support. She placed the call later that week when she'd sufficiently considered the possible outcomes. She knew he was married. She had met his wife. She knew he had other children; that was why she hadn't upset the man's family.

Nothing ventured, nothing gained, she decided.

Picking up the phone, she dialed the out-of-state number and asked to speak with Jerry.

"Hi Jerry, this is Melanie Finch. I know, a blast from the past, right? Well, I'm calling because I guess you have a right to know that you have a son in Colorado. I'm wondering if you want to see him or if you'd be interested in offering child support."

Jerry couldn't get off the phone fast enough. At first, he asked why she'd waited so long to tell him. Then, he denied the suggestion. Finally, he said, if he could see his son, that maybe he'd be willing to offer child support.

"No pressure," Melanie stated. "We're here." She hung up the phone and went to make dinner. Life was nothing but hard. Where was the fun of it?

Jerry never did pay a dime of child support.

Melanie let him go.

Elsie asked Melanie to attend a concert with her. She wanted to introduce her sister to a guy friend. When Melanie accepted, she immediately went to her sister's house, rolled her hair and sprayed it, adding barrettes.

Melanie rolled her eyes and muttered. "My hair won't take a curl. I know my hair. It will just fall out. You and Carlene got all the curl." But she let her sister preen and groom her and dress her up, and she even added some lipstick and eyeshadow. They were both impressed with the results.

The date didn't work out, but a bridge between the sisters mysteriously appeared.

This landmark event dredged up the submerged emotions of Elsie's rage at her mother during the adoption she upset, and the years of difficulties for so many due to that interference.

She loved and respected her mom in so many ways, but she also loved her father. Every time she mentioned her father within her mother's earshot, she felt a red slash of rage fly through the air and mark her person.

It was clear that for Elsie to be prioritized in her mother's heart, Gail would require complete loyalty and undivided attention. Gail had yet to tell Elsie her side of the events in the two divorces, but she required absolute fidelity without a story to inspire it.

Elsie's loyalty was to the family as a whole. Her aim was to mend family breaches. Other friends had parents who divorced, but their parents remained friendly. Their ability to get along helped the children with celebrations and holidays. Why could some families, even non-Christian families, manage to be so happy, when the Finch family, all who asserted the Christian faith, held each other's throats to the wall without a stool to stand on?

Elsie listened to a set of messages on forgiveness, and prayed regularly to be forgiving towards her parents, but memories renewed her anger and confusion, and neither of her parents seemed to feel any personal remorse or responsibility for the difficulties facing their children.

Seeing Kaida needing help at home with her children, she and Elsie became close. Elsie believed she could help care for Kaida's school-aged children if she moved into her sister's home. Her job in music therapy at the hospital allowed her to be available to the children much of the time when Kaida was at work. Elsie tried to be another stabilizing presence during the children's early years, filling in the gaps left by their father, and when Gail was not available either.

The thing missing was trust. While Elsie loved Kaida, she felt she could not trust her with her own needs. Kaida was too changeable. Sometimes, they cooked for one another, sang and played together, renovated furniture, rode bikes, and talked with the children. Sometimes Kaida talked about the Bible and the Lord, and worried about the well-being of her children.

Other times she threw it all out and called dating services, the certain avenue to find men for casual hookups. Kaida always said she was looking for a boyfriend, but she gave away the goods on the first night, and she never heard from any of them again.

The tragedy of her sister's choices caused Elsie much concern, but she couldn't reason with her. Elsie moved away when Kaida began bringing men home.

Very soon, Kaida decided to buy a different home due to an awkward situation. One of her ex-boyfriends lived next door.

Gail again found her a home and donated her real estate commission to her.

There were times when Gail seemed exasperated with Kaida's constant neediness. In those times, Elsie could claim her mother for a vacation.

Once absconding with her, they flew to an island and rented a house on a cliff wall. Mother and daughter played Scrabble over the crashing waves and watched fishing boats in the channel. All the while, Elsie felt a nervous duty to entertain her mother and please Gail while avoiding topics relating to family.

Didn't all mothers enjoy their children naturally? Elsie realized forgiveness was one thing but being reconciled looked more like the horizon, beautiful but unconquerable.

Trying to choose between Gail and Rich as parents and as people felt like trying to choose between onions. Which one would make Elsie cry the least?

I DON'T HAVE THE *THYME* TO BE ROASTED TODAY

In her music therapy groups at the rehabilitation center, Elsie met a man who stalked her by helping her take patients to and from the music groups. When he asked her out, she said "no" as politely as possible.

He first noticed her standing at the nurse's station, and turning to a coworker stated, "I could marry that girl." The problem was, he was in the midst of separating from his wife and had just graduated from a drug rehab unit. He realized he was a frightening prospect for any woman.

In no position to recommend himself to anyone, Miles slept on his ex-brother-in-law's couch, while his wife shacked up in their family home with his late best friend.

With no track record to ask for partial custody, Miles answered his wife's divorce proceedings in much the same way that Rich had first answered Gail's filing for divorce. He didn't fight it. Miles was barely hanging on, but this girl who showed up at the hospital unit inspired hope for a new beginning in him.

Elsie understood there were a variety of circumstances and motives for not fighting a divorce.

There was a time when Elsie had prayed for her future husband. She wanted to marry a pastor or youth minister or Christian musician. But while she was meditating on the lyrics to The Eagles' folk rock song, "Desperado," and the reality of the world she lived in, it occurred to her that the husband for whom she prayed may have a drug habit. In junior high school, she began praying for her future husband's salvation and that whatever he was doing, God would save him from it and give him a testimony that glorified God.

Elsie had several suitors from boyfriends at camp to crushes, friends, and boyfriends at college, including co-workers and boyfriends in Youth Corp, Denver and South Africa. None of them rose to her standard of being marriageable partners.

She'd become an expert at redirecting her almost-boyfriends into the arms of her girlfriends those more desperate or more interested in marriage. In this way, Elsie successfully set up six weddings with friends from her youth through young adulthood.

Miles was no different. When Elsie sat down at the table in the nurse's station, Miles said in front of everyone in the lounge, "So, are you dating anyone?" After a pause, everyone began laughing. He wasn't deterred, or even that embarrassed, but he didn't turn Elsie's head.

Between them was a deep ravine. The Sunday school song, "Deep and Wide," took on new meaning. She admired the fact that he worked hard to get clean, but she wasn't interested. She couldn't shake the feeling of Miles hovering nearby.

Whenever she had questions about tools, hospital chairs, or the layout of hospital land, the secretaries and nurses, even the doctors, would tell her to ask Miles. They respected him and his heart for the patients and their families. Maybe she should take another look.

In response to questions he'd ask, she began writing him letters about her faith and God. In them, she quoted scriptures and explained the reality of God's love for him through Jesus Christ's sacrifice and resurrection.

When she wrote these letters, it wasn't to answer his attraction for her, it was to lead him to a Savior. Every time he received one of her notes or letters, he'd come find her at work and take her to a quiet place where they could talk about reality and faith. He explained how his addiction to drugs happened, how his folks were so prim and proper that they called his Narcotics Anonymous program "Triple A."

"What? How'd they get that out of NA?"

"Since my dad is a dry alcoholic, when I told them that I was an alcoholic, it was something they understood. I told them that I was going to an AA group, and I was actually going to AA initially until I found Narcotics Anonymous."

"Okay, yes?"

"Well, they couldn't talk about AA openly with me. Instead, they'd always refer to my rehabilitation as 'AAA-Triple A' rather than AA-Alcoholics Anonymous. They're in denial, but that's okay. I'm the one who can no longer live in denial. My life was out of control, and I lost my wife and my family because of it. I'm the one who has to do the work. Not them. Nobody else, not even my ex-wife, is responsible for what I did."

Elsie had never heard anyone take sole responsibility for his own destruction and the ripple effects throughout a family. Her father and mother's model was to hang onto the ropes in the corners of a boxing ring and rise to fight until the opponent was knocked out.

Who could navigate the knots of lies in her family? Watching Miles work the twelve steps was the first time she'd experienced someone giving up territory and personal rights as the pathway to peace. No matter how much Miles was suffering, he accepted his responsibility.

He only needed to find his higher power. Up till now, he'd rejected the religious cross of Jesus scenario instilled by his upbringing. That Jesus seemed like a myth. He told Elsie the myth seemed powerless and lifeless to help him in the real world of job responsibilities, addictions, learning new habits, and reconstructing broken relationships.

Both his parents kept their religious views at the sideline of their lives, but here was Elsie, a girl who lived what she believed and offered him impromptu prayer and memorized scriptures to cope with his dilemmas.

One evening when she couldn't find someone to go to church with her, Elsie drove home in the ire of loneliness. Driving past the hospital, she had the idea that God wanted her to stop and ask Miles to go with her to church. The idea did not sit well with her, but the impression became insistent as she drove up to his street. At the last moment, she turned and parked in the parking lot of his apartment complex.

Miles switched off the football game and put on his shoes. They sat with each other at church that evening while Elsie tried to blot out the reality of him sitting so near her as she tried to concentrate on worship.

When she opened her eyes, she saw tears spilling down Miles's face. The lyrics "Lord, you are more precious than silver; Lord, you are more costly than gold; Lord you are more valuable than diamonds, and nothing I desire compares with You,"[1] had touched him deeply. He continued to cry with the next song, singing, "As the deer pants for the water, so my soul longs after You. You, O Lord, are my heart's desire and I long to worship You. You are more than my strength, my song; to You, O Lord, does my heart belong. You, O Lord, are my heart's desire, and I long to worship You."[2]

Miles's tears were not the tears she so often witnessed in her parent's acrid accusations, blame games, and sad regret. These were tears of wonder, gratitude, and a deep need for a Savior.

His natural generosity merged with the Narcotic's Anonymous doctrine of making amends to people he'd harmed and became a sincere expression of gratitude and service. The creeds came backlit with help and wisdom from someone who forgave him and a group of similar people. His understanding of his hard work was turned from earning salvation to working to help others understand mercy and change alongside him.

Miles didn't seem to have a need to always put his best foot forward like Elsie's parents did, like so many churchgoers and performers did, and like she herself often did. He didn't mind talking about his struggles. He embodied "gratefulness" and something else described Miles that kept escaping her until she finally landed on the words "meekness," and "humility." No one had so fully exhibited those character traits in her world.

She became captivated by him. If he didn't ask her to marry him, she worried that she would have to take the initiative.

Miles said things to her like, "There's no hope for a better past; there's only hope for a better future." It was similar to the scripture verse, "Leaving what lies behind, I press on to the high calling of Christ Jesus." Miles's focus, though, was on the practical daily interactions between himself and others, practical acts of integrity, confession, and honesty. Thanking God for forgiving his sins was a deeply moving and regular prayer.

She was deeply attracted to his commitment of making amends for how he'd done wrong to others in the past. This made sense to her because when people do wrong, it isn't only a sin between a person and their Maker, it is often an act against someone else that causes a wound to fester, trouble, trouble, and more trouble, until the act is confessed and amends are made to the best of one's ability.

These twelve step doctrines had the effect of her asthma inhaler, opening up her breathing, calming her heartbeat, and bringing hope and healing to her anxious mind.

Elsie didn't believe she could marry this man she'd fallen in love with because until his ex-wife remarried, there was still hope to reunite his family. She prayed that Miles and his ex would reconcile, though she believed she might die of grief if they did. He accepted the blame and even wrote a letter of sincere repentance to his ex-wife, though Elsie reckoned his failed marriage had not, of course, been a one-way street. His ex-wife married Miles's friend anyway, and Elsie felt at that point, she had a green light to accept Miles's romantic overtures.

Elsie knew she would end up defending Miles when he met Gail. There in the white carpeted, white couched home, she explained this beautiful thing about her love. His meekness in accepting the work he needed to do in his own life and making amends in his relationships; how well-respected he was at work and how his gratefulness, in the middle of honest reality, refreshed her and lifted her up from her bitterness.

Gail listened nervously then moaned, "Oh, Elsie, are you sure?"

When she joined Miles in his revved-up, autumn red Camaro to meet her mother, her mother's body armor immediately tightened down, and later, she voiced sincere concerns.

The old hotrod coming through her neighborhood and being parked in her driveway was the cherry on a long list of reservations ruffling her feathers. The long-haired young man was nothing like she had imagined Elsie would marry.

He had only just become a Christian, and he had no talent, not even that of simple conversation.

Elsie's impish sisters, Kaida and Melanie, told Miles about Elsie's prudish nature, about her obsessive-compulsive tendencies, and how they were surprised that the two could kiss each other since Elsie had always been a germaphobe.

Elsie, shamed, felt the anguish of a bird surrounded and pecked at by a mobbing flock.

The mean comments, nevertheless, were continually met with gentle smiles, a word of love, a squeeze of her hand, a kiss of enjoyment, and the shining eyes of deep admiration from the enamored boyfriend, Miles.

A DOG THAT SWALLOWS AN ENGAGEMENT RING IS A DIAMOND IN THE *RUFF*

Seeing her dad lit up in a red flannel shirt felt unreal, but dressing the part of an outdoorsman, he turned up at Miles's apartment to go hiking and shooting. When Miles paused for a cigarette break somewhere in the hills, he posed the marriage question to Richard.

As much as Elsie knew her dad despised guns and cigarettes, she tried to imagine how the two men's hike together was going as she sat and waited like a nervous, scratching hen that Saturday.

Rich stood bravely in the threshold of Miles's humble apartment, surreal, nodding his agreement as Miles detailed their hike through the woods, the turkeys they saw, and the eagles overhead. Elsie handed them each a glass of water and offered a meal. "Dad, Miles took to the Colorado foothills from the moment his folks moved them here. He's shown me all kinds of places. We love to explore."

Elsie experienced Miles's retelling of their hike as his true nature laid bare his delight. Her father's reserve fell from his shoulders in the warmth of Miles's inclusiveness and refreshing lack of inhibition. Perhaps Miles would be the key to getting her father to shed his inhibitions and live life on life's terms.

After this Saturday hike, it was clear that Miles became the recipient of Rich's gratefulness with the simple honor Miles had offered to him by inviting Rich into his life and asking for his daughter's hand in marriage.

Elsie readily accepted a proposal that evening after her father's nod of approval. She'd become her own person during her years away from home. It was a formality, really. Her mother's approval was as important as her father's. But Elsie valued the traditional rites of passage. Life would be easier if Miles could find acceptance.

Miles, in fact, was her safe boundary between her life and her family members.

Elsie's mom's continued disapproval of Miles mattered less now that she had become married to her fancy real estate brokerage, but Elsie would try her best to turn her mom's head.

After their first failed introduction, Elsie prepped Miles with how to keep a conversation going in the company of strangers and hungry wolves.

"Just ask my mom a question or give her a compliment. When she responds, use whatever she says to lead into a new question. As long as you keep asking her questions, the conversation will flow." She also prepped him with her sisters' backstories so that he would know how to talk with them.

He listened and learned quickly.

In fact, Elsie, so well nurtured by her boyfriend that she appeared before them as a blooming sunflower, nodding in the sun, full-faced and smiling. She astounded her mother and sisters. How did she deserve happiness? They wondered among themselves, why Elsie was the one to find true love. "Just wait till those two really get to know one another," they said. "They'll see how different they are. It won't last." Elsie wore her fifty-five complex emotions as petals, lilting in the breezes of her family's envy.

The Lord had given them each a great rescue. Elsie told Miles that though he was her prize, her sweet prince, she wouldn't be alive to marry him if it wasn't for the Lord lifting her out of her despair; without Jesus being the door to her faith, she would not be experiencing life's goodness, including him. God the Father, God the Son and God the Holy Spirit could be found in nature, in people, in the events of this world, and in scripture.

She kept feeding her foundling with scriptures. He kept feeding her with his unbridled gratitude.

The first time Miles introduced Elsie to his parents, she wore her favorite dress that her mother had given her. She always trusted her mother's choice of outfits because, number one, she hated shopping and her mother's spiritual gift was finding incredible clothing at unbelievable prices, and number two, her mother understood how to emphasize her daughter's best features.

Standing at the door, with both of his parents looking her over, they said smiling, "You look every bit the girl Miles has been telling us about. We'd like to pay for a nice dinner at our favorite restaurant for you both."

After they had exchanged pleasantries and thank yous, Miles's parents posed the strangest question Elsie had heard in a long while. "You don't have any mental illness in your family, do you. . .that you know of?"

She frowned. After a quick mental inventory, she rallied. Admitting that her aunt Lou had been in the mental institution once felt intrusive and, well, none of their business. She felt like an ant under a magnifying glass.

"Come on, Elsie, let's get outta here!" Miles said pulling her away.

Then, back in the car, headed to the restaurant that would soon be her favorite romantic venue with Miles, she contemplated the time in childhood when she almost slit her wrists to punish her father; the time Melanie had two emotional meltdowns in high school; the time her youngest sister almost died in her drunken vomit, rallied and married a man she despised, then screamed her way through a divorce. The china doll face painted on her eldest sister slid through her mind, laughing lips opening to reiterate Carlene's claim that the delivery of her daughter had exposed her to a whole classroom of medical students who raped her during the birth.

"Dear Lord, please help me. Save me. Don't allow me to let Miles down in our life together because he's a far, far better person than I've ever known. In all my days of church, I've never truly known someone so refreshingly honest and grateful, someone so willing to do common everyday work without drama or acclaim. My anxiety drops to zero around him. Keep me sane. Keep us tenderhearted toward one another."

On the way to their special dinner, she pondered, "Am I one of those people who retreat into religious experiences when life becomes threatening? That's a mental illness of sorts, isn't it?"

"You sure are serious, sweet'ums." Miles nudged her.

"Why did your mom and dad ask me that question about mental illness in the family?"

"Because it can be genetic. They're just concerned about protecting me."

"Well, I started thinking about how dysfunctional my family is, and it crossed my mind whether every one of us is wacky. What if I do go crazy on you, honey?"

Miles snuggled close and kissed her. "I don't care. You've changed my life and introduced me to my higher power. I know that you are saner than any of my friends. You're what we call a "normie." I love you good, bad, and crazy. You'll never be that scary ugly muffin."

Kaida sliced through the scheduled wedding plans for Miles and Elsie by deciding to have her own small wedding in her mother's house three months prior to theirs. Elsie tried not to lock horns with her sister even as Kaida pilfered away her mother's attentions and frittered through the joyful season of her own wedding preparations.

A guy from an internet dating site, with two boys of his own, joined hands with Kaida in a Hawaiian styled celebration. He was a local chef who enjoyed all kinds of outdoor activities.

Rich did not attend Kaida's second wedding.

Kaida and her new husband purchased a new home from Gail who handed over her real estate agent's commission toward the down payment as a wedding present.

The exciting love of Kaida's life delighted her with his cooking and swept into her active lifestyle, so much so, that when he and his boys began abusing her two children, she turned a blind eye, refusing to believe it.

DON'T ROAST THE CABBAGE TILL IT FALLS APART—YOU'LL NEVER GET *AHEAD* LIKE THAT

Beryl Hudson flew out to Colorado from Arkansas to honor and celebrate Elsie and Miles's wedding nuptials. "Will I be getting any great-grandbabies this year, sweetheart?" She smiled sweetly, though wrinkles creased her lips and eyes as her face lifted to Elsie's.

"I don't think so, Grandma. Miles can't have children, and we are a little older than most newlyweds."

"Oh, I'm so sorry to hear that…who will care for you when you're old like me? Children are what made my marriage fun."

"Grandma, may I ask you a very personal question?"

Beryl paused. She studied her granddaughter as a rabbit studies a family dog let loose in the same yard.

"Well, it's just that Mom told me that you and Grandpa had a major issue in your marriage, but that somehow you must have worked it out because you both moved to California and stayed married."

"Are you talking about Dorjan and my sister, honey?"

"Um, well, yes, actually, and Grandma, you have been more talkative now that he's gone than you ever were while he was alive. So, I thought it might be okay to ask you."

Beryl grasped Elsie's arm with both of her hands and held on.

"My dear, have you read Genesis chapter three? Animosity between the man and woman and between the snake and the offspring of Adam and Eve was begun back there in the garden. Animosity is *not always* what is done to you. It can be the *reaction* that people have to slights, insults and offenses. Animosity begins when those fiery darts are thrown at you and they burn and wound and maybe even leave scars. I had a choice, and so will you, someday, honey, to either live in bitterness, spite, and animosity toward your husband, or to remain tender-hearted, forgiving one another as Christ Jesus has forgiven you."

Elsie felt the warm oil of gladness for her grandma's wise counsel rolling over her head, coating her heart.

"Did Grandpa ever confess to you what he did?"

"Some people can't bring themselves to talk about their sins and dredge all that ugliness up again, but Dorjan moved as far away from my sister as he could by moving to California. And he did his best to start our family fresh there. He tried, honey. He tried. And, you know, on his deathbed, he prayed to receive the good Lord's forgiveness."

"If he hadn't moved to California with you, do you think you could have forgiven him?"

"Well, honey, I kept trying to forgive him there, but it was a lot easier in California!" Both women laughed and hugged.

"I think if he had never turned away from it, I would have been practicing the '70 x 7 method of forgiveness' forever, or maybe, I would'a eventually broke it off, like your mama did to save herself from being poked with a firebrand again and again."

It was a precious time to have so many of their friends and family members involved in the celebration.

Melanie shut down her Walkman, took out her earbuds, and handed over her own wedding dress. She let Elsie alter it, embroider gold threads into it, and wear it. "I won't ever use it again. You may as well." She smiled.

"Where have you been storing this?"

"In a box in a drawer."

Elsie noticed Melanie had absorbed the accent of her best friend from New Jersey. Drawer was "draw." Orange was "arnge." This was not the Finch family accent. Melanie spent as much time with her best friend's family as possible. Maybe there, she could disassociate with her own messed up family.

Gail offered to buy all the flowers for the end of the pews, for the bridal bouquet, the bridal party and groomsmen's corsages, and the front of the church. Elsie's artistic friends provided a bell choir, a mime of God introducing Eve to Adam, and the music, some of which were love songs written by the bride.

When the doors to the chapel opened, Elsie's nervous face and pinched mouth looked identical to the mask worn by her stiff father, her escort. Looking into the faces pressed on that photograph a few months after, and long after, Elsie recognized her many features knit together by Rich and Gail. Knowing that she had been given the best and the worst characteristics of both parents would become a surreal joy and the bane of her existence.

Afterwards, a photo was taken of Elsie in her wedding dress with Rich on one side and Gail on the other. The parents had each contributed $2,500 to their daughter's wedding, $5,000 total. Still, she had to use her credit card to cover the surprising costs and ongoing wedding expenses.

Miles had warned Elsie. It had taken some persuading of his parents that Elsie was a good catch between minimizing the virtue of frugality and maximizing the virtues of purity and decency. They didn't want him to marry a girl carrying debt.

"Oh, my word. I had to pay for the wedding, Miles!"

"I know."

"Thankfully, using Melanie's wedding dress, I didn't have to purchase a new one."

They looked the part of the perfect family, Elsie, Gail and Rich. It was a joyful image Elsie longed to frame and present to the world as real, but she never would.

She felt honored to have her grandma standing by like the cherry on top of a sundae.

A home can be built in three arenas independent from the others or all three kinds can be interwoven as a strong fabric for making into a protective covering. The first kind of home is built of sticks and stones with mechanical parts and can be viewed even by imbeciles as a residence and a mile marker in life. Back in the day, Rich said he felt he had arrived when he stood on the street viewing the home he and Gail had built together with their talents and ingenuity.

A home, as Gail later learned in her real estate courses, is the cornerstone of financial success. Having her name on a title to a home could build community trust, business credit, and responsibility of character as it becomes the foundation of a personal portfolio of power and choice. Paying faithfully on a home, builds one's secure asset, one's rights, and one's independence for the future. Even the simplest budget can build an inflatable investment.

But the third home type embodies a hidden strength that can be enjoyed by the meek, the most influential, and the righteous alike. Without title, even without sticks and stones, a homebuilder can tie a rope from the chimney to heaven...heaven, by the tether of the heart.

Elsie was beginning to realize how embracing others in proximity, teaching them skills and wisdom, equipping them by being kind, praying with them and for them, is building her house. The pillars are the people, the children, the friends whose arms become the protective siding. The strength of this home is impermeable to rain, hurricanes, and earthquakes. The place of belonging cannot be stripped of its framed memories and hopes by financial crises, injustice, or even death. It is a spiritual home that lives forever. It may be hard to see from the street and it may not add up on a spreadsheet, but it is the most fortunate of realities, founded and roofed, and automated, nonetheless. This is the most vital home anyone can ever build for themselves or offer to another. It is the sacred home.

It was Elsie's turn to try her hand at homemaking.

After their honeymoon, they arrived back at Miles's family home to open presents only to discover that every piece of china, purchased mostly by Gail and Miles's mom, and some pieces by the bridesmaids, was missing. Someone had stolen it all!

Elsie was confounded considering the value of the loss that she and Miles could never replace, but Gail had an idea. She thought she may have a way to claim it on her homeowner's insurance because her insurance covered things in the trunk of her car, where they had carried the china after the wedding.

Gail paid the deductible and replenished her daughter's set of china with the insurance money. Covering the loss was a touching gift. It humbled Elsie that her mother would do something like that for her.

While she was in Colorado, Beryl spoke with her daughter about appointing either Gail, or Coalbert as her representative for her last will and testament. What did Gail think?

Gail thought about it and answered, "Mom, I'd be happy to do it, but Coalbert is right there, living near you. He's also the eldest. I think he'd be the likely choice, but if he doesn't want to, then, of course, I'll do it."

Four months later, Beryl, happy and satisfied with life, came home to her small but elegant third floor apartment after sharing her favorite meal, a catfish dinner at the local diner with friends. She sat down in her favorite recliner, pushed back, and put her feet up. She felt wealthy and at peace with the family and the world.

She thanked God for all His goodness to her and for bringing so many of the children and grandchildren into the kingdom. When she began to feel a familiar pressure rising in her chest, she dialed Ivy, her daughter-in-law, who called 911, which triggered the ambulance from the hospital across the street, but by the time they arrived, she was gone.

It was clear to everyone attending her funeral that Beryl had gone home to be with God the Father, the Son, and Holy Spirit.

To every grandchild, she left a thousand dollars, which in her day felt like a mint. The rest of her stocks and savings were divided between her four children. Everything she owned had a piece of tape with a name on the back or bottom of the item saying to whom each gift was intended. Only her linens, her Bible, and her oil paints were argued over. It was a tense but fair distribution between all of the families because everyone got to pick in order of birth for the remainder.

When everyone found a time to eat a meal together, they decided that Beryl had created a way to make distribution of a parent's assets as easy and comfortable as possible. During the meal, Laila, who now spelled her name Laela, told the story of her mother taking her in to live with her for a few years. She had gone from doing drugs to dealing drugs, and after several arrests, the county judge pointed his finger at her and said, "Young woman, I have the right to put you away for life." She laughed and her head went back to remembering it. "I don't know, maybe in his heart, he felt compassion for the wayward young woman I was. Anyway, he told me that if I was to leave California and never return, he wouldn't send me to prison."

"Well, of course I agreed to that, and I went to live in Arkansas with Mom. I say 'Mom' because, of course, Daddy did not agree. I was an embarrassment to 'em."

"I became a born-again Christian at Mom's church, so whenever I went back to California," she said, "I went back with a different spelling to my name, L-A-E-L-A, instead of L-A-I-L-A. If you change the spelling of your name, you can start over. That's what I did."

Elsie felt that if there were ever someone deserving of sainthood, it was Grandma Hudson, ever patient, ever kind, a prayer warrior and miracle getter. She often sensed her watching in the great cloud of witnesses cheering on her family.

Gail told the story of Grandma Sander's little house in Western Grove before she moved to Harrison. She said, "Mom dropped us kids off with Grandma for a while, and it was raining. Her house was no bigger than a living room in a typical suburban house, but she had added the bedroom with a tin roof onto the side. I remember all of us kids laid in there on Grandma and Grandpa's bed together as we listened to the rain plunking on her tin roof. It was so peaceful."

Elsie's first official holiday dinner at her home came that Thanksgiving, one of many to follow. The entire Colorado family was invited. Carlene and Foreman and their two children came up from Lake Charles. Miles's mom and dad came offering flowers and desserts. Kaida's family showed up with vegetable dishes.

Thanks to Gail giving the couple a realtor's housewarming gift, they had a moon-shaped, velvet couch for seating the first arrivals to the party. Elsie felt grateful to her mother. She appreciated this perfect anchor to her living room décor.

That morning, Elsie made the turkey and dressing under her mom's tutelage at the kitchen table. Elsie had shopped for the ingredients from the list her mother gave her, and now, she boiled giblets, potatoes, eggs, gravy with chicken broth, flour, onions, herbs, and celery.

"I'm glad you wanted to come help, Mom. You were always such a good hostess. That's why I want to learn to be a good hostess. I love hospitality, I just don't love cooking, and it may be because I don't know the tricks and shortcuts yet. I wouldn't know, really, how to cook a holiday dinner without you."

"Oh, nonsense. I taught each of you girls how to cook a turkey and stuffing!"

"No, you didn't. I'm learning right now."

"Well, I guess you're motivated to learn now, but I did teach you how years ago."

The last thing Elsie wanted on Thanksgiving morning was to argue with her mother, yet her mother had taken a compliment and turned it into a dig. Searching her memories, the things she remembered doing at holidays were cleaning house, table settings, preparing the stuffed dates or celery appetizers, peeling the potatoes and helping to roll up yam balls. For the life of her, she could not recall her mother ever teaching her how to cook a turkey or gravy or dressing.

She let it go.

"I received my check, you know, Grandma's thoughtful gift to all of her grandchildren. She didn't have to do that, but all of us feel blessed. What a nice surprise! Have you gotten your own distribution from Grandma's estate, Mom?"

"Not yet. Coalbert said he's taking out what Daddy owed him for his unpaid half of the partnership with Daddy."

"What's that?"

"He said when Mom and Dad moved back to Arkansas, he'd helped Dad build his house. Then, Dad was supposed to help Coalbert build one, but it never happened."

"Oh, did you know about that?"

"I don't really care. It's probably true. I only care that it keeps dragging on. He keeps promising to send the rest of the life insurance and investments, 'cause Mom had made a bundle on Walmart stocks being an early investor, but he sure is taking his time. When the rest of us asked him for an accounting, he sent a computer file none of us could read, with a jumble of numbers and no headings. We're going to have to be all right with whatever he decides. I have an aching feeling nothing will be the same in the family after this."

Gail helped Elsie put all of the dishes on the sideboard of her beautiful old-fashioned dining room. Then, she welcomed her Thanksgiving dinner guests.

Kaida arrived in a foul mood.

"What's wrong, sweetie?" Gail hugged her daughter.

"Oh, Celia's mad at me again. She won't return calls. She's depressed, but she blamed me for doing something, like her chronic depression is my fault."

"Well, you're both adults now. Why don't you find another friend?"

"Because, it isn't that easy, Mom. Whenever I start getting close to someone at work, and we start having a little fun, they back away, like I repel friends, or something."

"Your family loves you, so come on in and let's share a nice Thanksgiving together, okay? That casserole will be yummy, and thanks for the pie!"

When everyone but Melanie was seated and the dishes were lined up for service, they decided to pray and dig in. Just before dessert was served, young Ricky opened the door with Melanie trailing behind, an appetizer in hand. Melanie saw everyone sitting around the table. "I'm sorry I'm so late, but, I brought a dish!" Ricky looked crestfallen to see he'd missed dinner.

"Well, come on in! We'll dish you up some plates."

It seemed Melanie just couldn't make any event on time these days.

Miles and Elsie rescued each other. They celebrated life and love in silly ways. They purchased matching robes their first Christmas and matching bicycles for Elsie's birthday. They took his parents' direction for saving money and for spending a little bit to have a special date night together every so often. Whenever they did, they pretended they were rich. They'd clean up, dress up, and hold hands, complimenting the other one and often humble tears would spill expressing their gratefulness to each other and to God.

They experienced wonder at strange blessings like when they stumbled upon a free concert from someone practicing violin, or bagpipe, or guitar.

"Pretending they were rich" spilled over to their families as well. They saved up and splurged on Miles's folks' fiftieth anniversary with a limousine ride to their favorite restaurant. Celebrating Gail's birthdays like la-de-dah events at the Brown Palace, the Boulderado Hotel, the Lake House, and the Broadmoor atrium were family landmarks.

Their taste in music would never line up, but they learned from each other's preferences, laughing, teasing, and challenging one another's musical choices.

Nothing much had to happen for the two of them to erupt in joy and curiosity for a new adventure.

Quickly, Miles became Gail's new favorite son-in-law due to his eagerness to please, and for the help he provided with Elsie's sisters' children.

Being a kid at heart helped Miles easily relate to the children at play. He understood what divorce felt like, how irreparable the rifts were in relationships. He would initiate cleaning her gutters, organize family garages, give manly advice, do the dishes, and he was the grill-master during summer gatherings. He kept the children occupied so that the sisters and their mom could talk and try to figure things out amongst themselves. Everyone loved Miles

Inspired by her daughter's happiness, Gail found a historic arts and crafts styled bungalow in mint condition to show to Miles and Elsie for their first home. Miles had always been a renter, but he had also learned to save funds from his mother and father. With Gail's gift of her agency commission, the young couple were able to buy a beautiful first home in town.

Soon, Elsie began hosting a writer's group in their new home and later, a book club.

They loved their vacations together. Sometimes Miles packed a tent. Sometimes Elsie planned a holiday on the coast. Miles's parents also invited them to join them on long weekends away, or to a beach in Mexico. They almost always invited Miles's son, watching him play and explore the world with them.

Miles was never going to be a high wage earner, so Elsie worked alongside in their marriage to be frugal among themselves and to help pay for what they needed. It seemed when she was working, they had plenty of money, but no time to get away; when she changed jobs, she often took some time between work for family vacations, but of course, the money was shy as a kitten. They made do.

When Elsie asked Miles's parents why they spoiled them by helping pay down their mortgage, his parents said, "We adopted Miles not for eighteen years, but for a lifetime. When he married you, you became another daughter to us." They rarely used the phrase, "We love you," but they showed their support by being benefactors and sharing their lives and wisdom. Elsie often thanked Miles's parents for their advice on financial choices.

Two years into Elsie's marriage to Miles, when Rich came for a springtime visit, he began to understand how much Elsie appreciated Miles's parents. They sat on the porch stairs of the couple's bungalow smelling the juniper and hyacinths and watching the tulips bloom while she talked about her new family planning a long weekend getaway together. He looked around at the peaceful home, a classic in the arts and crafts tradition, the woodwork glowing. He whistled.

"This kinda reminds me of the woodwork in our house in Pennsylvania!" Rich said. She agreed. She remembered it fondly. She mentioned Miles's parents' generous payment on the bungalow's mortgage given as a Christmas gift and described how Gail showed them that the amortization schedule changed due to the gift.

Elsie talked about Miles's parents inviting them to posh restaurants and even ordered desserts. She mentioned how much she'd learned from Miles's parents about saving money and choosing priorities through logical assessments and comparison.

"We went up to Steamboat and looked around at a timeshare there, because we love the hot springs and we love the whole gorgeous drive, but his mom and dad told us not to get involved. They said, 'Why let a corporation tell you when you can take vacation and where? A whole world awaits you, and your tastes will change.'

"His mom told me that she purposely doesn't buy a hotel room with a kitchenette because if she is on vacation, she wants to be served. All of that made so much sense to us."

Thinking her father would be interested in her married life, Elsie blabbed on, but she was hurt to see it bothered him. He shrugged, grinned, and hung his head.

"I recently heard a quote that goes something like this. 'Don't you dare let the young man you are today make decisions that limit yourself as an older man.' I wish I'd heard that years ago. I regret to say that I have too many limitations and too many regrets."

Then, Elsie's father tried to hold her hand, but she gathered courage and told him she was an adult, a married woman now, and she didn't want to hold his hand anymore.

THE BROTHER WHO TOOK HIS FAMILY ON A SHARK FISHING EXPEDITION LOST AN ARM AND A LEG

When Kaida divorced her second husband, she began calling and visiting Elsie. The two sisters became very close friends. One day Kaida said, "Let's go to the Aspen Folk Festival together."

"Okay, let me ask Miles."

"Can't you make your own decisions?"

"Geez. We're married!" Elsie thought of several reasons she'd likely run ideas past Miles, finances and vacations included.

She was giving Miles a backrub that evening, her adept fingers finding the swollen muscles around his aching joints as her father's backrubs had taught her to do, when she broached the subject of a sisters' getaway to the music festival with Kaida.

He agreed to the sisters having some fun together on his dime. Miles's graciousness often included generosity.

It was only six hours into the girls' weekend when Kaida looked at her sister and asked, "What would you be doing here if you were with Miles?"

The girls were enjoying the hot tub, having arrived at their condo, and Elsie nodded. "Probably just this. Maybe reading. Maybe exploring."

"Really? You don't take tours, rent bikes, dirt bikes, four-wheelers?"

"We went up in a hot air balloon once, but there was no wind that morning. No, we just enjoy each other."

Kaida couldn't comprehend her sister's life or her marriage. She spent the weekend trying to figure out why her own marriages had collapsed. "My children are in counseling. They hardly speak to me."

Elsie prayed with her sister for God's help. Then, the two left to see Bob Dylan's show. The weekend turned out to be nothing much for the sisters, each, for her own reasons.

Gail and Elsie invited Melanie out to lunch at The Crab Shack.

Melanie agreed, but by the time she arrived, her mom and sister had placed their orders. "We thought you'd forgotten."

Melanie pulled one of her ear buds away from her ear, set her phone on the table and kept talking to the guy on the phone. Pretty soon, she found a moment to order a line of shots. "I don't have much time for lunch. I think I'll drink mine today." She smiled and continued her work conversation about who said what, who was filling in, how it happened, and what the boss thought.

Gail looked at Elsie, and Elsie looked at her mom. There was no point in trying to converse over Melanie's conversation.

Melanie ordered another row of shots, even though Gail said, "Don't you have to go back to work?"

When the meals were nearly finished, Melanie said goodbye to her work associate. Shaking her head in big circles and placing both hands on the table to rock back on her chair, she apologized.

"Sorry! I just couldn't get him off the phone."

But Gail and Elsie had listened to her draw out the conversation repeatedly exasperating their goodwill. Drinking two rows of shots for her lunch was certainly meant to annoy them as well.

When the two were back in the car together, Gail turned to Elsie.

"I didn't know Melanie even drank beer, much less liquor, did you, Elsie?"

"I'm as shocked about the hard liquor as you are, Mom. She's had to have been drinking for quite a while to be able to put all of that away and still go back to work."

Melanie didn't have to worry about her mom asking her to lunch again.

Rich's last official job in Colorado was designing the nuclear response system for Fort St. Vrain. When he finished that, he was asked to remodel the Front Range Emergency Response System into the new computer coding required by the latest software language and programs, but he said, "It's too late to teach this old dog new tricks."

The utilities company was being bought out and all the upper management and personnel had been given a similar alternative. When Elsie asked what her dad's decision would be, he said, "Take early retirement or get laid off. I've watched my managers and bosses refuse retirement and get laid off, so when it comes my turn, I'll choose the forced retirement."

Maybe he thought the endings should coincide, but it seemed like a perfect time to discard his second wife, Polly. "Biggest mistake of my life," he said. "She took everything I had saved, and I have to pay her support until she can get a job!"

It seemed the women were always the ones to blame for burglarizing Rich's house. On all accounts, he should have been a better policeman.

Rich packed away this spent chapter of his life, with 60s and 70s love songs playing as his soundtrack. His stereo was the last item to be packed.

When Rich divorced Polly, he left all his tools in Miles and Elsie's garage. He also left a chest with a few pictures and memories in case they wanted them.

Hanging his head, he hugged Elsie. "All my choices have been chiseled down and depleted!" He sang bass in his own operatic tragedy to his audience of one. "I'm moving to Iowa to work on designing websites for the remainder of my career. See ya later, gator."

One day, Elsie found a small brown briefcase in the garage that seemed familiar to one from her childhood, so she unzipped it. Inside were artifacts from those two years in Pennsylvania, when life was rich and poignant for her, but miserable to her parents. She remembered how she'd felt God had saved her for something special.

That time and inclination felt like a reel-to-reel film playing.

Curiosity called. She rifled through the papers. Instead of good memories, however, she found her dad's packing list and diagram, his map to Colorado, the mean notes on a third-grade report card from her sister Carlene's first teacher in Pennsylvania, and stockpiled letters of ill will written in her father's draftsman print about and to her mother. Then, there was the humiliating letter of being let go from Fields

Mission Corp. together with a job offer from Electric Service Company of Colorado.

Why had he left this briefcase in her garage?

All the illusions about her dad, her excuses made for him, came crashing down. Her father had always been a plotter, a schemer, and a man of stubborn ill will, collecting the pain and hiding from his past, blaming his wife for all his failures, and spinning the truth for the benefit of his children. He was a conniver, not someone flying by the seat of his pants.

Not a victim.

She sat down on the garage floor and wept more bitterly than she knew could be possible.

Elsie grieved this strange form of depravity of her father. Not only did she disrespect the fact that her dad had never gone to be with her mother during childbirth, or afterwards in recovery, he'd never visited her the entire six weeks she was laid up for back surgery and recovery in the hospital. She was disgusted that her dad refused to support his own children when he divorced and had put the full weight of support onto her mother's shoulders. It confounded her that for someone so creative in woodworking, machinery, electricity, and music, the man who loved beauty such as ice-skating, and the way he thrived remodeling and helping her mother decorate their home, why then, when he divorced her mother, did he live like a mole?

He enjoyed thoughtfully planned, extravagant dates, but he lived in small, dark, empty apartments using card tables for a dining room table and made a single bed frame of pine two-by-fours for his own bed. Sometimes, there wasn't even a couch or chairs to sit on besides the folding chairs at the kitchen card table when she came to visit. At least, he'd enjoyed a real house in Golden for a few years where each of his daughters had experienced time alone with their father before Polly and her children moved in.

"Don't you have some equity built up in your house, Dad?"

"Nope. I have to sell it in order to pay the attorney fees and court costs."

For a moment, she felt sorry for her dad. She had made excuses for his strange behaviors and failures, thinking that his upbringing had cultivated and predetermined his limitations. Now, she in no way blamed her mother for riling whatever freedom and happiness was possible apart from her dad's clouded life, temperamental judgments, and silent treatments.

She hoped the best for Polly and her kids.

Elsie told Miles about her father's most recent woes in their evening walk in the park. They clamored to the swing set smirking at the children nearby. "I'm six and she's four years old. We like to swing, too!"

The children stared back at Miles and scattered. Next, the couple hopped on the teeter-totter bouncing each other up and down. Then they found a softball and played catch before going home. Elsie hoped the best for her sisters who were growing more and more estranged. "Lord, please heal all our wounds. Show each of us the way to live the abundant life You've promised to those who walk with You."

Miles said, "Amen!"

HE PAID THE FARE, FAIRLY WELL

"You always thought your father was the gallant one."

"He was, to me. Did I ever tell you how I candy coated his kitchen?"

"No."

"Well, I tried to pressure cook a can of condensed milk to turn it into caramel. Then, I forgot about it and went to the store, and the thing exploded all over his kitchen. We cleaned it for a week, but he still had to scrape off the caramelized rock candy from behind the fridge, when he sold his house."

Elsie tentatively explained, "It was always Dad who played with us, biked with us, treated us to root beer floats with Papa Burgers, Mama Burgers, and Junior Burgers on mountain excursions to see the colors changing. It was Dad who built bedrooms for Carlene and me and then let me work alongside him building out the church basement and roofing our house. He helped so many other people and by golly, he could fly an airplane!

"Seriously, though, he bought me my first car and showed me how to change the oil. He taught me how banking works.

"Dad was the one who flew out to New York to find the scoundrel who stole my car, Mom.

"He wrote me letters, was my power of attorney and called me occasionally while I was overseas. Mom, I didn't know anything about what he did to you. I was in the dark as to how you lost the baby brother I always wanted.

"When he left, I kept feeling it was an anomaly, and when I was angry enough to pray that lightning struck him dead, it didn't happen. All I knew was I didn't understand what was going on between you guys. He just kept moseying along.

"Even now, you admit that the story you told everyone about him being a deadbeat dad was really an honorable trade in real estate that you concocted, and he accepted. You spread a falsehood that colored my impression of him my entire life."

Gail shrank a little.

OKLAHOMA, 1994

WELCOME TO THE FINCH NEST, A SHADY NEW HOME WITH BEAKS, CLAWS AND WINGS TO FLY

After Rich was forced into early retirement from the Electric Service Company of Colorado and he moved to Iowa to work, Elsie lost touch with her father. She hardly knew him anymore. A few months into working as a book manager in a large retail outlet, she was having her lunch in the staff lounge when one of the clerks led Rich and Noeleen to where she sat.

"Are these your parents, Elsie?"

Elsie stood, abruptly hiding her half-eaten microwaved lunch under a magazine and greeted her dad and the pretty lady he embraced. "What are you doing here, Dad? You didn't even call me to say you were coming…we could have gone to lunch together."

"Well, I wanted it to be a surprise. You see, this is Noeleen, my childhood sweetheart. Her husband died awhile back, and I happened to be visiting her brother, a judge in Oklahoma City. He told me to look her up and the rest is history."

Noeleen greeted Rich's daughter with an Oklahoma drawl.

Elsie tried to be polite and return Noeleen's greetings as the realization sank in that this woman was soon to become Elsie's new stepmother. She was saying, "Yes, I was in the middle of a piano lesson, when there was a knock at the door. When I opened it, there stood Rich! I didn't recognize him at first, but then he smiled, and I did. What a surprise! I let the student go home early, and Rich and I got caught up."

She felt the panic of intuition, not for her dad but for his unsuspecting bride.

Elsie had no idea how to absorb the news or her feelings, much less did she know how to talk to either of these strangers. When she started working at the Christian store, she sent her father a present of a woven throw blanket featuring the words, "I'll raise you up on wings of eagles" for Christmas. He hadn't bothered to call and thank her, and there had been no letter or card till now. Here, he stood before her with a new woman on his arm.

"Would you like to see the store?"

She showed them around and made small talk. When they got to the woven blankets, Noeleen looked through them and pulled one out smiling. "Look, Rich! This is the same one I just gave to you for Christmas!" He smiled and turned to Elsie. She looked away. "Yes, I got one from you and one from Elsie, too. Best Christmas ever!"

The afternoon shifted as puzzle pieces from her family's transition from Pennsylvania to Colorado via Oklahoma fell into place. As the realization dawned on her, she said to her father, "That time you took us to Oklahoma City, you looked her up, didn't you?"

"Well, yes, in fact, I tried to, but her brother said she was married at the time, so I had to wait." The lovers giggled and smiled sheepishly.

But, you were our dad then. She didn't use her voice. She only absorbed the implications.

Rich said he needed to "move along pretty quick" to see his other daughters and introduce Noeleen since they were celebrating their engagement. "This is super exciting for me because I've never been out of the state of Oklahoma, Elsie!" Noeleen exclaimed.

"Thank ya', kindly," Rich said, nodding to his daughter as though she had served up something special for him.

As they left the store, they left Elsie full of disturbance, a surreal combination of revulsion and wonder overwhelmed her, the feeling of betrayal lodged as yet another scrape of a bear's claw.

"Women ought to interview their prospective partner's children, don't ya think?" She spat, "I mean, from their first marriage to see if the man they say they want to marry is really the man they want to marry!" She turned to a fellow employee. If not for Elsie's bitter reaction, the surprised clerk would have been none the wiser.

When Rich and Noeleen's imminent marriage became an Oklahoma reality, Miles and Elsie were, of course, formally invited to witness the vows, but Elsie couldn't find it in her heart to celebrate her errant father finding life so far afield of the lives of his real children.

It was only because Elsie liked Noeleen the minute she saw her, that her heart closed against the marriage.

Miles concocted an excuse for his wife. Elsie held her breath at the implication of their decision and then muttered, "I can just see the moment when the officiant says, 'Does anyone have any reason that these two should not be married today?'" She would have to stand up and try to articulate a life of dashed promises, broken women, and irreparable harm done to the groom's real family, probably mentioning his divorce and isolation from his second wife, Polly, and her family, too. No, she may as well stay home. She didn't want to meet the children who would one day blame her or accuse her. Besides, she didn't know anything about any of them except that Noeleen was devoted to each of them.

Noeleen set a dinner table of humorous goodwill, quiet love, and inspired a house appropriately decorated with a blossoming garden for Rich when they married.

His new love played the piano and the organ, so they sang in a quartet together.

Since Noeleen liked movies and country western dancing, they danced a few times and watched the occasional movie. She also played some mean dominos and Mexican Train, so Rich would occasionally stop working on his computer to play in a foursome.

ONCE YOU LET AN OTTER INSIDE, YOU *OTTER* GET THE SMELL *OTTER* THERE

The effect of the marriage fell differently on Kaida who decided she'd try again to develop a relationship with her father on account of her attraction to Noeleen's vibrance. Perhaps there was something to her father she'd been missing. True to form, Noeleen and Kaida spoke on the phone and made plans for the wedding. True to form, Rich removed himself from the girl's giggling. He left them to plot how the two families would meet and plan a couple of activities for mingling.

When her dad and Noeleen came to visit Miles and Elsie the first year, then each year after, the women bonded easily. Because of Noeleen, the young couple offered their home as lodging whenever they placed a call to alert Miles and Elsie of an intended visit. There was nothing to dislike about this spunky, open-armed woman. Elsie only regretted she or Noeleen had not possessed the courage to confer about Rich's adult life with those who knew him best.

Being the point person, Elsie placed calls to her sisters, as usual, to plan activities and meals with them so that they could all be together.

Rich, again finding the rhythms of life to his liking, eagerly showed off his new wife's musical talent to his previous family and to whomever would listen. He would record her playing all her favorite oldies on the piano ranging from hymns, to swing music and to love songs from the 40s-60s. One day he put all these songs played on Noeleen's piano on a compact disk and mailed it to the family. He became the new music minister at her church and they both joined a music quartet which practiced weekly and sang often.

Rich sang solos. Songs that evoked emotional memories or bolstered his internal strength were his main topic of singing or conversation. His previously clear, strong baritone voice, however, became diffused with the conditions of an asthmatic man.

With a laugh, Noeleen accused him of snoring *badly*. She learned to sleep with earplugs. Elsie explained to Noeleen, that when she was living with her father, he had undergone surgery to remove nose polyps, but the surgery failed to correct the fundamental irritation.

Rich's condition certainly didn't stop his musical ambitions.

When he found fault after fault with the minister at Noeleen's home church, he found another conservative church in the area where Noeleen knew some folks, and there, he worked his way into the music ministry and ended up leading the choir. During the couple's marriage, they church hopped five times to appease Rich's sense of blame, vindication, or being looked over.

He had once told Elsie that he believed God had put him on the shelf for his sins, but that belief, apparently, had fallen away in a new state where no-one but a forgiving wife knew of his other four children or his sullen, Eeyore years.

A WRITER BECOMES MORE *DETALED* WHEN NO ONE LISTENS

During the first and second year of marriage, Elsie had actively researched so many things that she needed to comprehend about marriage and her new adult life. She at first journaled the things she'd learned and then wrote a full manuscript for a book with her mother's help with editing.

"Mom, I didn't know you had copy editing skills. You're a much better speller than I am."

Her mother seemed interested and happy to help with her writing in a way she'd never shown interest in Elsie's music. Amusement with the editing process, as well as the questions and answers they discussed linked mother and daughter together in new ways.

When it came time to promote the book, Gail accompanied Elsie through the redstone parks of Utah and onward to a book expo in California. The time spent traveling Utah visiting the national parks with the arches and iconic red earth formations and conversing, eating out and dreaming together proved to deepen their relationship.

Nevertheless, when Elsie was especially missing a creative outlet and floundering as to what she could ever do to publish lyrics, record songs, or produce other forms of art in her wheelhouse, she wrote a poem that felt like crushing glass to read it aloud to Gail and Kaida.

Pathos for finding a path of fulfillment in the world of creative arts shook in the poet's voice. Comfortably seated in Elsie's living room, her sister complimented Elsie and talked over the essence of the poem, but Gail shifted nervously in her seat, reserving her opinion.

Expressing interest, instead, in how Elsie planned to buy a set of matching chairs, Gail mentioned that she'd seen a couple on sale for a doable price.

To Elsie, this movement reminded her how often her mom had run from the subject of her creative opportunities of the past. She took offense.

Another time when Elsie read an inspirational book about blessing others, especially in respect to parents offering blessings over their children, she mentioned, "Any blessing given to a child is an authorized gift imbued by the Father Himself through the parents."

Wide-eyed, Gail seemed not to comprehend the concept of a parent's blessing being a dynamic legacy spiritually authorized by God. Nor did she grasp the importance of blessing her children at this stage. They were all adults. What did the archaic term "blessing" mean anyway? She changed the subject.

Feeling rebuffed on several fronts, Elsie considered that her mother's fancy Hollywood sunglasses blocked too much of the light of day. All she really wanted was to know the good that her mother saw in her. Did she see a future for any of her artistic assets?

Yet, the intangible picture of gifts such as spiritual authority, joy, peace, favor, success, or a happy family did not align with Gail's shopping lists and gifting routines, as they were blessing enough. She couldn't cope with another flashlight shining through a fracture of one of her children's souls.

This was not Elsie's intent when she mentioned the opportunity her mother had to bless her children's lives. A feeling of unraveling continued to occur in her relationship with Gail.

Surely Mom understood some of the holes that her own unhappiness had left in the wellbeing of the children. Yet, she seemed no longer interested in hearing about another struggle or another gravesite in their lives. Nor was she able to endure another implied critique. Was she a gardener to dish dirt into every hole the dogs had dug? She could readily warn them of the dogs occupying their areas of interest, but to call the dogs to their kennels to advance a place of healing seemed incomprehensible. She prayed for them.

If one of the girls suggested a better parenting skill for one of the grown children, Gail's eyes closed. Any implied remnant of need would have to be met by someone else.

Elsie recognized Gail had given and continued to give the girls material gifts as she saw fit. But words of encouragement, any forward counsel, offering praise, insight, or blessing were a commodity Gail could not afford. On Mother's Day, Gail was not the one to pull out family photos of her children and thank heaven or mention their accomplishments to friends.

Learning to form these words at this stage felt to Gail, a tad late. She'd done the best she could to raise her girls, given the circumstances, and now it was time for them to exceed her. She wished them her best.

On the other hand, some friends whom Elsie often referred to as her South African parents, sent them a beautiful and gracious letter encouraging them to listen well to each other and show honor for each other in private and in the public eye.

They said they were sure that the couple would be magnanimous in love toward one another as their Father in heaven had shown magnanimous love for each of them.

The feeling the scrawled word "magnanimous" brought to Elsie was that love could be lifted to a wide-open space, a place of vision, a place of trust, a place to grow and explore. Love was no place to demean. No place to control another. That one word offered a strange and wonderful transition to a new world defining love for both Miles and Elsie.

It was an interesting marriage because Miles and Elsie embodied such different strengths and perspectives that they kept doing things in different settings, for different sets of friends, and then coming together to talk about their lives in the evenings and on weekends.

They both loved the Lord, although Miles expressed his faith and love differently to Elsie due to his background.

Elsie sensed that without children, she and Miles needed something to draw them together in a mutual project or cause. She asked him whether he would want to adopt a child, but Miles was adamant that he already had a child by blood and didn't want to adopt. He said in jest that he didn't want to share his wife, but she knew the sentiment was more than jest.

Then, Elsie came up with another idea. "Miles, we could rent out a room or even both guest rooms to people in transition. You have a friend who is getting divorced. We could rent out the room, and you and I could both be available to help serve and counsel. Both of us like to cook, so sharing meals wouldn't be a problem. We have family over all the time. What would one more person in the house matter?"

Miles thought it over and agreed.

Pretty soon, they had two people in both of their guest rooms, and the plan began to develop in a way that satisfied everyone.

Then, Elsie read a book about passive assets and making money by flipping houses. When their house was paid off after only ten years of double payments whenever possible, he agreed to let her pick out another place and fix it up.

In this way, Miles and Elsie continued to make money on home renovations as well as keep people who needed a soft place to land in their guest rooms. They thrived on building into other peoples' lives, and the house renovations challenged Elsie's creative side.

Renovations were rolling along until a general contractor built all the windows in the home a half inch too small, and rather than fixing his error, he walked off the job.

Since Elsie had made the mistake of paying the general contractor directly as the project progressed, she didn't realize he hadn't forwarded the payments to the subcontractors. Instead, he had pocketed the payments himself. Miles and Elsie were handed a hard lesson when they had to find and negotiate with each of the subcontractors for a second payment of supplies from cement to lumber and settle the liens on their house from debts owed to the suppliers. It was a bitter pill to swallow at the same time the house needed to be finished.

As soon as the house was finished and only the settlement of liens existed, Gail and Kaida stopped by to see it.

Exhausted by all the effort and angles and schedules of construction, Elsie showed her mother and sister the parts for which she was most proud. One of these was the wooden inlays in thresholds from the main room to another. Stepping over one, Gail gasped. "Oh! What happened here?"

A *FROGMENT* OF HOPE FOR A *RIBBITING* PRINCE

Gail discovered another way to make money, through stocks and bonds. Her divorced friend from church, Adelia, had lived a middle-class lifetime already, caring for her children, while she held down a position as assistant to the president of a local office supply company. This company's president and board eventually determined they should go public. Adelia, being a faithful and creative main player in the company for years, was given several shares of the company prior to going public.

The men were honorable and faithful to her, more than her own husband had ever been. When the company went public, Adelia suddenly became a wealthy woman.

Gail, watching the before and after, began asking this joyful woman about stocks and how investments worked. The two became fast friends as Gail learned to invest her money. One day she said, "Adelia, if our husbands could only see how far we've come without them! Sometimes I want to get married again, but then I think about God's promises to me, and those verses that discourage women from remarrying in scripture. What do you think?"

"Gail, you know who would be waiting for us, if we started dating again?"

"No. Who?"

"Your husband and mine." Adelia's eagle eye looked sternly into her friend's face. "All those good men like the board members at my company are already taken, and they'll stay with their families and wives like they should. It's your husband and mine who are out roaming in singles groups."

That answer was enough to shake Gail's romantic hemlines down.

Adelia added for good measure, "I was standing right here, in the hall at church last week listening to two middle-aged men talking about finding their jackpot right here at this church in the single's group. You think they are interested in the Lord? No way. They're just here for their prey."

Gail told this story to Kaida and later to Elsie. She told it to Kaida to warn her about dating men, and she told it to Elsie to remind her how glad she should be with Miles's devotion. She'd been watching Elsie and Miles for several years and now realized that God had given those two a special gift. She'd been wrong about Miles, and she pushed those memories as far away as possible. When Elsie teased her with her warning not to marry Miles, Gail replied, "Well, I never thought that! And I never said that to you."

While Elsie was working a steady job downtown, she decided to reserve a table for two at a known hotspot to celebrate her now hoity toity mother's upcoming birthday. Sitting there, Gail seemed unimpressed.

"You are hard to buy for, Mom. I always get you things that you don't use. I still don't know what to get the woman who already has everything. Actually, sharing life together is what makes a thing special. I thought a special luncheon might be nice so we can catch up." Elsie kept trying to make conversation. Finally, she said, "Don't you like this place, Mom?"

"Usually when it is someone's birthday, you give them a card."

That evening, Elsie went home to a mentoring appointment with a friend. Miles went to his twelve-step meeting. When he came home, they shared what they'd learned and how wonderful life was when people kept putting one foot in front of the other and set themselves to unwrapping the little corrections.

Tucked under a warm quilt that night, Miles suggested they get away to his favorite place in the mountains. Elsie agreed to take the hike with him. She wasn't an avid hiker, but where Miles went, she liked to go with him. Maybe she would take pictures. There were always "Kodak moments" on the trail.

At the next church women's retreat, Gail was asked to pray with and support any women who asked for help. The first night, for entertaining conversation starters during the small groups, Elsie, along with Gail and all the women watched Amy Tan's *Joy Luck Club*, a movie made by Oliver Stone. It begins with the immigrant Chinese mama blessing her child this way, "May she always be too full to swallow any sorrow." Of course, the movie depicts female sorrow tagging the heels of all the women, especially the moves and countermoves between mothers and daughters.

Elsie burst into tears with the similarities in her own relationship with Gail, but Gail ignored her daughter's swollen eyes and her crises of missing blessing the entire weekend, never asking what had broken her heart.

AN ACCOUNTANT CAN ALSO BE DISCREDITED, YOU KNOW

One day Kaida called Elsie to tell her that she was going to take Melanie's son, Ricky, into her home to protect him from Melanie's lack of nurturing, and especially because Melanie's new husband had introduced drugs into Ricky's life. Melanie had agreed.

Pretty soon, Kaida began calling Ricky her third child, her son, and treating him equally with her own two children. The next thing Elsie knew was Kaida called to ask her to come over and sign some documents to adopt Ricky as her own. To be sure, Elsie hurried right over to discover what was going on.

This was not a simple adoption process. Instead, Kaida was building a case of Melanie's negligence and recklessness toward her son's upkeep. She wanted Elsie and Gail to sign as witnesses and add their own two cents to the story of Melanie's incompetence as a mother. Gail didn't like it, but she eventually signed her name, promising her aid in whatever way Kaida needed it. In disbelief, Elsie refused. It looked dirty, the business looked underhanded. Since Ricky was already living with Kaida, why did she feel the need to discredit his mother? It could only lead to alienating Melanie from the family. She said "No, thank you. What you are doing is wrong."

Again, Elsie grieved the fact that her mom had refused to allow Ricky's adoption by her best friend. Look where that short-sightedness had gotten them all. She prayed regularly for that boy.

When Melanie got wind of what was happening, she flew to court in a rage and defended herself appropriately. The stealing of a boy did not happen officially, but practically. Ricky stayed in Kaida's home and was content to be Paige and Grant's adopted brother.

Elsie felt she needed to get her mother away from the influence of her sister, and into doing something productive. She was on a board helping parents who were adopting children in need. Her mother would have ideas and resources, friends whom she could mobilize.

Gail headed up the next couple of fundraisers. She and Elsie spent time together as Elsie chauffeured and explained needs, and Gail brainstormed ideas and planned shopping excursions with her daughter. They were a great team as Elsie knew they would be. The parents were grateful. The organization flourished by gaining new donors and funds.

The only bar to their array of discussions was anything related to Elsie's concerns about Kaida overstepping her boundaries.

NO MARINA PARKING! YOUR CAR WILL BE *TOAD*

Elsie and Miles invited the family to join them on a railroad holiday to an island marina resort they called their "happy place" and frequented every other year. The destination was almost a sacred place to Miles and Elsie. They had enjoyed their reverie to the extent that they explored possibilities of moving there. Gail and Kaida had been so curious about this destination, they decided to accept the ocean side invitation taking along Paige, Grant, and Ricky.

Melanie, still feeling quite bruised, declined.

Since Kaida could go nowhere without her favorite box of wine, she brought it to the train and then left it with Miles to carry through the railway transfers and to the bus depot. Though he despised the power of alcohol, he said little and carried the box on top of his own luggage.

"Thanks, Miles. You see, I have to carry my own luggage and some of the kids', too," she explained, giggling.

"You know, wine can be found at any destination. They serve it right here in the dining car." The retort slipped from Elsie's lips. She was partly teasing until Miles's anger with Kaida sparked in their private compartment. Then, she suggested leaving the affronting box as a tip for the railroad staff and apologizing later to Kaida.

When the view of the private marina finally opened up to the family, the children ran for the cabin. After settling in, Miles escorted the children to the pool for an hour of swimming.

The women decided to make spaghetti and salad and talk over the maps and landmarks making plans for the week of fun.

Kaida plugged in her cellphone, but every time she checked it, she cursed the lack of cell coverage.

"It's okay, dear, we're on vacation. We only bring our cell phones for emergencies up here." Elsie smiled and patted her sister's back.

"No. I need to keep an eye on what's happening with my accounts. I funded this trip by moving some money around. I'll be in deep doo-doo if the funds tank."

Kaida had failed in real estate, but she had managed to divorce her husband as soon as she found a job in a retirement funding firm. As she learned to place stock trades, she tried her own hand at the riskier ones, and gambled on the family vacation. This week was to be a harsh lesson.

When the group went hiking, Kaida studied her cellphone. When they went whale watching, she missed the whales because she was searching her account options. When books were pulled out for reading and rocking on the porch, Kaida checked her funds and placed long distance calls. At every hiking and whale watching adventure, Kaida's lack of cell phone coverage and plummeting stock distractions caused a rash of irritations. She managed to offer half of her attention and tentative joy. Souvenir shopping was out of the question.

Miles played frisbee with the children, Elsie walked them through an outdoor art exhibit, and Gail footed the restaurant bill while Kaida, the detractor, worried at the cabin.

All in all, the vacation was a success for the children. For Miles and Elsie, it was interesting. But for Gail, she was ultimately very disturbed that her beloved daughter could not fully enter into such precious family time.

"They have two incomes!" Kaida complained. Elsie overheard her sister's envy and rolled her eyes. "So do you. In fact, you have three counting Grandma's support. Miles just knows how to save and budget."

Grant overheard this exchange and approached Miles. "Hey, Uncle, can you show me what a budget looks like? I'd like to learn about money, and what you do."

Miles sat down at the little table in the cabin and showed Grant what he did on paper, in categories, and how he separated accounts.

Miles and Elsie often took off for day explorations or short weekend getaways since these felt like everyday celebrations and didn't cost near as much as a full-blown holiday. "We celebrate life as much as possible together. Why wait for retirement?"

Grant nodded. "Can I save this piece of paper, Uncle?"

A FIREPLACE BUILDER WAS DISMANTLED

Richard soon visited Elsie and Miles again, "looking for a project," he said. Strangely, he had left his beloved wife at home, but of course, they always had a project for him. Gail had found a discounted fireplace mantle for the couple, and Richard mounted it to the wall. Strangely, he refused to trim it and left gaping holes.

"I'll fix it later," Elsie assured Miles. To thank her father, they took him out for dinner to a nice restaurant.

In the last few years, however, Richard had clammed up around family meals. He slept in the car on the way to dinner. He ordered the cheapest thing on the menu, either an appetizer or a piece of chicken. He looked straight ahead over the table and downed his food with monosyllables of conversation.

When Elsie said, "Dad? What's wrong? We want to thank you and celebrate with you."

"Nothing's wrong. I'm not a conversationalist. And I just can't stand paying these prices."

"We live in the city. It's just the way things are here. We're treating. Please don't worry. We want to thank you."

"That's all well, fine, and good. You did, and I'm ready to go home now."

BREAK THE *HOBBIT* OF *TOLKIEN* IN YOUR SLEEP

Elsie had the heels of her hands in soft dough when her sis called. "What ya' got going today?" Kaida had been seeing her sister more and more asking to sit in her hot tub, talking about the contractor issues, helping with the problems, and having lunch together. "Oh, I need gluten-free bread, so Mom bought me a bread maker. That was sweet, but I'm learning to knead my own dough," she answered. "Hey, did you hear that pun?"

Elsie also mentioned that when she'd been sick in bed, Gail had come to sit next to her all day and nurse her. "It was the beginning of healing for us, I think. It felt so good to have her care for me like that."

As they relaxed together in the chill of the morning, Kaida confessed, "I sometimes feel like Sméagol."

"Like what?"

"Ha-ha," Kaida giggled. "You know Sméagol, in *The Lord of the Rings?*"

"You mean, Gollum?"

"Yes. He's called Sméagol when he's good and Gollum when he's lusting for the One Ring. I feel like there are two of me. One is very sweet and nice; I'd like to be good and loyal and show people the way, but the other side of me is transformed when I am tempted by the ring."

Elsie wasn't sure what Kaida was haunted about. She finally said, "I think we all have temptations to deal with." This philosophical tact turned into a conversation about their parents and continuing family issues. Significant in Kaida's life was the question of what to do about her mom calling her seven times per day and hunting her down to chat if she failed to answer the phone.

Nonplussed at being taken for her mother's best friend, Kaida didn't want to be seen as unavailable to guys her age. "I don't want to be single; but Mom has me on a leash."

So Kaida was looking for another guy. She had friends of her own she wanted to go out with. Mother's tethers kept holding her back.

Kaida informed Elsie of the significant benefits to Gail's saddling up, on the other hand. Gail had purchased a car for her, one more appropriate for a businesswoman since Kaida had succeeded in taking her real estate sales license with her mom's prompting and coaching. Still, she did not enjoy the business or the same success as Gail enjoyed.

"In fact, I've sold nothing," Kaida confessed. "Mom continues to buy clothing for my children, buys me home décor, and pays my bills when things are tight. You know how she likes to shop, so I figure she's getting something out of it. I'm her source of entertainment." Kaida sniggered.

"Wait, are you saying even now, she buys like that for you guys? Even after she provided a new job for you?"

"Yeah." Kaida shrugged. "It isn't up to me. She loves living vicariously through me."

It seemed to Elsie that Kaida lived in a continuous loop of an emotional rollercoaster doing erratic things, saying she felt trapped. Kaida's sense of self-integrity was shaken after her last divorce, and she had always felt unloved by her father even as an adult. She railed against God and any religious morays, the Bible's quirky passages, and different family members whom she slighted with her entertaining tales of them at unexpected times.

Elsie asked Kaida often about her children's need for guidance and safety. Kaida, over the years, simply refused to discipline her children and shrugged it off if they needed help or from bullies or wisdom with friendships. She would tell them, "Figure it out yourselves. That's how you learn to get along in this world."

Sitting in the hot tub together, Kaida laughed and said, "I don't think God even sees me. Where is He when I need Him? You know, those religious bastards at the girl's boarding school? They taught us how the Israelites built the temple of God. What a waste of time! You know there's a group that built an amusement park with all that stuff, the temple, the ark of the covenant, Noah's Ark, and all that Old Testament stuff? What a crock. Don't ask me to go there! Stupid Christians."

Elsie didn't know what to say. She was quiet. Then, she replied, "I was just reading about all the details in the temple in Exodus. God told them to measure things by cubits. Do you know what a cubit is?"

"No."

"It's the general length of a man's arm."

"So?"

"He told them to gather wool, dye it, and make rugs and curtains for the temple."

"So?"

"God was very specific in His instructions, including what building materials to use. He instructed that gold be hammered over the décor. He wanted very precise gems and jewels, naming each one, and then He told them to dye a ram's skin in red and cover the top of the tent of the temple with it to signify His son's atonement covering those in worship there, I guess."

"He told them how to cover up the priest's genitals so that they wouldn't be exposed on the stair going to the ark."

"You notice the strangest things, girl." Kaida laughed.

"He told them how to make the bread for atonement, and how to cut up the bull and the rams for the offerings, how to dress each part of the priest, from the turban to the waistband, the sash, and the fasteners at each shoulder and the breastplate."

"What's your point?"

"Well, I found it all very interesting, all of these details relating to livestock, excavation, lumber, baking, butchering and even law."

"Why is that interesting to you?"

"Well, the Lord told them to kill the animals for their sins, but then, He had them shake some of the blood onto these brand-new priestly garments which He'd just designed for Aaron to wear. It was like He was saying, only the animal has to die, but I want you to feel the pain, and be forever associated with the sacrifice made for you. It's poetry and pathos. It's covenant and law. And it's a picture of Christ's atonement recorded forever and practiced by the Hebrews."

"I get that, but why so much detail? It's extravagant detail. He could have just told them a story, don't you think?"

"Well, yes. I was reading it and thinking it over, and I realized how intimately this Spirit-Father-God was being. The whole time He was reciting these blueprints and dictating details to reveal how holy He was, He was also detailing how personally He understood all His children."

"What?"

"He spoke of the intimate physical details and measurements of the human body, which He had incidentally created. He spoke of the work of farmers and ranchers, and excavators and gems dealers, tanners, lumberjacks and carvers, weavers, dyers, bakers, and lawmakers—including each one as though He lovingly valued seeing them in their elements. The pathos of the sacrifice spoke to the poets and musicians. God was telling each of them that He knew them intimately, not only in the way He designed their bodies, but He also understood their interests and vocations and blisters and delights. He understood what they treasured and what made them who they were."

There was silence in the hot tub, and Elsie held up her wrinkled palm to her sister.

"I think my takeaway from seeing these things is that God is intimately involved in our lives. He sees us and loves us. It's the grandeur of the plan to show His holiness, and salvation covenant, but it is also in Noah's case the Ark of salvation, that lifts those who believe up from the flood and from drowning in human degradation. When we miss out on the priestly sacrifices and covenant, there is still a lifeboat, if we want to get in it."

When Kaida was especially down and feeling guilty that week, yet still spiritually curious, she bought a case of beer and began to drink it as she lounged on her couch reading Genesis. Getting into the story of Jacob's trickery and then his wrestling with God, she closed her Bible and prayed. "I'm another Jacob, God. If You can forgive me, if You can make something out of me, I want to find You again. I want You to reveal Yourself to me."

She felt He did that afternoon, so she recommitted her life to Him flattered that she could call on Him like Bilbo Baggins called on Gandalf.

CURIOUSLY, PEOPLE TRANSFORM INTO DRAGONS AT THE FLICK OF A CAPE

On another hot tub day, the youngest sister began to lure Elsie into a business plan. This time, Kaida wanted to start up a mediation practice and wanted Elsie to become her partner.

Elsie flatly refused. Mediation was similar to arbitration, and the only arbitrators she knew of were judges and lawyers. Kaida was neither. Elsie had only paralegal credentials. It seemed a grandiose, but cavernous idea.

"You need to get a lawyer on board," Elsie advised.

When Kaida finally wooed in a lawyer for a partner and a human resource director as another partner, Elsie agreed to help her sister begin a mediation business by drafting documents to protect her financial installments and retirement portion.

Elsie did not want to engage in actual mediations or in meeting clients. She and Miles had set their sights on a hospitality ministry, and she was already immersed in this endeavor.

Kaida and her partners set about making a website, delineating duties and the type of mediation services they would offer, but Kaida kept running afoul of the partners' decisions with her. She gave different terms to the website designer than what was decided upon and then she unilaterally determined to take on a type of corporate arbitration that was not within the purview of her partner collaboration. No matter what they agreed to, she couldn't keep herself from moving beyond the decision of the partnership and instituting erratic point-of-the moment decisions.

Elsie tried to reason with her, but she wouldn't budge. She liked to spin a situation as though she were the victim. She was the owner; therefore, she could make whatever changes inspired her from moment to moment.

At the next meeting, when the partners gave notice of their resignation, Elsie also decided to quit. Kaida had become a bombastic autocrat. She'd run over everyone. There was no saving her sister's business.

Unable to face the consequences, Kaida poured herself a drink. Another. Another. She began crafting a lifeboat, one which would save her from herself. One which sacrificed each of her sisters yet provided for her children. One which took advantage of her mother's affections. One which exploited her loyalty.

When Kaida spoke to her mother next, she painted Elsie as a conspirator trying to take over her mediation company. Elsie called Gail asking how Kaida was doing, only to discover her mother's conviction that Elsie, who she expected more from, had betrayed her beloved youngest girl. "You and the other partners tried to steal Kaida's company! How could you?!"

Nothing in the stories of Kaida's behavior described by Elsie to their mother changed Gail's bias.

Elsie had never witnessed such erratic behavior. Especially not from her sister. Maybe it was beyond what her mom could imagine, too.

Elsie didn't know what to think. She assumed, if she just told the truth, the issues could be addressed. Things would settle down eventually. When the emotions calmed, the facts would reveal the truth.

She was wrong.

Miles wiped his wife's tears. "Believe it or not, there will always be those who want to go swimming with you just for an opportunity to drown you."

Gail had always valued honesty. Now, however, she introduced Elsie to relativism. Gail became loyal to the cause of Kaida's defense, though the cause was not worth the sacrifice of her other daughters. Gail's integrity and honesty no longer spun on the hub of truth.

Elsie cried and yearned for the mother she still deeply respected.

She would soon learn more about the hierarchy of loyalty: *"Loyalty is the only moral force that can exist on the same plane as the truth itself."*[1] Elsie went out to contemplate the unexpected distancing of approval from her mother, laying herself down in the grape fragrance of purple iris in her backyard, nursing her hurt. Things would be fine. Her aching heart reached to God.

WHY DO HOBBITS DESIGN BY *FRODO*-TYPES?

Most everybody in the family listened to Kaida's intricately spun stories unless they were the butt of them. Her entertainment won the heart of Ricky, her own two children and her mother.

Melanie couldn't care less what Kaida said. She lived out of the city now with her new husband. What she had heard about others, she kept to herself. She knew the stories she didn't hear usually concerned her.

Trying to keep Elsie away from her family milieu, Miles told other types of stories to entertain his wife. Every day, his stories of co-workers and problems that he managed to unravel with his history and inside knowledge of the hospital made her smile and lifted her heart. She also had stories of her friends and ministry events to tell. Together, they often entertained strangers who, in one way or another, they became saving angels for. They kept rooms for hospitality, and often had guests staying for weeks. Life wasn't dull in their household.

Carlene fed into the Finch family drama with her own whisperings—mostly about her mother and mother's favorite child. She was so far removed from the situation that the distance itself snubbed her ability to contribute anything helpful.

Elsie persisted in reasoning with both Kaida and her mother, but Kaida wanted her best friend back without having to reconcile the truth of what happened or to fess up to how she intended to use her mother's open hand and goodwill.

To secure her mother's favor, Kaida felt she had to spin the story with herself as the victim. Elsie, having sided with the departed partners who would perhaps begin their own mediation firm together, became the perpetrators in her version of what happened. "They've stolen everything from me, Mom. Elsie is a wolf in sheep's clothing." Having said so, Kaida could not retract her words or sentiments. She had to devise a different plan to show her heroic offer of forgiveness toward Elsie and Elsie's refusal to reconcile.

When Elsie caught wind of her sister's stories, she felt sick. Several attempts at solving the problem went back and forth between Kaida's house and hers. The conversations over a year's time went like this:

Elsie would say, "If I did something horrible to you, why would you want me back in your life? It doesn't make sense. You need to tell Mom and your children that I had warned you and I stood by you to the end. You need to tell them that none of us stole anything from you! Your lies are ruining my relationships with Mom and with my niece and nephews. I'm losing everything, Kaida, so I need you to tell the truth if you want me back in your life. You can't have it both ways."

"It's a matter of perspective," Kaida would cry. "Why can't we just start over?"

"Because I can't have a fake relationship. You've painted me to be the bad guy when all I ever did was protect you and tell you the truth. You use people until you find they are expendable, and then you throw them under the bus. Kaida, you don't love Mom the way she loves you. You're using her. You've told me how you can't seem to live your own life because she's always there."

"She's too valuable to me and my kids. I need her while I'm getting my business going."

When Elsie asked for a visit with her mother, Gail would show up accompanied by her sidekick, Kaida. It was Kaida who answered Elsie, accused Elsie, and Gail sat taking in the disputes perplexed.

One day Elsie's tearful angst spilled, "Mom! I was the good child! Why do you treat me like my very nature has changed? You always take me for granted. The only people who matter to you are Kaida and her kids. I'm an afterthought. Whatever did I do?"

Kaida got up from the table. "I'm leaving. Mom, if you want to stay here, Elsie can drive you home. If you want to come with me, you'd better come now."

Gail also stood up to follow her youngest. She flipped her hand at Elsie saying, "Have a nice life."

That was the last conversation between Elsie and her mother for five years, five of the hardest years of Elsie's life.

Miles and Elsie were dealing with two general contractors during that time who messed up two different remodels on their houses, and the liens and lawsuits followed.

In contrast to Gail waving off her daughter's friendship during this period, Richard sent a thousand dollars to help defray the costs of Elsie and Miles's legal issues. It was a thin slip of hope, this note of parental protection which she badly needed.

In the depths of Elsie's distress, she also had a dream where her father stood with a rifle in the front of their house defending it. "You'll come this far, and no further," he said, aiming his rifle toward the circle of aggressors. She knew that the image of her father signified God's protection of them, but the vision of her anti-gun-toting father defending her had a profound impact. It gave Elsie new confidence to do what she needed to do.

During this heartsore period, Kaida sent a bill for one thousand dollars to Elsie and Miles for what she called "helping you remodel your home" from two years prior. Although the sisters had regularly helped each other with painting and fixing things up, Kaida was obviously in a financial pit, so Miles and Elsie wrote her a check for what she requested.

Kaida reasoned she would put a mechanics lien on her sister's home if they didn't pay up. Either way, she'd win.

When her mediation business lost its web designer, its bylaws, and its partners, due to her erratic decisions, Kaida used the thousand dollars to file for bankruptcy while in the same instance, blaming Elsie for her company's demise. She also lost her rental home. She was forced to redesign her business limits more reasonably. She started from scratch as sole proprietor of a divorce mediation company. She took out a second mortgage on her townhome and carried on by leasing her primary home to her children and their friends.

Humiliation complete, she moved in with her mother.

Moving into Gail's home felt mortifying, but her mother had always been her anchor and supporting pillar.

Kaida then determined never to go bankrupt again. Now resting in a comfortable bed, sharing the privileged hospitality of her mother, Kaida used her favored situation as a springboard. "It isn't the favorite at the starting line, but the one who wins the race that matters." She smiled. She'd made up her mind.

During those years, it would have been a challenge for friends to determine who was the more tenacious bulldog, Elsie fighting her lawsuits with contractors and insurance providers to save their home, or Kaida fighting to hold onto her career and save her family home.

When her children graduated from high school, Kaida sold her townhome. She naturally used the proceeds to rent office space, buy a computer, pay fees, and build her new business.

She'd co-existed with her mom a year already. It was time to buy new bedroom furniture, and she had a door installed leading to the back garden from her personal three-room suite in her mother's home.

Things moved along according to plan.

On the other hand, combining households continued as a celebration for Gail. She enjoyed sharing chores and shopping with Kaida. She set aside her own style of décor by mingling Kaida's furniture in the joint living spaces of their household. She allowed Kaida to repaint several rooms.

Grant, Kaida's son, had been dating a girl and decided to propose to her. She accepted. The delight the family felt for the couple sitting in each other's laps barely able to keep their hands to themselves, hearing about Grant learning to dance, and the many other experiences the two enjoyed together was split. The aunties, Elsie and Melanie, were happy for the couple; Gail and Kaida saw the girl as having mental problems that would eventually bring Grant down. They schemed together to break apart the couple and verbally abused her until they succeeded.

When Grant's puffy white clouds in fairytale blue skies turned to days of rain, hail, and devastation, he would accept no explanation from either his mother or grandmother as anything but narcissism. He told them each, "You two are my Mom and Grandma, but we will never be friends again."

More than his heart breaking, Grant's optimism for the future was crippled. He would work extensively on himself for the next few years to find his purpose and a reason to abide in such a family even for limited dinner engagements.

During this time, Grant and Paige tried to confront their mother with her obnoxious interloping into their lives, namely that she had failed to protect them from her husband's abuse. Though Melanie was invited to air her anger at Kaida for trying to turn her son and mother against her, Elsie was not invited or included in the family meeting. Thus, she didn't hear about the longstanding issues with her niece and nephew's abuse, nor was she made privy to the fury over Kaida's junior high date rape. She didn't understand the nature of the meeting and had never heard about Kaida's rape. She again felt set off from her family.

Kaida made one attempt to fix her family's woes. She spoke with an attorney friend who offered to provide family mediation.

The attorney sent an online invitation to the Finch family members asking them to write a private email back to him each identifying the main problem in the family conflict. He would then go through the emails listing the issues. He'd listen if they wished to make recommendations, or he could write his own if they preferred.

Some family members were copied as the others sent in their letters. Others waited. Still others sent in private letters for the mediator's eyes alone.

In the end, the attorney sent a letter to family members stating that he didn't think he had the ability to navigate the complex issues.

"Have you heard of a river running in two directions? The Hudson River is one. Depending upon the rainy season and droughts, the sea tides, and runoffs of fresh water diluting the river, it flows one way and then the next. There are two high tides, and two low, every twenty-four hours caused by saltwater mingling with fresh water flowing into the estuary at different points. Even though it is an anomaly, it does exist. Apparently, so must your family."

The letter rippled through Gail because of her maiden name, her own deep tides by nature being Hudson. By giving up, the mediator succeeded in drowning her family hopes in the analogy.

Kaida then sent her own email blast to everyone saying, "The mediator feels our letters were too caustic and that our family is too toxic to help. It's really too bad that it didn't work out."

This outcome stunned every member of the family who had worked on a letter. The time, vulnerability, questions, and personal analysis that they had put into the process made the outcome even more frightening. An isolating war enveloped each of them separately, as a chilly veil fell between them.

For all, except for Kaida's world.

Kaida still had her mother and her children's affections. From this vantage point, she sold or gave away everything that Elsie had made or given her mother in the process of moving in and redecorating Gail's home. Having recently dated a sailor, she accompanied him on a race across the water. In a race of sailboats, there is a term called "dirty air." It means that a boat pulling ahead of the others can tilt the sails and set them to cut the air current so that the following boats catch filtered wind and lose power, unless they manage to break away from the turned current.

Kaida drafted a beneficiary deed in her own hand and convinced Gail it was to her benefit to alleviate the competition of her other daughters at the time of her death. "This acts like a trust, Mom," she said, "for me and my children. They will forgive you and me if you sign it."

When Kaida read the sentence at the bottom of the legal form, however, she realized the deed was revokable. "Revokable" made her a tad nervous, so she convinced Gail to write a last will and testament to specifically disinherit Elsie. "Elsie will fight me on the beneficiary deed if she finds out and, with her legal knowledge, the attorneys will get everything. She has Miles's parents' home coming to her. She won't need yours. I will though, and my children will inherit from me. Now that I've put money into renovating our home, it's only right that I inherit it."

Of course, Elsie knew nothing of this. All she knew after her mother rebuffed her attempts at reconciliation, was that her mother had not once run after her with a mother's heart or attempted to contact her.

Elsie had read *The Sermon on the Mount* recently. She was baffled by it. How could she turn the other cheek? How could she give anything more to Kaida or her mother than they'd already taken from her?

Kaida kept life interesting for Gail, shopping and redecorating, so why bother with the other daughters' rancor when she could simply move along with Kaida?

Forgiveness is one thing, but reconciliation takes two. It also cannot be achieved without significantly renewed trust. Trust crushed and eggshells in the nest, the entire Finch family tried to flee except the big birds, Gail and Kaida.

A book of receipts kept between Kaida and Gail noted figures and balanced the costs of living and extra costs of goods that they would agree to whether it was in trade for value from one to the other, or in actual deposits and withdrawals.

DIRTY DEEDS DONE DIRT CHEAP

Gail had been losing her vision for quite some time, probably since age sixty-five when she was unable to read real estate contracts in print any longer, and the computer became blurry. When she was diagnosed with macular degeneration, she retired.

For six years, Kaida and mother lived as near to being a married couple as mother and daughter might. Emancipated Paige found a military man and married him with a huge celebration in his hometown. Neither Gail nor Kaida was very excited about the man's post-traumatic stress nightmares, but they couldn't dissuade Paige from her choice. There was never going to be a man who was good enough, and Paige had grown into a very independent woman. Kaida and Gail smiled as hostesses and celebrated outwardly, putting on the ideal wedding reception. Even Rich and Noeleen tried to socialize cheerfully. Secretly, Gail and Kaida hoped for the best, but felt a gnawing fear for Paige. Had she thrown away all the benefits they had so carefully provided to her in life?

Meanwhile, Kaida continued to hide her personal disdain for her mother's controlling affections and embroiled lives. They enjoyed each other's company openly, finding happy hours around town, eating out, buying and selling, spoiling Grant and Paige whenever the kids could spare a couple of hours for their elders. Yet Kaida, oh, so carefully, staked out future aims.

I SHOULD BE UPSET THAT A BURGLAR STOLE ALL MY LAMPS, BUT I'M DE*LIGHT*ED

There is a tree called a strangler fig. The bougainvillea-like trunk of the fig wraps itself around a host tree and feeds from its nutrients, eventually killing the host tree. What's left is an intricately laced columnar fig tree, a towering work of skeletal twines for a trunk. The beautiful empty filigree is crowned with a thriving green bush of leaves on top.

Kaida extolled her exclusive relationship with Gail and the grandchildren she loved, comparing herself and her children to Gail's other unworthy children and grandchildren. There was a pile of ammunition for Kaida to choose from.

She reasoned, "Elsie had her education handed to her on a silver platter and then never had to work, really. She's made her home with Miles's family since. I am the only likely child to care for you, Mom, in your old age, I should be the one to inherit the house. My kids would get the benefit when I die."

Gail considered her options. There had been the time just prior to buying her home, that Elsie had asked her mother to buy in her neighborhood so she and Miles could be nearby to help, but that seemed ages ago. For some reason, her relationship with the adult Elsie had been shy of gold. There'd been those silent years. Elsie had a fault of siding with Carlene and defending Rich at times. She had no children and probably didn't need the money. Melanie had refused her mother's help at every turn. She could not recall a time they were close.

Gail's main asset had always been the home, and more specifically, the location of her home. Savvy always in business, she knew that the location determined the difference in value of any two identical structures. Gail made her choice in a reputable and safe neighborhood. Kaida had proven to be the daughter she'd always hoped for.

Still, it seemed Kaida was a bit too anxious and consumed with her estate, all of it, to be exact. It worried her.

In a lucid moment, considering that Christmas was again approaching, Gail devised a quit claim deed giving her property to herself, Elsie and Melanie with Kaida inheriting her mother's share at her death. She filed it in a cabinet, meaning to ask an attorney about it with her potential bequests and concerns, but it slipped her mind. Instead, she shopped for gloves and slippers and bought other novelties that Christmas. She forgot to bring the deed to light.

Once Gail had purchased a beautiful home with a solidly rising value in a safe and upscale community, Kaida wanted that house. She approached her mother again with the idea of creating a family trust or a right of survivorship contract for her estate. Gail told Kaida to do the research and show her what it entailed.

Kaida eventually contacted an attorney who was the consultant for her mediation business and engaged him to draw up a trust document called a life estate regarding her mother's home. After all, she'd already signed the previous beneficiary deed now filed.

Carefully considering Kaida's interests given the age of her mother, the attorney suggested a quit claim deed as the best vehicle for transferring Gail's home into her name with a limiting clause for a life estate for her mother. The single page was drafted on his computer.

When Gail asked Kaida why her beneficiary deed and her will were not sufficient, Kaida told her the new "trust" was more complete. It ensured that Grant and Paige would finally inherit her property at the end of Kaida's life. It would also substantially help her build Kaida's credit back from the bankruptcy to have her name on the deed.

Gail certainly loved Kaida and her grandchildren. Gail trusted Kaida's promise to care for her in her old age, and she believed their funds had become hopelessly co-mingled, so that sitting in the attorney's office that day, she finally agreed to sign the trust document with a "joint tenancy life estate" on her property. It felt like a business transaction. It was only right to incentivize Kaida for her promise to care for her in her old age.

To clarify her rights and ownership of the house, Gail started to decipher whether she still had the right to sell her property if she needed to, and Kaida's attorney assured her that she did. The attorney placed the document in front of Gail.

Kaida showed Gail, nearly blinded by advanced macular degeneration, where to pen her signature. Kaida then escorted her mother to the waiting room. She went back into the attorney's office and finished her business, adding the title, "Quit Claim Deed."

Blinded, now, in more than one way, Gail made Kaida co-owner and the sole beneficiary of her home, secretly, away from her other daughters and their heirs.

Kaida told her children that she and Gail had created a "trust bequest" for them but advised them to keep the secret from the rest of the family.

She had given her mother a life estate.

When the Quit Claim Deed was filed in county records, it was returned to Kaida's name, not to Gail.

This mother-daughter relationship had become so intertwined and interdependent, it was difficult to see which one was the host tree and which one was the strangler fig.

The tree, now grown tall, would bloom in the foreseeable future. Only a death certificate and affidavit needed to be filed in order for Kaida to claim her mother's full estate.

DON'T CHANGE YOUR MIND AFTER COMPLETING A DEED OF TRANSFER, FOR THE DEED, AS THEY SAY, IS DONE

Although Elsie was not speaking to her mother or to Kaida, and being unable to dispel their punishment of slander, Melanie continued to navigate family waters and would visit with them as though no scars or misgivings existed. Melanie watched and listened and smiled and asked questions about Kaida's children, Gail's grandchildren, and enjoyed the occasional family holiday or outing with Gail and Kaida's mutual friends.

She knew what normal, appropriate family relationships entailed, and she spoke the talk and walked the walk to get herself included. But, when she looked toward her fiftieth birthday year, it was Elsie whom

Melanie asked to join her on a vacation in Italy in celebration. Miles gave his wife his blessing, and in October, off the sisters went.

The two stayed on a boutique cruise yacht by night and took walking tours of cities around the peninsula by day.

The fall weather remained gloriously blue and gold, reflected in the gondola canals of Venice; the sisters marveled. What they had only seen in pictures, they experienced in languid channels around the glass island of Murano. They witnessed the intrigue of orange persimmon polka dots covering green residential trees, fields of green olives, and orchards of purple grapes. These images painting themselves onto their hearts with all the illusion of Brunetti and Montalbano.

Inquisitive sisters attended a pasta making class in a traditional Bologna café. Breathless, they discovered and rode the highspeed Italia rail to the red and white striped city of Florence. They drank the bewitched espresso, and savored gelato between visits to cathedrals, palaces, operas, and Dante's gravesite. This exotic trip went a long way to repairing the sisters' rift. Laughter, good meals, fun explorations to open up history and art in their minds. Sharing each other's pictures and historic perspectives of their family burdens ignited a new camaraderie.

"Do you think Dad would have enjoyed this trip, Elsie?" Melanie asked. "I mean, besides all the wine?"

The girls laughed. "No, I don't. Did you ask him to come?"

Melanie was taking a picture of yet another cathedral. "Yes, but he said he was too busy, of course."

"Mel, Dad likes to conquer things, but he doesn't wonder about them. He doesn't want another culture to influence his thinking. Even when his thinking doesn't serve him well," Elsie finished in a halting voice.

"What do you mean? He enjoys traveling."

"Yes, but I think traveling calms his nerves. And the music calms him too. It makes him all sentimental. He's completely in charge. He doesn't enjoy his destination, though. He doesn't stay long—always cuts his visits short—and he doesn't ask personal questions. He'll tell you what he thinks on religion, politics, mechanical stuff and techno lectures matter-of-factly, but he doesn't really let people know him. He can be a hero to them, short term. He doesn't converse well because he has no real interest in anyone else and he's afraid they'll discover his hang-ups. What if they confront his way of thinking? What would he say then? He can't risk the vulnerability."

"He'd duck and hide! He wouldn't say anything!"

"That's what I mean. He doesn't allow anyone or anything to challenge him. He can't stand change. He can't afford to wonder about things—go down a rabbit hole with someone a little different—or wander too far from home for that matter. He has his patterns, and he has trails. That's where he operates."

"Maybe that's why Noeleen has gone quiet lately?"

A *DESCRIPTED* COMEDY IS MOST LIKELY A SILENT MOVIE

The week after Christmas, when Melanie's car was parked in Gail's driveway, Gail backed into it. She blamed this on Melanie's parking, but Elsie broke her rule of silence. She told her mother that she shouldn't be driving if she couldn't see another car in her own driveway.

One day in January, Kaida made one less car to navigate on the driveway. She sold her own car and began driving her mother's, since Kaida reasoned that she was serving her mother now by taking her to doctor's appointments. They also enjoyed many of the same things from restaurants to shopping the local Goodwill and recycling stores.

When tax season came around, however, Kaida discovered that she no longer had the vehicle deduction for her car, so she asked her mother to add her name to the title on her car. Gail agreed.

Melanie divorced again in early spring when the ice lay melting on the tarmac and snowflakes decorated the air. Elsie drove her to the divorce proceeding in a decided show of support. The confident articulation and preparedness of her sister in the stand answering the judge's questions, opened her eyes. Her underdog sister was no idiot. Melanie's preparedness also impressed the judge, who in turn lectured the new girlfriend about men who use women and take everything they have before dumping them. He granted everything Melanie requested.

Melanie confessed to Elsie at lunch that day that she had given up her second child, a little boy, for adoption.

"What are you talking about, Melanie?" How could Elsie have remained in the dark about a pregnancy?

"Yes, he and I got pregnant four years ago, and I thought it would save our marriage, but he only wanted me to freeload off of. He didn't want a child."

"He's a gigolo, Melanie!"

"He's the best thing that ever happened to me." She began sobbing. "I had no self-respect until he came along. He gave me self-respect." Her hands went over her face. Her shoulders shook with the pain of a lifetime.

"He's an alcoholic and a drug user. You just told the judge how he lived off of you your entire marriage and couldn't keep a job. You heard what the judge said." Elsie paused, unable to absorb the perspective of her sister. Finally, she said, "You deserve better."

"I know. I know. It's terrible when the best thing that ever happens to a person is a gigolo!" Melanie wept and laughed intermittently from the irony.

Elsie tried to take stock of the situation. "What happened with your baby, Melanie?"

"I gave him the pregnancy test result, and he said, 'Choose me or choose that.' So, I chose him. I thought I could save us."

"What became of the child?"

"Oh, I get to visit him every so often, as long as I don't tell him who I am. His parents tell him I'm a friend of the family."

"How old is he?"

"He's three and a half." Melanie began to smile with tenderness. "I know I did the right thing for him, but now I have nothing."

A DOUBLE-CROSSED STRAWBERRY IS CALLED A *BL*UE*BERRY*

Rich came to Colorado and he and Elsie helped Melanie move into an apartment complex with a community barbecue pit and dog park. It promised some possibilities of making new friends. They renovated some furniture for her, but Melanie's loneliness became desperation. No real community developed, and the depression pushed her to seek out company even with her mother and Kaida.

While not completely in the dark as to the amount of control Kaida had gained over their mother, Melanie was willing to take the risk in the name of camaraderie. She didn't realize that to them she was little more than a potential renter, someone they thought they could manage because they knew her, someone who presented them with another financial buffer for occupying the empty basement apartment.

The two offered Melanie the basement apartment for below market rent. As soon as her lease agreement expired, Melanie began moving all her possessions, including everything she had in storage, into her mother's basement; she wanted to be nearer the inner circle.

With the arrival of Melanie's boxes, Gail and Kaida became alarmed. The entire garage filled up with stackable plastic boxes of quilting material piled to the ceiling. Cardboard boxes of things saved from early childhood, and every stage thereafter, piled up. Then, Melanie's motorcycle appeared. She had barely moved in, helped by her nephew Grant and a friend, when Kaida drafted an eviction notice, signed it and had her mother sign as well.

"What are you doing?" Melanie asked, confused.

"You can't take all the garage and fill the entire basement with your junk. You just can't stay. We can't have it. You have thirty days to leave. Take all this stuff out of here," Gail demanded, her words embellished by Kaida's.

Melanie began weeping. "All you had to do was tell me you'd changed your minds. This is horrible. Horrible!"

When Elsie heard of her sister's humiliation, she agonized. She could expect the treachery from Kaida, but it was unbelievable that their mother would stoop so low.

"Why couldn't they give you a month to sort through your things and give them to a thrift store or put them in the trash or something?" she asked, horrified.

"I don't know. I wanted to send some of it to Ricky, but some of it, I just couldn't get rid of."

To this end, Melanie and all her belongings were tossed out the door with her mother's signature and blessing.

THE SINGER FELT *DENOTED* BY THE LACK OF APPLAUSE

Carlene also resonated with Melanie. She felt she'd been tossed off the same mommy-boat years ago. This was evidenced by the fact she was no longer welcome in her mother's home, and she hadn't spoken with her mother in several years. So, Melanie's humiliation fanned the flames of family gossip all over again as she told her woes to Carlene.

Whenever Carlene could, she rehashed how her relationship with her mother had turned out so differently to her relationship with her father, and when Elsie tried to change the subject or introduce mitigating factors, Carlene would clam up, believing Elsie to be playing both sides. Carlene continued to be very careful about what she shared personally with members of the Finch family.

In the past, whenever Gail had tried to defend herself to her eldest or tell instances of Rich's insidious side, Carlene cut her off with her own understanding of the story. Gail had no voice.

Carlene intended to punish her mother judiciously.

She could never accept that family choices, family layers more like, had formed outside their household first, while she had been away at the girl's school. Further, each of her family members now lived lives she did not understand because they continued stretching their wings and building lives long after she escaped them herself. After she married Foreman and left the family home behind forever, their lives were comprised not of mirrors to the past, but of new experiences and viewpoints and motivations other than her own.

She couldn't imagine how rooms were emptied of her father, or that now these rooms were reappointed by Gail and her sisters. No, Carlene was the oldest Finch child. She knew more about the family. Her perspective deserved respect. Carlene thus busied herself with turning the disgruntled siblings against their mother.

However, when Carlene's first daughter left home, refusing to speak to her ever again, the unexpected truth appeared like an apprehension of her treatment of Gail. Her own daughter's treatment appeared like a ghostly apparition, an eerie mirror of her past.

Carlene also busied herself in potentially worthy political causes, health and wellness research, and militia lawsuits. Carlene became so absorbed in her causes, she failed to notice Foreman or her daughters' needs as anything more than distractions to her causes.

Carlene's goodwill for the living flesh of needy family members drained away with the water from her long daily baths where she lay pondering the mysteries of life before migrating to her computer.

Like Gail, Carlene wrote off her own daughters' complaints and perspectives on homelife, saying how small these complaints were lacking in reason or substance. When they were older, they'd understand. But had she ever changed her own mind about her mother?

Growing older, they sensed Carlene's constant distractions in different ways, naming the whys and wherefores according to their experiences.

Carlene also recognized a pattern of dysfunction in her home but took no responsibility for it. She pointed fingers at the discontent instead.

When Carlene telephoned, or came to visit for the holidays, Elsie wondered at the ever-serious nature of her elder sister. Was it due to being mired in land and water rights actions and philosophical politics? Carlene lacked the levity to laugh and treat her loved ones as precious individuals. She resented that her responsibilities for her children kept her from making a name for them all.

Uncorrectable, she took every comment that differed from her perspective as a personal slight.

Carlene's list of enemies continued to grow. First was her own mother, then Foreman's parents, then his medical siblings because they wouldn't give her credit for her medical contributions. Her list of offenses included the students at the teaching hospital who touched and examined her during the birth of her two daughters. She added the water district, and for good measure, her taxing authorities.

Her youngest complained, "Mom loves her dog more than she loves me. She hugs her dog and takes her dog to the vet, and otherwise, never leaves her computer to cook a meal. I am her slave in the kitchen and in the garden, but I never feel loved by her," Meryl confided to Elsie.

Gail learned of this drama from her other children and grandchildren. She wasn't allowed to communicate with Carlene's daughters directly, apart from Carlene supervising.

By way of getting more involved with land causes, medical causes, and militia lawsuits, Carlene lost touch with her second daughter's needs in much the same way as she had her eldest.

Carlene delayed the daily cause of mothering her own family year after year, until her second and final daughter graduated from high school and left the home never to speak to her again.

Carlene said, "I helped heal a guy from Legionnaire's disease…from cancer…from tuberculosis…from meningitis…"

"How do you know they had those diseases?" asked Elsie. "Did a doctor diagnose them? Did they have blood tests done?"

"Oh, no. But I researched all the symptoms, and I was able to find cures for them. So, they got healed."

Carlene continued to sit at her computer, researching light and energy wave healing techniques and arguing causes she believed in while growing all the more stubborn, singly focused, and fat.

"Physician, heal thyself," Gail said whenever she heard about one of these stories.

To her youngest sister, Carlene was no more than a ghost. Kaida could put her hands into Carlene and come away empty. Why, she could walk right through her.

CONJUNCTIONITUS IS CAUSED WHEN AN INFECTION JOINS THE EYE

At church, the pastor offered Miles and Elsie, with the rest of the small congregation, a message on loving one another. Having arguments, even heated ones, did not dissuade the couple's admiration for each other or their open handedness allowing each other to thrive.

As Elsie searched other corners of her soul, her mind wandered to Gail and Kaida's treatment of Melanie by inviting her into their home, only to immediately serve her with eviction papers.

The thought still made her stomach clench. How could her mother have stooped so low?

Elsie and Miles also had their differing approaches to life, and therefore, their own arguments, but she felt grateful for the good humor she and Miles shared. Nothing came near the reproach she felt for her birth family's drama. There could be no comparison, really. If she mowed the lawn for him and soiled her soles with grass clippings, Miles chided her, but he'd clean them up. In the summer, Miles liked to leave the garage door open to keep it cool. This drove her crazy, so she warned him about tool thieves. In the winter, they could never come to an agreement about how to program the thermostat or prepare taxes. "If you loved me, you'd wouldn't do this or that." None of these arguments rose to the level of the Finches' ruckus.

Her mind wandered over what her youngest sister had done repeatedly to Melanie, and the burning hatred her mother displayed toward all three of her daughters while spoiling the youngest. How could she maintain the duo's professional face, the happy-go-lucky ease and friendship with their mutual friends? Everything in the Sunday scripture and exhortation to the church congregation that morning, poured water over Elsie's hatred of her birth family and made her long for reconciliation for each of them. It would take a miracle to mend fences at this point. So, that's what she prayed for.

Perhaps she'd moved away from them due to the longevity of her birth family's mistreatment and suspicion of one another. They'd tried to create a separate peace, each in their own worlds. Was this how the new world was founded? Broken families running to seek their fortunes elsewhere? Maybe there was some purpose to the things that happened to families like hers.

After the worship and teaching ended, Elsie insisted that Miles drive her down to her mother's place. She hadn't seen or talked to her mother in years. She felt a certain urgency today.

There, when Gail and Kaida's curiosity welcomed them, she opened God's word and reiterated the pastor's message and the sin against Melanie once again at the hand of her own mother and sister.

Kaida's gaping mouth leered as she pointed at Elsie, saying, "You tried to steal my company. You're one to talk!"

Elsie turned to her mother. "Look at me, Mom. You know what the Bible says. It is foolish for a woman to tear down her own house. You know you've done the wrong thing."

"I couldn't live with all that mess in my house and my garage. I just couldn't."

"Didn't you consider any other ways to settle it? You could have given her a month to sort through her things and give them away or have them picked up for donations or by the trashmen."

"Well, I hadn't thought of that."

"You didn't have to do an official notice of eviction either. You are her mother, for goodness' sake!"

"We had to make it clear. . . She's depressed and we didn't know if we'd ever get her out."

"Yes, she is depressed. She doesn't believe you love her, and you may have just sent her over the edge. You want that on your hands? Mom, you need to find a way to make it right, and we need to stop this bickering and slander against the others in the family right here, right now."

Gail looked to Kaida, who stomped out of the room.

Gail said, "I think your arrogance in trying to instruct me after keeping me out of your life all these years is ironic. Frankly, it astounds me. Even if I agreed that the Bible was applicable to this situation, I don't know how to fix it. What's done is done."

Elsie asked to pray for the situation and Gail agreed. Together they bowed and asked the Lord for wisdom. Elsie confessed the sins of the family and begged God to help them all fix it. Then she told her mother, "It wasn't I who broke up our relationship, Mom. It was you who told me to shove off and have a nice life. It was you and Kaida who dropped off all the goods, pictures, and gifts I'd given you and then you sold the painted furniture I made you. It was never me. It was you."

"Why is it always my fault? Why am I the one everyone blames?"

"Because you are the mom, Mom. You set the tone. You have the power to comfort, the power to help, or the power to cut people off in your judgment." She paused. "I want you to remember that you have four girls, Mom, not just one. I need you to remember who I was and still am. You wield the power of 'queen of the family,' and only you can turn the tide."

"Where is this coming from? Have you looked at my will?"

That comment stunned Elsie like being nudged toward a shrouded ravine, but she stayed on task.

"What? I haven't even been in your house for years. Take responsibility, Mom! This is your doing. You act like Kaida gets to determine what you want, but this is your doing. You've ganged up against Melanie twice now, after setting her up. You know better!"

Gail sat shaking, her focus down. "I don't know. I don't know."

Elsie embraced her mother and said, "It's up to you. I have never stopped loving you. Though, because of the way you've been acting, I've wondered whether my mother is really a Christian."

"To be honest, Elsie, part of what came between you and me was because I paid for your college tuition, and you never gave me credit for that. Then, you ran off to your dad's and shut me out."

Elsie gasped. Was that occurrence after her return from South Africa the beginning of her mother's animosity?

"I know you helped me, Mom. I've thanked you for that and I felt so close to you at one time. But Dad helped me too. You were two sides of a ladder, the rungs between you were what enabled me to climb into my own life. A mom doesn't right off her child just because her child doesn't understand her sacrifices. I've continued to need my mom. So has Melanie. Yet, all the rungs on the mom-ladder are rotted or broken these days. Since you have been the one to shut us out, you are the only one who can fix this. Please, think about it."

Then, Elsie and Miles left.

Miles had cried through the entire meeting. He got outside and hugged his wife. "You are so courageous. I can't believe you did that. I was praying the whole time, but I don't think anything will change, do you?"

Elsie pondered the meaning of forgiveness again. "No, they won't make good with Melanie, for sure. The thing is, I didn't do myself any favors either. Miles, I got a loan and a grant and worked my way through college, too. She acts like she paid my way! How can two people see things so differently?"

Sometimes she felt she could be altruistic and forgive no matter what harm had been done. She could offer unconditional forgiveness. At other times, she felt she needed a real standard, a meeting of the minds, a real apology, a return to devotion, and proof that a family member was moving away from a harmful way of thinking and behaving. She felt this time that her offer of forgiveness was conditional, and her wariness felt justified.

Her mother, not being one to accept blame, kept the dynamics of their relational parts in a centrifuge.

If Gail were to forgive Elsie, she would only do it as a pragmatic way to move beyond the awkwardness, a means to safeguard her from further embarrassment and to help the family get along. The benefit to making friends with this daughter was that Elsie's faith closely resembled her own, but she stepped carefully. While a part of her longed for Elsie's fellowship, she felt she'd done nothing wrong. She deserved obedience and respect.

A DRAGON'S *TALE* OF 3.14 FEET IS CALLED A PIATHALON

When multiple diets failed, Kaida determined to have bariatric surgery to regain her sporty, petite physic. She had no problem undergoing the series of elective surgeries required, considering the medical advances. She stopped drinking by attending A.A. meetings and cleaned up her act.

Flagrantly after she healed, Kaida brought a date home to bed, much to Gail's chagrin. Gail had just stepped out of the shower and was dressing in her bedroom with the door opened when a man scooted past to Kaida's bedroom. Gail's tantrum was unbridled. "Get out of my house! This is my house! You cannot bring men in here to sleep with you! I'm so angry right now, I could throw you out on your ear!"

Afterwards, there was a widower in the neighborhood who opened his door to Kaida's compassions. That fall, she began going to his house in her pajamas, and, in an effort to halt the neighbors' gossip, Gail said, "This has got to stop."

When the widower broke it off with Kaida, her sharing at the A.A. meetings became vicious. When warned, her laughter and arrogant mocking of others who shared their own struggles turned caustic.

The leaders of the meeting tried to corral Kaida and reason with her. Unable to get through, they simply told her not to return. She'd have to find help elsewhere.

She renewed her dating profile online, modeling in a sleek black dress. There, she met several guys and eventually narrowed it down to one man she particularly liked. That man lived an hour away, and he wasn't ready for a long-term relationship, at least not with Kaida. There was a backup choice, however, and she pursued the young man, Brian, several years her junior.

A LOBBIEST TO CONGRESS WAS *DISMEMBERED*

As Gail's anger toward Kaida grew, snippets of conversation arose between Gail and Elsie, and Gail and Melanie, like remnants from a memory quilt, prompting Elsie to begin inviting the whole family back to her home for Sunday dinners, then Easter, Independence Day, Thanksgiving, and Christmas. Just as she had in the past.

In addition to the regular driving of her mother to doctor's appointments that year, and chauffeuring Gail to things they enjoyed doing together, suddenly Kaida also had to drive her mother to Elsie's house for the special dinners. There were board games for hours after.

She asked Elsie to meet up for lunch. Elsie was excited and nervous to be making up with her sister. It soon became clear, however, that Kaida had an agenda other than making good. She set the tone by saying she was getting counseling to get over their toxic family.

This was good, Elsie acknowledged. Yet, Elsie had journeyed so far beyond any Finch bitterness that she was taken aback by the vitriol that began pouring from Kaida's mouth, rising in volume from the other side of the table. She acknowledged that Kaida had grown up experiencing a vastly different family than she had, but when Kaida started talking about physical beatings, and accusing Elsie of being an abuser herself, her jaw dropped.

"Kaida! When I was put in charge of you and Melanie, I was a child myself, and your arguing and bickering drove me crazy. I didn't know how to make you stop. I only spanked you one time. I'm sorry for it, but I'd hardly put that in the category of abuse."

Kaida reminded Elsie of the time their dad had pulled her from under the table and beat her with a belt.

"That, again, was one time, Kaida. It wasn't a regular thing. I know you weren't close, and that disturbs me greatly, but it wasn't like he ever sexually abused us. Our parents always told us how many licks and why we were getting them. So many people deal with being starved for food or being physically abused repeatedly. That isn't the story in our family. We were emotionally starved."

Guests at the other tables glanced at the sisters.

Elsie said, "You know, I was so excited, hoping to have a good time here together, hoping to be reunited with you, but I'm going to leave you here to think about it now because I totally disagree with what you are saying. You've been spoiled rotten by Mom, and she's more than made up for Dad's lack of support." Unhinged by grief and shock, she pushed away from the table and left.

Elsie didn't know the half of it.

To prevent arguments about difficult family matters during family visits, Elsie bought a straightforward game, Ticket to Ride, and another, Skip-Bo, to engage them after the dinner dishes were washed. These games offered little opportunity to punish or steal from another player, and Elsie protected herself that way from the conspiracies of her mother and Kaida's style of playing. Kaida's son, Grant, the gamer in the family, also brought games he'd learned to play with friends at local coffeehouses. Laughter, and a view to new possibilities, filled the house.

Miles was turning hamburgers on the grill at the next family visit with Gail and Kaida, when Kaida saddled up to him and, giggling, told him about being ousted from her A.A. group. He stood over his grill for a time shifting his feet as she doubled over in laughter. He couldn't imagine such a thing, from his own years of experience in the accepting nature of twelve step groups. Finally, he spoke into the rising smoke.

"Those groups are about taking responsibility for being out of control. They're about making amends for your wrongs against others. If you are still blaming people, places, and things, then you aren't ready to be a part of the program."

Kaida turned, rolling her eyes. She rejoined the family.

Kaida kept digging at Elsie's character, as she'd done with all three sisters, but she was losing influence over her mother. Maybe it was Gail losing control over her daughter.

In any event, Kaida decided she wanted a newer model of car. She traded in her mother's car by forging Gail's signature and signing her own as co-owner. Then, she bought the car of her dreams. The only problem was, she had no insurance, other than being a rider on her mother's insurance, and since she had not added Gail's name to the ownership of the new car, she could not drive it off the lot.

She called Gail, fessed up, and asked her to phone the insurance agent and ask for coverage on the new car for a week—just until she could get her own insurance coverage. Then, the dealership handed over the keys and let Kaida drive the new car home.

Gail questioned her daughter's irregular vehicle trade-in of her car, but in the end, she agreed with Kaida's purchase because she assumed she would enjoy being the passenger.

Family members each received an Easter invitation by phone. Elsie failed to understand how broken her mother's relationship with Kaida had become. She invited them both. They were to have crepes on the back patio for Easter.

Kaida brought her new boyfriend, Brian, to the gathering. Now that his hair was cut and neatly groomed, Brian was beginning to satisfy Kaida's preference.

Melanie arrived. Grant brought Grandma Gail. Paige and her children came all the way from Montana for the holiday specifically to meet Brian.

Miles and Elsie had only met Brian once at Gail and Kaida's home for an introduction party, and Paige and Grant felt it important to get to know their potential stepfather.

As when Elsie welcomed her sister with a hug, Kaida's arms again remained at her sides. Elsie recoiled from her sister. How strange the slip of a sister had become!

The meal went well, but as soon as the crepes were demolished, Kaida excused herself. She and Brian had another Easter engagement.

Melanie and Grant agreed to play a board game anyway. Melanie immediately grabbed the bank assets, saying, "I'm banker." She took the color red.

As competitive as her family was, Elsie saw this as an opportunity to let Melanie control and shine. Melanie was a good banker.

Elsie also let her mother win where she could unless Grant was playing. To her, it was a time to rebuild by making good memories, enjoying laughter, keeping old family curses at bay.

A CAMERAMAN *DEPOSED* THE MODEL'S STANCE

When the annual Mother's Day planting-and-gardening-clean-up-party arrived, Kaida told her mother that her boyfriend had offered to help in the garden after he moved into her bedroom. "He's planning to share the house and expenses with you and me too, Mom." She explained, "He's living in a house with some friends; it's become so annoying for me and him to find privacy."

Gail gasped. In her daughter's recent absences from the home, she realized Kaida had turned her back on sexual purity again. The lack of privacy came with her choice. A much larger issue than the lack of fidelity to Gail, was the fact that her daughter, who now owned the title to the home, would willingly violate her sanctity. It carved a hollow in her soul.

"Kaida, you know my stance on living together. You are not going to bring your boyfriends here to my house to sleep with you."

"Sorry, Mom, but this is just as much my house as it is yours."

"It is not! You moved in with me! This is my house!"

Shutting her mouth for the time being, Kaida consulted with her attorney friend. The attorney explained that in the State of Colorado, Kaida's mother had absolute right to live in her own home as long as she survived. What they had drawn up was a quit claim deed reserving a life estate for Gail, not a simple gift deed. It was Kaida's home at risk for the time being, not Gail's.

Although Kaida's interest in the property would continue to accrue with the market, she would not inherit any rights to use the property until her mother died or vacated the premises. The news came as a blow.

Gail separately called the attorney. She wanted to get out of the quit claim and life estate plan, but she was devastated to learn that the deed she'd apparently signed was an absolute gift. The attorney calmed her by saying that she still retained the rights to who could come and go from her home until she passed away or no longer lived in it, but she couldn't sell it or gain back her investment if she moved into assisted living. She'd have to find a place that accepted someone without assets.

Gail, gutted of her wealth, was far from pacified. She began calling a number of attorneys to see if there was a way out of the quit claim deed, by citing fraud and elder abuse.

The fact that she was able to call and explain the situation put them on notice that she had been in full control of her faculties when she signed the deed. Besides, she still had full control of her home while she lived. Was that elder abuse?

When they asked what her career had been and she offered her business information as a real estate agent, they explained the court battle would be less than 50/50 because the judge would hold her to a higher standard of knowledge given her career. She should have understood the terms.

Gail cried, "But, I'm blind! She stole my car, too! She's taken everything from me!"

They each advised her one way or another, that unless she sued her daughter, she would not be able to void the deed. A gift was a gift was a gift.

Suddenly, far from getting along, the two argued about who owned the furniture, the appliances, and kitchen equipment. Which one had actually paid for the new flooring and windows? Digging up receipts and trails of trades, they went at each other. Gail scrawled in a diary every fact she could recall.

Kaida stopped recording purchases in the budget book and abused the credit cards by buying a closet full of jewels and jewelry, flaunting them to guests, without sharing the amount of deficit with her mother. Gail would discover it as soon as the credit card bill came through. With all of Gail's rage, Kaida appeased her by giving her a contract promising to pay half of the homeowner fees, taxes, and service repairs.

Then Kaida quickly moved in with her boyfriend and left her dog for her mother to feed and care for.

A month later, Kaida and her boyfriend were buying kitchen cabinets and furniture for a kitchen and study in a new house. They opened Gail's garage with the code and began storing it all until the sale went through.

"What are you doing?" Gail said.

"Isn't it clear by now? We've bought a house, and we're going to store our new cabinets and furniture here until closing. I'm moving on since you won't allow me to live here in my house any longer."

"I never said that. I never said that!"

"It's the same thing. When you love someone, you love everything about them. You accept them as they are. I need to have a love life, Mom. I'm not an old woman like you, and I don't believe the Bible says what you say it says. So the way I see this is that you're operating the way you've always operated, making me abide by your rules under your roof, or I'm out."

"Why are you doing this to me, Kaida? We've been best friends all these years. I gave you the house because you promised to take care of me."

Kaida laughed. "We've never been best friends. You've suffocated the life out of me. You disgust me, Mom, with all your religion and moralist rules. You may be able to live without sex, but it isn't natural, and I'm not going to live the rest of my life like you are, as an old maid. I won't allow you to starve, but I'm moving along."

"You have no savings or assets. How did you qualify for a house?"

Kaida shrugged and smiled. She'd used the quit claim deed.

Deeply shaken, Gail called Elsie to ask for help. "She's using my garage to store all their stuff, but she's saying terrible things to me! I need help!"

Elsie hastened across town to her mother's side and the furniture was still being offloaded for storage. She told Kaida and her boyfriend that they couldn't fill up their mother's garage with their things without her permission.

The boyfriend stopped working when he heard Kaida calling her mother vengeful names, and Elsie felt the whirlwind of words as scratches of tumbleweed against her skin. Did Brian take notice of the kind of gal he'd chosen to live with? When Kaida told her boyfriend, "Unload the goods. This is my house, too." A vision entered Elsie's mind of a parched lawn, once well-watered and cared for, now baking under the sun. A burnt field the color of rage. This is what her sister's life amounted to.

Kaida lunged into Elsie spewing flames. "You have absolutely no right in any of this. You're the biggest jerk I've ever known. What, are you going to start taking care of Mom now? Are you her big hero? We're storing these things for six weeks, and then we'll come get them, and then you'll never see me again."

The wave of bitterness borne by Elsie couldn't be absorbed. She shut the garage door and sat with her mother until the truck left. Her mother explained the whole situation to Elsie, who listened, stunned. The more questions she asked, the more she grieved and became sickened at the answers.

"So, you are saying Kaida owns your house and also stole your car, and you have nothing left to give any of the rest of us when you pass?"

"I'm sorry! I'm sorry!"

"Why, then, why did she call you all those names? Why is she doing this? She already has everything. That's what she meant about me having no say in the matter. I don't have any rights at all, do I?" Elsie's old feelings of being forgotten and taken for granted resurfaced with vengeful, soul-eating gnashers.

"She didn't steal from you. She stole from me. Now she can't wait for it. She wants to live with her boyfriend, and he didn't have a house, so I guess she figured out how to get one on his credit, and she's remodeling it with the cabinets in the garage."

"But, I was the good child, Mom. I was the one who didn't give you any problems! The one who tried to help you, the one whom you relied on to babysit, the one who came home that year to help you with Kaida and Melanie when you got that second divorce! I've honored you my whole life, and this is what I get for it?" She didn't realize how enraged this made her.

"Why, honey, you didn't come home that year just to help me. You came for your own reasons."

"Sorry, I need to leave now." Elsie got into her car and tried not to drive erratically home. She had a mind to leave her mother with the effects of the dragon she'd nourished so well. *"How ironic that Mom called me to save her from Kaida,"* she thought.

Elsie had to do some fast self-talking. *No child has any guarantee that they will receive an inheritance from their parents. Your mom is right. Kaida stole from her alone, not from her sisters.* Still, Elsie grieved the tryst between her mother and sister, and utter betrayal to the other girls to such a degree, that it had been a complete secret for how long—? It especially hurt that Mom could discount her motives to help the family over the years. When she was in trouble, she used Elsie to lean on, but when things were good, she only had heart for the cunningly strategic Kaida.

After Kaida's closing, Gail called Elsie in alarm to announce that Kaida was now stealing her furniture, her pots and pans, and dishes from the house. By the time Elsie arrived, Gail was wailing that Kaida had also stolen their mutual expense book, and a diary from the study in which her mother had been listing details of all that occurred, all she had lost at the hands of her daughter, the betrayer, the fraud.

Just to be sure, she said, "You didn't take my file with my wills in it did you, Elsie? You didn't take my diary or anything from my office, did you?"

"Mom, this is the second time you've asked me that. I hardly know where you keep anything. Why would I do that? No. Of course, not."

"Well, she's taken my important papers, so everything I've been documenting is gone."

Elsie immediately recognized that she had been promoted from being a non-entity to being the one her mother wanted, a shoulder to cry on, and the one she hoped would protect her.

HEAD AND SHOULDERS, KNEES, AND TOES ARE WHAT YOU FIND LEFT IN A SHOWER OF CANNIBALS

Knowing she had to stay mobile, Gail finally accepted the knee surgery she needed.

In recovery, both Melanie and Elsie spent days with Gail to get her through the confusion after anesthesia, through therapy for the frozen knee, through the pain, and the extenuating effects of her diabetes.

Meanwhile, Kaida took advantage of the unoccupied house. In her mother's safe she found, among a litany of legal documents, the jewels reserved for other family members. Rifling through her filing cabinet, she found the General Power of Attorney her mother had enacted for Kaida due to the recent development of heart issues. Behind that, was the Medical Durable Power of Attorney. Kaida grabbed it all and shut the filing cabinet drawer.

While Melanie and Elsie sat in their mother's hospital room, Kaida took the Power of Attorney to the nurses' station, showed her identification, and tried to adjust the medication being given to her mother. Then, she called Gail's doctor and reported her mother's faltering memory and patterns of anger reporting that she'd turned on Kaida and kicked her out of the house. Then, she cited her mother's inability to care for herself. She asked for a review of Gail's mental health.

Kaida again drove to her mother's home, combed through their gardens taking everything she wanted, and made another round inside the house, spending a little extra time on her mother's computer.

Once Gail moved back home and reckoned with her pilfered belongings, she changed the locks on her doors and began again to write in a little notebook the numerous ways her daughter Kaida had set her up to steal her car and her assets. Even her internet access and bank accounts were hacked by Kaida asserting that the "B" in Gail's middle name stood for her own middle name, Kaida Beryl.

When her Fidelity bank account statement arrived, Gail realized that bills and notifications were coming to her address with the name Gail Beryl Finch rather than Gail B. Finch. Her estranged daughter, knowing all her passwords and codes, had inserted her own name as Gail's middle name to control all her business accounts, or at least track what her mother was doing.

A bank agent alerted Bertie Gail of Kaida Beryl's request for a change of address. Another bank alerted her that her checking and savings accounts had also been breached. Gail immediately cried fraud.

"Don't worry," the banking representatives told her. "The fraud department is on it."

Gail believed that scripture taught taking another believer to court was prohibited. But, she was so distressed about depriving her other daughters of any portion of her inheritance that she wanted to consult with a Christian attorney. "Can you do anything legally to help me, Elsie?"

"No, Mom. It wouldn't be effective even if I tried. I'm also the wounded party, so my conflict of interest in trying to help you would look as suspect as what Kaida's done. I'm sorry."

"You can look up some Christian attorneys for me though."

Elsie looked up an association of Christian attorneys and sent it to Gail.

Before long, her emailed list of attorneys and phone numbers was answered with an out-of-office message saying, "Kaida B. Finch is out of the office until the twenty-first." Elsie's gut twisted to think that her sister was stalking their mother.

Elsie called her mother. "Kaida has some kind of hold on your internet services, Mom. I got an "out-of-office" response from her mediation business when I sent you the list of attorneys!" When Gail tried to fix the internet problem with her internet service and later with her computer itself, she saw Kaida's craftiness infiltrating her communications.

Gail bounced theories and ideas off Elsie. Yet, every time Elsie mentioned that Kaida had not only stolen everything from her mother, but also from her sisters, Gail ignored the suggestion. She kept saying that Kaida had treated her so awfully, so shamefully.

"You know she got into my safe and into my jewelry in my bathroom cabinet? She stole it all. She's probably pawned the pieces she didn't want."

"You mean even the Krugerrand gold necklace you were keeping for me?" Elsie asked.

"Yes! That and pieces I was keeping for Carlene's girls and Melanie and Nena."

"You're kidding."

"No, I'm not kidding. Go check my cabinets. Check the safe. It's open."

Elsie got up and opened her mother's bathroom cabinets as instructed. She went to the closet and found the safe gaping open.

"My preciousssss," she sneered at her sister's ghost. Gollum, the fictitious Hobbit of Gladden Fields, had embodied Kaida after all. The "One ring to rule them all" had disappeared with all the rest.

Rich called Gail in response to all the news he was getting from Carlene, Melanie, and Elsie. "Howdy, Gail," he began. "I'm calling to clear up a story I've been told about. Have you given your whole estate to our youngest in a quit claim deed?"

When there was silence on the other end of the call, he started again. "If you really have given everything to Kaida, I'm fixin' to even the score a bit by deleting Kaida from my will in order to try to balance the scales."

Gail admitted to her short-sightedness. She further explained, "Even though I've tried to undo the quit claim deed, it's a legal gift, and I can't undo it unless I take Kaida to court to prove duress or fraud, and I believe that scripture says we aren't to take other believers to court."

"Well, I don't think any hell fire in this life or the next really scares that gal. You sure she's afraid of Almighty God?"

"I guess it isn't up to me. We aren't to judge, but there was a time when she'd given her life to the Lord, and so I still pray for her every day. With all my mother's heart, I do hope so, Rich."

"Okay, then. I guess I got my answer. Thank you very much. Catch ya later, 'gator."

THAT AWKWARD MOMENT WHEN YOUR CHEMISTRY PROJECT DOESN'T GET A REACTION

To acknowledge her mother's post-surgical recovery, Kaida sent Gail a get-well card with a note saying, "You think your other daughters are going to care for you after what you've done to them? You make me laugh."

Gail's other daughters did pick up the pieces and did care for her, regardless.

When Elsie and her mother discussed her mental health test results, Gail surmised, "I think she was trying to get me committed to assisted living or to hospice or something so that she could take over the house!"

"Maybe she wanted to show that you were of sound mind when you signed the quit claim deed."

"Oh! Maybe. I hadn't thought of that."

Grant had been strangely silent and out of pocket since his grandmother's physical needs had presented themselves. Soon enough though, Grant let the family know that his mother seemed happy. She was stable and had finally married Brian.

"That's nice," quipped Gail.

"Well, she kinda had to. You left her homeless when you kicked her out of the house, Grandma. The only good thing about this is that Brian will kick her out as well if she drinks. He had an alcoholic mother, and he won't put up with that."

"Grant," started Gail, "I didn't make your mother homeless. I didn't kick her out of this house. I was counting on her living with me always but I couldn't take in her new lifestyle of men trailing like ants in and out of my house. This is my home. I need it to be secure."

"Hmm. I guess I'll never know which one to believe, will I?" he responded and turned away.

Gail then turned to Melanie and apologized for her previous behavior in handing her the eviction papers while blaming Kaida for being the mastermind and pushing the idea.

The flimsy apology made Melanie roll her eyes, but she finally moved into the basement suite.

Gail reckoned to Elsie, that she had given her despondent daughter a square opportunity to figure out her life in a safe and normal environment.

Melanie would not have said the environment was safe or normal, but she desperately needed to prove her worth. This opportunity would keep her on her toes.

The arrangement was nowhere near as happy or cohesive as it had been for Gail living with Kaida, but the pragmatic benefits for both herself and Melanie were unquestionable. On Gail's part, Melanie would drive her to appointments, take her shopping, bring in the groceries, keep the yard, do odd jobs. And Melanie was already familiar with Gail's house rules, so Gail didn't have to risk breaking in a newcomer so long as Melanie agreed to the conditions.

Besides doing odd jobs around the house and yard, dressed like a workman, Melanie nevertheless had a traditional female interest. Her quilting hobby had become her claim to fame in the family.

Many beautiful quilts graced the bedrooms and walls of each of her family members and their friends, her work associates, and others who needed baby quilts or wedding quilts.

Melanie often brought up one of her quilts from her basement suite to finish in her mom's living room as the two of them watched a show together. She would lace on the binding of the quilt and listen to the movie with one eye open.

Sewing the binding felt comforting to her, her needle working, the wonder of finishing a quilt, imagining the joy in the recipient's face. She kept searching her soul, but there was no real love left for her mother, only the occasional longing when she witnessed her mother's interaction with friends or the youth in the family.

Melanie kept pushing away a strange temptation to punish her mother, to poke her with the pins removed from the bindings. She used superficial, yes and no answers to Gail's questions instead. These rebuffs proved to be apt social weapons, piercing her mother's gregarious nature over, and over again.

Though the relationship was rocky, it was better than living alone for each of them.

When Melanie couldn't take Gail to her doctors' appointments, Elsie would. Elsie soon became her mother's confidant because they often went for a meal together to chat afterward.

Elsie also regularly invited Melanie, but often, Gail would call her to say, "Can we go out, just you and me?" And when Elsie arrived, she was awaiting her outside.

"I just needed to get out of the house. She shuts me down and corrects me for anything I say. Even if I offer to make enough food to share with her, she gets angry and tells me to quit obsessing about what she eats. I don't know. I tell her I love her and try to talk with her, but she tells me I've never loved her, and she seems to be taking it out on me however she can without hurting me physically."

Sometimes, Gail would burst into song to lighten the atmosphere. She'd sing old familiar hymns from the passenger seat like "In the Sweet By and By," "What a Friend We Have in Jesus," and "Jesus is the Sweetest Name I Know," and the Sunday school song, "Roll Away, Roll Away, Roll Away"...every burden of my heart, roll away. Tentatively, Elsie would smile and join in.

Witnessing Melanie's animosity toward their mom, even when playing table games, belittling her, grandstanding her mental mistakes or blind sightedness, indeed it seemed a precise form of punishment for Gail's past marginalization of Melanie throughout her life, and the years when she preferred Kaida.

"Don't get involved," Miles told her.

There was nothing Elsie could do but continue to pray. She kept trying to help the others give a little grace. Okay, a lot of grace.

One day, Kaida called her mother to say that she was willing to make a deal with Elsie if Elsie and Miles would sell their home and buy her out of Mom's quit claim deed.

Gail replied, "Why would she want to do that? She's perfectly happy living in her home."

"I've had a real estate property market assessment done, and she could buy me out for at least half of the value of your home."

"So, you are saying you want her and Miles to move into my home with me, sell their home, and buy back half of the value of the quit claim deed that you finagled and are using to steal her inheritance?"

"I wouldn't put it exactly like that, but yes."

"I can't ask her to do that."

"Just ask her. You don't know what she'll say. I need the money."

"To renovate your new house with Brian?"

"Yes."

"Of course, you do. Now I see."

"Just ask her."

Gail called Elsie and explained the offer. Both Miles and Elsie were amazed once again at the chutzpah of her sister. "She had an appraisal done on our home?"

They politely declined to enter into any kind of deal with Kaida.

"Why would she dare ask that, Mom? I just don't get why she would think I'd be interested."

"Honey, I don't know."

Miles said, "Your sister is treacherous. She can't be trusted. Stay as far away from her as possible."

"Well, I just won't call her back. She'll get the message," Gail said.

A NOTARIZED LAST TESTAMENT IS A *DEAD GIVEAWAY*

For full family occasions, Melanie would remove the audio book speakers in her ears. Laughter and conversation filled them instead.

Elsie and Miles's home became the destination for family meals. Always worth the effort, lots of good conversations, and games came from these times. Playing games was Elsie's way of building relationships in a measured way where warm memories could be built without speaking evil.

A letter came in the mail for Gail with a copy of her old will. Gail had trouble seeing the small, attached document, even with her magnifying glasses and the lens she now used to read. She asked Melanie to print it out. They brought the letter and the attachment over to Elsie's home since they were already scheduled for Sunday dinner and games there.

Elsie read the letter aloud to her mother. In it, both Gail and Elsie were bad-mouthed as well as Melanie, but Kaida's letter made excuses for Melanie.

Next, Elsie read the attachment which was sent to confirm Kaida's assertions. The attachment was Gail's Last Will and Testament, which Elsie had never seen, the one in which her mother had disowned her.

Melanie got up from the dining room table and moved into the kitchen where she could smile privately. Elsie noticed her sister's movements. She had undoubtedly already read this will.

She looked at her mother and hated her.

Throwing down the letter, she shouted, "After all I've done for you, Mom! You know, I used to name you as my beneficiary in my jobs on life insurance policies before I got married, and before you were so successful in your business. What did I ever do to you to make you write me out of your will?"

"Elsie, I trusted her. She was like a husband, a best friend, and a business partner all rolled into one. When two people are that close, you just don't question their judgment. Besides, you weren't even speaking to me."

"I wasn't speaking to you because you believed Kaida and wouldn't listen to me. I tried and tried. The last time I tried, you came to the restaurant with your sidekick. We couldn't even talk privately. Kaida answered every question I posed to you and called me a liar. You followed her out the door, telling me to have a nice life!"

The old rage at not being seen by her mother, at being misunderstood, at being taken for granted, even eventually cursed when her mother took sides with Kaida's story and gossiped in front of the grandchildren, all this came flooding back in waves of anguish.

"It was that time when my heart was giving me fits and you said you couldn't rearrange your schedule to take me to my next test."

"MOM! I took you to the first test, and we were having lunch when you asked me about the next test. I already had plans the next day, and you were living with Kaida, remember?"

"Well, I felt you didn't love me."

"Oh, God!" Elsie sobbed.

Gail sat across from her daughter, her head bowed in shame. Tears began to wet her face. "I'm so sorry, Elsie. Really, I am. You have no idea. I love you so much. How can you ever forgive me?"

Elsie hurried from the room, but in passing she noticed her mother's wretched condition. Slouched in her chair, she couldn't even lift herself on her own or drive herself home. Pity, fine misted pity, and fumes of compassion sprayed over the flames of Elsie's wrath, dampening it. They'd made so much progress. They'd forgiven so much.

She found herself in the kitchen looking aimlessly at cabinets for help. She nearly ordered her mom and sister out of the house. She wanted to evaporate. Her anxious movements wound her feet into small kitchen circles.

Yes, her mother had created a monster, but the monster had eaten up her mother along with the rest of them.

In a few moments, she came to understand that Kaida's letter and revelation changed nothing. Elsie had known about the quit claim deed for two years now, and she'd developed a relationship with her mother anyway because she wanted the relationship. Kaida's letter simply established the animosity she and their mom felt towards Elsie was an old feeling.

Determined to honor her mother, praying for help to do so, she stopped her anxious circles and took a deep breath. This was just one more window to her sister's wickedness. One more offense.

Elsie, weeping, went back into the living room and bent down to hug her mother. "It's okay. I forgive you. It changes nothing. You love me now, and I love you. That's all. Let's play a game, shall we?"

Yet, it stung that Melanie knew, and most probably all the grandchildren too.

After they had gone, she collapsed in her easy chair. Elsie remembered her grandmother in the great cloud of witnesses cheering her on. Trying for years to cut out the dead wood from her family tree while enjoying the parts still flourishing, had been counterintuitive. Maybe the whole tree was poisoned. She remembered the pre-wedding chat about tenderness and forgiving one another from great offenses. She picked up her computer and searched for the phrase "animosity in scripture."

Another passage, other than the Adam and Eve passage, appeared in Geneses 27. It was after Jacob and his mother managed to steal Esau's birthright, Esau being the elder, and Jacob the younger was favored by their mother. She read how Esau harbored animosity toward Jacob because of the way his father had blessed him and how Esau plotted to take revenge on Jacob by killing him.

Elsie checked her heart. She had no thought to kill her sister hidden there. So far, so good.

"Oh, Lord, I can't love this family enough, and I can't even pray for them. I am not impervious to spite. In the coming years, animosity may well take root in me. Already, I'm slogging through it. There's no end to it that I can foresee. Please don't leave me in this despair. Preserve me from acting with malicious retribution because I feel its roots creeping around my heart. Thank You for shining a light on what this darkness is. Take my hand. Lead me on."

COMPRESSION SOCKS ARE A REAL *HOSE* TO PUT ON

That week, Grant telephoned his grandma to let her know that Kaida was bedridden from a mysterious malady.

"What happened?"

"My mom said she woke up one morning last week and couldn't feel her feet or her ankles. She tried to walk to the bathroom, but she fell. She called Brian and he helped her, but for some reason, her feet are completely numb. She said it's like walking on stumps and she keeps falling."

"Both feet?"

"Both of them."

"What's she going to do? Surely, she's called her doctor."

"Of course. They're doing a lot of tests. She won't be able to ride bikes with Brian anymore. She can't go to work. For now, she's working from home via the computer, but her doctor said she'll have to learn to walk with a cane if they can't figure it out and it doesn't get any better."

RECORDING THE PAST WITH A DULL PENCIL IS *POINTLESS*

Carlene had a practice of calling Elsie to touch base.

She didn't disclose anything much about herself. Foreman was always fine. The girls were always doing okay. She continued to write pleadings and complaints for her enemies in the water district, in the county, in the taxing authorities, and they continued to be ignored or denied. Sometimes she talked with Elsie about her legal philosophy or premise, but Elsie had become apt at ducking.

"Dad has finished updating my website."

"That's nice. Which one?"

"Oh, the water rights one," or "Oh, the land patent one," or, "Oh, the health and wellness one."

Did Rich ever consider the value of what he was doing to enable the path of his eldest? While he ignored his own wife, working on behalf of his daughter's causes, Carlene depleted her husband's resources and ensnared his.

Carlene was tearing down her own future, saying, "God showed me this. God confirmed that for me."

Elsie had learned over the years that no one argued with Carlene and won.

"Are you coming up for Christmas this year? I'd like to start making plans."

"Well, we never know until the last minute. Foreman's boss needs him during the holidays."

"Okay, well, I'd appreciate it if you would let me know as soon as you know because I need to be able to plan."

"Oh, you don't have to do anything for us. We'll be doing our health routines and buying most of our meals at restaurants."

"Okay, but for Miles and me, we still need to be able to plan, so if you could just let us know…"

This kind of conversation had been going on for the last five years preceding Carlene and Foreman's visits to Colorado. Elsie longed for a day when she and Miles could maybe just get away to Mexico for Christmas or visit some quaint Christmas village in Europe. She was sure holiday romance awaited her somewhere other than her kitchen post during the holidays.

ROCK, PAPER, SCISSORS: THE FAVORITE GAME OF TOM, DICK, AND HARRY

In the last three trips Rich and Noeleen made to see Elsie and Miles, it became obvious that Rich had worked silent curses over his childhood sweetheart.

In one earlier visit, Noeleen confided to Elsie that she was taking anti-anxiety medication because "I kept feeling, unreasonably so, that Rich was planning to hurt me."

She had developed a healthy fear of the man. "Of course," she confessed, "the whole thing is unrealistic, so I accepted my doctor's prescription."

Since she was practically deaf, experiencing tenderness and pain by using her hearing aids for more than a couple of hours, he simply refused to speak with her. As she grew fully deaf, she lost her usefulness for playing the piano at church services or for accompanying his solos.

Her solo singing at home with the piano were like the wandering tones of the obscure theremin, driving him nuts.

Now, when traveling together, he put on his earphones and closed her out for hours at a time. When at home, he called her a puppy dog because she lay on the single bed in his computer room waiting for a free moment that he might make for her. She stopped cooking because the only time that he would talk to her was over a meal, and meals lasted longer if he had to take her out.

Still, Noeleen meant a lot to her friends and family. She would make cakes or meals for them in sickness or grief and would drop off bouquets or do chores for shut-ins, but her husband was not a party to this goodwill. When Rich was having heart problems, extreme exhaustion, dizzy spells, and bladder cancer, Noeleen made sure to get him the medical care he needed, even in the middle of the night.

Yet, on her final visit to Colorado, Noeleen showed her extreme exhaustion. She felt faint. Elsie watched Rich ignore his wife. Incensed, Elsie tried to mediate the appalling way her dad treated Noeleen. "Since Dad is busy working, would you like to get a massage? I know someone who is really good with Swedish massages," Elsie offered.

"Oh yes, I'd love that, but only if they have a velvet hand. I don't want any poking, pounding, or prodding."

"Of course." Elsie booked the massage for her stepmom mentioning, "That's one of Dad's best gifts. He gives such relaxing massages."

"I wouldn't know. He won't touch me." Noeleen revealed this in a moment of vulnerability.

"What?" Horrified, Elsie realized up to that moment, she had assumed her father had enjoyed a pretty normal, loving relationship with his exceptional wife. Now, the picture of why Noeleen was frightened, was clear. There was no tenderness for Noeleen left in Rich.

When Rich did manage to take Noeleen to the hospital, he forgot to grab her purse with her ID in it, and the list of medications. It took just that much longer to get treatment. She called Elsie from the hospital room to tell her that she was frightened. Elsie assured her that she was in good hands and reminded her they'd put stints in Miles's arteries and in her dad's. Surely, she would gain back her energy like the men had after a stint procedure. She prayed over the phone with Noeleen that she would feel the presence of the Lord's great love and care for her.

A massive heart attack had occurred, and it was irreparable. The staff used paddles three times that night to no avail.

When the doctors made the ending clear to Rich that night, they asked if they could remove life support from her. He refused.

Elsie called the next morning.

"Dad, you must take her off life support if she's gone."

"I suppose so, but I don't want to be the one they blame. I don't want to have to tell anyone that she's gone." He'd never been one to support the tears of another. Instead, he called Noeleen's family and best friends and told them to come quickly because she was barely holding on.

They each came to pay their respects, but when her best friend came in, the one whose career had been in nursing, she knew immediately what was going on. She advised the family to remove the fluids, bells, and other devices.

Noeleen had been gone for ten hours.

During this time, Rich stood in the hallway chatting with friends and Noeleen's daughter. A nurse asked if the two were married, and Rich laughed to be considered not the husband of the deceased, but the son-in-law. Repeating the story to others provided a pleasurable distraction from that night's tragedy.

Elsie and Melanie drove down to the funeral. When they were able to view the body, Noeleen did not look like herself due to the heavy fluid retention. "Dad, you are a despicable coward," Elsie muttered.

GETTING THAT PURPLE HEART, AFTER MARRIAGE, WAS SECOND TO NUN, SPEAKING POSTHUMOROUSLY

The number of tearful mourners filled the church to overflowing. Friends from a variety of churches, square dance groups, music ensembles, and retired co-workers attended. The sweet woman had planned many a family reunion. There was no one left who loved them in total like she did. It was only fitting that their last time together would be to honor the one who had kept them in good spirits.

Rich appropriately received visitors and flowers until the funeral. He shook hands with hundreds in the full church for his wife's send off. He was asked to sit in the front row, and Elsie assisted him down the aisle. Because there were so many children and their spouses and families, the children of Rich ended up sitting in the front row with him for Noeleen's funeral, making Elsie wonder about etiquette. It seemed unjust to be taking a seat belonging to one of Noeleen's children.

When the service began, Rich's eyes drooped. When his breathing grew heavy, Elsie nudged him hissing, "Dad!"

Sitting next to her sleeping father during his wife's funeral was the transitional moment that moved Elsie, by jet engines, down the track from her father. No more making excuses for him and no more kid gloves.

Carlene, quite heavy-set at this stage in life, wanted to sit in the folding seats beside the burial plot as well, but there were only enough seats for Rich and Noeleen's children and their spouses. Elsie stood in front of her sister and instructed her on the number of chairs and the right of Noeleen's children.

"But, I can't stand for the whole burial!" Carlene cried.

Foreman managed to get his wife to stand. She fretted and groaned and finally made her way back into a chair when a male family member took pity on her.

When the children gathered at Rich and Noeleen's home to write thank you notes and try to comfort themselves, Rich disappeared to his study and got to work on his computer.

All told, Rich and Noeleen had been married two years more than Rich and Gail, yet the children had never melded into a blended family; it was likely that they would not recognize each other on the street outside of the context of their parents' home.

When it was time to leave, Rich filled their car with gifts and knickknacks that they had given to Noeleen over her lifetime. He had no use for them.

The husband, free to live again and still physically fit for work, went to see other gal pals, making himself indispensable. When Elsie called to check on the wellbeing of her father, he described how busy he'd been with the widow who needed things moved into her forever home. Then she required the occasional dinner out. Another widow, Rich confessed, was after him even though he knew he could *never* measure up to her deceased husband.

He said, "That man worked at the headquarters of the Conservative Baptist Denomination. If she were to marry me, she'd discover what a loser I am compared to him. No, that would be a huge mistake! I'm going down to see her now only because she needs a handyman."

Then, there was the woman whose husband made her promise to publish his theological dissertation after he passed. "I'll help her. I can edit that and get it published through Amazon for her, but I'm never going to move to South Carolina." Rich laughed.

Elsie listened patiently, agitated.

Rich's cache of sentimental music, however, became the bane of his existence, sometimes causing a watershed of tears often when he was driving here or there, listening to the love songs that reminded him of his childhood infatuation and his middle-aged married life with Noeleen, and his failed attempts at love with the infectious Gail.

COMFORT AND CARE TO COVER A DARKNESS

One pantry door Rich made from a warped plywood panel turned out six inches wider than the counterpart and it wouldn't lay flat. It wouldn't even latch. "You win some, you lose some." He shrugged telling Elsie and Miles. "I must be feeling my age." He packed his bags.

Abruptly leaving Elsie's home, Rich drove straight to St. Charles, Louisiana via New Mexico, Texas, and Missouri. Three days later, Carlene called and left a steaming message with her sister.

"You used Daddy so badly that we had to take him to the E.R. when he arrived. He couldn't even climb out of the van by himself! You tried to work him to the bone, so he ran away. You should be ashamed of yourself. I saw the pictures of your new pantry. Why can't you just be grateful?"

Elsie listened to her sister's accusation and deleted the message. She didn't return the call. Her father had asked for a project, and she had given him one, but per usual, he hadn't listened to what she wanted.

When his own way turned up a mistake, his ego deflated, and he evaporated.

Her father's work was becoming as sloppy as his attitudes about his children, his wives, the nation, and his pastors. When she invited him to eat, he sat and shoveled salads into his mouth but wouldn't touch the bread. Nor would he respond when she informed him about Kaida and Melanie's latest. He would not engage in any conversation other than to pronounce judgments over the world and say, "My mind is slipping."

She had not enjoyed his surprise visits for some time. Where had her father's gallant armor fallen off? She nevertheless kept him fed and watered attaching, please and thank you when appropriate. It was only when he rolled off her driveway that she fell apart.

"I'll bet being in that empty house without Noeleen is like living with the ghost of Christmas past. He's going a bit crazy!"

Elsie's husband listened to her embroiled emotions until he interrupted.

"Your five minutes are up, dear. It's my turn to share."

Elsie arched her back, stunned, then collapsed in laughter. Her husband's good humor always managed to distract her.

LONE TREE, 2018

PETER PAN ALWAYS FLIES BECAUSE HE *NEVERLANDS*

Rich tried on two further occasions to stay at Elsie and Miles' home in the basement bedroom he had built for just this handy reason, his trips to Colorado.

On the first of these visits, Elsie begged her father to call Kaida and Melanie and make plans with them. He refused. She gave him a book to read called, *The Story of With* by Allen Arnold. It was a compassionate but compelling allegory about a father gone astray from his real world and needy child. Rich stayed up and read it weeping throughout the night, but it did not change his behavior.

"Kaida told me she wants to dance on my grave! I have no interest in calling that girl."

"But Melanie, Dad. She doesn't even know you're here."

"Well, you call her and tell her. I don't use the phone to call anyone, you know that."

"You used to call on our birthdays, Dad. She's your daughter, too."

"It was Noeleen who called you girls. I just stood by while y'all talked."

That much was clear.

Elsie called Melanie to tell her about her father being in Colorado. Melanie brought over meals for the rest of the week. "I just want to help."

"My dear, our refrigerator is already full."

"I just wanted to help out. I can take it home if you can't find a place to store it."

Melanie had begun to do this when Carlene and Foreman came to visit. She also gave up her timeshare week for Elsie and Miles a couple of times. Melanie's gifts of her beautiful quilts were a prized item causing the siblings to display fits of jealousy over what gorgeous fabric art piece was given to another. *"Melanie's gifts are always welcomed,"* thought Elsie, but they came accompanied by the disease of buying her way into others' hearts. Elsie had tried to talk with her sister about what motivated these gratuitous displays, but the extravagant gifts continued.

"You know you don't have to pay your own way for a visit with family. I've already bought meals…"

"I just wanted to help out."

Elsie kept having the uneasy feeling that her sister was bolstering her worth, her place in the family, by her habit of over-gifting. She couldn't pinpoint what was going on, but she shrugged and thanked Melanie. Then she tried to find storage for the bags of goods.

Twice, Elsie had an older friend visiting at the house when her father came to the table.

"My! Your father is a handsome man!" said one.

"Does he intend to remain single?" said the other, "Because, he's apparently a helpful man and good looking."

To both of her friends, she said with a pounding heart, "You stay as far away from him as possible. There is a lot behind his looks that I don't want to have to say to you."

The "Me Too" campaign, being all over the news, became the topic of a family dinner conversation. Were both girls ever surprised to hear their father decry the accusations against Bill Cosby. Rich put down his fork and looked straight ahead through the dining room window, cleared his throat, and said, "He is a fine, upstanding man, an American family actor who has been widely respected his entire life. . . who is having his entire career and future ruined by these girls' false accusations."

When he didn't get up and leave the table, yet blew his nose and continued his meal, Elsie looked at Melanie and said, "How do you know, Dad?" before she could stop herself. "Do you personally know the man? Let's let the courts decide what happened."

Melanie looked at her meal in silence. They dropped the subject.

Then, Melanie asked her dad to help her assess damages and costs to repair Gail's fence. He agreed.

She'd been living with her mom, driving her to hair appointments, pedicures, doctor's appointments, and she shared living expenses ever since Kaida had abandoned her. Melanie's help was appreciated, but her silent treatment, rolling eyes, and mockery of her mother's opinions, was not.

Gail couldn't see very well anymore, so it was only when there were guests in their company that Melanie's disease with her mother became noticeable.

A parasite lives on a larger, more complex organism and survives by living on, or by invading into, cells of the host. Melanie had two parasite mates eating at her: first, her mother's lack of nurture and second, her father's lack of nurture. No matter how she tried to shake off these burdens, they continued to eat away at her and drag her down. It is the most natural thing in the world for a child to respond to a parent's open hand, but when the hand closes against a child's request, or when the hand holds fruit from a poisonous tree, how can a child survive?

Yes, Gail could hear Melanie's frustrated tone, feel her continued attempts to please and fail oiling her pores. But Gail honestly felt they were adults now. For goodness' sake, let bygones be bygones!

It was a simple business arrangement to help them move forward, and she wasn't about to face her own demons or engage in family counseling. Certainly, she wasn't going to rehash history or tell her truth to someone who barked at her for simply saying, "Good morning," as Melanie was prone to do.

Why cut down the poisonous tree at this stage? Why couldn't they just reroute and avoid it?

"Perhaps it was her attempts to right a wrong," thought Elsie, reflecting back to when their mother's invitation was extended to her sister, but more likely it was her mother's sense of good business prompting the offer. It was a stable and clean place to live with an offer of companionship while watching a movie or eating a meal together in exchange for sharing living expenses.

A few years into Melanie's living arrangement with her mother, Kaida came for a visit, and Gail let her in the door.

"I'd like to make peace," she began, looking around at all the familiar furniture and décor.

"How is that?"

Gail's daughter handed her a large bottle of her favorite perfume saying, "Well, I don't know, but I want to have my family back. I'm cut off from my kids and my grandkids and you. Nobody's talking to me, so I want to make peace."

Gail took the bottle, opened the stopper, and wondered that it was unsealed, but it was worth saving until she could hear out her daughter's proposal.

"You mean, you want to give me back my house?"

"No."

"Are you going to return my jewelry?"

"No."

"What are you talking about, then, dear?" She set the perfume on the window ledge.

"I've been thinking that I could buy out the remainder of the value of this house from you. Brian and I could move back in and you would have a bundle of money."

"Where would I live?"

"In a retirement facility, I guess."

"You've got to be kidding, Kaida! This is my home. I don't need your money to keep living comfortably here. According to our contract, you are supposed to be paying the house taxes and insurance, and apparently you can't even afford to do that."

"You're the one living here. Why should I?"

"What a piece of work you are, Kaida." Gail shook her head. "You offer to buy peace with a deal that only suits you!"

"My daughter is withholding my grandchildren from me!"

"How is this going to solve that?"

"That's for me to worry about."

"With another one of your lies?!"

Melanie heard her mother's raised voice in the living room and quickly went to check on her. Seeing her younger sister sitting stiffly on the easy chair, a heron on a stick, she poked her.

"Are you here to apologize?"

"No."

"Then, I think you should leave."

The bird flapped her wings and stood from her perch. She was expertly herded to the front door and ushered outside. "Goodbye."

Gail sighed out her relief, but also despair. How long did she have? Which precarious position would topple first? She flipped her iPad screen to her audio Bible with the nice man's voice to distract her. The reading helped to refocus her mind on a higher perspective. She was losing hope for her daughter.

The next day, after the mail came, Gail discovered that her savings accounts were again mounting to new heights. Her stock investments had also been doing very well. She leaned back in her computer chair and surveyed the discolored ceiling of her study. Yes, the roof was leaking, but it hadn't yet destroyed the ceiling. Even if it did, she would not replace it with her own money. Kaida could inherit the leaky roof with her house.

Her plan to live more creatively, and frugally, showed off in these financial advancements. She decided to stay put in her own home until her final breath. Even if it fell down around her.

Although the adjustment was difficult, she took a cue from Miles and Elsie's hospitality house and rented out a second room in her own home.

Neither Melanie nor Elsie enjoyed bargain hunting as she did. Thus, Gail had stopped shopping as much.

There had been tax refunds, and she also saved stimulus package refunds.

She clicked her tongue with satisfaction. Taking out a second mortgage was a successful ploy so far, even if she had to spend some of it for upcoming medical expenses.

A WOLF WHO KNOWS HE'S A WOLF IS *AWARE* WOLF

Melanie planned a quilting vacation along the historic Route 66 by cajoling her father to break free. "You don't have to come into the shops, unless you want to. I just want to take a trip with you. You can show me the historic sites. Deal?"

Melanie managed to convince Rich to drop his computer enterprises and volunteer building work to accompany her on vacation. Then Melanie managed to take him to every quilting store on the route, per her goal.

He slept in the car as she browsed and bought what caught her eye. She had the time of her life.

Rich agreed to help Melanie rebuild her mother's fence. There were two sections of Gail's fencing that had toppled onto the garden, and the neighbors refused to fix their fence. Rich flew up to Denver and he and Melanie spent an entire day getting new posts, fence planks, and screws. They fixed the fence and the gate to boot.

After Gail fed and thanked Rich and Melanie, she moved to the living room where she felt most comfortable in her chair and put her feet up on the ottoman. She'd wash the dishes later.

Rich followed her and sat on the ottoman, piling her feet onto his lap. Gail, so vulnerable, and not knowing what to say or how to get him out of her house was taken aback when, with a grin, he began to massage her aching feet.

The experience turned against him, however, when he said, "Gail, you have an extra bedroom here. Wouldn't you like me to come help out around here when I come to Denver? I could just sleep there."

Gail laughed from nerves and said, "No way! Rich, are you joking? How many years have we been divorced?"

"Well, my granny and my dad's mom hated each other for years, but in their old age, they learned to care for one another, and that's what they did until my granny passed away."

"That's nice, Rich, but it won't work here. I need all my space for my grandchildren and their families when they come. You know Melanie is staying in the basement apartment, so it really wouldn't be possible."

Melanie, who was cleaning up in the kitchen and eavesdropping, said, "I could sleep on the couch, Mom!" The drama between her parents intrigued Melanie. Perhaps, an unrealized longing for her parents to peacefully cohabitate, piqued her interest. Could her dad pull it off?

"I don't think so," came the reply.

Both Rich and Melanie were disappointed to hear the verdict. They had been talking throughout the workday. Rich stopped his foot massage and went to say his goodbyes to Melanie.

When Gail called Elsie after Rich left the house, Elsie was surprised and disgusted. "Did you like the foot massage at least?" she teased her mom.

"Augh! I was trapped! You should have seen him grinning at me like a ghoul. It frightened me that he presumed I'd appreciate him touching me that way. My back is so bad that I didn't have the strength to pull away! And, it was like he had forgotten all the things he did to me. But, I hadn't forgotten."

"Well, Mom, I'm glad you stood up for yourself. Though Dad does give good massages."

"I wouldn't know. He never gave me one. How do you know?"

Elsie felt incredibly awkward. "He used to give me really good shoulder massages, Mom. He never gave you a shoulder massage?" She didn't dare mention the one time…

"No. Never."

"That's so strange. Noeleen said the same thing the last time they were up here. She was aching for a velvet glove massage, and I told her that Dad could help with that, but she said he'd never touched her like that. I was surprised."

"To be honest, I'm surprised he gave you massages."

"Well, yes. I am now, too. I'm sorry, Mom."

"It isn't your fault."

When Rich came back to sleep at Miles and Elsie's home, he stood in the kitchen for quite some time, arms crossed, trying to reason it out with Elsie.

"She'd never want to leave her fancy house and live in mine."

"Dad, Mom doesn't love you. That ship has sailed."

"If she wasn't so dadgum materialistic, I could'a lived with that woman forever. She was a good mother to you kids."

"Yes, she was, Dad, but when you left, God became her husband, and He spoiled her rotten. Just like a groom who loves his bride. That's why her house is so nice. It has very little to do with being materialistic, or maybe God doesn't hold things against her. She's a very generous person, you know, and you can't outgive God. Really, Dad, she's satisfied with her life as it turned out. Her church is only a few blocks away. She still has a lot of friends and family here, and her doctors. Why would she want to give all that up to move to Oklahoma, where she's never lived before? You aren't thinking straight Dad, I have to tell ya."

"Well, my granny and my dad's mom lived on the same block, and they figured out how to let bygones be bygones."

"Dad, she's eighty-four-years-old. She can hardly see, and she uses a walker. It can't be that you are attracted to her, and she's certainly not attracted to you. She wouldn't be able to care for you. You'd have to take care of her. Why are you talking like this?"

He shrugged in his flippant way. "Huh. I really don't know, but I guess you must be right." Then, he walked out of the kitchen, down to the basement bedroom, and turned on the heater.

When Elsie came into the living room where her husband sat with the television on mute, he turned his head toward her with saucer eyes and an "O" of a mouth.

"So, you heard."

"What's he thinking?!"

"I have no idea."

After she settled in next to Miles, it occurred to Elsie that her dad was frightened of living alone. "He probably wants someone there when he dies. Otherwise, he may die alone with no one to check on him. The things you do to others do come back to you."

THE COWBOY WAS *DERANGED*

Rich decided to visit Colorado again. He didn't bother to call Elsie until he was an hour away.

"I would have waited to serve dinner if I knew you were coming, Dad."

"Well, I'll pick up something before I roll in."

"No, we had soup. I'll heat it up for you when you get here."

Arriving, Rich opened the front door quietly, and put his bags in the entryway. Elsie heard him and turned on the stove top for the soup to reheat.

Then, there was nothing. Finally, a bit of rustling, clinking, and slurping.

"Is that you sitting at the table in the dark, Dad?"

"Yeppers. Soup's good!"

She went in to say hello personally but what met her was a hobo of a man with a scruffy beard and long hair. She decided not to comment on his unkempt appearance.

"Dad, I just turned on the stove. It isn't even hot yet."

"It's okay as is."

"We're sitting right here. When were you going to announce yourself?"

"I didn't want to bother you."

His white chin-pincushion moved in waves of cactus hairs pricking the air as he chewed. She'd never seen her father unshaven before. How often had he said one of his lifelong fantasies was to be a hobo? Maybe he was trying out his hobo side. Where would he find a train to hop? Did he have a plan? Her dad's long hair looked crazy. Was he trying to impress her outdoorsy husband?

As a youngster, she could have drawn her dad's "nerd" image by heart. Always in a white shirt and pencil holder with his record keeping pocket diary.

Her sheepish dad now looked like a scraggly werewolf.

Elsie stewed on the situation all night, wondering how she could honor her father and still make him behave. She realized if her dad kept a key to their home, he would start abusing the privilege, and she had begun to fear and despise him.

"If someone takes your shirt, give them your coat also. If someone asks for a mile, give them two."

The last thing she wanted was for her father to dig into her private computer without her knowledge like he'd done several times in past visits. She imagined he'd become the third wheel, the guest to every meal no matter who they invited over. He'd been giving her and Miles the silent treatment during meals the last few visits, making her a prisoner at her own table while she fed and watched him munching away. This not talking and staring at the wall thing was not going to happen whenever he was feeling uncomfortable at home and on the hunt for change. She would not become another of the female casualties he left drowning in the wake of Richard Finch.

"I'm taking the key back tomorrow, honey," she told Miles turning towards him in bed.

"Don't be rude." His finger touched her lips.

"I'm not being rude. Did you see how he looked? There is something wrong with that man. He's not asking, he's assuming, so he's the one being rude. And he's just using me like the other women he's used in his life. I think he thinks I owe him since we used to be so close, and because he built that bedroom downstairs."

"Well, he did build the bedroom, and we do kind'a owe him."

"No. We don't." She paused. "It was a gift. Okay, why don't I go on vacation, and you can host him for a while."

Miles snorted.

"See? He shows no respect for anyone's boundaries. I know his games. I'm not going to have the rest of my life sideswiped by him. My life is not at his disposal."

The next morning, Elsie told her scruffy haired father, "Dad, I don't feel right about you coming and going at will from my home without even asking. We have our own plans, too. It made me feel weird to have you sneak in and not announce yourself last night, then you took what you wanted in my kitchen. In the future, I'd like to keep my housekey, and I'd like you to call me if you want to come visit so we can make plans together."

He hung his head in mock shame. Then he felt around in his pocket, took the housekey off his key ring, and placed it on the table. "Talk at ya later, 'gator!" He stood and went to pack his bags. He left the house without a word.

LEMONY YOGURT WAS TOO CULTURED FOR THE RODEO

Rich wrote two more letters to Gail. In one, he recognized her as a terrific mom.

"I didn't know what I was leaving behind after you broke your tailbone and when we divorced, and I regret everything that's happened to the family since. I take full responsibility for it. I've tried to make up for it, but no one is forgiving me. What can I do?"

He went on to write his own recollection of things that happened as though to excuse himself in her eyes.

She immediately called Elsie. "Can I read this letter to you? I don't know what to think about his account on the events of our lives. His letter is a sweeping work of fiction! He also thinks we should share a house together."

"No Mom. I don't want to hear any more of his propositions, blame games, and excuses. Why do you think he is writing to you? He's still calling your broken back a tailbone injury. He wants you to allow him to come stay with you. If I were you, I'd just file that letter in the trash bin, and don't write back. It would just be an exchange of he said, she said. The last thing you want is to rehearse a lifetime of bitterness with him. How would that help your situation or his?"

"You're right. I'll ignore it. It's just so disturbing."

Elsie couldn't stand the thought of her parents' soap opera continuing, or that she would be forced to parse out the implications of one more scene. She was sixty years old, for goodness' sake. They were in their eighties! Why did this keep circling back?

"The chips have already fallen. Let them lie."

The second letter Rich wrote was much the same. He didn't offer to correct Carlene's persuasion against Gail. He didn't ask her to correct Kaida's persuasion against him. He only said he had regrets and he wanted to apologize. Why couldn't she forgive him?

In his program, Miles had talked about the need everyone has to work a fourth step, take a fearless moral inventory. Now, it passed through Elsie's mind that when a person takes the time to list their sins and omissions against self, others, and God, they give themselves an opportunity to make amends, to give others another opportunity to forgive them, and to live apart from an awful burden, to live with freedom and goodwill.

Taking the inventory requires no excuses. No blame. A person can either make an honest apology about the suffering they've caused or make amends to someone for their behavior. Forgiveness is such a precious gift, or an honest wage for doing the work. It can be either. Some people cannot offer it unconditionally. There has to be a remembering and a reckoning for the damage done, and a true apology. In a human world, some things should not be glossed over.

A man who goes his entire life without defending his wife, or taking any blame, or setting the record straight, a man who enjoys the drama of competition, tallying which child will love which parent most without considering the lifetime harm he causes, is a selfish man who ruins his own children.

A woman who changes the details of what happened, who won't remember accurately, who refuses to apologize or adjust to the truth and makes no effort to reverse her weapons' wounds, continues to tear down her own house.

Over the phone, Gail said, "I have forgiven him. I just don't want to have him in my house."

Elsie said, "Yes, now you get it. Forgiveness is one thing, but reconciliation is quite another. Parents should confess their sins to each other and to their children somewhere along the line, beyond confessing to a priest or a friend. It's the kids who need to know the truth, not God; He already knows.

"There are so many reasons why two people cannot go back to the beginning or start over, Mom," Elsie said, "Dad has made a lifetime of bad choices. He hasn't changed. To allow an abuser and a taker to come into your home and stay while you are blind and walking with a walker, that's just stupidity."

"I don't think he'd try to hurt me, do you?"

Elsie didn't even want to think about that. Noeleen was afraid of him. She had become afraid of him. Sometimes the fear did seem irrational. Elsie herself felt the fear of living with her father. She half expected the DNA police to come ringing her doorbell asking questions of her father's whereabouts from one year to the next, but nothing like that had ever happened.

There was nothing to substantiate the roiling anger that lived inside of Dad's gut. There was no way to explain his form of manipulation and silent punishments after he got what he wanted.

Instead, she said, "I don't know if he thinks you are soft in the head or soft in the heart, but you just keep your boundaries up, Mom. They are healthy boundaries. Melanie and I can help you with whatever you need."

"He does have that Eeyore side that drives me crazy. He's either got to be someone's hero, or he's the silent, misunderstood malingerer with a cloud over him."

"Oh, so you do remember. It's gotten much worse than that. There really is a smoldering anger inside him. He feels betrayed by everyone in life, including God. You won't be able to convince him that anything is his own fault, and you won't be able to save him. If he hasn't encountered redemption by now, I'd say it isn't coming. It's far bigger than you. So, just don't answer him."

When Gail didn't respond to his letters, Rich picked up the phone and called her. They talked over their wills, and he said he'd taken Kaida out of his to even the score, but everything else had remained the same. She told him that she had forgiven him, but that she was in no condition to play hostess at her age and his.

Cycling through both Gail and Elsie's hearts were the sentimental birthday and holiday greeting cards featuring eye-catching vistas, even anniversary cards featured with country paths leading into the unknown horizon, words reciting any number of landmark memories in a typical life. These routinely came from Rich.

He could pick out cards to compliment and flatter like no other. Sometimes Elsie imagined how long her father stood in the card section looking for the perfect words someone else had written. He never used his own pen to add to the store-bought cards. The signature space was always filled with, "Dad," "Love, Dad," or "Rich". Sometimes there was a stock Christmas letter from him and Noeleen.

Over the years, Gail had learned to overcome the shock she received when these odd missives appeared, and she tossed the cards into the bin as one swats at a fly.

Elsie had saved many of her dad's cards. Now, looking through her stash, she saw what they omitted. "Mom, do you realize the beautiful sentiments to me and Miles always came with a check for $50 but, not one of the cards included a personal note, a letter, a story, a prayer, or a scripture?"

Gail said, "I don't think your father had it in him to actually love someone. He was a very sentimental man, and he liked to play the hero, but he just didn't know how to love. Maybe it was his childhood. People are often scarred from poor childhoods."

"Mom, many people who have come from bad childhoods make a new life for themselves and learn to love others. There are many others who have all the benefits of a good family, and some of them just become mean and foul. Who knows why people make the choices they make?"

Elsie compared the many Fathers' Day and birthday cards she'd agonized over, searching her heart for something honorable to say to the stickman existing so far away. A man who busied himself with his computer in isolation from his wives, past and present, as well as his offspring. Why must she find something gratuitous to write her father every year, hiding her abiding grief and disappointment? Why not simply sign her name to someone else's classic words as he did? With the realization that the cards were nothing more than pretty compliments, Elsie said, "Thank you, Dad."

She then dumped her collection of sentiments where her mother had habitually tossed hers. She would not allow them to prick her with rolling surprises in the future.

THE CRUSHED GRAPE ESCAPED THE FLASK WITH A SMALL *WINE*

The day Elsie and Miles enjoyed a lunch with her father's brother and his wife, Luster told a story about Rich that chilled them all to the bone.

"Your dad called me from basic training one day. He was in the infirmary."

"Basic training, like way back when he was in the Air Force in Arizona?"

"Yep, way back then, but I'll never forget it. He was in the infirmary because he had been attacked in the shower. All the guys had brushes and brooms and they had scrubbed his body raw."

Elsie couldn't speak.

Finally, she looked up and said, "Why would they do that? That is incredibly horrible." Her mind filled with images of her father's suffering, curling up and kicking out, with harsh brushing being run over his body.

He was quiet. "I know. That's exactly how I felt."

"But why? Had he played one of his practical jokes on someone?"

"I never found out why. He wouldn't tell me."

Elsie abruptly left the table. She had to go to the garden to hide her grief and think. Her father had run away from his poverty and father and motherlessness every day of his life. He was so busy trying to be free that he lived a life without trust in God or a willingness to stick with someone who had something fearful stacked against them. He sabotaged love with those who helped him and loved him because the risk of them dragging him down again was too great a fear. Maybe he had experienced an emotional or psychological breakdown.

What did all his sentimental tears mean, then? Music, movies, and good books still brought him to his knees. Was there such a thing as tears that don't lead to turn arounds? Could he not see that God had always sustained him and given him mercy and hope throughout his life? Why? Why? Why?

GROAN UNDER GOD'S HAND OR *GROAN* UP

Elsie and Miles had moved into his parents' home to care for them in their old age. Their care over these seven years, being successful, had kept them living in their home into old age. This situation, however, limited what Elsie and Miles could do to help Melanie and Gail.

Since Gail's diet required no salt, the learning curve became difficult for both girls. Ricky sent his grandma a no salt cookbook, and they tried chicken on the grill, using thighs for flavor, and a sweet rhubarb sauce. They tried frying purple cabbage and onions in sesame oil, garnished with peanuts. They bought fresh foods with flavor bursts such as radishes, salmon and bok choy. They used herbs like anise and basil and rosemary.

Nearing the end of the fifth year of Melanie's living arrangement with Gail, Gail complained to Elsie that Melanie had stopped using their budget and record book to note her purchases and record rents paid to her mother. She also started taking several extended vacations away from home, leaving Elsie to drive across town, buy groceries for their mom, massage her legs and back, get her set up for the evening, and during daytime hours, take her to doctor's appointments and blood draws.

For Elsie, this commitment was becoming costly. The fifth time that year, when Melanie informed her mother that she was planning another extended trip the next week, Gail responded, "Melanie, you are gone more than you're home this year!"

Melanie didn't want to explain her thinking or plans. She just needed her own choices unquestioned; she craved freedom.

When Gail told Elsie, Elsie confronted Melanie. "What happens if Mom falls? What happens if she needs eggs or milk, or hot packs for her leg cramps? Why are you leaving so often?"

· Melanie retorted, "It's none of your business what I'm doing with my time or travels. Mom is not without options."

Gail explained, "Elsie, I'm afraid I'll fall one night, and no one will be here to help me. Melanie either forgets or avoids asking me about my needs. If I call her phone from another room, I have to leave a message for help, but she will likely not respond until after I've gone to sleep."

Gail endured excruciating leg cramps from her long-term back issues. Her leg, over the last few years, had become twisted and deformed, but even if Melanie was in the same room with her, she would ignore her mother's tears and groans.

Elsie understood, from conversations with her mother, that her sister worked long hours now, shut away in her home office, similar to Rich's treatment of Noeleen. Melanie had good cause. Elsie gave her that much. It was just so painful to watch.

The problem was twofold.

Melanie's wheels dug through heavily rutted feelings that her mom was merely using her. She simply could not reconcile having to pay rent while being her mother's servant. Yes, the rent was basically a shared expenses agreement, but paying it became the rocky, worn trail of Gail's inequitable treatment amongst her sisters convincing Melanie that her mother had never loved her.

Their mother-daughter relationship was in fatigue and now, the sisters also stood at odds with each other.

Gail additionally complained that she was tired of Melanie buying huge quantities of canned food, storing it at the house, and making meals to be given away to people Melanie wanted to care for. Often, she failed to leave any portion of the meal for her mother. "If you want to do that, Melanie, it's fine, but the costs should be coming out of your own money, not mine. I'm on a fixed income."

Elsie knew it must be emotionally troublesome for her sister but punishing their mother with sullen treatments and last-minute escapes was not an honorable way to live. Although Elsie struggled with a similar feeling toward their mom's lack of blessing or nurturing, while she instead, used them, and Elsie felt compassion for her sister, it was becoming harder to believe in a good outcome under the circumstances.

Elsie invited Melanie along with the family to Miles's birthday celebration, but there was no response. On the day before the party, Elsie asked Melanie to confirm.

"*I'll come, and I'll bring mother.*" Melanie texted back.

"*Well, we were planning to come pick you two up.*" Elsie texted.

"*Okay. What time.*"

"*4:30*"

"*I'll have her ready.*"

Elsie gritted her teeth. Her mother was perfectly capable of dressing herself. She only kept a few garments in her closet these days, but they were her typical elegant style or casual and tailored pant suit combinations.

When they picked the two up, there were terse yes—no communications. Melanie, wearing lanky hair and a strangely angled shirt over dirty jeans covered by a jean jacket sat in the back seat with Elsie. Thankfully, her usual pocket device and ear buds did not further accessorize her getup.

Gail dressed to her usual nines. Miles, spruced up with his wife, played host for the family on his big day.

After dessert and the bill paid, Melanie walked out with Miles to get the car. Grant, Gail, and Elsie waited in the restaurant foyer.

"Hey, what's going on with Melanie?" Grant asked.

Gail spoke up, "I've asked her to pay two hundred dollars more per month because I'm going to have to hire extra help if she's going to keep traveling. She's moving out because of it."

"Oh!"

"What, Mom?" Elsie was shaken.

"Yes, she says she's packing up this week and moving out."

"It's the week of Christmas! Where's she going?"

"I don't know. I'm not going to stop her. She doesn't want to help me, so she may as well leave."

Later, Elsie asked Grant if he could just spend one evening a week with his grandma, and only if he really wanted to. She promised he wouldn't regret it. She'd take care of the rest.

He stepped up, said he wanted to, and he immediately visited and began cooking with his grandma on Wednesday nights to prove it.

TO THE ONE WHO INVENTED ZED, ZERO, AND NAUGHT, THANKS FOR *NOTHING*

Elsie stayed away the week Melanie moved out. Two days before Christmas, though, Gail called Elsie to tell her, "Rich is in the hospital with a bad lung infection."

"Why hasn't Carlene called me, or Melanie?"

"Carlene's been calling Melanie repeatedly with updates, and I'm afraid, with all the pressure of her moving out, she's going to have a nervous breakdown! She can't get everything packed and out of my house in time for the deadline she gave me, but she wants to take Rich out of the hospital for Christmas."

"She's moving there?"

"I guess. I don't know, but I'm afraid for her. Carlene's last call said Dad was spitting up black blood from his lungs and they had tied him down, even though he was having leg cramps."

Elsie shuddered at being tied down with leg cramps.

"I told Melanie she should just go and come back later to get the rest of her things." Gail said.

"I still don't understand why neither Carlene nor Melanie have called me about Dad."

"I don't know, but Carlene is threatening the hospital staff with a lawsuit if they don't release her dad and treat him with the homeopathic medication she wants for him."

"Oh, my word! So, she's calling from Lake Charles trying to demand treatment and release and trying to get Melanie down there to do her dirty work, yet no one is telling me anything."

"Pray for Melanie, will you, while you pray for your dad?"

"I'll try Mom. I'm struggling with every angle of this situation right now." Elsie didn't feel inspired to pray for anyone but herself. She couldn't even find words for that.

They celebrated Christmas Eve with Gail, and while there, Miles, playing around with Gail's pulse oximeter, discovered that his heart beats were reporting only thirty-four pulses per minute.

Throughout November and December, Miles had been experiencing episodes of faintness and changing heart rhythms. Elsie took him into the E.R. on Christmas morning. The issue was diagnosed as bigeminy and precipitating pulse rhythms. He and Elsie spent that day in the E.R. rather than sharing Christmas with others.

Melanie had driven to Oklahoma City as fast as possible two days before Christmas to try to get her father home for Christmas, still not calling or texting Elsie about their father's condition. Elsie decided to let her sister cool down. She didn't call or text her to complicate things.

On Christmas Eve, Melanie was able to obtain oxygen services through the nurse network so that she could take her dad home. Rich's pastor helped them get his wheelchair in the door, and Melanie cooked a meal for two. After they ate together, Melanie called Carlene to say he was looking better and breathing better. "He's so thin. You can tell he's pretty sick, but his eyes are twinkly and he's happy to be at home." She giggled to realize that her wildest dream was coming true on Christmas Eve; she would finally start living with her dad.

Over Christmas dinner, she filled her dad in on the decision to leave her mother's home and she told him she intended to stay with him until he got better. Previously, he had made it clear he couldn't support her there, and that he didn't want her to move in with him, but today he was a man in need, and at the moment, she was there to help.

The next morning, Melanie checked on her dad. He said he needed to use the restroom. She helped him into his wheelchair and rolled him into the bathroom and left him for the sake of privacy. She heard him moving around, but when the process seemed finished, she knocked. There was no answer. She went in. His body lay on the floor. He had finally outgrown his skin and shed it.

Rich, the main joint of the puzzling family, was removed allowing the other members to fall where they may like an interlocking burr puzzle falls apart when the key is removed. Other pieces of the puzzle, strewn about, left Melanie with a cruel ending.

In shock, she at least knew to call 911.

As reality began to grip her unhinged situation, she backed away and called Carlene. Nothing but screams and cries came from her mouth. She didn't know what to do next. Carlene promised to come up as soon as she could, bringing Foreman. She stayed on the phone with her distraught sister until the paramedics arrived.

When the ambulance came, the medics pronounced her father dead of a heart attack, and gathering up his body, they moved it to the hospital morgue.

Richard Finch's pastor was next to be notified, and he began to prepare a funeral for the following Sunday afternoon. *Who would be leading the music at church and for Rich's funeral?* He'd have to figure that out.

Carlene called and left the time of their dad's death on Elsie's messaging system. No sisterly words accompanied the message. No tears.

Melanie called her mother. Her mother called Elsie.

The triangulating scheme of things felt surreal. Elsie shed no tears. She was numb. If anything, she felt relieved. She texted her sisters, "I plan to stay in Denver and grieve Dad's passing on my own." She heard nothing from either of them.

The reason she would not be going to the funeral was layered, as everything always was with her family. She wasn't going to offer the information about Miles's heart to the feral family of cats.

She couldn't allow bitterness or resentment to create more strife at a time like this. There was no place for fault-finding now, or stories that always wound up in more supposition and slander. She would put Carlene and Melanie's malevolence far from her. It was time to live in peace with her husband by keeping her sisters at arm's length.

LACKING A SMOKING HOT BODY, HE ASKED FOR CREMATION

Carlene and Foreman arrived the next day at Rich's house. Carlene didn't call Elsie or their mother while driving through Texas and Oklahoma to ask about their feelings regarding Rich's passing or to help process her own.

Arriving, she took stock of the yellowed spots on his white carpet, the faded and scuffed walls, the broken burners on the stove, the leaking sink. Richard had been living in his head and on his computer since Noeleen's passing.

Happy to support Melanie for her loyalty to their dad, Carlene came to help organize the memorial service. The two sisters also began to order flowers and find the necessary documents to submit to the county for a death certificate. Foreman began to assess the structure and presentation of Rich's house for sale.

By phone, Carlene hounded the county and the hospital to change cause of death so that Covid would be the attributable cause in order to get the funeral expenses paid for. She went so far as to ask the neighboring county to amend the death certificate. Eventually, in need of the life insurance policies, Carlene applied for and accepted the death certificate of her father as first presented: pulmonary embolism.

Melanie called Noeleen's children, who offered their condolences. One of them let herself in with a key to rifle through Rich's notes and papers in his desk. It became apparent that Noeleen's child was looking for leftovers. The stepchildren were not as close to Rich as he had made them out to be. Calling him "Dad" was perhaps a form of pandering, but Noeleen and Rich had settled the issue of the children by signing pre-nuptial agreements, and her children had already received their mother's portion of the estate. Carlene and Melanie paid to have the locks changed. Only one of them materialized for his funeral.

The memorial service was filled with the pastor's praise for Rich's valuable help at church, help with the bulletins, help with the website, help with the song leading, help with teaching Sunday school.

Miles and Elsie remained in Denver watching the funeral from a streaming link. Since funerals are mostly about supporting loved ones as much as praising the deceased, Elsie felt neither need nor obligation to attend. Rich had prepared his own obituary and service as well as his final will and testament in his final years. He wasn't about to leave these details to his heirs. In doing so, he made sure that he ended well by winning some.

Carlene, very large in size, sat in the front pew with her husband absorbing the mounting conflicts.

Melanie took the podium and said she'd never seen so many Christmas cards piled on her dad's bookshelf. "He loved every one of you. When I called you to tell you about his funeral, so many of you told me how he had helped you with a project, whether it was fixing a refrigerator, remodeling a basement, putting in new bathroom or kitchen cabinets, or adding shelves to a garage. He showed his love through serving you, and I thank you for showing up here today."

It occurred to Elsie that Melanie held herself straight and spoke very well for having all her emotional joints dislocated. She had survived to tell the story Rich would want to hear. Elsie considered all the praise her sister was giving to her dad for all the work he did for so many. This truth being the pure irony of her sister's longing and lifetime of loss.

Once again, as on the day of Melanie's divorce, Elsie sat in awe of her sister's composure under immense pressure. She pointed out Melanie's speech to Miles saying, "Look! She isn't stuttering, she isn't waffling, she isn't telling wandering backstories. She made an appropriate and honorable speech there, in the appropriate amount of time. That girl is cunning, I tell you. She is not what she portrays herself to be generally. She is very much in charge of herself."

Carlene made sure the service ended with military honors.

All of this was completed without a personal phone call to Elsie or Kaida.

For the next two days, Carlene helped organize and clean out the house. Foreman appraised the value of the needed repairs because Richard had left his house with a broken floor support beam under layers of dust and grime.

When Elsie called to say the funeral had been honorable, and that Melanie could have the music her dad had told her was to be her own inheritance, both Carlene and Melanie spurned her by not responding. Melanie did text and say, *"Is there anything you want of Dad's?"*

"Not really," Elsie replied. Later, Elsie called again to ask about one of the vehicles. She had already agreed Melanie could have the Winnebago, and she assumed Carlene and Foreman would take one of the cars, but who would take the other car? Could she have it?

A long pause at the other end of the line informed her that a decision had already been made. *"Um, Foreman and I are taking the cars,"* came Carlene's reply. Her hobby of suing the water district, the state, and the county for over ten years had impoverished them. Her husband, though at retirement age and riddled with arthritis, continued to work, and he had to use the company car because they couldn't afford to purchase one for him, although Carlene had a car.

Miles said, "We don't need to buy more car insurance or new tires or anything. We don't need another car. Let them have it." Of course, she would. She was just wondering if they intended to include her in anything or whether they would work out the value of the estate between them.

"You can have both cars." She texted Carlene. *"I would just like a death certificate."*

"Why do you want a death certificate?"

"Because he's my father."

"Since you won't tell me why you want a death certificate, you'll get one when I get around to it." Carlene texted.

The next thing Elsie heard was from her nephew wondering why Elsie had refused to help with the clean-up of Rich's home and the funeral preparations.

"You've got to be kidding. This story is moving so fast and they are already disbursing his things? Neither of them even let me know they needed my help with anything. Now, they're telling Mom and the grandkids that I refused to help? All I said was, I wanted to grieve in Denver."

What she really wanted was to understand her father's story. She wanted to be able to put the pieces together and lay the effects of his influences on the family to rest. She still had so many questions. She'd been surprised to see and hear military taps played at the memorial. Her father had said so little about the Air Force that she didn't know whether he had been honorably or dishonorably discharged.

Elsie had never felt entitled to either of her parent's estates. It seemed likely that she would be included to some extent, though she hadn't considered until the last couple of years that she might be disinherited by both of them. It had certainly come true in her mother's case, and now her sisters were leaving her out of the division of her dad's valuables as well as accusing her of not helping them in their hour of need.

She didn't feel she owed them any explanation, nor did she believe they should judge her for what they understood her relationship to be with her father. She was wrong.

THE WINDING STAIRCASE WAS *UP TO SOMETHING*

During the first week of January, a Christian retirement specialist offered a dinner on biblical stewardship. Elsie was curious. Perhaps she had something to learn about giving to the poor or helping the earth more. She signed up for the event for herself and Miles.

The message that evening was taken from Luke 12:13 and following.

"Someone in the crowd said to him, 'Teacher, tell my brother to divide the inheritance with me.' Jesus replied, 'Man, who appointed me a judge or an arbiter between you?' Then he said to them, 'Watch out! Be on your guard against all kinds of greed; life does not consist in an abundance of possessions.'"

In all her reading of the Gospels, Elsie had never noticed this exchange in scripture. Though she was a dreamer, she wasn't a particularly greedy person. She had experienced enough love. She had learned to be content. Perhaps because she'd never considered her inheritance to be problematic until Kaida stole it, but also because even then, she'd experienced sufficiency. Trusting the Lord to provide for her welfare and happiness, she'd seen His faithfulness.

Yet, with a beating drum, her beating heart reciprocated.

She realized that she'd been asking God for two weeks now, since her father's death, and even since she'd seen the evidence of her mother's treacherous bequest of her estate to Kaida, that He would intervene and make the division of her parents' estates equal and just.

She was that young man in Luke 12! She sat up.

Miles and she had been blessed with all kinds of good things in their lives from his parents, from amazing times of travel and conversation, to enjoying great friendships, discussions, and deep meaning in life. They'd also enjoyed hosting people in their home and learning about the world while helping others. And, unlike so many other spouses, Miles was always telling her he loved her, how she was beautiful to him, and often asked whether she needed something he could provide.

He had been an honorable spouse and had also received honors from work. His good humor and acts of service for bolstering her in her times of need were exemplary gifts she'd enjoyed. Beyond all of this, Miles was proud of his wife's accomplishments and listened to her spiritual views, and also her values and perspectives on life decisions. She knew she was wealthy and rich in ways that money couldn't account for.

It was the blessing of her own parents she kept missing.

Her entire life, she'd longed for them to be honorable themselves in parenting and in the public eye. She'd tried to honor them, but it was difficult to show respect where respect was not due.

She'd longed for them, even as they were, to see her for who she was, to converse with her, help equip her, and bless her with practical strategies, but all her adult activities had been accomplished in a struggle marginalized by her family.

At her mother's eightieth birthday, she wondered how many of the guests had heard Kaida and Gail's slander.

She kept making her peace with the truth that a mother's respect and a financial bequest are not always what proves a person's worth. A woman is not defined by her family. Yet others do discover these awkward results.

Besides the injustice of the money distribution, it was the fact that her mother and sister had dragged her reputation through fraternal mud that bothered her most.

When she told a friend about this, her friend reminded her of Joseph in the Bible whose brothers had stripped him of his father's love and sold him into slavery. Joseph survived imprisonment, and because he could decipher dreams, the Pharoah made him a ruler over all the nation's food distribution. When his brothers came begging for grain from him, not recognizing their grown and decorated brother, Joseph wept in agony wondering whether he could forgive them. Finally, he said to them, "You meant it for evil, but God meant it for good."

She comforted herself, comparing how the heat of the journey would purify her character, similar to how smelting metal lifts the impurities in the fire, making the vessel valuable. She counted on the process providing memorable results in her life like a debt collector counted his tears.

She was surprised to find herself struggling with this. Money did make a big difference, especially in travel opportunities and in healthcare, but God had worked many miracles giving her a peaceful life, and it was also full of joy.

While she had been making frugal plans for retirement and aims to travel and budgets for medical care, was God laughing at her? If He watched her wrestling for her parents' reward, would He vindicate her?

Could she trust God now?

Here was a bronze mirror, presenting her wavy reflection in an hour of vulnerability.

The rest of Luke Chapter 12 was being read. When she later studied verses thirteen to the end, it spoke to her of the watchfulness of God for her needs, and His promises and good intent to provide for them. Anything the world or her family might promise or withhold from her was not a matter for her concern, nor was the Lord concerned. He was able and willing to be more than fair with her. She only needed to keep this perspective of His sovereignty and care.

A week went by. Perhaps she could.

One night Elsie curled into a ball in bed. She'd been unable to stop her leaking tears. Suddenly an image of herself as a little child in pajamas came to her, hidden under a magnificent wing.

The Lord was simply helping her to recognize her soul was the real prize. She was securely held by His tender keep.

A GRAVITATIONAL MOON CAFÉ HAS NO ATMOSPHERE THOUGH IT ORBITS AWAY

Gail's eighty-sixth birthday was approaching. Elsie asked her mother to celebrate it at a fancy hotel atrium, lit with reflections of past celebrations and fine dining. She would buy.

Her mother happily agreed, and they made plans.

Then, Kaida lashed out by sending a letter to her mother, "Happy eighty-sixth birthday, Mom! Remember the party I threw for you on your eightieth?"

Kaida's pen went on to remind Gail again of Kaida's year spent in the girl's home in ninth grade and accused her of kicking her out of her home and depriving her of furniture when she had every right to move her husband into her house.

"He wasn't her husband then. They had just met."

"I know." Elsie looked at Miles, and he nodded.

"Now I take my claim off all our jointly owned furniture." Kaida wrote. She listed each item she thought belonged to her in detail, like an insurance claim.

"Where did this list come from?"

"Probably from the documents and records she took while I was in the hospital."

Of course, Gail, had an argument and an understanding about each piece leaving only two of the controversial pieces in limbo saying, "Perhaps she's right on that table, but she could have taken it at the time she moved out, and she didn't. The others, she bought to replace the furniture she got rid of when she moved in here, my furniture! Sometimes she bought them with my credit card when I agreed to it. She's exaggerating or outright lying!"

Kaida's letter accused her mother of slandering her to her children so that they had turned against her. Of course, seeing it from Elsie's side of the aisle, she knew this claim was false because she had pleaded with her mother to set the record straight for years so that she could have a solid relationship with her niece and nephews. Her mother had recoiled saying, "I don't want to turn those kids away from their mother, and I don't want to get involved anymore because it could turn out badly for me. I don't want to lose them!"

Elsie knew her mother had been very careful not to say anything bad about the grandkids' mother.

Finally, Kaida accused Gail of trading favorites amongst the children again and attached a court document. It was the court docket of construction filings from Miles and Elsie's ordeal during the six-year trial of two renovations. Kaida and Gail had also done their worst to her then.

Gail now knew the hell Elsie had endured, so she discarded the court docket enclosed by Kaida. Nevertheless, it acted as the bite of a rattlesnake to both Gail and Elsie, and to Miles, who saw firsthand the effect of Kaida's venom in his wife from Kaida's repeated strikes.

Kaida's letter ended, "When you die, Mom, I am coming in and changing the locks and selling that house. No one will stop me. I will take it and buy my own house with the proceeds, and when I die, the proceeds will go to my children."

Elsie wondered if the Lord would be that patient, but it wasn't up to her. She didn't begrudge the grandchildren an inheritance. She just hoped it would still be there for them by the time Kaida and her husband had finished with it.

Two weeks prior to Gail's eighty-sixth birthday, Elsie received notice that her father hadn't forgotten her. A month after her dad's passing, Elsie opened a packet stating that she was an heir to several of her dad's life insurance policies. It was a relief not to have been written off. Her dad's goodwill for her was sealed to the end.

True to his word, he included his three daughters in all four policies, leaving Kaida out.

Elsie experienced a bit of renewed goodwill and tenderness for her father. The wisdom of the policies was that the payouts would bypass her sister's administration of the trust.

Gail sighed with relief to know her girls had been given something of an inheritance although she couldn't change anything in her estate. There was that opportunity she had seen to take out the full extent of her HELOC on the value of her home, paying the interest only. She'd transferred the proceeds to an account set aside for Elsie and Melanie.

Elsie had an idea. "Mom, why don't you take out an insurance policy like Dad did?"

"I don't believe in insurance policies like that."

"Well, I guess you can believe in them now."

"It's too late anyway. They only go to age eighty-five, and when I inquired, I could only get three thousand dollars."

Elsie thought there must be something else out there. She put her mother's details into a comparative insurance search engine. Instead of spilling out offers and terms, her inquiry spun out to ten other insurance companies. She closed down her search.

Three hours later Gail called Elsie to say her phone was ringing off the hook with insurance calls.

Elsie didn't fess up.

After she hung up the phone, she couldn't stop laughing. It had become an incidental joke in her intent to not allow her mother to forsake her. Once again, she'd mistakenly tried to fix her mother's fault in her own strength. Why couldn't she just trust the Lord that He had promised never to forsake her?

Elsie called her mother back and told her the truth, apologizing for the incessant phone calls.

After much consideration, Gail finally explained to Elsie the reason her heart had first hardened against her. She was once highly offended when Elsie denied knowing how much she had paid for her college education; this issue became a significant reason she had broken faith with her daughter. "I even went through my check to show you the pile of them, and you refused to even look at them. You may not like it, but you need to know from my side, why I did what I did." Gail explained that she had continued her perfunctory habit of writing checks throughout the first two years of her daughter's education, "at quite a sacrifice to me and the younger two living at home, so much so that it was one of the reasons Kaida continues to nip at your heels."

Kaida, over the years, openly described her envy of her parents having underwritten Elsie's college tuition.

"I'm sorry, Mom. I knew you had contributed a lot, but I thought you were trying to take all the credit. And, I remember working my way through school, and getting other help, too, grants and loans. I guess because we misunderstood each other, unnecessary years of hard feelings and resentment built up. I'm so sorry that I let my ego get in the way of looking through that stack of checks. I remember being stunned that there were so many. Did you send them directly to the school? Because I don't remember receiving them or taking them to the school office."

"Well, yes, a lot of them went directly to the school office, so I guess you wouldn't have known."

"Mom, do you recall that you had worked a trade of child support for sole ownership of the house? Meaning, you took on Dad's divorce decree order to support me during college, and in return, you got the house, right?"

"Let's close the door to this, shall we?" Gail suggested.

Gail and Elsie came together often these days, laughing at the past, looking over each gem in the family affairs. They adjusted judgments upon the crimes, making excuses for human frailty. They permitted or denied excuses and bolstered their unity. Weaving in threads of tenderness, they laced their walking shoes. Elsie, a loyal character by nature, had forgiven her mother for disinheriting her in the will and then the quit claim deed, but sometimes, she had to remember the seventy times seven.

Their family pastor preached on getting out of Egypt while the Lord fights His children's battles for them. Elsie and Gail learned that being still and knowing that the Lord is God doesn't mean you don't obey His voice and expect miracles. You put on your walking shoes and pick up your armor. You don't get too comfortable or fail to march into battle. It simply means that you are still and confident in your spirit that God goes before you and picks up the rearguard, too.

There were still things to be done if the Lord would help her.

Ten days before Gail's eighty-sixth birthday, the grandchildren said they'd like to come to the celebration, but they couldn't afford to have lunch at such a fanciful place.

Elsie changed the venue. Miles made plans to pay for the party.

Then, Elsie got word from her mother that Melanie was coming to stay at their mom's for a work week, and she hoped to attend Gail's birthday party as well at the end of the week.

Turning the timing over in her mind, Elsie understood their father's insurance payments would be arriving in the mail, and with Melanie's son coming to the party, she realized that Melanie was using her mother to stay the week at her house, and deposit the checks, all while claiming her intent was to celebrate Gail's birthday. What a sham.

Rage claimed Elsie.

"This is my party, Mom, and Melanie is ingratiating herself with you not because she loves you but because she wants to freeload in your house that week."

"I know that" said her mom.

"She didn't even bother to ask me and I'm hosting it."

"I know."

"Why aren't you saying anything? Why are you allowing it?"

"Because she's my daughter and she needs a place to stay."

"After all she's done to you."

"I guess so. I've been reading the 'turn the other cheek passage again…'"

"But, Mom, don't you see how she's treating me too by not calling or talking to me for six weeks about my own father's death?"

"You'll just have to forgive her, Elsie."

"No! Not like that. If she wants to celebrate your birthday, she can call me or make her own plans with you. I can't do it. It's one thing to forgive her and wish her well. It's another thing to allow her to keep walking over both you and me, gossiping with the grandchildren while making herself look good, and I'm left to clean up.

"Mom, you keep leaving me out of every equation. It's like you think your daughters are only hurting you. So, by not putting up boundaries, you allow their wickedness to plow through my life as well. You don't protect me. You've cut me out of your will, for all practical purposes, twice! You've never provided for my wellbeing since childhood. You will never defend me. You don't see me, and you never have! You don't think anything that they do is costing me anything. It's like I'm nonexistent to you, and yet you claim you love me! I — I can't deal with this!" She hung up.

Elsie felt wretched. In her heart, deep furrows were picked and pulled through the long fields of thorns and briars by the many alliances of the family plowing machine.

She wanted to be gracious and float above it, but she just couldn't.

She began wailing.

The grief came from deep inside her own inability to stand on any part of the fractured foundations of her family or to put back any of the walls of their felled house. She was so enmeshed in the crumbling structure, that she had become one of the errant building contractors herself. She didn't want that guilt to cover her.

She didn't want to be the buckling loadbearing wall, or the cracked joist. She was not the bad person behind the wrecking ball. But, at this moment, she also couldn't deny her own piece of earth upon which she needed to stand.

Her mother called her back.

"Elsie,—" her mother began, "I do see you. I see your beautiful house, the houses you've built, the way you decorate them and your hospitality towards everyone. I love your cooking. I've given you all my hospitality silver and tablecloths. You've kept your love for your husband, and he loves you. I see that. You are so talented with music and the arts. I do see you and I love you. I'm so sorry for everything that has happened. I'm sorry that I didn't see how this was hurting you. I will call Melanie back and tell her that she's welcome to stay, but this is your party, and she needs to make other plans."

Elsie went silent. In those few words, her mother told her that she saw her and loved her. Not for what she could do serving her, or for her entertainment value, but just for being herself, for her character and gifts.

In those few words, her mother apologized. In those few words, she agreed to set a boundary, if for nothing else but to protect Elsie.

"Okay. Thank you, Mom."

And there was peace.

The Sunday before Gail's eighty-sixth birthday, the family pastor opened his message with the words, "A person will not change unless they want to change." Elsie's family members paraded before her mind's eye. A scripture followed: "I am the vine; you are the branches. If you remain in me and I in you, you will bear much fruit. Without me, you can do nothing. – John 15:5"

The verse seemed to provide the core reminder of Elsie's dilemma. Family animosity was eating through her personal peace. She had niggled both Carlene and Melanie to do the right thing in handling their father's estate, and she had called them out on their hard hearts and silence towards her. What began as a bit of goat prodding took on the fury of an underground gas explosion in the shadowy caverns of their sibling relations.

It was her own furious texts to her sisters that felled the fragile beam in the family caves, finally collapsing the escape route from the room in which she found herself.

Then, she'd told her mother the cold truth—as she saw it—about Melanie's intent, even though it only added to her mother's anguish. Yes, she was guilty of generating her own form of malice and spite.

Although she wanted to hear from the Lord and continue to work in tandem with Him, she felt continually distracted by family dramas and sideswiped by problems too big for her emotions or resources to handle.

Beyond that, surveying her ministry in the arts as though from a circling helicopter that Sunday, showed results which were not what Elsie hoped for, and she was winding down and getting ready to retire. Without Miles's resources in their retirement, she would not be able to continue to fund her ministry. She hung her head and confessed again to the Lord, "Besides my animosity toward my family, I'm honestly disappointed with the result of my life's work and years of labor for others in Your name."

"Just abide in Me." The verse promised that she simply needed to abide in the Lord. "Yes, abide in Me and you will bear much fruit. Without Me, you can do nothing. With Me, all things are possible. I've adopted you. My blood runs through your veins. You can stand on Me and My kingdom for your foundation. I love you, and I'll keep you."

Whatever she did, Elsie mused walking through the exit doors of the church, treasuring an overwhelming knowledge, it needed to be done through a connection to Him. Her work would bear much fruit. It would, because He promised it would. It was a realization that had the effect of lifting her hair with a chill from her scalp and sending a refreshing thrill down her neck.

Elsie would continue to learn to manage traumatic interactions with her sisters and remaining parent. She would practice keeping her focus on the Lord and on the race she was running, and she would see the blessings He showered over her. If she allowed the distractions, accusations, and the drama to overtake her, she would be operating in her own weak, one-sided perspective. She had already lost a higher perspective several times as of late. She confessed this to the Lord and renewed her commitment to live connected to Him and to her husband and to the blessings in her own backyard.

Miles always called this process his "God bag." Everything that he couldn't deal with, he simply stuffed it into the bag for God to sort out.

A fine peace spread through her body, releasing the tension as easily as a spa day might do. And the peace lasted much longer than she expected.

Two days before Gail's eighty-sixth birthday, Gail called Elsie with a list of groceries she needed. Although Elsie had set her mother up for delivered groceries at her local grocery store, the first two experiences had proved confounding with items switched out and the bill being far greater than originally indicated. When she called the store for an explanation, the clerk said, "That delivery is provided through a third party and oh, the billing is actually handled by another credit card service."

That was it. "I refuse to participate in a service where I get the runaround by a second, third, and fourth party in a dilemma!"

Elsie sighed. "Okay, I'll get your groceries for you and the grandkids, Mom."

"Well, I also have a problem downloading and printing that contract you wrote for my new renter. Pages and pages, some blank and others full of writing are shooting out of my printer."

"Mom, shut your printer off. Tomorrow when I come over, I'll look at it."

"Okay. It's shut off now. It's stopped. I'd like to have the contract printed out tonight so that if I need to make corrections, I can complete them before she comes."

"Mom, I've showed you how to download an attachment and print it. Are you trying to print the email or the attachment?"

"I don't remember, and I can't figure it out. It's messed up."

"Okay, well, I don't speak your computer's language, but when I come tomorrow, I'll look at it and see if we can get it printed. If I can't figure out what's wrong, then one of the grandkids will likely know how."

Gail pouted on her end of the phone. Her daughter wouldn't make the trip over that night. There was nothing more to be done. She'd have to wait.

BABIES ARE DELIVERED BY STORKS BUT LARGER CHILDREN NEED A *CRANE*

The day before Gail's eighty-sixth birthday, her grandchildren Paige and Ricky drove a snow-blown course from Montana to Colorado through the winds of Wyoming to celebrate with their grandma. They brought Gail's beloved great grandchildren from Paige, Nena and Cormac, and Ricky's dogs.

With her mother's grocery list in hand, Elsie went shopping for the special weekend. Rather than going to several different stores, she picked the organic produce store that also offered her mother's favorite blueberry pie. This meant the bread her mom wanted was not available, so she picked the closest alternative.

A gorgeous bouquet of red and pink flowers greeted her at the door of her mom's home.

"Wow, Mom! Who sent you those?"

"I don't know exactly. The card just said, 'Happy Birthday' but not who sent them."

"Someone loves you!"

"Or, hates me."

"Why would you say that? They're beautiful."

"Well, I don't know."

"Maybe they're from Carlene. She sends you flowers every year."

"No she doesn't."

"Yes, she does. Most years, at least."

"Really? Maybe some but not all."

"Okay, whatever, Mom. I think Carlene probably sent them to you."

"See, like I thought. They're from an enemy." Gail finished the discussion.

Elsie picked up the vase and added water.

When she brought in the groceries, her mother picked through them commenting, "This isn't quite right, this is too much, why did you get that? Oh, thank you for remembering the pie and coffee and getting the cheese and eggs."

"Honestly, Mom. You are going to have to accept what people can give you. If you can't drive and pick out the things you want, you are going to have to be thankful for what you get. Now, let's look at your computer settings and printer."

Gail padded into her study and offered the captain's chair to Elsie.

Elsie pulled up the email, clicked the attachment to "save" and then clicked the tab for printing out the new shared expenses housemate agreement. A string of other documents being printed came up as well as a notification that the printer was paused.

When she un-paused the printer, large print emails, along with her mother's emailed codicil from months ago, began shooting out of the printer like disks for target practice. She hit pause. She unplugged the printer. She picked up all the papers and put the clean ones back into the device. She asked her mother what the large print emails were all about.

"They're letters between Kaida and me and you and me. I want to save them because there's important information in them."

"Mom, it makes me sick to read these letters about who harmed whom. I'm throwing them away."

"Okay, but I want a copy of that codicil."

Elsie clicked the little x for "delete" on the emails. Then, she allowed the codicil to print as she printed the housemate agreement.

When the codicil came out, it stated in Gail's words that there were consequences for behaviors, referring to Kaida. She was cutting her out completely from her will and from all her possessions.

"Mom, you should probably update this, especially since Kaida sent that letter dropping her past claims to all your furniture and appliances and because she's threatened to change the locks and keep everyone out when you pass. You'll have your housemate here with rights of her own. This place could be a battlefield if you aren't specific."

"I know. I plan to give this amendment to my will and the codicil to Paige when she comes because she's my personal representative."

Gail spread her hands over her new rental agreement and thanked Elsie for printing it out.

Elsie felt sick in her soul having seen all the words, all the words her mother saved and ruminated over even when she was forced to use a magnifying glass on letters of 24-point font. Her mother's fiery critique of her ousted sister, her sister who remained the focus of their mother's heart created petrified wood of her heart.

She'd challenged her mother about disinheriting Carlene a couple of times, but her mother had remained adamant. Her heart was closed because Carlene, from childhood, had always fought against her. In Carlene's letters over the years, which could be counted on one hand, Carlene had lectured and accused her mother relentlessly. Gail's eldest remained unwilling to ask clarifying questions or allow any mitigating factors to change her bent heart.

Why couldn't her mother see that she continued to treat both Melanie and herself as non-entities a cast above Carlene?

Even as Gail desperately tried to right her wrongs, all her focus was to punish Kaida. Her codicil did nothing to right the wrongs done to Melanie and Elsie or to recognize her helpful grandsons, Ricky and Grant.

Elsie mentioned that Gail had overlooked Grant and Ricky in her codicil regarding the household goods and might want to reconsider because they were the ones most likely to need furniture.

"Oh, can you add them in?"

"Yes, I can, but you really need a professional's advice." Elsie fixed the codicil to include Grant and Ricky equally, and she referenced Kaida's signed letter relinquishing her claims on all of Gail's possessions.

"That's good. Thank you," said Gail.

Then she reprinted it for her mother to see. Her mother did not see that now Grant and Ricky were on the same level as Elsie and Melanie, but now Elsie could only blame herself for that. She held nothing against her niece and nephews. She hoped the best for their lives. It was her mother's birding binoculars and the blind spot she lived in that irked her.

She fixed the grandchildren's lunch and made a bowl of guacamole as a snack for them, but her mother's attitudes, focus, and behaviors made Elsie feel invisible again, except for what services she could render. Maybe Melanie had felt this every day of her life. The age-old sickness overtook her.

"Mom, I can't stay. I can't wait for the kids to come in. I'm just not into it today. I'm gonna go."

"Why? What's happened? Have I done something?"

"No, Mom. You have done exactly nothing. I just can't stay. I'll see you for your birthday tomorrow."

"Honey, I wish you'd read that passage on turning the other cheek in the Sermon on the Mount. It's been helping me so much."

All evening long, Miles tried to wrangle out of Elsie why she was sleeping through the television shows. She was unresponsive. Elsie just couldn't name it; she wished her throat would close up.

The morning of Gail's birthday, she called Elsie at half past ten. "Hi, Hon!"

"Hi, Mom. Happy Birthday to you! Did you sleep well?"

"Oh yes. I slept so well, I overslept!"

Elsie had also overslept, but she was rejuvenated this morning. "Well, you gave yourself a happy birthday present, then."

"Yeah, I guess so! Hey, what time are we supposed to be at the restaurant?"

"At eleven."

"You're kidding! It's ten thirty! I best get dressed. We'll be right over."

The party started at 11:30. The air between and among them was clear and fresh, like the blue sky above.

"Little Cormac asked about you first thing when he came in the house yesterday," Gail offered.

"He did? Why?" Elsie looked at little Cormac standing in his chair, leaning over the table to see everyone and everything. Her heart swelled.

"I don't know. He was looking forward to seeing his great aunt!"

Miles was the perfect host, offering suggestions, appetizers, and drinks. Elsie asked Paige about her graduation date and law school. She asked Ricky about the trip from Montana.

He said it was great, except that he had to drive the whole way because Paige was listening to juries and doing schoolwork.

Paige rolled her eyes, sputtering, "It's true, but we also had to take care of his dog."

"Oh, you brought your dog?"

"Yes. I couldn't leave her there for a long weekend."

"How's Mom with your dog?"

"She's been great! It was so cold out last night, that Grandma let her sleep inside."

"Really Mom? You did?"

"Well, yes, I hear about people who make their dogs stay out in subzero temperatures and they freeze to death."

"You mean like Bandit did?"

Her mother went quiet. "I forgot about that. Is that what happened?"

"Yep. Well, I'm glad you let her in, Mom. And they say old dogs can't learn new tricks."

Ricky laughed.

Nena said, "I couldn't sleep. He ran around for a long time and then he went into his kennel and gnawed on a bone all night."

"Aww..." everyone cooed. Paige patted her daughter's back.

"One thing I learned though," Grant interjected, "is a big dog can fit through a little doggie door."

"Really?"

"Yes. Really." Grant practically shouted.

Ricky laughed. "You know Grandma's doggie door? Well, I showed it to Shiva, and she scooted right through it."

Grant belly laughed. "I saw her do it. It was hilarious to see that huge dog scrambling through there."

Gail chuckled. "I saw it too. I couldn't believe it!"

"So, a big husky can fit through a little doggy door. Nice to know," Elsie said. "I've been thinking about getting a large doggie door installed, but now I know I can get a small one."

Still laughing, Grant said, "Yes, you can, but it wouldn't be polite."

The whole table laughed with him.

"Guess what Cormac did this morning?" Gail said to Elsie.

"What?"

From the other end of the table Cormac shouted, "I fixed Grandma's Rumba!"

"What?"

Gail nodded. "He did! He's only in second grade and he figured it out. And, all this time, I've been wondering why the house cleaners kept leaving the rugs dirty. But it was because there was so much hair in the roller that it couldn't go 'round."

"Yeah," said Cormac standing up in his seat to command the proper attention. "I turned it over and I pulled on the door, and I pulled out the roller and I cleaned it and put it back."

"Well, are you a clever boy!" Elsie congratulated her great nephew with true admiration, then she added a vacuum cleaner story of her own and

Miles's. Of course, other hair-raising vacuum cleaner stories added to the conversation.

When Grant saw the receipt for the food, he pulled out his wallet and asked if he could contribute. He typically contributed anything he could to family celebrations, making him a most welcomed guest. This time, Elsie and Miles refused. "This is our gift to Grandma," Miles insisted.

"Well, let me get the tip then...Please?"

"No, we've talked about this. It's our treat."

"Please? Please? Purty Please?" begged their nephew, his pleases going up the scale.

"Nope. Absolutely not."

"Please? I can hit even higher notes!" Again, everyone laughed at Grant's levity.

Elsie's heart filled with deep joy and satisfaction. This was the party she'd envisioned. Her mom glowed. She invited them all over to play games.

"Why don't we all go back to Grandma's?" Ricky suggested. "My mom dropped off some boxes of records from Grandpa's collection, and Grant is bringing over his record player so that we can listen to them."

"Oh! Those must be my inheritance from Dad. I didn't know Melanie had brought them up."

"Well, she thought you didn't want them, so she brought them up for me."

"Well, I do want a few of them from my youth. You can have the rest."

Miles took Gail's arm and she hobbled towards Grant's car while both Ricky and Grant opened doors for her, honoring their grandma.

IF YOU DON'T KNOW WHAT APOCOLYPSE MEANS, IT ISN'T THE *END OF THE WORLD*

Back at Gail's, Ricky brought in a box of records for Elsie and Grant to look through. For a couple of hours, they played albums and talked about bands, singers, lyrics, album covers, album notes, and the lack of years printed on the release of these precious commodities. Tears were shed, jigs were danced, and many laughs and groans at warped records followed.

"You must be exhausted, Mom." Elsie handed Gail a blanket and a glass of water.

"Oh, I am, I am, but this is the best birthday, and I'm going to enjoy it to the fullest!"

The desires of one's heart are often hidden behind layers of all the things that don't fit in.

When a photo album was found in one of Gail's drawers, the two grandchildren began laughing, sharing photos and stories with the rest of the party, grabbing the ones for themselves they felt they couldn't leave behind.

Elsie started squirreling away some herself. Gail didn't protest. She smiled blind smiles. She swirled in the happiness.

They each searched and found more albums and envelopes of old family pictures. The family spent hours reviewing baby years, vacations, holidays, graduations, weddings, and more babies, all the phases of their family's lifetime.

Elsie's chest constricted when she saw her sister Melanie in the photos Melanie always swore had never been taken of her. Elsie saw her sister's belonging, love, and beauty. Melanie was cherished, held by her father, and dressed up by her mother. She shook thinking how important this moment would have been if she would have allowed her sister to come to her party. Elsie would have to wrap these up and send them to her sister hoping for the best.

Each of them traced facial expressions that showed the characters changing in each of them growing up. There was mocking, amazement, fun, and awe.

Then, the most personal memories that Gail had saved from her teen years with friends, with her siblings, her portraits from high school, working at the Ford Motor Company, and early marriage were found when Gail and Richard seemed to touch, embrace, and lean into one another. Elsie swallowed.

It was a time of awe for all of them viewing their Mom, or Grandma, in her elegant youth, laughing wholeheartedly with boys she loved.

Four large portraits of young men who each danced with her at the ballroom, were beguiled by her, and left for the war, intrigued the grandchildren.

"Those boys hoped I would wait for them and write to them," Gail said with a smile of regret.

Elsie was able to tell her sisters' kids and her mom's grandchildren the stories that she had been telling her this year. Gail answered questions recalling further details.

Gail could only participate by trying to recall these portraits but seeing her deep sadness and great joy over these pictures, Grant declared, "Grandma, you have always been classy. You will always be the classiest of us all." The imprint on his heart transferred onto the group when he said, "Look how beautiful she is! She hasn't changed one bit."

Finally, Miles asked Elsie to go home with him. She did so with a heart full of wonder.

The next day, Grant and Miles put in pull bars for Gail's bathrooms. They removed Gail's bed from her room to make way for a mechanical bed. At Elsie's niece's insistence that her grandma spend her money on a good bed, Paige used her time to search for one, find it, and get it delivered and set it up. Each of them took turns laying on it and playing with the simple control, heads up, heads down...approving of her initiative.

"Oh! This is like downtown!" Gail refused to get up from her new bed, so everyone took turns piling on next to her. "Hey, this bed's seeing some good action, too." She laughed when the children said, "Grandma!"

The morning after, Elsie laid in bed soaking in the memories of yesterday. The weekend of being together, basking in their lives so deeply intertwined with each other, listening, and deferring to one another was the answer to Elsie's deepest desire. She was so grateful. So grateful.

That night, an email came to Elsie's mailbox from Gail. "Paige helped me rewrite my LAST WILL AND TESTAMENT," read the email.

The will was attached.

THE DIFFERENCE BETWEEN A RAVEN AND A CROW IS THE DIFFERENCE OF *A PINION* IN THE TALE

It was another month before Melanie called her mother from her father's home with the clear memory of what had happened to her last November's rent. "Mom, you told Elsie that I was overspending on groceries and that I wasn't paying you the November rent, so you upped it by $200, but, remember in October, when you hired a tree-trimmer and garden assistant?"

"Yes."

"When it came time to pay, you said you didn't have the money, so I offered to pay the bill, and I took it out of what I owed you for rent that month. Do you remember that?"

Gail felt the strike of an arrow. She did remember that. What she had meant by saying, "I don't have the money for that" was that she didn't want the gardener to clean up the side yard, only the back yard.

Melanie had misunderstood, and then they'd both forgotten the whole thing. It had been six months! How could she go back now and resolve what she'd told Elsie? Yet, how could she continue to charge Melanie with failure to pay rent when it had only been failure to place the payment in their budget book? It was a misunderstanding?

"Are we square, Mom? Do you remember that?"

"Um, yes, I guess so." Gail didn't want to admit her error. After all, it had been Melanie who had misunderstood her meaning.

"Do you or don't you, Mom? I need a yes or a no, because if you 'guess so', then, you'll change your mind later."

Gail was furious to be pinned down. She'd lost a month's rent to whom, a gardener? So much love had been lost between her daughters and herself over this lapse in memory, this mistake. She couldn't recant her story, the story that bolstered her bias now!

"Yes. We are square, Melanie." What she really meant was, "I forgive you," but how could she explain all of that since so many wrong notions had blown into the river of the family?

She hung up the phone, turning all this over in her mind until distractions claimed her thoughts.

HAVE A NICE TRIP – NOT OVER YOUR OWN FEET

The next time Kaida called Gail, she said, "Mom, you could find peace if you would just meet with me. We could compromise on the house in a way that would satisfy us both. I'll promise something as your legacy to each of the grandchildren and to Melanie in a secondary agreement."

Gail mustered her own courage. "Kaida, you are not the giver of peace. Christ has given me peace. I have repented, and the Lord has forgiven me. You also don't have the right to determine my legacy. I choose my own legacy, and to whom I want to give it. I hope that one day you will be included in my legacy to the family, but that will take your repentance as well. Honey, are you ever going to deed my house back to me?"

"No. That's not why I want to come over."

"There's quite a bill you've racked up by not paying the homeowner association fees, the taxes on the house and other things you promised me in our life estate contract…"

"Drop it, Mom. You are living in the house. You kicked me out. Those bills are yours to pay."

"I didn't kick you out, I simply wouldn't allow you to bring your boyfriends here to live. You've left me with so little to live on."

"Forget it. I never thought you would live this long."

Another arrow struck Gail's heart. "Then, there is no reason for me to let you in. We have nothing to say to one another." It was the hardest moment for Gail in her growing new experience of coming to terms with her own mistakes about her daughters. The terms of truth and reality begged a hard bargain. Standing on her own, not manipulating, and not being manipulated.

She blocked Kaida's phone number once and for all. It occurred to her that she had very little time left on the earth. If she refused to pay her taxes and homeowner's association fees, she could put more into the pot for Elsie and Melanie, and Kaida would have to pay those liens or lose the house.

SPLITTING A POLAR BEAR POPULATION MAKES THEM BI-POLAR

"Hey, Mom," Elsie laughed, "Do you remember the time in Pennsylvania when I saved a shrew from a cat's mouth, and I almost had to take rabies shots because it bit me?"

Gail chuckled too. "Yes, Carlene held up the cat and called you over to pull the mouse out."

"I remember the doctor said if shrews were the size of dogs, they'd ransack the whole world. I still have a scar from that so-called mouse!"

"Some things aren't worth saving!" said her mother.

There were other, more difficult truths.

Elsie and Gail braved the hard questions from stories of their past.

"Why were you so upset about me influencing Melanie to keep Ricky when he was born?" Gail ventured.

"Because, she wasn't able to mother him. It was a selfish and shortsighted thing you did when she couldn't manage—"

"But how did that concern you? Why couldn't you forgive me?"

"Because of Melanie's rippling pain. As I watched her depression year after year while she mishandled her son, you became the enemy. I couldn't defend you both. I also lost my deep confidence with my best friend until years later when she miraculously had her own baby. I was ashamed of my family's behavior and caught in the middle of everything. I lived in the anxiety that Ricky's life would be ruined."

"It isn't. He's a healthy, young man and doing well."

"Yes." Elsie waived a white flag. "Miracles never cease."

While her mother challenged Elsie's standing to hold a grudge, Elsie challenged her mother's everlasting effects of betrayal.

Her voice wandered off. "You make yourself small, Mom, like an innocent fluffy cloud, barely moving in the breeze with the rest of the clouds offering shade, but there's always a bomber flying around in the mist. You control the family by what you mention to one and won't say to another. Shading one and not shading the other. You drop your opinions like hail destroying rooftops."

"That is an awful thing to say about your mother!" Gail sputtered. "I don't intentionally do anything like that!"

Elsie slapped her knees and leaned forward. "You aren't careful with what you do and say. You just go on with whatever feels right in the moment. Now, I have to manage the damages!"

"Elsie, it's true that I didn't have a close relationship with God while I was busy working. I must have made a lot of mistakes. Now that I've had many years to review my life and to listen to God's word on my audio tablet, I realize the precious life I left behind. I must have hurt my children terribly."

"All the trees you so carefully seeded have fallen hard, with felled limbs and strewn boughs, we've all landed outside the family circle until there is no family loyalty left. You've felled your children at the very time you need us most. All I can think is, *'what a tragedy!'*"

"What a tragedy, you're right about that." Gail lifted her chin.

When Melanie drove up to Denver for the meeting with her mom, Elsie, and the attorney, she unblocked Elsie and called her. She wanted to talk over their dad's estate, and the upcoming visit with Gail's attorney.

"The last time I talked with Kaida, she said she would pay off the house she owns with the proceeds from Mom's property, and then give me the rest, so it would be about the amount I would have received if Mom had divided the property equally. Of course, I can't trust anything she says."

Elsie gritted her teeth.

"In one of Dad's boxes, he had the court records from when Kaida had tried to steal Ricky from me. Mom was helping her. I noticed that you weren't involved."

"That's right. I couldn't."

"By the way, did Mom tell you that I remembered how I paid my November's rent?"

"No. What do you mean?"

"In October, she didn't have the money to pay the gardener, so I wrote him a check in lieu of November's rent. She admitted it, and now she says we're square."

"Oh! Why hasn't she told me yet?" After a moment to absorb her own error, Elsie spoke again. "I'm so sorry about me taking her side and yelling at you. So many problems could have been avoided if ..." *if what? If she hadn't defended the wrong person.* "I'm sorry."

Elsie immediately called her mother, but Gail seemed reticent to tell Elsie the squareness of the deal she'd offered Melanie.

"Out with it, Mom. Did she or didn't she trade November's rent for paying the gardener?"

"Well, I told her I didn't want to pay for cleaning up the side yard, and she paid for it."

"She said you just didn't have the money."

"I didn't have the money because I didn't want to do *that*, is what I meant."

"You're admitting this was all a misunderstanding, Mom. You are calling it square though. Is that right?"

Gail paused. Finally, she said, "Yes. Square."

"Okay then, Melanie and I are good. She thought she'd paid you in that way. I'm not going to say that she was in any way dishonorable financially toward you anymore. A misunderstanding should be forgiven. I'm dropping it."

"I guess that's right. You and she should be friends," Gail said thoughtfully.

When Grant's birthday rolled up on the first day of June, Elsie swallowed in a dry moment and fessed up. "I created a new problem in a spate of problems by reporting an inaccurate account against Melanie to you six months ago, and it has created the most recent spate of arguments in the family. I inserted myself, you see, into Gail and Melanie's rent dispute, where I had no place and no player in the game. I've been wrong and have caused unnecessary hard feelings and bias against Melanie." She looked at Melanie with pale-faced sorrow. "Please forgive me?"

"It's okay, Elsie. We've all moved along. It was time."

Gail quietly looked at her plate of food.

Grant leaned over and hugged the sisters. "It's okay, aunties. I love each of you and bear you no ill will at all." He blushed with happiness and relief.

Small corrections matter. Just as small misunderstandings had splattered their family with filth, small corrections mattered a great deal.

Every time a check came from Rich's life insurance policies, Elsie experienced out-of-body sensations. At first, profound joy danced to the initial relief that he hadn't disowned her. She and Miles paid down their mortgage with it.

Then came another in the midst of nasty stories she was writing about her dad's behavior. She checked herself after making the deposit.

Additional checks came, each one feeling like a smile from her beloved father. This being compensation from a man whom she'd come to see as a twister in her mom's life, a possible inciter of her brother's death and a conduit of dear Noeleen's death, someone who repulsed Elsie in his final years, but whom she had loved and idolized throughout childhood. The only sense she could make of this came in a phrase from a verse in Matthew 7.

"So, if you who are evil know how to give good gifts to your children..."

There was a final surprise check, one she did not expect. On her way to deposit it, she felt she wanted to kiss her father and apologize to him for the mistaken way she'd viewed him and represented his personal conflicts as hypocrisy. *Each of us are conflicted human beings, aren't we, Dad?*

He was a blur of pure, white starlight, coming midday for a delicate kiss on her forehead, all the strangeness peeled away from him. He was just a free soul, grateful and free. Then, gone. *God must have forgiven him.* She stopped at the bleeding traffic light, tears blurring undeniable sentiment. Gratefulness, it was gratefulness. She wanted to run to her dad, chase him in flight and hug him for being honorable. For being stalwart and true to her, unlike her mother.

When she got home, she hugged Miles. "I cried with this check, honey."

"You did?"

"Yes. I still get so confused when these checks come in the mail. I'm so grateful, and I think I understood nothing about how sentimental he was, that maybe he did want to be fatherly to all of us. But, with so few navigating tools, and life's temptations, he just couldn't give anymore.

"I remembered the time he kept bringing back that toaster he'd bought me for a birthday gift. I kept taking it back, leaving it on his doorstep because I despised him for leaving the family. He'd tenaciously kept bringing it back to me. Today I felt his hugs, without any weirdness.

"I remembered in childhood how he read to us, drove us around Pennsylvania explaining history, and then in Colorado, how he took me to the stadium events and concerts, and as an adult how he put gas in the car when I went to visit him in Oklahoma. He was gallant in many ways. Then the awful memories come flooding back. The checks make me feel compensated somehow for all the incongruencies, for everything he did to our family. Do you think that was his intent?"

"I don't know," answered Miles. "He admired the way my dad kept giving us gifts, and I think it instilled a bit of competition in him."

When Elsie explained the tears with the final check, Gail listened with a blistered ear. Then she asked, "How much was it?"

"Not much, Mom. It was just the fact that he kept trying to do something over the years. That is really what touches me to my core somehow."

Elsie's wet face was a stone tossed over the surface of Gail's placid lake, skipping, creating small disturbances of doubt. Elsie knew her mother did not allow her any feeling of loyalty or kind thought toward her father. She deflected her mom's detachment with learned conversation that could reunify their bond.

The information gathered by Gail regarding Richard's insurance payments helped her to assess whether her own bequest scheme would be sufficient to outdo her ex's gifts to the Finch heirs. She wanted to come out the clear winner in this final race. She was the good guy, and she would prove it.

After breakfast with Elsie, Gail's cane and the shelf beside the garage door helped her boost herself into the house.

Gail had never denied her tears were only crocodile tears for Kaida's deceptions. She was the one who was shocked and betrayed. Kaida had managed to put her lifestyle in a vice-like grip. How it irked Gail!

Kaida's unjust enrichment was bad news for her sisters, but she hadn't stolen from them. The question now was had she saved enough to provide compensation for Melanie and Elsie?

A few days later, after hours of magnifying lens research on her computer and downloading forms, Gail felt she had an answer. She called Elsie. "Can you take me to get something notarized?"

"Sure, Mom."

After, the notary, Gail said, "Do you have time to take me to the county clerk and recorder?"

"Okay, Mom. What's up?"

"A revocation of beneficiary deed in this envelope."

Elsie pulled over to a nearby parking space. "What is a beneficiary deed, Mom? Did you give something else to Kaida?"

"I'm sorry to say, she was never satisfied with whatever I gave her, and she just kept asking for assurance, so I kept signing her beneficiary deeds. She knew the beneficiary deeds I signed for her could be revoked, and that's why, I'm sure, she connived to have me sign the quit claim deed representing it like it was a trust document."

"You're telling me that you've filed multiple beneficiary deeds to Kaida, like, um, a succession of gifts to her, eliminating me and Melanie over several years? Do you know how that makes me feel, Mom? That you, someone I've always held in high regard, my own mother, did this to me repeatedly, year after year, and Kaida's children knew it, but I didn't?"

Elsie seethed at the years of her mother's ongoing treachery. Years of betrayal began replaying in her mind, all the hospitality she had offered her haters! She and her mother had been serving the orphanage together just before the first beneficiary deed was signed. The swooping shock of this was an asteroid slicing through the earth's atmosphere, to land on her house.

"Mom! I have no family!" she fumed. "You were not only complicit with Kaida's schemes, but you are also culpable if you intentionally disinherited me so many times. What were you thinking?! Oh, I always knew something was wrong between us, between me and you and my whole family, and I kept trying to fix it. Now, you admit it's true."

The duplicity of her mother! Elsie raged at her mother, for the longevity and secret hatred held close in her mother's heart for years. "I just don't get it!"

"But, I want to undo it now. It was a mistake. I was wrong, so wrong, and I want to make it right, honey."

"How can I ever trust you again, Mom?"

"There's another beneficiary deed in this envelope giving you and Melanie my remaining property and use, rights, title, if possible." Gail was talking quickly now.

"I'm just trying one more angle. Maybe it will help. Maybe it won't. We'll have to contact an attorney. Again, maybe it will help, maybe not."

Elsie's heart pounded. As surely as she'd been hit by a car, she was incapacitated by shock. She looked closely at her mother. "Why are you admitting this now? What's gotten into you?"

"I've had to forgive myself. The struggle is real." She muttered. "There's so much to forgive in the animosity we've each held for one another...all our failings. But if we can't forgive ourselves for the struggle of it, the animosity will track us down."

"Yes, it is doing just as you say, like a mountain lion sniffs for its prey, Mom, and I am the prey. When it pounces, there can only be death. If you were to die now, knowing what I know, I might not survive it. You've devastated me!" She hated admitting how much her mother meant to her.

"I don't have much time to make this right, honey, and I can't sit still."

Isn't it interesting how wide and clear the sky becomes when all the trees beneath it are felled? Barely breathing, and ever so gingerly, Elsie pulled into traffic again, her face puffy, her eyes swollen.

"It doesn't matter whether it works, Mom. Thank you for trying to correct it. It means a lot." Then, she began to worry.

"If working with an attorney can reverse the deed, Kaida may be furious, she might come after me with an avalanche of new schemes, Mom. Your estate is not worth my life. Money has never mattered as much as the assurance that you loved me, and that you'd fight for my wellbeing. I went to a Bible school, remember? I was a missionary. I married an average wage earner. What has always mattered to me, and still does, is that my mother tried to bless me, but I have no assurance that you ever really loved me now. You disinherited me multiple times!"

The difference between mother and daughter was Elsie assessed her loyalty to her mother and to the family's wellbeing as the typical loyalty to one's tribe. Her mother's loyalty, on the other hand, had attached itself to her sister exclusively, likely because both of them were absolutely committed to protecting the first granddaughter, Paige.

"I get it Mom. I'm 'C.'"

"What?"

"Nothing. I didn't have to do anything wrong to get disinherited by you. I simply had to represent an outside competition, a potential risk to be forfeited."[1]

Elsie, ever curious about the inner workings of the family loyalties, landed on research that week that had discussed the phenomenon of loyalty, that loyalty can most often be expressed as $A + B = B + A$, but sometimes, B demands that C be eliminated because C is identified as the competing challenge to the expressed cause of $A + B$.

"I don't understand."

"I know. It doesn't matter. Except that when you forfeited me, you forfeited your own best interests for autonomy in your old age and your quality of life, Mom. I have feelings. I'm not a robot. I have integrity as a member of this family, but you keep shredding it by treating me like a servant or a debtor, not like a daughter should be treated. You chose another, and I can't love you now like I would have, knowing what I know. With the amount of rejection and hurt that you've piled over me, I have to betray myself and what's best for me in order to keep spending hours and days helping you. I have to take some time to sort this out.

"I feel that the only reason why you say you love me and why you call for me is to keep your own supply of resources, help, and entertainment coming, but that kind of love is a business transaction. It isn't the way a mom is meant to love a child."

Elsie continued, "It can't make up for the years of betrayal I've experienced because of your choices. I'll find a way to help you, but it isn't going to look the way you want, Mom. I'm sorry, but that's the truth. I'm going to have to raise a boundary so that you can't keep hurting me."

Gail looked quizzically at her daughter.

"I'm trying to undo my mistakes. I'm trying to fix it. I think we really do love one another."

Matthew's full gospel words flew like a flock of squawking ducks through Elsie's mind. "So, if you who are evil know how to give good gifts to your children, how much more will your Father in heaven give good gifts to those who ask Him!"

"The one thing I do know, Mom, is that God gave me Miles. My husband has given me psychological balance in all this. I also have quality friends who are healthier and more loyal than my family ever was to me. I can trust my Father in heaven to keep blessing and treating me well. You knew how to give good gifts to your children, but I feel like you've given me scorpions and snakes."

Gail grasped Elsie's hands looking into her daughter's eyes, searching for threads of fragile trust with which they might continue to try to stitch their lives together.

Finally, Elsie said, "I'm sure whatever you do, these things you're doing with the deeds, will go a long way to make good with Melanie, but you forfeited her too, treating her like a business in trade, and that's why she had to leave you."

"Can't we do anything? Can't we do anything to fix this?"

The two prayed together asking for help, for forgiveness, for a way forward. Then they decided to visit Gail's attorney about their many distresses, though Elsie finally understood how little could be done. She had to take some time to process who her mother, the real Gail Finch, was. Beyond that, healing would take time.

FAIRYTALES DO TEND TO *DRAGON*

The attorney drafted a medical durable power of attorney and an advance medical directive for Gail's safety in Elsie and Miles's name sharing responsibility with Gail's granddaughter, Paige. He drafted a general power of attorney, and he notarized Gail's Revocation of Beneficiary. He took Gail's affidavit. Then, he took Gail's previously written quit claim deed in hand. "I don't know if Kaida will return a quit claim back to you, but I'll look into that possibility, too." He noted his duties to himself on a short list.

"I will write a letter of demand to Kaida mentioning the evidence of elder abuse we have. I think she might return the property under the circumstances. If she doesn't, we'll at least notify the taxing authorities that she needs to be the one paying taxes—Take that off your mother's plate. And, as a professional, I will take it upon myself to report Kaida to the department of elder abuse."

Melanie let out a deep sigh. The weight on her shoulders rolled away. She felt vindicated, almost prioritized to the place of a daughter. Was it the hint of her mother's love she felt?

Gail smiled. She'd done the best she could.

If Gail could revoke the seals of hatred, her signatures of betrayal, could she manage to soften the long scars she'd inflicted on her daughters' souls? She lowered her gaze through blurred vision to the pen moving in her hand. Her distressed scribbles on the notepad could not alleviate the awful situation, yet the Holy Spirit waited in the wings. Comfort was available to them all.

Elsie felt such hope. She'd been asking, seeking, and knocking as Matthew chapter 7 advised, and didn't the story of Zelophehad's five daughters prove that God cared about land and inheritance for the tribe and for women? The women had asked Moses for a determination because they stood to lose their father's legacy. Moses had inquired of God, and God said, "Give the women their father's land." She'd also read the Genesis story of Tamar, whom the Lord blessed for seeking her own place of honor after her husband died. Elsie saw that God approved of cleverness to secure one's rights in the family.

She had also finally read and meditated on her mother's favorite passage, "Turn the other cheek, go the extra mile, give away the comforting provision of your warm coat." Among these passages, the path to her blessings of reconciliation and honor lay.

She and Miles knew they'd been cats lapping at life's cream. They often reminded each other of their escapades. They knew, "The point of making money is to enjoy some of it along the way." A wealth of friends had become family members to them. They weren't suffering. In the moment, should Kaida refuse to be reasonable, Elsie was prepared to hand over the hefty happiness tax her sister and mother had required of her. The maxim she'd heard throughout life, she knew now to be true: "To whom much is given, much will be required." God would help her. She'd take her cue from her father who so aptly understood, "You win some, you lose some."

She could envision Jesus out on the stormy waves calling her to join him, not looking around at the laws of nature. She'd just need to keep her focus on the Savior and walk over these tossing waves. To look down on the watery sprays trying to drown her would be her undoing.

Elsie spoke. "I'm at peace with this. It feels just. To be honest, I think my sister did make my mother happy for a very long time, even though she did it for her own personal enrichment scheme. I'm thankful for my mother's happiness during that time. I just want Kaida to stop torturing herself and torturing the rest of us with her poisoned pen. She needs to take responsibility for her breach of terms owed to Mom. If you can find a way to hold her accountable for over-reaching without charging her with a criminal offense against mother, it will be mercy. To peel the layer of stolen goods from Kaida's back is an act of mercy. Mercy can sometimes lead back into healed relationships."

Gail bowed her head and said, "Amen," as if to a prayer.

Kaida did not respond to the attorney's letters of demand. He was shocked, but Gail's family members were not surprised.

Within two days of a report being filed with the division of elder abuse, a handsome county sheriff visited Gail at her home. While there, he called the county assessor. The new deed required both signatures.

He provided a quick abstract for solving the problem. Legally, Gail would simply sign another quit claim deed from herself to herself as both grantor and grantee cancelling the life estate. Kaida was relinquishing her swindled title to settle in the face of prosecution said the district attorney. State rules made a way out of the gift deed transfer if obtained by fraud, duress, or deceit.

"How can this be?" she asked. "I've waited ten years for an answer, and now all it takes is for me to sign another quit claim deed?"

"There will be a note on the new deed that says its purpose is to revoke the life estate. Kaida will save face and not go to jail."

Gail's ears were on fire. The house could finally be put back into her name? If she would have died, the gift would have effectively transferred to Kaida, and it would not have been possible for her other heirs to sue or revoke the deed. Instead, the Lord had looked down with pity on the nest of Finches and granted her prayer for help. "If I can get my house back, I won't press charges. That will be my gift to Kaida."

In her amazement, she phoned Elsie to come hear the news.

When Elsie arrived, she sat and listened calmly, but Gail began to hear her daughter weeping. She stood and made her way to where Elsie sat, then she caressed her daughter's back. "Are you crying for relief, dear?" Gail finally asked.

Elsie couldn't answer. She recognized God's mercy, but why did life have to be so hard. Why?

Gail murmured, "I know. It's a miracle I can hardly grasp myself. I've been existing in an imaginary prison cell with Kaida holding the key. But when she was finally apprehended, all I had to do was open the door and walk out!"

"I can't believe it, Mom! I've laid this down a hundred times and picked it back up to wrestle with it because I couldn't let the injustice of it alone. Now, I think about the wasted years of hurt if we could have only known better!"

"Then, we wouldn't have had this year, Elsie. You wouldn't know what you know now, and I wouldn't have known forgiveness and freedom. If you wouldn't have helped me make things right, the entire family would have suffered after my death. We've come full circle through the suffering, and I love you dearly."

It wasn't over yet, but Elsie could see it would be soon. She wished she could simply erase the scars of memories in her mind. She wished forgiveness was the same as forgetting, and forgiving was the same as reconciliation, but she had grown wiser than to believe that.

Eventually, she would thank the Lord for changing the shape of her future and the future of other family members, but in the moment, all she felt was the weight of a page turning like the demarcation of picture frames in a quickly moving reel of film, and she was unable to see through the dark haze lying between good and evil, lying as a ghost of good intentions and bad.

EPILOGUE

"The history she's tucked inside her belt, like a traveler carries cash, means she's handing me Finch secrets like rationed bits of treasure for trade. I'm the only one remaining to help her. I'm hoping the truth is explorable, but even as I cup my hands to capture the streams running to the ocean, water leaks through the crevasses." Elsie reviewed what she'd said back in counseling.

She closed her finished document and leaned back in her recliner with fingers clasped behind her head. She digested the evolving facts. Her mother never sat this way. Elsie mimicked the same position her father often sat in, musing about the meaning of life. She wondered if loyalties are kept in a gene pool, or if they really can be changed by divine intervention and a warm reality.

As life can imitate art, Elsie envisioned herself camping with the children of Israel, chased by the Egyptians, about to be overtaken, turned back to slavery, and their provisions confiscated. Trapped on the beach, she saw the Red Sea part and rise as walls opening to make a way to new life. She felt the wonder of walking right through the waves on dry ground and tasting freedom on the other side. "Father God, You had a purpose for forming me in my mother's womb, and even though my mother forgot me, You will never leave me or forsake me."

Just last week, after Elsie saw the palliative doctor leave Gail's front door, her mother explained why she didn't believe in offering apologies. "I believe in repentance before God, but apologies can make things more complicated between people." There it was! Another secret as to why her mother never apologized for anything was handed over. It wasn't a blind spot. It was a creed!

In the same conversation, Gail told Elsie, "Now that I have my house back and I've put everything safely into a trust, I'm ready to go. I have peace. I have no regrets." All was well until that last bit shriveled

Elsie's heart. Her mother had no regrets? She was touting this to a daughter whom she'd intentionally jilted year after year passing judgment under a false premise against the one whom she now needed to perform the daily tasks of a personal nature for assistance.

Yet Gail had made amends. As far as she was able, she had righted her wrongs. After signing her trust documents, she returned home to show off the papers and percentages of her new divisions to her daughters and grandchildren waiting there. The gaunt flesh of her cheeks turned rosy as she leaned back in her chair and breathed, "Hallelujah! I feel like the woman who searched and searched and finally found her lost coin!" Then, she began quoting Bible verses, "Delight yourself in the Lord and He will give you the desires of your heart… For by grace you are saved, through faith, and that not of yourselves, it is the gift of God lest anyone should boast…"

"That's a little out of context, wouldn't you say?"

"It's still true! It's still true!" Gail laughed in her freedom and joy.

It was only last year, she was taking her mom to get her nails clipped, running her to hair appointments, worship services, and bringing her a half gallon of milk with calculated reserve. Now that Gail was experiencing heart failure, Elsie additionally needed to set aside several days each week to sort her mother's meds, cook meals, and attend home appointments with the palliative care team. She was glad to be the one to do it now. Her heart, free. The wall had crumbled between her mom and herself, and she served Gail as a daughter who is no longer a slave.

Elsie's mind wandered toward her husband. Miles was the one who trimmed Gail's trees and cleaned her gutters. She had not been able to give her mother grandchildren, but she had given her a son-in-law to help care for her in her old age and help her at home. *You are my greatest gift, Miles. You are the reason I survived this. God moved me from my family to your family, from emotional abandonment and being a wallflower not worthy of my mother's love, to your family who treated me as a daughter giving us thoughtful gifts all along the way. You helped me do right when I couldn't help myself."*

Elsie wanted to start practicing a new way of thinking, processing things from a grateful spirit, not from betrayal and poverty, not keeping tabs of wrongs and slights. She would think about the good and pure things in life. She considered the few noble examples of grace and mercy she'd seen. These images washed through her stress. She was desperate to break away from her deadly family traps, and trust the Lord, who says, "Be anxious for nothing. Bring Me your cares and worries because I promise to care for you as always."

She felt a shift with this new perspective. Elsie made a promise to herself and to her family. *"I will learn to be a better person because of the grace given, because of my happiness and provisions of resting in God's hands. Hasn't He proven Himself?"*

That, He had.

Endnotes

1. "*Loyalty is the only moral force that can exist on the same plane as the truth itself.*" – Peter Mitchell, Murdoch Mysteries, Season 8, episode 7, November 24, 2014

2. It has sometimes been suggested that "*A can be loyal to B only if there is a third party C [...] who stands as a potential competitor to B*" Fletcher, George P., 1993, *Loyalty: An Essay on the Morality of Relationships*, New York: Oxford University Press P.8.
https://plato.stanford.edu/entries/loyalty/

3. For more information on pollution along the front range near Denver, CO visit: https://earthlab.colorado.edu/blog/air-quality-data-and-transportation-related-emissions

Biblical quotes used were from The Revised English Standard Bible

Lyrics
In subchapter, I Don't Have the Thyme to be Roasted Today, two song lyrics are quoted.
1. "More Precious Than Silver" was written by Lynn DeShazzo circa @1982 Integrity's Hosanna! Music
2. "As the Deer" was written by Martin J. Nystrom circa @1984 Maranatha Praise Inc.

For further reading on understanding complex loyalties, I found this college syllabus by John Kleinig, who is also an author on similar issues in policing and criminality. The short syllabus itself is enlightening.
https://plato.stanford.edu/entries/loyalty/#Bib

For further reading on the subject of going back to one's family roots to become a whole and healthy person, I recommend reading, EMOTIONALLY HEALTHY SPIRITUALITY: It's Impossible to Be Spiritually Mature, While Remaining Emotionally Immature by Peter Scarzzero, Zondervan (April 25, 2017) ISBN-13: 978-0310348498

GLOSSARY OF TERMS

1. **Beneficiary Deed**: a revokable statement of a property or estate gift from one party to another to be granted and transferred after a person has died. It is notarized. This form of deed is easily revoked or amended at any time prior to the death of the owner-grantor.
2. **Codicil**: a notarized note of a benefactor's items made as an official attachment to a Last Will and Testament for specific bequests to individuals, may be a handwritten letter. It is often used as an amendment to the Will when the grantor realizes he or she has forgotten to name something or someone in the Will.
3. **Last Will and Testament**: the official, notarized statement of a person's identity, heirs, and devisees with the deceased's last instructions and intent for the distribution of his or her real property, bank accounts, life insurance policies, vehicles, animals, jewelry, division of corporate ownership, stocks and bonds.
4. **Quit Claim Deed**: a simple but irrevocable title deed of land, estate, or real property usually used as a gift between family members at any time, not dependent upon the demise of any party. It sounds like quick claim, and that is the way it is often used, but there are step up issues and capital gains taxes in that kind of a transaction to consider for the beneficiary of the title and there are other bars the grantor should consider.
5. **Trust**: a complex legal document wherein certain states regulate or limit taxes on a person's assets for the benefit of those who may inherit valuables.
6. **Power of Attorney**: a notarized document giving someone else the right to act as your attorney in fact, your official representative for legal and financial decisions.
7. **Medical Durable Power of Attorney**: a notarized document giving another person the right to make medical decisions for you in the event that you cannot make them for yourself or you don't have a living will controlling how you would like to be treated.

AUTHOR ACKNOWLEDGMENTS

To Bernice Wassell, the first to finish reading this manuscript when I was in doubt, incredible relief washed over me to hear you report the initial story made you check your own small matters. Your interaction with the characters in your coalescent manner helped me to understand the necessity of publishing this generational story. Bernice, Tonya Blessing, Karl Wheeler, and Sue Summers, you were four pillars in my house of emotional support during the year of discovery and development of this story.

To Sandy Fisher, for your enormous heart to coach the full story out assuring me the characters were provocative and believable, it couldn't have been easy to keep drinking this wine four times. Cheryl Bostrom, your experience did not lead me wrong in adding "Elsie" in snippets along the historical way. I'm grateful for your advice in how to accomplish this.

To readers Rosie Duggins, Charmayne Hafen, Bobi Muldrow, and Brieanne Smart, I needed each veracious reading helper's savvy slashes, tics, line edits, votes, and comments. Thank you for being kind. I am forever grateful that you sent your insights to Capture Books. You honored me with your valuable tips and encouragement and winnowed out the awkward passages; for this, I am humbled.

The book became salable with Kathy Hoffner's line editing, alongside Crystal Schwarzkopf's punctuation marks and Sue Carter's persistent questions and redlines. Thank you for your constant encouragement while focusing on the purpose and intent of the manuscript during your own family matters. If only I had your attention to detail!

My husband, William Paul, is the kindest soul of all, allowing me to rave and write and question the futility of life while I split our face time with the screen of my laptop every day for nine months.

To Reinhold Niebuhr for his helpful Serenity Prayer (original is printed on the following page).

God, give us grace to accept with serenity
The things that cannot be changed,
Courage to change the things which should be changed,
And the Wisdom to distinguish the one from the other.

Living one day at a time,
Enjoying one moment at a time,
Accepting hardship as a pathway to peace,
Taking, as Jesus did,
This sinful world as it is,
Not as I would have it,
Trusting that You will make all things right,
If I surrender to Your will.
So that I may be reasonably happy in this life,
And supremely happy with You forever in the next.
Amen

—Reinhold Niebuhr

ELSIE FINCH BOOK CLUB QUESTIONS

Q: What desires or fears defined Rich's life and Gail's life?

Q: Should Gail have been more vocal with Rich or more transparent with the children regarding Rich's effect on the marriage in the children's formative years?

Q: What kind of confessions would a child not be able to forgive in their parent?

Q: What is the nature of forgiveness? Should forgiveness be offered unconditionally, or does it require a true apology and renewed devotion?

Q: How does forgiveness differ from reconciliation?

Q: Does timing or keeping short accounts provide a more likely outcome with giving or receiving forgiveness?

Q: Do you believe the days of your life, your motives, or the results of your choices are recorded anywhere, by anyone?

Q: Do you think that after years of bias, Gail honestly felt regret and sorrow over her fractured relationships with her children or was she only protecting her end-of-life aims?

Q: Which do you think played a larger role in helping Elsie overcome her neuroses: art and music or her strength of discipline?

Q: Which Finch family members struggled with personality disorders?

Q: What was the saving grace offered to Gail? To Kaida? To Melanie? To Elsie?

Q: What does Matthew 5:38-42, the Sermon on the Mount, have to do with the members of the Finch family? As Jesus said, "You have heard that it was said, 'An eye for an eye and a tooth for a tooth.' But I say to you, do not resist the one who is evil. But if anyone slaps you on the right cheek, turn to him the other also. And if anyone would sue you and take your tunic, let him have your cloak as well. And if anyone forces you to go one mile, go with him two miles. Give to the one who begs from you, and do not refuse the one who would borrow from you." — Jesus Christ, English Standard Version Bible

Q: Do you agree that studying the past and remembering details can be helpful to wounded individuals?

Q: What takeaway from this book will make you change something in your own life?

Q: Can a commitment to virtue become dangerous? If so, does the promise of heaven or some other thing make virtue worth it, and why?

Q: What do you think happened in Gail's mind to create her character arc, and was her compassion for her children and behavior towards them mostly tied to her spiritual health, or to what they did to her, or to how she viewed herself?

Q: Do you think Elsie would be able to maintain her altruism in the real world or would she need outside props?

Q: Do you think the Biblical injunction to not oppose an evil person pertains only to personal attack or does it extend to mediations, legal representation, and duties to report or to interventions?

ELSIE & FINCH

CPSIA information can be obtained
at www.ICGtesting.com
Printed in the USA
LVHW110320241122
733898LV00017B/483/J